ELLY UNCOMPOSED

ELLY UNCOMPOSED

A Novel-Opera

VALERIE NIEMERG

Contents

A Note... About the Notes... About the Notes

When I first presented this project to non-musicians, the reaction was confusion. *What is this? Who is that? I don't know what any of this means. . .* Mass hysteria in the streets, sleepless nights, the whole fall of Western Civilization. The more Elly test readers, the more opera terminology, composer references, and musical/theatrical terms were questioned.

Is this really necessary?

When I asked Elly, she was adamant. She must be accessible to the Gentiles, she said, to spread some healthy opera around on the toast of this contemporary culture of electronic screens. After much discussion, we settled on the glossary. So, let this forward serve as an apology of sorts. When you arrive at a **bolded** vocabulary word like **Chopin**, or **piano crook**, or **coloratura**, please don't be horrified or offended. If you like, you may look it up in the glossary at the back. But understand that it was only added because a highly intelligent, extensively educated and well-read person ... had no idea who Verdi was.

That poor, poor soul.

OVERTURE

Chapter One

The Druid Virgins were becoming restless. Fastidiously prepared and preserved, the ceremonial maidens encircling the sacrificial altar, no longer focused on their high priestess with statue-like sanctity. Among their ranks a mutiny brewed, and their long, stately robes now undulated with the tell-tale signs of the revolt: a wiped nose, an unnecessary cough, a fly shooed away. Finally, a pair of restless fingertips ignited a storm of ripples beneath the vestal gowns in a sad, desperate search for a cell phone.

From her piano bench, Elizabeth studied this ritual of mandatory chorus time. Beneath each dark hood, a young singer stood yearning for her turn to be the soloist at the front. Each one dreaming of that fine day, to be the one easing through the great opera composer Vincenzo Bellini's buttery **melismatic** flourishes under the warmth of the bright lights, while a new crew of Virgins could fight the urge to scratch their noses.

But today they were all just chorus girls at a Saturday dress rehearsal, doomed for two more hours of stiffened silence in their heavy costumes.

The revolt was escalating. With their minds wandering further and further from the Druid ceremony and the prayers of their high priestess, the rehearsal would soon terminate in genuine operatic disaster. At this moment, someone was assuredly forgetting to unlock her knees and would inevitably wobble into unconsciousness off the back risers. In fact, one second alto was already exhibiting the beginning signs of an impending doom, her glazed eyes swimming beneath the hooded headdress.

As Elizabeth's fingers continued to accompany the scene on the piano, a serious quandary stirred inside her. She might have to stop the rehearsal.

Charlotte Maples, the soprano singing Bellini's heroine Norma, presently stood at the front of the Druids, spinning golden strands of sound. The director and full technical staff sat well-hypnotized. Terminating Charlotte's singing could be considered criminal. The call could wait, the soup grow cold, the rain ruin the carpet, but one should never interrupt a young soprano in the middle of such a triumph of human beauty.

Elizabeth noted that the overheating second alto was on the third riser, a good six feet off the floor, and those ceremonial robes were so long, the slightest wobble and she might trip on her own hem.

With agonizing reluctance, Elizabeth leaned to her left.

"Reggie, red alert on Virgin Number Five."

Reggie Greene pulled his directorial eyes away from his twenty-three-year-old opera star. "Hold!" he called out, breaking the room's stupor. "Sorry, Charlotte. Everyone, take five. Go outside and cool off. Get something to drink."

The Virgins released great sighs and dispersed. The ancient burial grounds melted away into the university's box-shaped band room, and the Druid hordes crumbled into folding chairs, commencing the more current ritual of staring mindlessly at their little glowing screens, half of them texting classmates ten feet away.

A dazed Charlotte stood alone in the center of the rehearsal space, stunned by the abrupt return to twenty-first-century tech-

nology. *Poor girl.* Elizabeth would pay her a compliment. Nothing
was so easily manipulatable as a soprano's ego.

Before Elizabeth could even rise from her piano bench,
Reggie pulled a folding chair up and sat backward, eyeing her over
the rim of his long-cold mochaccino. Apparently, Charlotte
would have to handle the slings of outrageous fortune by herself.

"Is something wrong?" Elizabeth said.

"Lizzy, why don't you have a car?" Reggie asked.

What could it have been about Charlotte's entrancing resonance that made Reggie Greene think about cars? Was it a male
thing? *No, Elizabeth, that was sexist.*

"Goodness. Where'd that come from?"

"You're twenty-seven, and still riding a bike everywhere."

"It's good exercise, and I like the fresh air. You'd be surprised
how much you miss while speeding around in a three-ton can of
steel."

"So that's it? You like the air? That's why you take hours to
get everywhere, and you're always sweaty and frostbitten?"

"Oh, come on. I've never been frostbitten. Plus, I tried once. I
went to a store and picked out a cute little red thing with four
doors and a built-in GPS. Then they handed me this enormous
stack of forms. I mean a stack like this." She held her hand a foot
above her keyboard. "I couldn't possibly read all those, let alone
understand them."

"You don't have to understand them."

"Well, how do you know you're not signing your life away?
It's not safe."

"Yeah, it's much safer to bike all over Wichita in two inches of
snow. Do you even have a license?"

"Good grief, Reggie, where is this going?"

"Okay, okay, forget the car." Reggie reached across the piano
keys and snatched away her **score**, the spiral bound piano reduction of Bellini's orchestral music. He slid a small ivory envelope
across her music stand, and she recognized the return address with

professional curiosity. "Open it," he said. "It's from New England Conservatory."

"I can see that."

"Please don't be mad. I just can't stand it anymore."

"Can't stand what?"

"Watching you fade away. For seven years, I've let you fool me into thinking it was me; that you couldn't let go of me. But it's not me, it's everything. It's the bike instead of a car, it's your hatred of all things cellular, it's those plants at your place."

"What's wrong with my herbs?"

"Nothing. It's just..." Virgin Number Fourteen passed him with a trailing ceremonial robe, and he grabbed her Druid sleeve. "Hey, tell the seamstress to raise that hem. You're gonna break your neck on those risers."

Elizabeth bristled. Reggie Greene was a walking opera façade. He loved to put on the appearance of a meaningful conversation, but his head was constantly backstage.

"You're unhappy with me," she said. "I'm not doing well enough?"

"Well enough that I could sleep at night. I'll probably be tortured by rotten pianists for the next six years trying to replace you. But every time they can't **follow the stick**, I'll just smile and pat myself on the back because they aren't you." He took the papers from her. "NEC wasn't just here to watch a master class last month. They were here to meet you and see you play. They're offering you a full assistantship, free ride for your Doctorate, plus a living stipend, reimbursement for rehearsals, lots of contacts, concerts, real experiences... You won't even have to buy a car; you can take the subway everywhere. You'll meet lots of new people. Maybe even go on a date or something."

"Or something? I can't go on a date. I'm in love with you."

"Lizzy, I'm gay."

"You can't be sure. And don't call me that."

"I've been married to Josh for six years."

"That can be annulled."

"And that's another thing. How come you go to church every week like it's dialysis, but don't know the first thing about your own religion?"

"Hasn't it been five minutes? Shouldn't we call them back?"

She slid the envelope aside and snatched back her Bellini score. The pages flipped randomly between her fingers, because she really didn't need them anymore. That's how her memory for music worked. She could play a piece once and have it forever in her, like it had been carved in stone by a great artist. The extravagant nuances of pitch and rhythm were only recorded in the seemingly chaotic blurs of little black dots and stems. Recorded like a message from a long-gone generation. A secret code of simple beauty and its unearthly power. Bellini wouldn't fade from her once the production ended. Bellini should never fade. Just to look at the piano reduction was to hear the whole mesmerizing combination of sounds, the orchestral harmonies, the human voice soaring out above it, like a cry through eternity, or a heavenly bird on a—

"Lizzy, you should take this offer. You should go to Boston."

Elizabeth had known that it would be an irregular day. Nothing traumatic had taken place. Her neighbor's dog remained notoriously silent before her alarm went off. Nice clean ride to work, no one sent her reeling onto a sidewalk. Quick line at Java's café and aside from having to tragically interrupt a soprano, everything else had been music.

But now she understood. Everything had gone so easily, so smoothly. The day was saving up for something big, buttering her up, like overly friendly relatives marching an unsuspecting loved one to an intervention.

"You want me to go away."

"No. I don't want you to go away. Never. I just want you to— go on. Listen, when are you done here today? Maybe we can go out for a drink."

The stage manager entered, hollering orders. Reggie sighed and returned to his seat while students stowed technology in purses and backpacks, and the sounds of gossip and cajoling began to fade.

The Virgins shuffled back onto the risers. Elizabeth noted their ceremonial robes were recycled from last year's production of *Dido and Aeneas*, and if she wasn't mistaken, *Magic Flute* before that. They had been dressed up with new collars and belts, but the fabric seemed to be turning a mistier shade of blue every year.

Once all the singers were in position, Maestro McDanials, perpetually hunched over, shuffled back into his seat and lifted the stick. Elizabeth's hands surrendered to Bellini on the piano with sweetest pleasure.

Regrettably, a few bars into the music, the maestro again lifted a silencing hand, and the band room grew uncannily quiet. Alice Shearman, the main office secretary of the College, approached and whispered something in McDanials's ear. This was certainly odd, because the main office stood a full, four blocks away, and Alice Shearman was a sixty-something maternal prototype with a great love for cream pastries. But the silence festered, and worry lines dug into the conductor's brow.

Elizabeth stayed put on her bench, waiting for some announcement. *Was there a problem with the building? An event on campus?*

The conductor nodded, and Alice approached the over-worked and under-tuned spinet, with every Druid eye watching. "Elizabeth, honey," she said, **sotto voce**, "you need to come with me. Something has happened."

"Me? I'm needed here."

Alice leaned over the keys and laid a hand on her shoulder. "Honey, we just got a phone call in the office. It's your father."

"My father? Well, can't it wait until after rehearsal?"

Alice leaned in even closer while waves of whispers scattered through the Virgins.

"They sent me over to tell you, sweetie. Something happened this morning, you know, from the side effects of his treatment?"

"The—wait, what are you talking about?"

"The treatment for his cancer. I'm so sorry honey, but your dad is gone."

They stared at her: Alice waiting for some response, the cast curiously motionless in their long ceremonial fabrics, the stick resting immobile on McDanials's music stand, and Reggie like a memorial statue at the center of it all.

An urge seized Elizabeth to move. Get up. Run back to her studio. Shut the door and play something wonderful. But words rushed in, necessary words catching in her throat, choking her with urgency, forcing her to speak, to look back at Alice and ask,

"What cancer?"

Chapter Two

A week later, Elizabeth withered into an uncomfortable, high-backed chair in her late Father's house. The table before her resembled a digestive battlefield where a legion of finger foods lay defeated, half-eaten, gooping and crumbling through the lace cloth. She marveled at the carnage, though she herself had eaten nothing.

Josh came in from the kitchen, wiping his hands on a dish towel, while Reggie scrambled around the front parlor picking up stacks of paper plates.

"Thank you, Josh," she said. "You're a living wonder. I don't know what I would have done without you two."

"We'll stay until this is all cleaned up. Why don't you go lay down upstairs?"

"No, you two have done enough. My gosh. You've been here all day. I really don't know what I would have done."

"You said that already."

"Well, it's a day for repeating things, I guess. Thank you for coming. I'm very grateful. I'll be fine. Yes, he was a good man." Elizabeth considered all the necessary exaggerations of truth she had muttered in the last hours. "This whole day just feels like another production, with everyone saying their lines and stuffing themselves as if the parade mattered. It's like in dying, we all suddenly become heroes and saints."

Reggie sat beside her, placing his stack of plates on the table. "Did you know any of these people?"

Josh and Reggie had showed up before dawn and begun cleaning. By the time people arrived, all the clutter of her father's legacy had been hidden away: stacks of papers, dusty books, old records for which there was no player, and a quantity of knick-knacks that had lingered since her mother's death sixteen years ago, chipped and covered with the grime of cigar smoke. For the first time since another funeral, the rooms looked a bit like her home.

"Sure," Elizabeth said. "Some of them. Mostly from that school."

"Baker. Was he a professor there?"

"And the librarian. Books were his world."

"Yes, I know. We moved about two hundred out of here this morning," Reggie said.

That didn't surprise her. The stacks had been steadily growing throughout the house since her mother's death. Elizabeth's father, George Arlan Kirtenpepper had lived his life in books and wanted to be buried in books. In a way, his passing felt like the end of an era, with the world moving on to electronic things and abandoning paper and ink.

"You're going to have to do something about this place you know," Reggie said, "now that today is done."

"Right." Elizabeth regarded the vaguely familiar space in which she had grown up. The thick mahogany table and hutch stood like stone edifices from her childhood. The cabriole and Chesterfield still sat facing each other in the living room, rather contrasting, but the same, like her parents. The carpets, the window dressings, all familiar in an eerie time-warp kind of way.

"What do you think?" she asked. "Should I throw it all away? Go through everything? Burn it down?"

"There are companies you can hire to clean and sell the place for you," said Josh. "All I know is, I'm not doing it."

"What if there's something important hidden in all those stacks upstairs?"

"Like what?"

"I don't know, something from my mother, or money or something valuable maybe? And I mean it's a house. It's not close to school, but it's a house, and it's paid for. Maybe I should keep it, you know, as a backup sort of place."

Someone knocked at the open front door, and a tall bald man in a London Fog placed a foot on the threshold. "Elizabeth Kirtenpepper?"

"Yes?" she said. "Come in." Elizabeth stood, and the man stepped inside and shook her hand.

"I'm David Ginnis, the attorney in charge of your father's estate."

Reggie and Josh ducked back into the kitchen.

"I'm sorry to intrude," Ginnis continued. "This must have been a very emotional day for you, but I tried reaching you at your home and I couldn't find your cell number in your father's—"

"I don't have a cellphone."

"Well, I knew you'd be here today, so I thought maybe we could sit and talk."

"Of course. Today is the day for chats. Can I offer you something to...?" She gestured towards the food devastation.

The lawyer raised a hand. "No, thank you."

They sat together on the Chesterfield, and he opened his briefcase. "Most of the details of your father's estate can be dealt with in my office over the next few weeks. It's pretty much the usual routine. I wish I could say you have a big trust fund coming, or a secret investment portfolio, but your father wasn't much into money, as I'm sure you know. But this," he took out a large bubble-wrap envelope and passed it to her, "he was adamant that this be delivered to you as soon as the services were over. I don't know what it is, or what it's all about. He gave it to me in that envelope just like that when he was still mostly lucid and insisted that I keep it at our office until now. Was afraid it would get lost in the house, I guess."

She took the package in her hands. A book. Could have guessed it. But the rest: the lawyer, the sickness, such careful preparations, all the while undergoing his treatment, knowing he was going to die, and yet never telling her anything?

When Mr. Ginnis left, Elizabeth shut the door and carried the parcel up the stairs to where Josh and Reggie had stashed the hiding chaos. She imagined there were worse hoarders in the world than her father. There were no unopened packages, or piles of rotting food attracting rodents. Just books. Books and papers and records, like a massive personal library to support the walls.

She nudged the door of his room open for the first time since his death. Stacks of books everywhere, dirt, and the stagnant smell of cigar and death. He must have had a nurse coming in to help him. Orange med bottles lay toppled on the nightstand, and the bathroom smelled like hospital sanitizer. The sheets were also relatively clean, and someone had cleared a path to the front window to let air in. Withering flowers in a vase dropped browning petals onto the desk. A card from a co-worker at the college read, "Get well soon."

So, people had known. Just not her.

The indent of her father's sleeping body remained sculpted into his side of the mattress. The other side lay mostly unstirred beneath the mustard-colored spread.

She moved aside some papers and plopped into the old armchair her mother used to knit in by the fireplace, now long cold and blackened. He had always said he was going to clean it out, kept meaning to get to it, move all those books and start a fire again. Now Elizabeth was grateful he never did. Better this than an inferno.

Right?

VALERIE NIEMERG

She listened to the clinks of dishes and water turning on and
off while Josh and Reggie cleaned up downstairs. She clutched the
packet, unwilling to tear it open just yet, knowing well what was
inside.

Chapter Three

Josh and Reggie had finished cleaning and left while Elizabeth napped. The house donned a stifling quiet, an emptiness unheeded by the books and clutter.

She huddled in her mother's chair, still hugging her father's packet and listening for some remnant echo. Surely the spirit of her childhood self still danced for her dying mother somewhere in these rooms. Couldn't she hear another cough, a breath, someone rustling the sheets? She might have even welcomed a disembodied spirit to break the silence, but the old Victorian didn't proffer so much as a wall-creak. She was a relic in a tomb of stories.

She lifted the envelope, and the book slid out and dropped into her lap. Of course, it was a book, her father's answer to everything. It felt corpselike in her hands: cool, lifeless, and heavy.

Gold lettering stitched across the red-thread cover declared her name like a marquee. *Elizabeth.* What did that mean? Had her father written this and named it for her? He never wrote anything that she knew of. Still, it looked fairly new: the pages neither worn nor earmarked, and the binding almost perfectly unbroken.

On the inside cover, a note in his familiar hand had been hastily scratched.

Elizabeth,

I almost forgot. Be advised, this book CAN be stolen. Can you imagine? Who would do something so horrible? But it does happen. I had a book stolen once and had to cross the Atlantic to get back to it. At that time, no easy feat! Keep it safe!

-Dad

She shook her head. How deeply medicated had he been when he wrote these last words to her?

The oddities of the book continued: no title page, no publishing information, no author bio, preface, introduction, copyright date, dedication. Just the words *Read Carefully*, printed like a warning on the first page.

How ridiculous, she thought. Did one have to be careful when reading now? Crossing the street, cell phones, strange cities, falling in love, all yes. But reading a book? Wasn't there anything left in the world that a person could relax about?

She began reading.

Chapter Four

Figaro, the most renowned of itinerant barbers, that rogue of former years, once friendly with both noble and peasant alike as the swarthiest of fellows, the champion of impossible causes, the Saint of medicines and cures, indeed none other than the wonder of Seville incarnate: Figaro, had taken to settling down.

A handful of fireflies erupted forth from the pages, though Elizabeth only saw them in her peripheral, and waved them away with a careless hand since she wasn't even certain she saw them.

No longer itinerant and self-employed, Figaro had accepted a steady position as the Major-Domo in the household of Count Almaviva. Goodbye to the days of wandering to and fro in all weathers, piecing together a livelihood through the gossip on every tongue in Seville. Figaro-su, Figaro-la! A settled man he was now, working in a steady employ, serving his lord and master in an honest manner, restricted to a routine, and rather liking it.

A warm breeze swept Elizabeth's hair around her cheeks, and she brushed it back while she read.

Of course, being so persuaded to a settled situation, it naturally followed that Figaro, after so many years of passing the gauntlet between the promises of others, should at last nod his own head in a romantic direction.

As the object of his most intimate desire, Figaro had chosen the clever and charming Susanna, personal chambermaid to the Countess. Really the situation could not have been sweeter. Susanna would serve her Mistress, while Figaro served their Master, and together they would share the grinds and laughter of their days. And at night, well. . .

Oh, Dad, Elizabeth thought. *You sent me a novel version of* The Marriage of Figaro. *How useless.* She shooed a fly away and ran her fingertips over the seams of her corset.

While the Count's family had withdrawn to Cadiz on holiday, Figaro resolved to ask for Susanna's hand by the seaside. She accepted him with a smile so sincere, it made him shudder.

It was so like her father to think that a book would be enough to mend everything. She snuggled herself down into the grass and leaned back against the trunk of a large tree.

The story progressed with a lengthy introduction describing the holiday in Cadiz, and a few flashbacks to the home manor, where a servant girl was let go for being pregnant.

Elizabeth pursed her lips. There were no seaside vacations in *The Marriage of Figaro*, or chambermaids getting sent away pregnant. What was this? Some kind of mockup? *Oh no.* How horrible. Not one of these "contemporary rewrites" of a masterpiece. She had once suffered through a production of *Hansel and Gretel* in which the entire second-act ballet of angels had been replaced with supernumeraries in monstrous rubber-chef costumes, plodding around the stage alongside fish heads and tree stumps. She repented her previous thoughts about harmless books.

"That's just not the way it happened in the opera," she said aloud shivering to think where this novel-form of *Figaro* would take her, because she would have to read it. She would have to read it. *Oh, Dad.*

Elizabeth's feet were feeling squeezed, as though held prisoner in tin slippers. She reached down through her skirts, struggling against an intense constriction on her torso, and removed her very foreign-looking shoes. After a lengthy process of unwinding laces, she pulled them from her grateful feet with a sigh of relief and held one up. Sort of a cross between a boot and a pump, but with a frighteningly angular heel about two inches tall, and a nonsensically pointed sole that would get stuck in any sidewalk crevice. Maneuvering on this miserable thing would be a balancing act akin to tightrope walking.

What a stupid shoe.

She was just about to cognitively process that she had removed it from her own foot, when she heard the horse hooves, and that's when she looked up.

᪥

Elizabeth gasped and jumped up, wobbling on the uneven forest floor. She jabbed her foot on a protruding stone, then tripped and fell backwards onto the trunk of a large elm.

Her senses exploded with information that her mind couldn't process: sounds, scents, and visions that didn't make sense. A warm breeze whispered through the leaves above her. A fly crawled across her arm. An unseen bird chirped nearby. All began turning circles, as an onslaught of nausea overwhelmed her. She rolled over and threw up on the tree's roots.

When the spasm had passed, she hung over the retch, gasping air in and out between hiccups, clutching the tree like an anchor as everything around her continued spinning while the sounds of the horse hooves climaxed and faded.

Her hand gripped the bark of the tree. She dug her fingers into one of the deep grooves, its coarse fibers sinking into her fingernails. She scratched at it and rubbed the grains, slowly, slowly, round and round. She looked up.

Her father's wingback chair was gone. All his stacks of books and papers were gone. The bed where he died, the whole room and house gone, vanished as though never existing. Only trees, shrubs, and dirt. Woods. Green woods, with a dry, reddish, earthen floor and the dark scent of pine warmed in an afternoon sun.

She tried to calm herself, to stop the hiccups. It all felt so real. It sounded real. The pain in her foot and the grit on her fingertips couldn't be more real. Was this some delusion brought on by the trauma of her father's death? Yes, some dissociative disorder causing a traumatic hallucination. She hadn't really reacted to his death at all, had she? Wasn't that unnatural? He was the last living member of her family. She should have been traumatized, or at least healthily upset.

Dissociative disorders. Elizabeth had heard the phrase, but she had no idea what it meant. It sounded right though, didn't it? Dissociative disorders? She shuddered. There was something wrong with her. Something so wrong that her mind could transport her senses to another place, without feeling anything so upsetting as a bump on the head.

A bump on the head. That's probably what happened. She had been reading the *Figaro* book when she must have fallen off the chair and hit her head. That must have caused some kind of temporary memory loss. Or perhaps she was completely delusional and imagining, with exquisite clarity, a strange place she had never been to, or heard of, or seen, and...*what was she wearing?*

Her black chiffon mourning dress, the one with the flowing sleeves for concert appearances, had been replaced with a massive pile of heavy fabrics and refinery. It was a lady's costume, probably eighteenth century: slip, stockings, hooped petticoat and what could only be described as a torturous cage, fixed like iron around her ribs and waist. A corset. How did singers breathe in these things?

But this could make sense. She had been reading a mocked-up version of *Figaro* when she hit her head, right? So now she was probably in a hospital somewhere, dreaming all of this up. She searched past her massive skirts for the shoes she had taken off and saw the book her father had given her. It lay on the forest floor at her feet, the golden, cursive letters of her name sparkling in the sunlight.

She opened it. "Read Carefully." Right. She found where she had left off and continued reading.

Custom required that two servants notify their employer with the intent to marry before any public announcement, so Figaro would have to approach the Count. But there could be no objections to the match. Susanna and Figaro were both eligible, and able to carry on with their jobs. Not to forget either, Figaro had been instrumental in securing the heart and hand of the Countess Rosina for his employer. No doubt, Count Almaviva would delightedly convey upon Figaro his permission for the same joys of matrimonial bliss.

Well, this was useless. But she read on, hoping to ignite some unseen trigger, and find herself home again.

But Count Almaviva was not of the same mind as he had once been. After a year or so of marriage, the fascinating allure of his lovely wife had waned. The Countess Rosina sat now amongst Almaviva's possessions, a living trophy to envy and admire, while Almaviva, lord of his estate, allowed his interests to stray outside his wife's bedchamber to the next most convenient conquests. Whether willing or not, those under his authority, through his employment, security and all that contemporary social dictates decreed, owed him such small inconveniences.

Elizabeth looked up. Still in the forest. Still in the corset. What the hell was going on?

Even the day before leaving for Cadiz, the Count had decided to take what was due from one of his youngest kitchen maids. Amada de Suria, newly come of age, was by all rights on Heaven and Earth surely his for the taking. But the infernal girl got her pride up and resisted him, fleeing into the woods. She would have to come back eventually, of course, or she would starve. What on earth was she afraid of? This had to be dealt with swiftly. If Almaviva left for Cadiz, there would be rumors. The girl would talk, and the time was ripe for talking. Servants and lower classes all across the lands were standing taller, speaking louder, and adopting unspeakable attitudes of impudence in the face of those to whom they owed much. They called it Enlightenment, perhaps to disguise its wicked promise of societal chaos. Or so thought the Count as he got on his horse to track the girl down and subdue her one way or another.

"Again, none of this happened in the opera," Elizabeth said out loud. Just then, she heard voices, a man muttering obscenities, while a smaller voice whimpered. The tall man in formal riding attire appeared in the clearing, dragging a young girl by the hair. He threw her to the ground, mounted her, and began to sort through her skirts. Elizabeth didn't need a diagram. Whether or not this alternate reality was imagined suddenly seemed irrelevant. She crept out from behind the tree, picked up a conveniently large branch from the forest floor, lifted it like a baseball bat and gave the bastard a good solid whack on the head.

For a breathless second, he hung suspended in gravity-defying stillness before collapsing onto the forest floor.

"Well," Elizabeth said, making sure he was really out. "That's enough of that. Are you okay? Are you hurt?"

The girl trembled with terror, writhing away from the fallen man.

"It's all over now. You're safe." Elizabeth bent down and offered her a hand. She couldn't have been more than fifteen years old. Definitely servant class. "You're okay now." She brushed the girl's skirts off and pulled some twigs from her hair. "Who was that man?"

"He was—did you kill him?"

Elizabeth looked back at the man crumpled on the dirt. She hadn't even thought about whether or not it might kill him. Goodness, now that she thought about it, she'd never done anything like that in her life. Had she killed a man? She bent over and felt his neck for a pulse.

"No. I didn't kill him. But I suggest we get out of here before he wakes up."

The girl's eyes widened with renewed terror. She lifted her skirts and tore off through the trees.

"Wait! Wait! I don't even know your name! Can't you please just—"

Elizabeth wanted to follow her, but in her haste to prevent the unthinkable, she hadn't even put her shoes on. She went back to retrieve them and her father's book before pursuing the girl through the trees.

She quickly learned that one doesn't "run" anywhere in formal eighteenth-century garments. Beyond the absurdly geometrical shoes, the large hoop and the cage around her waist made navigating trees and shrubs nearly impossible.

She pushed on, hopeful to catch the girl, but her clothing was incredibly hot, and moving through the woods, constantly stumbling over things one couldn't see, was only making her hotter. Why on earth had women put up with these costumes for so long? She yearned for the facility of a pair of Keds and her bicycle.

After only a few minutes, she had lost all trace of the girl, but she trudged on. After about a half hour, she realized she was hungry. She hadn't eaten anything at the funeral, and her long-neglected stomach now gurgled impatiently with each inhale. Upon recognition of this, her mind, like a well-programmed search engine, instantly launched into a reflex analysis of what type of food she would like: Italian? No, too heavy. Mexican? Too gassy. Chinese? Possibly, some stir-fried veggies in a garlic sauce. But no rice. Too many calories. Definitely no rice...It was at this moment in her habitual menu search that she paused, perplexed.

How am I going to get something to eat?

Wherever she was, it wasn't anywhere near a strip mall or corner deli. And her freezer, in which she stored half of everything she cooked, was all the way back...home. With mild panic, she realized she wasn't in Kansas anymore. No longer a beneficiary of twenty-first-century American convenience, with fourteen ethnic options to choose for lunch, she was hungry, and there was nothing she could do about it. Hungry. Imagine that.

A veil of shame descended on her while she continued on her trek. She had always kept her diet to a civil rate, eating to live and not the other way around, but she had never been hungry. Not real hunger. Of course, there were people in the world who were hungry. She knew that, saw the ads on TV and the internet, sponsored a family in India, or was it a child in Africa? She did her part. But now she realized she had never actually been hungry herself. As a Catholic, she was supposed to fast twice a year, or was it every Friday? She vaguely remembered something about Fridays but didn't think it was supposed to be an actual hunger-inducing thing. And what did they really mean by fast, anyway? They didn't mean not eat anything. Surely not. For working people? What about sick people, and pregnant women and elderly and children? Did they all have to go hungry too? For an entire day? Twice a year? What nonsense.

Still, lost in those woods, Elizabeth wished she'd had not lived her whole life so spoiled. It would have been nice to have some experience with hunger before being dumped into it against one's will.

However, the hunger answered a question. She wasn't dreaming. When in dreams, fantasies, or hallucinations, did one ever feel something as grounding as good old-fashioned hunger? Delusions

24

were never so real as that. Goodness, if she really had hit her head and been sent to a hospital, surely someone would have hooked her up to a feeding tube. Even coma patients get food.

Indian. She loved Indian, especially that creamy spinach with the blocks of cheese curd, or those wonderful deep-fried pouches of potatoes and peas, or some chicken in a milky-curry sauce, or— *Elizabeth, you must stop this.*

It did her no good to think about food. She should control her thoughts. Stay focused on the task at hand. Find some signs of life. She wasn't alone in this universe, and couldn't be too far from some civilization, *so keep moving, just keep going forward.* If she was going forward. What if she was going in circles? *Oh dear.* What if she ended up back with the unconscious rapist? It would be impossible to defend oneself while constricted in all this wardrobe nonsense.

Her foot caught on a tree root, and she stumbled to the ground again, banging her face and scratching up her hands. She probably looked a mess in these dirty clothes, smelling of sweat, with dirt and scrapes all over. But of course, there was no mirror or handy shop window to glance into for a vanity check.

She got up again and wiped her hands. When visions of chicken tandoori came into her head, she shook them off with another horrible thought. Unless she was mistaken, the forest was getting darker. And cooler. Assuming time worked the same in her present realm of oblivion, this particular day was winding to an end. She was alone and hungry, in a strange wilderness, and soon it would be dark.

She wished she had invested some time in learning to survive outdoors, like watching some of those TV survival competitions or internet classes. Why had she wasted so much time on stupid, useless things like **Verdi and Puccini**?

Elizabeth stopped. *What a terrible thought.* She mustn't think that ever again. She promised herself that no matter how hungry she got, she would never again allow that thought into her mind. Even chicken tandoori was better than that.

If she couldn't find civilization by nightfall, she would just have to sleep in the wild. On the ground. What if it got cold at night? This hoop skirt was absurdly uncomfortable, but she could try to remove it and use it as some sort of covering. What if another rapist came along? Were there wild animals in these woods? Wild cats or bears or snakes?

Poisonous spiders?

Elizabeth shivered, then applied all her mental faculties towards a pungently vivid recollection of a warm plate of chicken tandoori.

Chapter Five

❧❧❧

E lizabeth lay curled into a ball, hidden within a cluster of large boulders. The waning hours of the day had brought a variety of enlightening sensations, like cold. She had removed her outer layer of skirts, just to get the ridiculous corset off, and tossed the hoop cage away, wrapping the fabric over herself. But the cold night air was penetrating, and she shivered endlessly, warming her hands with her breath.

The hunger grew nerve-rackingly intense. How acute hunger could get when one didn't take care of it within a decent time frame. Without food for only one day, it was all she could do to continually stop from jumping up and running to her non-existent kitchen. Was she shaking from the cold, or dehydration?

Under some of the skirts, she had found a crescent-shaped pillow tied around her waist. She used it as a head rest placed atop her father's book.

As darkness descended between the trees, the woods became a perfect palette of blackness. Elizabeth couldn't see so much as her hand before her face, let alone the rocks she leaned on for some warmth and shelter. Anything could be inches in front of her, staring her down, drooling. Creatures crawled all around. Every so often one scurried up a limb, and she'd flinch back in horror, shaking her skirts, and opening her warm cocoon to more cold air. She had never known such terror. It consumed her like an unearthly possession, heightening her senses to every branch crack or bend, every scamper, and every strange horrific gurgle of the wilderness. She wept from the fear, quietly, lest anything in the darkness find her huddled there. She could hear her own heart beating heavy and frantic inside her ears. She could hear her breaths, and she could feel her nerves under her skin tingling with a new and foreign agony. Had she died and didn't know it? Was this hell?

She couldn't let herself go to that place of panic. No, she was not dead. This was not hell. It was just...solitude.

Elizabeth lived alone, but then it wasn't really alone, was it? One always knew one's neighbors were right upstairs, or next door, or a phone call away. The whole fabric of society was always there with a police officer or a soup kitchen or a welfare program, or even a church one could go to. But this was not like that. This was real solitude. Wherever she was, she was abandoned and isolated, with nothing but some ridiculous clothing and a useless book.

She wept, shivered, and slapped at the critters through the horrible, darkened hours. There might have been moments when she dozed, but mostly, she wept.

When daylight came, Elizabeth found several lumps on her legs where critters had sampled her wares. She and her skirts were a mess of dirt and leaves. Her fingers got stuck trying to sort through her knotted mess of hair, and she smelled like something on its way to a morgue. Her hunger had evolved into a sinister companion, constantly writhing inside both gut and mind.

But at least the woods were warmer, and the light had returned. Blessed, beautiful, shimmering light. Elizabeth was newly grateful for the gift of eyesight.

And there, she thought, *I'm alive, warm, and not blind. See?* Not hell. Definitely not hell.

Not yet anyway.

A few minutes later, she was standing, extremely perplexed over the five layers of clothing she had removed before going to sleep. Which one went on first? She had on her stockings and what could only be described as a white cotton nightgown, but the rest lay scattered on the forest floor like puzzle pieces. She despaired at the thought of putting it all back on. For goodness' sake, it would probably get hot again today, and she surely had more miles to walk. Could she even get back into the corset without help? She had wiggled and writhed for half-hour the night before, trying to get out of it. She put on one of three petticoats, tucked her nightgown inside it, and carried the rest in her arms.

At least an hour of trudging passed before a most satisfying sound softly rippled through the trees: horse hooves. Her heart jumped as though it were a motorcycle or a lawn mower. She plunged through the trees toward the sound, tripping over a rock and falling face first onto a dusty road, where all her garments and her book spread around her in the dirt.

Fortunately, the horses had the decency not to run her over, and two of the three veered around her, while the third, more directly in her line of fire, simply jumped over her head and kept going.

"Wait!" She dared to raise her head after the spattering of rocks and dirt had landed. "Please wait! I need help, I'm lost! Oh come back!"

A cloud of dust quickly faded into an echo of the pounding hooves.

Elizabeth sat up and started to cry again. She couldn't eat, or sleep, or find any decency in humanity. So, she might as well enjoy some good old, dependable, self-pity. Quickly admitting that crying wasn't going to get her so much as a drink of water, she picked up her clothes and started down the road the way the horses had come. But she allowed herself the pleasure of crying while she walked.

It wasn't long before she heard more clip-clopping from behind. A dilapidated wagon approached at a labored crawl. The driver sat so hunched over that, besides the dark and worn hands holding the reins, all she could see of him was a smoky beard dripping down beneath his threadbare straw hat.

This time, she took no chances. She marched out in the middle of the lane and planted herself directly in his path. The carriage came so close that she could feel the warm stinky breath of the horses on her forehead before the man finally pulled up on the reins.

"What the hell are you stopping for now?" a woman's voice squawked from behind him.

The man remained fixed like a stone sculpture, only lifting a reluctant hand to shoo Elizabeth out of the way.

"I'm very sorry to bother you," Elizabeth said, "but I'm lost, and I haven't had anything to eat in almost two days."

The woman's head popped up behind him. Beneath her dark red mop of hair, her face testified to a colorful variety of life's beatings, from scars and burns to warts and moles.

"Get out of the way, you hussy, before I have my Ramon run you through!"

"Oh no!" Elizabeth cried, tears returning. "Please, I don't mean any harm, and I don't want anything, really, I'm just lost, and I haven't eaten. I've been walking so long through these woods, and can't you just please help me find some civilization?"

"Civilization?" the woman hollered back with raucous laughter. "Why don't you have no clothes on? Walking around with nothing on but a shift and under-petticoat. What kind of hussy are you, out here in the wild? Now get out of our way!"

"Oh, but I do have clothing, see?" Elizabeth held up the bundle of garments. "You see, I was just so hot and tired that I found it easier to take them off. I'm not a hussy or anything like it, I swear to you, I just..."

Ramon stood up in the wagon next to the woman. Elizabeth imagined Ramon must be about seventeen years old and very tall. A tuft of coarse black hair seemed to stand erect atop his bulbous skull, but the rest of his angular structure was ashen with sun-stained skin. His large white eyes wandered over Elizabeth as though she were a roast in a butcher shop, while his mouth hung perpetually ajar. A small, rusted axe swung back and forth in his left hand.

"Them's some nice clothes," the woman said. "Come here and let me look at 'em."

Elizabeth walked around to the back of the wagon, unable to take her eyes off Ramon and his axe. The woman snatched one of the skirts up and examined it.

In the back of the wagon a third passenger lay, a hand resting on the beginning hump of a pregnancy. She was very young, younger even than any of Elizabeth's students at the college, and her eyes glanced up at her with pleading despair.

"I tell you what," the older woman said. "We'll give you a ride into the nearest village. In exchange, you give me this here skirt and gown. Awful nice this is. I'll take it for a deal."

"Then I won't have any clothes!"

"It's your choice. But there ain't nothing to eat in these woods, and you won't last another night against the critters."

Elizabeth didn't have to think too hard. If she didn't find shelter by this evening, she might as well starve to death as freeze.

"Now hurry up then." The woman concluded the deal, reading Elizabeth's expression. "I don't have all day."

Ramon stepped forward and took Elizabeth's hand. His strength surprised her, pulling her up into the wagon with one easy gesture. She retracted her hand and sat down on a pile of hay as far from Ramon as possible. The cart smelled like sweat and excrement.

"Hello," Elizabeth said to the girl. "My name is Elizabeth. What's your name?"

The girl's eyes settled with curiosity on Elizabeth, as though she was surprised to be noticed. "Frescura Bascal—"

The older woman cut her off. "I'm Laia, and her name don't matter. She ain't no need for it no more. All done with all that, you hear? Now shut yourself up!"

Elizabeth swallowed her horror and hugged her father's book. Perhaps she was in hell after all. "Laia, could you please tell me," she asked, trying to avoid Ramon's perpetual stare, "if you don't mind, where we are?"

"What do you mean, where we are? You are lost."

"Yes, I'm afraid so. I really have no idea."

"Where you from?"

"Kansas. Wichita, actually."

"Kansaswitch? You a witch?"

"No. Wich*ita*, it's a city in Kansas."

"Well, Kansaswitch. You're on the road to Seville."

Elizabeth gasped. "Seville? Surely not Seville, Spain?"

The woman released another haughty roar. Ramon stared. Laia replied, "Well, I don't mean Seville, England, hussy witch."

Seville, Spain, England. Elizabeth felt a momentary lapse of relief. She might be in a world created in the bliss of a coma, but at least it was her home planet.

"Do you mind telling me what the date is? I mean, I've been lost for some time, and I need to make sure I haven't missed anything. Do you know what day it is?"

"Course I do!" Laia said. "You think I'm ancient? It's Sunday, first in November. How long you been in them woods?"

"Some time, I think. I wonder if you could possibly tell me also, what the year is?"

The woman's eyes widened. She pointed a jagged finger. "Now you listen. We don't need no trouble from any witch or hussy or loon, you understand? Who doesn't know what year it is? I'll tell you who. A looney. Escaped from your dad's attic, did you?"

"What? No! I'm not a loon! I'm not any of those things. I just need to know what the date is. I mean, I know that's a ridiculous question, but these clothes, and everyone riding horseback and pulling wagons. I was. . .sick. Yes. I was sick and in a coma."

"Where's acomba?"

"A coma. It's when you fall and hit your head and go to sleep and you can't wake up. I was asleep for a long time, and now I need to know the date."

The woman's boney finger waggled loosely in the air between them, ascending in slow motion to her forehead. She made a quick gesture toward her son. "Get her out. Get her out now!"

Ramon stood in the wobbling wagon and lunged for Elizabeth. He grabbed her arm with knife-like fingers and dragged her up.

"She's a witch, she is!" Laila ranted. "In a comba, in some kind of spell. I knewed I shouldn't picked her up! Throw her off, quick now!"

Ramon lugged Elizabeth's reluctant body to the rear of the wagon.

"No, No. please. I'm not a witch. I'm sorry. I won't ask any more questions. Please, please don't throw me off!"

With a heedless shove, Ramon sent her flying and she landed, skidding on the road, her book tumbling in the dust beside her. A searing pain ignited in her shoulder and hip as she rolled over and hit her head.

Chapter Six

Her head throbbed wickedly. She reached a hand up and felt a gash, the hair around it hard and sticky. Other parts of her cried out, her right arm where she had landed, her shoulder and left wrist. She moved them cautiously. Not broken. *Kirtenpeppers don't break bones*, her father had always said.

She pulled herself up, but it was a terrible mistake and her head reeled in protest. She lowered back down onto a soft pile of hay.

A soft pile of hay.

She lay still, rubbing some of the dried, cracking straws between her fingers, relishing them and their heavenly smell. Hay was a marvelous thing. Its very presence implied so much, the way a tiny **fermata** drawn over a music staff can indicate all the inner complexities of a human soul.

"Why is that fermata there?" She had asked that question to many a student, but today it was Devon, a junior and aspiring baritone at the college who stood beside her piano. He answered her with the look of indignant disgust only a college boy can summon when asked an entry-level question. It amused Elizabeth because they all made the same face, and they all thought they were so unique about it.

"Hold the note longer," he said.

"How long?"

"It's a fermata. I don't know. As long as I like."

"Really. As long as you like? So, all day?"

"No," the youth replied as though she was an idiot. "Not all day. I don't know, until you run out of breath or get bored."

"Oh dear. Is that what you think? Devon, we don't just stop because the composer told us to. We figure out why the composer told us to stop."

"Well, ask Mozart then. He put it there."

"Okay. Take a sarcasm break. You can do this. Why did Mozart put it there? Why over that particular note? Was the fermata just arbitrary? It just seemed like a good place to hold the note?"

The Socratic method was failing. The young singer just wanted to learn his notes and be told where to breathe so he could join his friends at Java's Cafe. If he was going to get his money's worth out of her (whether or not he wanted it), she would have to employ an alternate tactic. Throughout the centuries, one approach had never failed with any singer.

"Here," she said, reaching into her purse, "let's go get a snack, and I'll show you why that fermata is there."

"A snack?"

"Yup." She held open her studio door. "Leave your score here; we'll be right back."

"A snack."

"Patience. All will be revealed."

Together, they trod down the linoleum hallway to the well-loved and deeply abused campus vending machine. She passed him the money.

"It's on me. Go ahead."

He put the money into the machine.

"Okay, right there!" she said suddenly.

"What?"

"What did you just do?"

"I put the money in the machine?" he answered with a wedding cake of sarcasm layered so profoundly that she suddenly suspected he wasn't accessing his whole range. "Like you told me to?"

"No, after that, you stopped for a second. Why did you do that?"

"I don't know. I was just thinking about what I wanted, I guess."

"That's a fermata."

Slowly, almost imperceptibly, the dawn of understanding bloomed on the young baritone's features like a morning in Spring. "So, you're saying, Mozart put that fermata there so I would ... stop and think?"

"Not you. Your character."

"So, the fermata means that he stops to think about something for a second? But what's he thinking about?"

"Well, what's the last thing he said, and the next thing he says? The fermata should carry him from one thought to the next."

"Oh, come on. You really think people can tell all that while you're holding a note?"

She entered the numbers on the machine to drop some pretzels. "Much more effective than thinking about the position of your soft palate."

‖: :‖

The appearance of pretzels in the memory forced Elizabeth back to her present entanglement, where her stomach gurgled. But she returned easily, for hay was a fermata.

People made hay piles. People did. And she hadn't landed on

hay; she had landed on a rocky road. That meant someone had brought her to the hay. A repentant Laia, or perhaps a passing good Samaritan, had lifted her unconscious body from the road and carried her to some hay. And that meant kindness. Hay was more wonderful than a warm bath, Ibuprofen, and a plate of steamy chicken tandoori. Someone had been kind.

There was a heavy wool blanket atop her, and even better, a roof. She could smell animals and hear their stomping and grunting. Wherever this was, it was not hell. The other mysteries could be solved as they came, so long as the stings of hunger, pain, and fear could all be quickly vanquished by something so simple, so humble, so primitive, as a pile of hay.

Her father's book lay beside her. *Elizabeth*, it proclaimed in golden, cursive across the cover.

"I am still Elizabeth," she said, reaching for it as though it were suddenly a blood relative, "and together we do not make any sense."

She lifted the cover and passed the title page with its strange precaution, though she didn't remember it being in such large print. She turned the pages back and forth to find her place.

It was about mid-day when he found her, shivering in a cave. If she didn't submit willfully, he would take her by force. But even in this he was thwarted, when a stranger encountered them both, and knocked him unconscious. He awoke a half hour later with a wretched headache and a sorely bruised ego.

Elizabeth blinked and reread the passage. Perhaps she had gotten it wrong before. In her frantic state, maybe she had just mis-read it. Still, the chapter's final paragraph felt oddly scolding.

Furious, he returned home to finalize the arrangements for his journey, while both girls strode off through the wilderness, independent and headstrong, lunging into matters, circumstances and forces without proper knowledge, counsel or preparation,

37

*causing general chaos for themselves and much unnecessary labors
for the universe at large. Read Carefully.*

Despite feeling oddly reprimanded, with hay and a warm
blanket and a throb in her head, Elizabeth let the book slip from
her hands as she drifted again into sweet, healing sleep.

The second time Elizabeth awoke, hunger attacked like a rabid
animal, more fearsome than the pain in her head and shoulder. It
was night. A glass lantern hung on a nearby post, casting golden
shadows on the barn's beams and cobwebs. A small plate of food
rested nearby: bread, cheese, and a white fleshy fruit with tiny
black seeds. She devoured it in a wild, uncivilized manner.

However, even in her gorging, she had to stop and pay a
particular deference to the wedge of cheese. This was no grocery
store mozzarella. This cheese was unique, mild but with a tangy
character she had never tasted. She savored each small, delightful
nibble, closing her eyes and then almost choking from giggling at
how ridiculous she was.

"Do you like it?" a man's voice said. "I make it myself."

Elizabeth started, then turned. The voice was mature, but less
aged than the cheese, definitely a baritone, with a warm depth and
slight rasp. The voice's owner sat about fifteen feet away on a
small bench, his hands hanging loosely between his knees and a
lengthy piece of straw dangling from his fingertips. He was probably mid to late fifties, well-darkened by years in the sun, his thick,
gray hair pulled back in a low ponytail. He was a short man, she
could tell that, even sitting, and his figure suggested he not only
made the cheese but enjoyed it as well.

Elizabeth sat up, and her head screamed out again.

"Whoa, easy there. You've taken a nasty bump. Go slowly
now," he said. "Got no need for concern. Safe here."

"This is your barn then?"

"Yes, yes, and I'm sorry. Shouldn't have said that last part. I mean, the part about me making the cheese. What are you supposed to answer? No? Was vanity. Just vanity. Can see you enjoyed it well enough."

"I did. It's a very unique cheese and, and...I don't know how to describe it."

"Of course not. If you did, wouldn't need the cheese."

"Goodness, there's a quandary," she said. "If I could describe it, we wouldn't need the cheese. Are you saying that the word is more powerful than the cheese?"

"More the opposite. Can hear someone tell of the cheese for months, listen to relatives describe it, read all the cheese papers, sit through sermons on the subject of the cheese. None will be as good as just tasting it for yourself."

"Still, the words are necessary."

"Are they? Can't we just eat the cheese?"

Elizabeth considered. "Well, I can't. Part of an experience is putting its effect into words. Sort of the ode of gratitude. We describe because we're grateful. And surely gratitude is the best of all experiences. Yes. That's it."

The man leaned backwards on a beam, then placed the straw between his lips. He crossed his arms and slowly spun the straw back and forth between his teeth. "All right," he said, "perhaps you're right. But just don't get stuck and forget to eat the cheese."

Elizabeth laughed. "You're not going to throw me off a wagon."

"Ah. Is that what happened to you? Explains why you were in the road, knocked out and half-naked. Imagine you'd been there for some time."

"Oh," Elizabeth answered, wary. "I was lost in the woods. For a long time. I was very hungry, then this family picked me up, promised to give me a ride if I gave them my clothes."

"Took your clothes and threw you off first chance they got?"

"Something like that." She took another nibble of cheese and noticed that he seemed to wince and look away briefly. "Thank you," she said. "For picking me up. You could have just left me. I imagine there were others who had. . ."

"Uh now. Don't do that. Can't do that. That's the one rule. No one has ever cried in this barn, and we're not going to break the tradition tonight. Now take a deep breath, and we'll deal with all that in the morning, or whenever. Just one step at a time, right? Probably need another good bout of sleep for that bump on your head to steady. Now I live alone you know, and much as I'd like to take you in, don't think that'd be appropriate, understand? So, you stay out here. You'll be safe. Can show you how to block the door from the inside. Never too cold in here, and it's better than the side of the road."

"Most certainly. But, if you don't mind my asking, why did you take me in?"

The straw teetered in the corner of his lips. "You were in my way," he said. "Had to move you anyway, so might as well pick you up. No trouble. No trouble at all. Now there's fresh water in a pitcher on the table there, and a wash basin with a clean towel, and through that back door, you'll find the necessary. I think that's everything you should need. That bruise on your head will be much better in the morning. Wasn't bleeding too bad. Not too deep. See how it looks, and then maybe tell your story."

He stood and rubbed his jaw with one hand, like massaging a sore, while he looked around, imagining what else he could do.

"I spent last night curled up under my skirts between some boulders in the woods," she said. "I think I will be very comfortable here, thank you."

"Well, can leave the lamp burning if you want, but might attract the bugs. Up to you. Good night."

Chapter Seven

✦✦✦

E lizabeth dreamed of her little apartment in Kansas with her herb plants on the tiny patio off the kitchen. She rubbed the leaves between her fingers and held them up to her nose: rosemary, sage, chives, mint, thyme, dill, parsley, and four different types of basil. In the morning, the barn door remained blocked from the inside. She didn't want to sleep late. Farmers generally needed to get into their barns early: rooster crowing, cows milking and all that.

When she opened the door, the bright sun ignited only a minor throbbing in her head.

Around the side of the barn, drifts of fat, gray sheep meandered across a well-chomped hillside. A plump swine snored in a dusty pen, and a handful of multicolored goats skittered nervously through a bruised and battered yard, much more brown than green. Elizabeth assumed it was a yard. The fence supposedly serving as border and containment lacked sufficient posts to prohibit the simplest of escapes.

A handful of rusted farm tools had been tossed in a pile next to a mound of buzzing manure, and somewhere there must be chickens. She could hear their squabbling and noticed the feather fluffs wafting around her feet.

The house was small and quaint in a stucco kind of way, with a pale brown stone that had probably once been white. Patches of straggling greenery edged the walls, rising from long-neglected flower beds overrun with weeds. The whole property was in desperate need of an HGTV remodel. Surely no woman had touched the place in decades.

No, Elizabeth. That was sexist. She wondered if it was okay to make sexist assumptions in this fantasy version of Spain. Passing a rotting tree stump on the pathway, she deliberately decided it was a male stump, and took a naughty personal pleasure in knowing that no one could do anything about it, except accuse her of being a loon.

He waited for her on the front stone step, sitting against the door frame with his legs stretched out and crossed as he sipped from an earthenware mug.

"I haven't kept you waiting, have I?" she said.

"No, no, though grateful you're an early riser. How are you feeling?"

"Oh, hay and cheese. The whole world is looking brighter."

"Sleep well enough?"

"Yes. Thank you. A thousand thank you's."

He gestured to the stoop, where a new plate awaited: a healthy chunk of dry toast, another piece of cheese, and some fried meat she didn't recognize but which tasted like prime rib. From a pottery cup, she sipped the creamy milk of some animal.

"I am so much in debt to you, and I don't even know your name."

"Gaspar," he said extending his hand, "and you don't owe me anything."

"Elizabeth Kirtenpepper."

"That's a name you don't hear every day. Now I know you're not from around here."

"No. I'm not."

"Well now, where is it you're supposed to be then?"

Elizabeth silently fiddled with her toast, while a pair of birds whistled away in the branches of an old tree.

"I see. You're in some kind of trouble. Trouble with the nobility? Or family? You're not an outlaw, are you? Not that it would matter. Laws aren't always to be trusted, but...would be nice to know all the same."

"No, I'm not an outlaw," she said.

"You have any family? Someone we could send for?"

She shook her head, and he rubbed his jaw, puffing out a snort.

"I thought you said I wasn't going to throw you off any wagons," he said.

"I was intoxicated by the cheese. Sleep has sobered me up, I think." She smiled up at him, squinting in the morning light. "I even bonded with those two horses in there."

"You're easy to please. That's something."

"The truth is, I just keep hoping I'll wake up somewhere else."

"We've all wished that from time to time. Where would you like to wake up then? Home?"

"Oh, I'd settle for a hospital bed. Or someplace that just made sense. At least that would mean I'm not crazy."

"What doesn't make sense?"

Elizabeth finished her cheese while a nearby cricket complained about morning coming too early. The swine apparently had woken up as well and released a series of furious snorts across the yard.

Elizabeth answered his question with one of her own. "Gaspar, why did you pick me up? If I'd been laying there for some time, I imagine others rode past. But you didn't."

"Can't a man just do the right thing? Christian duty, that sort of thing?"

"I suppose. Is that why?"

Gaspar finished his drink with a lengthy series of gulps. He rose, wiped the crumbs off his pants, and picked up a new piece of hay from the nearest gardening chaos. He placed it between his teeth and winced. He stood there, chewing the straw, his thumbs hanging on the edge of his pants, his eyes floating over the hillside of gray sheep.

"I've got to feed the horses," he said suddenly, and trod off towards the barn.

Elizabeth bit her lip. She hadn't meant to offend him. So, one nutcase threw her off a wagon, others drove past her, and a man tried to rape a young girl in the woods...She forgot where she had been going with all that.

She couldn't tell him the truth. He'd boot her out for sure, or send her to the witch hunt or the Inquisition, or the First Republic. *Wait, what century is this?* She clasped her head in her hands and took some deep breaths. The clothes. The clothes were certainly mid-eighteenth- century, and she already knew she was in Spain, not France or colonial America. Hopefully, this imaginary European community followed ordinary timeline laws and couldn't jump from one persecution to another at random. She was trying to sort all of this out in her head when she heard Gaspar's footsteps on the path again.

He passed her a basket. "The coop's around the corner there," he said. "Go in and collect the day's eggs. After that, I'll show you how to milk the ladies. Get your strength back, you can shovel the stalls and help with the horses too."

She nearly jumped up and hugged him but found enough restraint not to embarrass them both.

"Oh, Gaspar, thank you. I promise I'll come up with some solution soon, and I won't live off your kindness."

"Not worried about that. Just might get too comfortable, that's all. Now go get those eggs before the foxes."

Chapter Eight

It's amazing what one can do in three days without a job. The memory of her night alone on the dark forest floor still inspired a fresh, cool sense of terror. Her gratitude to Gaspar for hay, cheese, and shelter stretched beyond words, and Elizabeth made up her mind to be useful. Gaspar's decaying and neglected property provided ample projects. Surely, she could contribute somehow.

After collecting the eggs, of which she only found half and he had to go back and show her the rest, and the milking, which was surprisingly difficult, Gaspar demonstrated how to feed the horses, pigs, and other animals. He then released her with strict orders to rest. So, she explored the property and began the intimidating task of making herself useful.

What could she do? There was no piano. Of course, there was no piano. Elizabeth wracked her memory for when the piano had been invented, or even evolved into something she could recognize.

How useless she was in this world of earthly past. There was no music to be made here, no score to bury oneself in and interpret for the pleasure and enrichment of others.

The pleasure and enrichment of others. Was that what she

had spent her life doing? Certainly, she could do something useful here, couldn't she? She had a master's degree for crying out loud. She could translate five languages and generally make beauty where there was only strain and screeching. Well, okay she didn't actually make the beauty. But she could be the one to guide the screeching singer to find some inner beauty. Or find some reason to beautify — goodness, she wasn't even the screecher.

Elizabeth suddenly felt ridiculous. She didn't know how to fry a simple egg without an electric stove, a non-stick pan, and some coconut oil. She couldn't even clean her clothing without a front-loading machine, and some stain-lifting, concentrated, odor-killing laundry detergent.

Something in her life had to be useful. She refused to believe she was a total waste to the eighteenth century, or that opera had taught her nothing besides solutions to other people's screeching problems.

Gaspar's house was like the rest of the property—neglected and trodden upon. For a caretaker, he had very large and comfortable living quarters. Two stories with three bedrooms on the second floor and three chimneys. On the first floor was a sitting room that served as a drop-all, a dust-laden dining room, and what she could only assume was a kitchen, in which she found pots, countertops, and a sink, or at least something shaped like a sink, but with no spout for running water.

Gasper directed her to a long-unopened closet where a few women's garments hung, settling the matter of her clothing.

Elizabeth stood alone in Gaspar's bedroom alongside a familiar eerie silence, like there had been in her father's room after his funeral. Life had happened here. Then it had stopped. At a humble vanity table, an old brush and comb lay beside a fancy hand mirror. A frosting of sticky dust coated everything, reminding her of the trinkets in her father's living room, gathering residue until Josh and Reggie came along to disrupt them. Perhaps that's what it took to get on with one's life after a death— someone coming along to disrupt things.

Gaspar's bed lay undisturbed beneath piles of dirty and tattered clothing. She suspected the pillow had not seen slumber in years. Hanging from various locations in the room were other items of clothing, mostly torn, stained and tattered, like the ones he wore. When the room had become silent, Gaspar had ceased caring about his appearance, ceased mending the clothes, ceased pulling the weeds, even ceased sleeping as he had before.

She took the lady's garments outside and whacked them with a broom until she was certain all inhabitants had evacuated. She returned to the quiet room and passed an hour trying to solve the puzzle of how to put the clothes on.

What had become of Gaspar's wife? Of course, she had no right to pry, especially since she wasn't willing to share the smallest shred of her own story.

"It's terrible. I can't do it right," Elizabeth had once whined to her mother.

"It's not so bad as all that. Try again."

"It looks awful. Nothing like yours. I'm terrible. I'll never get it."

"I've been doing this for years, sweetheart. You're just learning. Everything takes patience. Patience and practice. Not just this. Everything. Now, now don't do that. You can't do that. That's the one rule. No one has ever cried in this barn and we're not going to break the tradition tonight. . ."

Elizabeth shook her head. No that's not the way it had happened. That was what Gaspar said to her the night before, in the barn. Her mother had said something different, something more sensitive, more, feminine, if it was still okay to use a word like that. Feminine.

"Honey, are you crying? Oh sweetheart. No one is born knowing how to do things. Everyone must learn. One small step at a time, that's all. Now here, stop that, wipe yourself off or you won't be able to see. There's a girl. Now let's try again."

"I don't want to. I can't do it. I'm terrible."

"Of course, you're terrible. Everyone is terrible their first time doing something."

"Mozart wasn't."

"Well, Mozart. Who was he? Could he sew a seam? Fix a button? Make embroidery? I bet there were things he had to work hard to learn too. We'll do a little every day, until you can sew it together perfectly by yourself. You'll see. One day, you won't even need me."

"I keep pricking my fingers. I don't like it. This is horrible."

"Now. Let's not write an opera about it. This isn't horrible. A few little pin pricks to learn how to sew? What a small price to pay for such a gift, right? Horrible? No. Horrible is eating raw chicken livers on toast. That's horrible. Horrible is spaghetti with rats' tails mixed in. Would you rather do that? No, I didn't think so. Here's a new square. Try again. In and out, over and down, in and out."

"Ouch! I hate this! Can't I stop?"

"Just a few more minutes Elly. Just a few more. . ."

<hr>

Elizabeth had to be honest. She wasn't completely sure her mother had said that bit about writing an opera. Her memories had so dissolved with time that she was adding her own details to keep them alive.

Elizabeth sat on the end of Gaspar's bed, clinging to the bed post. Did that mean she was forgetting her mother? *Oh God no. Please not that.* But it was true. Her scent, once pungent like citrus and gardenias, her voice a dulcet lyric mezzo, her touch a warmth so powerful it would envelope Elizabeth with just an elbow nudge. It used to fill her memory with vivid colors. Now, she almost had to rewrite it all, like a daytime television show. Telling the same story so many times, it needed spicing up with abductions, rapes, and murders to add back a little drama.

Her mother had definitely never said that about the opera.

Elizabeth stood, then straightened her corset. Piece by piece, she collected Gaspar's long-neglected clothing and set out in a search of a needle and thread.

Elizabeth mended everything she could find, from curtains to footwear. When she wasn't sewing, she followed Gaspar and watched him do simple chores around the farm. She learned how to clean the stalls, pump the water, and feed all the animals.

She tidied. Straightened up rooms long steeped in dust, clearing up piles of papers and broken projects. A rag doused in water became her dearest friend. She wiped murky residue off windowpanes, layers of film off tables and bookshelves, and after a frustrating hour with an ineffective straw broom that only seemed to drop its own innards across every floor it touched, she got down on all fours and went at each room with the rag and the water. She pulled up braided rugs, nearly choking in their resident clouds of filth, then hung them outside, beating them with sticks until they swung clear in the sunlight, and her face felt thick with dirt and sweat.

In the gardens, she picked a spot of chaos and attacked it as though it were a piece of **Stravinsky**, weeding flowerbeds, straightening stone paths, and trimming overgrowth. She even hunted down a hammer and nails and set herself to mending the dilapidated border fences. She whacked away for hours, undaunted by the wrathful bleats of a furious goat who followed her to and fro, nudging and jabbing at her with his bent horns.

Once she heard Gaspar chortling behind her, the customary straw dangling from his lips.

"What's so funny?" she called, but he just waved her off.

She returned her hammer to the barn and stroked the horses like she had become a member of the clan. When Gaspar called her for dinner, she came out to the unglorious vision of her fence-mending experiment, glowing in setting sun, like a random cubist painting.

She longed for a hot shower and some scented body wash. Cherry blossom or ocean breeze. She had never felt so dirty, and she admitted a certain inner pride at sinking to such a grimy stench. By the end of the third day, Elizabeth was both exhausted and pleased with herself for settling in. If life had thrown her into this situation permanently, she could probably tolerate it.

She and Gaspar ate meals together, during which they would inevitably launch into some absurdly philosophical conversation that mattered to the universe at large, but no one in particular.

"Do you ever wonder if the hens mind us stealing their eggs?"

"Have wondered often," Gaspar said. "But that would imply a right and wrong to the collection of the eggs."

"Do you suppose they think we're any better than the fox?"

"Right, wrong, better, worse. All judgments beyond the hen."

"Judgments? Well, I'm certainly not judging anyone," she said.

"Hey now. Not a bad word. Somebody's got to judge something."

"Not where I come from. Judgment is reserved for those who get paid to do it."

"And who would they favor?" he asked. "The chickens, the foxes, or us?"

"I suspect the chickens. But someone could argue the case for the foxes."

"And us? Who argues for us?"

"Well, no one really. No one would dare."

Laughter felt as pleasurable as it had in twenty-first-century Wichita.

Neither party asked for a single personal detail. Elizabeth found this the most intriguing trait of Gaspar's character. If either of them had any rights to knowledge, it was him. She could be an outlaw, a murderer, a con artist, or a leper! (Were there lepers in eighteenth-century Spain?) Still, he had full rights to know who he was willfully allowing into his home. But he never asked. Not once.

She had to admit the favor would not have gone the other way. If Elizabeth had picked someone up off the street (which of course she'd never do), she would have been a genuine nag, pestering and hounding for every detail before they were out of the bed, just so she could have the pleasure of justifying her actions, and not feel a fool for taking in a leper.

Only twice in three days did anyone visit Gaspar's farm. On day two, a slow horse came clip-clopping up the dirt road and emerged from the woods. Elizabeth peeked out between the straw and feathers of the chicken house as an older woman with pointed features and leathery skin pulled up in a wagon. The woman chatted with Gaspar softly for a few minutes, but when she moved to climb down, Gaspar raised a hand and passed her two rounds of cheese. The woman seemed mildly put off. This was not the customary ritual for the exchange. Nevertheless, she curiously scanned the property before giving the reins an indignant snap and turning back down the lane. Neither Elizabeth nor Gaspar mentioned the visit.

Late in the afternoon of the third day, two teenage boys came riding bareback atop one horse. Elizabeth spied their dirt-darkened hands and faces through an upstairs window, her hands busy with thread and seam. Gaspar came out from the barn to meet them before either could dismount, and after some brief utterances, they left the property at a dusty gallop. Again Gaspar said nothing of the visitors.

Nevertheless, it was on the fourth day that her impending eviction arose, due to a series of unfortunate issues concerning oral hygiene.

"Gaspar, whose land is this?"

They sat together quietly after dinner, watching early evening rays light up a field of hay just outside the dining room window. "I mean, whose farm is this?"

"It's my farm."

"This is your farm? You're not working it for someone else?"

Gaspar shook his head, winced, and rubbed his jaw.

"So, you're a landowner then? Can't you have someone to work the farm with you?"

"Could. Do, usually."

"Usually? Oh, I see. You mean you don't have any help right now because I'm here."

"You're plenty helpful. You are. House looks better than it has in years. Wearing all my clothes again, thanks to you. Nice to have a woman around. Forgot how nice."

"So, you let your regular help go."

"Oh, not like that. Usually have those two Mendez-Rodrigo boys come every day. They help out enough. All I need really. Will send word for them when we're ready."

"You mean when I leave. Oh dear. I've taken away someone's source of income."

"No," he winced again, and groaned softly, cupping his jaw with a large, calloused hand. "No, still paying them. Just told 'em to keep their mouths shut and wait for word, that's all. You stay as long as you need. That's what I want. Long as you need." This time he groaned longer.

"Gaspar, are you all right?"

He rubbed the left side of his jaw, shut his eyes tightly and furrowed his brows. "Oh, just this darn tooth. Soon as it comes out, will be fine again."

"Soon as it comes out? Gaspar, you can't wait until then. It will only get worse."

"That's how it goes. First few times it just hurts a little, keep hoping you imagined it, or it will go away somehow. Sometimes it does, sure enough."

"No!"

"Just got to wait it out. Suffer a bit."

"Gaspar, for goodness' sake, you can't wait for that tooth to come out. You're already in agony."

"Sure thing, that. Might ask you to take care of a few things. Might need to bring them boys back. Don't know what I'll do, come to think of it."

"Don't know what you'll do? You have to go to the dentist!" Elizabeth realized her mistake so quickly that she could almost see the bubble hanging above her in the proverbial pages of her coma-induced stupor. There were no dentists in eighteenth-century Spain. Across the entire planet at that hour, there wasn't even a solitary strand of dental floss.

Gaspar eyed her across the table curiously. "What's a dentist?"

"I mean, someone who can take that tooth out. Surely there's a doctor of some sort you can call...on."

"You mean the barber."

Elizabeth cursed her foolishness. She knew these things. A barber meant something far beyond a shave and haircut in eighteenth-century Spain. The town barber was sort of a jack of all early pharmaceutical trades.

"That's the problem," Gaspar continued. "There's this new fellow in town, but never had to call on him. Keep my own whiskers clipped, and was used to the old fellow. Liked him. Don't know about calling on someone different. Feels wrong to take a man's barber away."

"Well, where's the old fellow?"

"Figaro?"

Elizabeth's breath sucked in so fast that it made a wretched gulping snort in her throat. She had to steady herself from nearly falling off her chair.

"He's got a big fancy job for the Count now. Head of the whole house, if you can believe it. Left us all to scrap with a couple of yearling amateurs. Rascal." He moaned again and rubbed his jaw.

"I'm sorry, Gaspar, but did you say Figaro? I mean, that's an odd name for around here, isn't it?"

"Funny you should ask that, but it's the only name he's got. Someone found him on a convent doorstep or something when he was a baby. Had no family, no connections, made him perfect for his job, staying out of business and not choosing sides, until the right one came along of course."

"The right one?"

"You really aren't from around here. Everybody in these parts knows about Figaro and the Count stealing the young Rosina— now the Countess—from that brute Doctor Bartolo."

Elizabeth's gut twisted wretchedly with a surge of conscience. The idea that Gaspar's local barber (and how alarmingly coincidental that he lived right outside of Seville) could be the famous character from the opera of the very same story which her deceased father had so carefully selected a chopped-up novella version as a post-mortem gift, and was in fact, the only surviving relic from her home world, or land of consciousness, was of surmounting value to her, despite the obvious reality that her host, who had been so generous and in fact the only person to show her any kindness, without hesitation, question or demands, was obviously in increasing levels of agony such that should be addressed before he be reduced to an inhuman state of agony or devoured by some raging infection, that no matter the realization she might be on the precipice of regarding her own situation, Elizabeth knew she should do something at once: engage her morality for crying out loud, get up and act, defend the battlements, learn to milk the cow, stop the soprano, save the toppling alto, and help this poor, wretched, sainted-man get rid of that **damn tooth!**

"Gaspar, where can I reach this new man for you?"

"Oh no, can't. It'll start gossip. Don't want that. Want you to take your—ugh!"

The groans were rapidly ascending in pitch, far exceeding Gaspar's natural baritone range. The rate of his descent into agony accelerated as though his admission of the pain had released the furies.

"Gaspar, never mind that. We have to get that tooth out tonight."

"No. Tomorrow. We'll, no—I'll go tomorrow."

"You'll never make it to tomorrow, you poor man!"

"Too dark...thieves...bandits...too dangerous."

Elizabeth stood up from the table and pushed back the piano bench. She could feel the hot bright **Fresnel** beams on her face as she lifted her eyes unabashedly into the light and set her foot firmly on the stage beneath her.

"Then I will take that tooth out myself."

Without giving any leeway for argument, she marched out of the house to the barn. She found a bit of string and tested its strength. When she returned to the dining room, Gaspar sat exactly where she had left him, cupping his jaw and moaning, a new shadow of terror in his eyes. She went to the kitchen and got as clean a cloth she could find, wishing deeply for some antibacterial lotion or a triple antibiotic. She lit two candles and carried all back to her trembling patient.

"Sit up," she said, and positioned the candles on the table. She took his head in her hands, tilting it up and backwards. "Open please."

Immediately, the stench of a man's mouth which had never seen brush, floss, or rinse, assaulted her senses, and she steeled herself against it like a true Verdi heroine. She tried not to gag at the brown, jagged, chipped and otherwise horrific display of dental decay.

"Which one is it?"

He lifted a chubby, trembling finger.

Yes, it was swollen, with blackened lesions at the gum. She put her finger in and wiggled. Her patient whimpered but didn't move.

"I'm going to tie a string around it."

She gathered her will and wrapped the string around the

tooth several times, easing it between the swollen gums. Each turn of the string erupted another pathetic groan and tremble from Gaspar in his very awkward position, somewhere in the vicinity of her breasts. *Well, no matter that now.*

When she felt she had a sure grasp of the offender, Elizabeth stood back and lifted her left leg, bracing it against the chair. She wrapped the string around her fist.

It would have to be fast. Like swatting a fly with a folded magazine. Quick and merciless, no hesitation, wickedly violent, sinister with the clearest vision of absolute triumph.

"You can't do that," she had once said to Marta Claiborne, second year mezzo-soprano.

She was coaching her on the famous aria from <u>Werther</u> for her upcoming sophomore jury, a singing exam so rigorous that those who did not pass were asked to leave the vocal program.

"What? What did I do?"

"You're trying to put your toe in the pool," Elizabeth said.

"Excuse me?"

Elizabeth was seated in her customary niche, the three square feet between the black and white keys of her amputated piano and the wall of her tiny corner studio.

"If I may put it plainly," Elizabeth continued, "you want to make sure it sounds good before blasting it out for all of kingdom come. It's like you're running your singing by an inner bureau of critics who will decide whether it's decent enough to share with the rest of us." She pointed at the girl's head.

"You mean it sounds like that? Like I'm not really letting it out? Well, I don't mean to do that."

"Well, that's why I'm here."

The mezzo's face melted into the downtrodden expression of

an underclassman. "If I don't mean to do something, how can I stop doing it?"

"You can't do both at once: judge and sing. You must pick one. Now, sing that phrase again, and don't worry about what your voice sounds like, or even whether you're on the right notes. Give yourself permission to sound like a dying cat on a broken fence. Where are you supposed to feel the vibrations of that note?"

"Well, when I get it right, I feel it here and all back here." With a vague wave of her hand, the young mezzo indicated her forehead and upper skull.

"Then that's where your attention should be. Commit your thoughts to it. Don't leave any room for worry or hesitation. Just take the breath in and consign yourself completely to that one goal, all at once and right away."

Back in the eighteenth century, Elizabeth tightened her grip on the string and gave Gaspar a final confirming nod. She inhaled a deep, low, guttural breath, and one...two...three...

She pulled out the damn tooth.

Chapter Nine

❧

Two chairs had toppled to the floor. Between them, the victim of Elizabeth's grit lay brown and bloodied to its roots, interwoven on the string like a fish tangled in the line.

Elizabeth had been propelled to a corner of the room after yanking out the tooth. Sweat dripped unattended down her right temple, and her legs stretched out in an immodest position under her skirts, while the end of the string remained clutched in her fists.

Across the dimly lit floor, Gaspar lay on his back. The two candles that remained flickering on the table cast only a shadow on his body, which strangely reminded her of a sleeping Santa Claus. Elizabeth could not see if he was breathing.

"Gaspar? Gaspar?"

Gaspar erupted with a laughter so loud that Elizabeth jumped for fright. He sobbed a bit, wiped tears from his cheeks, then laughed again, giddily now. Before she could speak, he was whimpering so sincerely it wrenched her heart before it descended back to a naughty snicker. He moved quickly in and out of this delightedly wretched cycle that twenty-first-century medicine might diagnose as some personality disorder.

Elizabeth joined him, and the loose phlegm in her nose

spewed out onto her hands. She wiped it on her skirts, weeping as the dark agony of despair enveloped her before she realized she was senseless and doubled over in laughter, her stomach seizing up, her cheeks straining.

Eventually Gaspar rolled over on his belly full of jelly and pushed himself up. He stumbled into the kitchen and returned with a bottle and two small glasses. Crossing the battlefield, he put one glass in Elizabeth's hand, and she did not object when he poured something into it. She didn't drink as a rule, but there were worse ways to die.

Gaspar sat on the floor in the opposite corner and lifted his own glass. Elizabeth took a sip, but her host threw the whole thing back, like her friends in college had done at the bar until they became ridiculous and inhuman. Well, perhaps none of this was even really happening and she wasn't really human anymore. She slugged it.

The burn constricted her throat. She stuck her tongue out and gagged with a fiery agony.

"Do you like it?" Gaspar said. "I make it myself."

🌸

A half an hour, and three slugs of whatever was in that bottle later, their heads reeling, the room spinning and the floor feeling much more comfortable, Gaspar sighed three times and stared at the tooth with glazed, darkened eyes.

"I am responsible," he said, "for the deaths of my entire family."

Elizabeth willed herself into a frozen trance, despite any lingering giddiness and the alarming rate at which the ceiling was doing somersaults.

"My daughter, my wife, my grandson," he continued. "All dead. All because of me. And wasn't some accident, the kind you'd like to think, where someone is just looking the other way. Nice convenient fire, or something with the equipment maybe.

Even an illness would be better, wouldn't it? Just to be able to tell yourself you did everything you could, you were helpless, these things happen."

Elizabeth felt the room steadying beneath her at his soft, low confession. She felt torn between thinking she had just slipped into a slasher novel, or back to reality. She let him talk.

"My daughter, Mariella. Was perfectly beautiful. Don't blame boys for chasing her. Don't blame her for seeking their attention. She was so young, didn't know anything. But she was my only surviving child. One died just after he was born, and another when she was six, from the fever. This place," he looked around, "you must think it's falling apart, and dead, but wasn't always. Was a time when it was alive. And yes, could, fix it up, do something. But I destroyed it all. Why shouldn't I live in it?" He took another drink.

"... I remember so clearly the moment I realized she was pregnant. Outside of wedlock. That was too much for me. For my pride. My daughter carrying some boy's baby. Tried to get her to tell me who it was, but she wouldn't. Had someone forced her? She said no. Never know, I guess. That's another punishment. Never give them a chance to grow, never get your answers... She was so young. Had no need to control my temper before. Had a temper. You haven't seen that, but we show the best of ourselves, don't we? Got so angry, threw so many words. So many, rotten words. Seem so harmless when they're coming out, but then you can never take them back. Disgrace, shame to her mother and I, waste, whore... more. I threw her out. My beautiful Mariella. Her mother was so sore with me, didn't speak to me again hardly until she herself died two years later. That was all quite a bit after we found Mariella alone in the woods. The baby half out of her."

Gaspar kept his eyes devotedly on the floorboards, and the tiny villainous tooth in its tangled harness.

"The things we do," he said. "The stupid things in a flash or fury, a panic. We don't mean for it, but they become part of us. Like we've carved ourselves somehow. Only can't rewrite it, or tear it up, or burn it. Can only hope. Just hope. Hope that some-where, someday, maybe if you're very lucky, and God hasn't already damned you to another kind of hell, maybe someday you'll just come across some girl, hurt and alone. And you think, 'This time. This time I'm going to get it right. No matter what it takes. I'm going to be—better. For someone else's girl.'"

His little drinking glass tipped out of his hand onto the floor. The only sounds remaining were the flutters of a pair of moths, fighting over the candlelight on the table above them.

"My father had cancer and he didn't tell me," she said from her side of the darkened floor. "That's a sickness. I don't even know if you know that word yet. I know John Adams's daughter had it, but I don't know if that's happened yet, or if they called it cancer then, but it's a terrible disease that makes tumors in your body. And my father had it. He went through it all and he never even told me. Because we barely spoke, really. I was busy. And angry. So, he died, alone, and he left me this book. It's a stupid book. But when I opened it and began reading, I suddenly found myself totally alone out in those woods with no home and no food and no money. You see, I don't belong here at all. I'm from a very different place where people drive cars and use GPS and talk on little boxes called cellphones, and you brush your teeth twice a day. And the dentist has this wonderful needle that numbs your face so you can't feel a thing while he grinds a horrible drill into your jaw and saves your tooth. . ."

A lonely cricket had jumped up onto the windowsill. It stood alone in the opening to the cool night, twitching and turning back and forth between Elizabeth and Gaspar, postponing his nightly chirp like a judge summing up sentencing.

"It's the truth," Elizabeth said. "I promise you that I'm not a witch, or a loon, or anything like that. I play the piano for a small college opera program in Kansas, which you've never even heard of, because it became a state in 1861, and I don't know if you even know what a piano is, or an opera, or—"

With great difficulty Gaspar raised himself off the floor and wobbled over to her corner. Sitting beside her, he put a stinky arm over her shoulder.

"Well, that's just crazy," he said, and the cricket began its nocturnal song.

❧

Through the depths of drunken giddiness, both parties agreed that nothing more productive could happen that night. Saying many thank you's, Gaspar escorted Elizabeth to the barn, and left her a candle and the rest of the bottle.

In the morning she had a rotten headache and felt each footstep with a cranial pounding. Gaspar was sitting on the stoop with breakfast. She couldn't face the food.

"That bad, eh?" he said. "Don't do much drinking where you're from?"

"Oh, people do. Lots. We've a shameful variety of ways to drink our lives away. Whole stores, filled with every color and flavor, all aimed at the same thing. And they're everywhere, four liquor depots within two blocks of my apartment alone. Every time a new commercial plot opens up, I hope we'll get something useful like a UPS or a nice salon, but then it's just another liquor house or pizza parlor." She buried her head in her knees.

"You sound like you've lost your senses. Don't understand half of what you just said. Better not eat."

"No. I haven't lost my senses, Gaspar. I'm just telling you the truth. Finally. And it sounds crazy. I know it must. You don't know what anything is where I come from."

"I know what an opera is."

"You do?"

"Sure. An opera comes through Seville every so often. Even took the girls a couple times. Usually in Italian, but that's okay."

At the casual mention of his family, Elizabeth remembered through clouds of silliness the severity of the previous night. "How's your tooth?"

"Oh, much improved. Slept wonderful. That and the spirits didn't hurt."

"What was that stuff we drank?"

"Not sure there's a name for it."

"Well, it leaves one with a desire to self-decapitate."

Gaspar laughed. "Will pass soon. Better drink some water."

He disappeared around the corner and Elizabeth heard the pump clanking up and down. He returned and passed her a mug.

"All right," she said, "I know you have to get to work, and so do I, but first, I have a few questions for the wagon jury."

"Wagon jury?"

"Yes. I don't want to get tossed off again."

"Ah. No jury here, Elizabeth. But this is good. Proceed then."

"What year is it?"

"The year? You really did hit your head. Second Sunday in November, year of Our Lord, seventeen hundred and seventy-eight. That what you needed?"

"Yes. Thank you. 1778. 1778, *Figaro* premiered in 1786, so if this all is some delusion in my head, the dates are off a bit. All right, can you handle another one?"

"Straight on now."

"If we are in Spain, just outside of Seville"—he nodded—"then why is everyone speaking English?"

"English? Can't say I know the answer to that. Know I'm not speaking English. But your speech is refined, sure thing. Makes me think I was right. You are a lady. Aren't you? Noble born?"

"Noble born? Oh, how funny. No sir. I'm an American. The daughter of a librarian and a seamstress."

Gaspar's eyes widened; his whole face stretched. He sat up straight, pulling the straw out from his teeth. "Well, I'll be a grave digger. An American lady sleeping in my barn! *American.* Is that what you say now? Well good for you. American. Who would have ever imagined it? Are you from Boston? Where they dumped the tea?"

"No, I'm from Kansas, where they grow the corn."

"Kansas, never heard of that now."

"No, of course you haven't. So, let's just say I'm from Boston."

"Did you see any of the battles? That why you left?"

"Battles? Gaspar, we defeated the British in—oh yes, 1778. Of course. No. No, I didn't see any of the battles. I told you I'm from a different—"

"Your father died fighting for General Washington? Is that how he died?"

"What? No. I told you he had cancer. And anyway my—"

"Whoooo–!" Gaspar took out a handkerchief and wiped his brow. "I never imagined I'd have a rebel in my barn. No, sir. I mean, that's supposing you are a rebel. Aren't some runaway Tory now? Faithful to the crown and all? 'Course not. Right?"

"Goodness Gaspar, no! I can see which side you stand on. Now listen to me. The only time my father ever saw President Washington was on a one-dollar bill, and"—Gaspar's face fell— "actually, if I'm being honest, yes, my father would have most certainly fought with Presi— I mean, General Washington. Most certainly he would. He just wasn't born yet...during the Revolution, I mean. Gaspar, I'm from, oh goodness...I don't want to get thrown off another wagon."

"Steady now. I know you're not a loon."

"Or a witch."

"Or a witch."

"Or a leper."

"Assume that, since you were half-naked when I found you."

"So, there were lepers in eighteenth-century Spain!" Elizabeth also decided to again skip past the idea that a full-length skirt and long-sleeved top was considered half-naked.

"Gaspar, my birthday, I mean the day I was born, was June 14 in the year nineteen hundred and ninety-one."

The sun-darkened skin on Gaspar's face seemed to immobilize as though he were suddenly carved from clay. He stood watching her, unblinking, expressionless and expectant, waiting for her to say something else, finish an unfinished sentence, or maybe just go back to the part about General Washington.

"Nineteen hundred and ninety-one," she said again.

"Ninety-one," he said.

"*Nineteen hundred* and ninety-one."

"Here." She picked up a stick and scratched the numbers in the dirt. "Maybe it will help to see it."

"That's your birthday."

"My birthday, yes."

Gaspar stumbled backwards, clutching at the door frame. His eyes seemed to swim in and out of focus at the impossible accursed number scratched on his front stoop. Elizabeth began to speak, but he raised a hand to silence the court from presenting any further testimony. Time simmered past while she waited. On the hillside just beyond Elizabeth's cubist fence, the little woolen tufts of sheep meandered between the thickets, chomp-chomping mindlessly at their grass and weeds. For an eternal second, she envied their ignorant wanderings.

"Don't think I can help you with that," Gaspar said at last.

"Of course, you can't."

"But I swore before God Almighty I would see this thing through. Would help no matter what it took. Of course, when I picked you up on the street there, thought I was just helping a girl out. Didn't know, never suspected—"

"She wouldn't be helpable?"

"What does a girl need? Food, shelter, material things. You're sure you're not a loon? Well, how'd you get here then?"

"I don't know. I was just reading this book my father left me when—"

"You mean the book in the barn? The red one, with your name on it?"

"Yes. I was reading that when suddenly my whole world disappeared, and I was lost in the woods. That's what I've been trying to tell you."

Gaspar leaned over and pulled a long strand of weed up,

placed it between his teeth and again began rolling it pensively back and forth.

"Well," he said, "that's got to be the answer then. That book. Why else would it have come along with you?"

Elizabeth felt like someone had just hit the pause button on a DVD. "I hadn't thought of that. The book did come with me. Everything else of my home stayed behind. Even my clothes changed. I've been so busy dealing with hunger and shelter, it hadn't even occurred to me until now how strange that was."

"There's the answer then. We have to get that book and get you home where you belong. But first, got to feed the animals, so, drink your water, get about your chores, and we'll take a look at it together at mid-day."

Gaspar bounced off towards the barn. Surely, Elizabeth had come across the most sincere man of his time.

❦

They sat in Gaspar's dining room with the book on the table between them. Gaspar had taken out a pipe and meditatively puffed away. It was late afternoon, all the chores completed, which took significantly longer due to headaches and nausea.

"Gaspar, what if I can't find a way back home? I mean, what's so bad about that?"

Smoke billowed from his nostrils, filling the room with a bitter warmth. "You mean stay here? Indefinitely?"

"Well, yes. I don't mean here on your farm necessarily, but I'm not doing so badly, am I? I could find some kind of employment, couldn't I? Learn a trade?"

"A woman? Learn a trade?"

"Yes, well, never mind that for now. Let's take a look at it together. Do you read, Gaspar?"

"Yes, but rather not. Last time someone picked up that book, they disappeared into history. Brought you back two hundred years. Me, who knows what could happen? Might end up all

Inquisition and Moors. No thank you. Is your story, my dear. Explain it to me."

"All right"—she lifted the cover—"first of all, there's no printing information, author, publisher, like you would usually have in a book where I come from. All of that is missing and there's just this inscription that says '*Read Careful*'—oh dear, hang on. Where is it?" She fumbled through the opening pages. "Well, that's very strange. The inscription seems to have been replaced." Elizabeth returned to the opening page "*Stick to Your Story*"

"That there book is enchanted, that's what," Gaspar said. "Been cursed with something. Even if you're no witch, that book surely came from one."

"Now hold on, Gaspar. I am as skeptical about magic as the next person. But why does anything supernatural have to be evil? I mean, my own father willed me this book. Doesn't that mean anything? A lawyer came in with an envelope and documents and everything. He seemed perfectly legitimate. Didn't ask for my social, or smell of pot or incense. For goodness' sake, can't a girl trust anything anymore? The whole world has gotten so convoluted with Google this and Amazon that and passwords for everything from the library to the sushi shop. Just say two words to anyone anymore and you're sexist or elitist, or racist or whatever -ist has become the new rage. And you can't trust people who call you on the phone, or send you an email, or tell you they love you, but they're very sorry, they think they might be gay. So why bother at all? I mean, maybe this is where I'm supposed to be now. I'm supposed to live the rest of my days here in eighteenth-century Spain where the worst a person has to worry about is being thrown off a cart, or attacked by a pervert in the woods—"

"Or leprosy?"

"At least you can see those problems coming. You can depend on things being real, you know? Maybe my father sent me here because he knew I'd be happier. He knew this was where I belonged. I can help you on your farm, and live out my days—Gaspar, what day is it?"

"Today? Let's see. Have to go to the Manor tomorrow for an order of eggs and cheese. Do so every Saturday. So today is Friday. Why do you ask?"

"It's just that I usually go to Mass on Sundays."

"Now that's the first thing you've said that makes sense. Thank God Almighty. Had me scared for a minute there. Opera yes. Mass yes. But the rest of it, my dear, you can't stay here. You don't belong."

Elizabeth felt a rush of embarrassment. "Of course. You've already been so generous."

"No. Love having you here. Place feels alive again. Laughed so hard last night, I think I hurt myself. Haven't laughed like that in a long time now. Long time."

"Well, the scandal."

"Got that worked out too. Have a sister moved off years ago, no one in these parts ever hears of her. We'll say you're my niece. That'll pass. But that's not what I mean, Elizabeth. You can't stay here because this isn't your home."

"But I could make it my home. I know I've got a lot to learn, but I can learn to do anything. I'm a modern American woman, after all."

"You don't have to tell me. I've seen what you can do against a rotten tooth. But now that's not what I mean either." Gaspar rubbed his chin, considering his pipe. Everything about him felt safe, like the way he didn't rush into his words. "Isn't there anything you would miss? Anyone back home you would lose?"

Elizabeth thought about that. When her mother died, they had stopped reaching out to family. Now her father was gone. Reggie and Josh, they loved her, and she had a few girlfriends who loved music like she did, but they all seemed to marry up sooner or later and disappear. If she was honest, every one of them, even Reggie and Josh, were just **comprimarios** on the cast list of her life. They came and served some temporary purpose before going offstage to their real lives and families.

"I don't have any pets," she said. "I'm not opposed to them. I just worry. What would I do if they suddenly needed medical care? What if they got very sick? What if they had issues like peeing on the sofa or chewing up my herbs? I have some herbs, but I could surely grow herbs here too..."

"Herbs, Elizabeth?

"I'm sure I'll eventually miss Ibuprofen,"

"Who's that?"

"Never mind."

"Well, I'm no expert in any magical dealings, but that book there, good or evil, it's telling you what you need to do. Need to stick to your story. I'm not your story, Elizabeth. Neither is this place. You don't belong here. Just the way you talk about things. So open-like. I don't mind, but it's not customary for a lady. Not usual."

Elizabeth felt transported back to the rickety piano bench in the university band room, where Reggie coolly told her to go away to Boston, where she could ride the T everywhere and get a free doctorate, while hordes of Druids carelessly jabbed at their little screens in the distant corners of the room.

"I had a lamb once," Gaspar said. "Given to me by a nobleman passing through Seville. Make a lot of friends when you have good cheese. Anyway, gave me this beautiful little lamb. Not the same breed as my other sheep now, but that's no reason it couldn't mix in and do its part. Only it never grew. Always sat on the outside away from the others, ate very little. One day got sick and died. Couldn't save it. That lamb didn't belong here. Maybe he didn't know what he was a part of back home, but was a part of something that defined who he was. And when that got taken away—"

"But Gaspar, don't you think we write our own stories? Can't I just choose for myself where I want to be? Are we all stuck in some path paved for us on our birthday, with no options to change or break free?"

"Well, now see, that's what I did, isn't it? Didn't like the story I got sent. Wanted it to go just like planned and not the way it came to me. Don't think we get to, my dear. Think we have to stick to our story. And that book there. That's your story now."

"This?" Elizabeth lifted the book again and flipped through the pages. "This is just a dumb mocked-up version of an opera. I mean it's a mess. I can't stand a mess."

Gaspar puffed quietly on his pipe, gazing out the window at his property, at the sheep completely unaware of him, chewing incessantly at the grass, and the goats carelessly carving new dents in Elizabeth's fencing. "I'd like my daughter back, and my wife, and grandson," he said. "What I wouldn't give today for a little mess."

৩৯৩

Elizabeth steadied herself against the wobbling. She had ridden on a couple hayrides as a child, but never sat atop a cart next to the driver, or whatever Gaspar was at this moment. She had to stop herself from constantly reaching for a seatbelt.

"I don't know about this. I'm starting to think it's a bad idea," she said, clutching the side of her seat as the wagon shifted over some potholes in the road. She wondered if they were called potholes in the eighteenth century. Some problems never go away. Surely cavemen were confounded by the darn things ten seconds after they invented the wheel.

"Well, wasn't your idea, that's for sure. But's what you've got to do."

"But why would anyone hire me? I have no useful skills."

"Now that's not true," he said. "Gotten quite handy in the kitchen and the barn. Can stitch up nearly anything. I'd call that pretty useful."

"Are they looking for a seamstress? Exactly what position are they looking to fill?"

"Well, don't know quite. Mendez-Rodrigo boys just told me the Manor house let go of someone this week. Girl got sent away. Sure we can imagine why."

"Gaspar, that's terrible."

"Now see there. Do best to stop saying things like that. Nobody thinks like you do, not even the women. If this works today—"

"Which it won't."

"Just mind yourself and don't..."

"Make eye contact with any men?"

"Be careful the things you say now. I'll be back every Saturday to visit, early. That should seem normal. Got to bring the order anyway, and you're my niece. But if you need me before, send word. Anybody tries anything, we'll come up with another plan."

"I've been very safe with you, Gaspar."

"Now, don't do that. No one's ever cried in this cart and don't want to break the tradition today. First, got to get you the job."

Gaspar led the horses into a small gathering of buildings with signs hanging out front. Chickens seemed to run loose everywhere, and twice they had to stop for goats crossing the road. Children ran recklessly between the wheels and the horses' hooves. Elizabeth felt heat emanating from an open storefront where a man wearing thick black gloves worked over a large glowing fire. Two doors down, inside the same kind of open fronted structure, a soot-covered man sat, spinning a glowing orange bulb at the end of a long pole. They must have passed a baker, because something smelled enticingly warm and delicious. Through other windows, she could see sacks of food, rolls of fabric and tools. Adults looked up from their duties, nodded at Gaspar, and eyed Elizabeth with curiosity.

"Is this Seville?" she asked.

"Sikes no. City is on the southern side of the manor. Don't

have cause to go through that mess. You can in your days off if you like. But keep your eyes down there too."

"Don't worry. I'm very good at keeping my eyes on my score."

Their carriage turned a corner and they rode for about a mile before passing through a long lane of tall slender cypress trees. They were so well maintained and close together, they reminded Elizabeth of the stage curtain before a show, its thick red fabric hanging in waves of suspense beneath the soft glow of the preset lights. Taking one's seat, one wonders "what's behind there?" and the mystery itself is a prelude to the overture.

Suddenly Elizabeth heard the opening bars of a Rossini opera start up in her head with its unusual pizzicato opening. *Pluck, pluck, pluck, pluck.*

"What's behind these trees?" she asked Gaspar.

"This is the lane that leads to the Manor. You can see the full estate when we round the end."

The orchestra in her head blasted its first chord, full throttle.

As the end of the tree-curtain neared, the music in her head got louder. Elizabeth shuddered and clutched the tassels on her shawl. What would she find on the other side of those trees? Horrors? Violence? Powerful men with wicked ideals. Would she be enough? Would there be anything left of her when it was all over? Would it ever be over?

Rossini's overture took off into its ridiculous perky little passages of strings that suddenly sounded menacing. She took a full dose of the woody cypress aroma. The scents enveloped her, like no diffuser could have achieved. She took it in deeply while the overture flurried on through her veins without her willing it.

When they rounded the end of the lane, she could see the curtain open, backdrops ascended into the fly-space, and teasers fell into the wings as the magnificence of the view overtook all senses with a breathless awakening. Set pieces crumbled to dust, props blew away like the paper they were made from, and the arti-ficial glare of the strip lights disintegrated beneath the all-embracing celestial glow of a Spanish sun. If this was a coma-induced dream, it was a spectacularly designed one.

Gaspar stopped the wagon, and they rested on a hill crest. She could see for miles. Massive patches of greens lay across the land in so many hues, a painter would have to mix every color on his palette to represent them: grey greens, yellow greens, reddish greens, deep succulent purple greens. Elizabeth felt like she had never seen green before.

A few naked hillsides were randomly bespeckled with clumps of white, gray, brown, or black inhabitants, all stooped, heads down. Occasional bleats wafted over the acres like tuning woodwinds.

Structures dotted the landscape with dirt roads winding between them. The largest structure, the Manor itself, stood at the center, its two wings reaching out stony arms, curbing the land into submission.

"This side here is the olive groves," Gaspar said, waving a hand. "He's got four different varieties there, and beyond that crest, you could see the press and bottling house. They have their own staff there. I know he makes quite a bit of the oil, but some they save for the table and market, too." Gaspar pointed in the opposite direction. "There, just past that road, you can see the vineyards. They extend over the next three hill crests. The vineyard is a drive from the manor, but you can always get yourself some grapes to eat at the closest vines, those are for the eating, the ones nearest the house."

Elizabeth's nose felt rather assaulted. Every time the breeze shifted it brought a new contrasting aroma.

"I smell citrus," she said. "Is that the vineyards?"

"No, that's the oranges. See that patch of dark green on the west side there? Finest in southern Spain, I believe. Makes a massive supply of them, so much he's had to create things to do with the produce. Some years the fruit just goes bad. Got a good man now there, harvesting and deporting them. Ships them out to six or seven different countries."

"Ships? He owns ships?" Elizabeth had never fully considered the extent of the Count's wealth beyond what fancy clothes the costuming department had concocted.

"Yes. Four or five, but he's gotten into some land battles now, I understand. Property rights, that sort of thing. It'll take its toll eventually. Follow that road there about six miles, eventually you come to his barracks. Troops there training most times."

"Troops?"

"Maybe better just keep going." Gaspar shook the reins and the horse plodded down the slope onto the Count's property. "So, tell me again what this opera of Figaro is about where you come from."

"Well, the whole plot revolves around this horrible ancient feudal right called the '*droit du seigneur*' whereby a feudal lord, or a land owner had the right to, well on the wedding night of any women in his service he could, I mean, any woman beneath him, I mean, he had the rights to take her, or rather to—"

"Don't hurt yourself Elizabeth. Know what the ancient right is. But everyone in these parts knows the Count abolished that privilege."

"Well, you see, Figaro is now the head of the Count's household staff and he wants to marry a chambermaid named Susanna."

"Oh, I'm glad he's found a lady. Good for him. Is she pretty?"

"Is she pretty? Goodness, Gaspar."

"Man can wish his fellow a lovely lady. Can't a man do that where you come from?"

"Not really, no. Well, if you must know, she's always played by a **soubrette** in her early twenties with a tight corset and a large flawless wig. Of course, she's pretty. She's inhuman, she's so pretty. Anyway, Figaro wants to marry her, but the Count has taken to claiming all the ladies who find themselves in his employ."

"Naturally."

"And whether the Count wants to assert himself over Figaro,

or just finds Susanna too delicious, remains debatable, but he goes to great lengths to stop the wedding."

"Oh, the bastard. It's not enough that he has all this, is it?"

"Apparently not. Anyway, after a series of escapades involving a variety of characters and about two hundred pages of **recitative**, they publicly catch the Count cheating on the Countess. He begs forgiveness and leaves the newlyweds alone. The end, drop the curtain, go home and have something nice to eat."

"Is that what's in that book of yours?"

"No, not at all," Elizabeth said, pulling the book from beneath her shawl. "This is all wrong and miserable. The opera is a comedy, for crying out loud. Even without a dead soprano at the end of this, the reader wants to kill herself. No, in this twisted mockup the whole plot gets thrown in the very first scene. Susanna is supposed to tell Figaro about the Count's advances, and then they plot it out together. But in this version, she doesn't tell him for some reason, and tries to fight the Count on her own. I read the whole thing through last night. It ended very bitterly with Susanna being violated in some corner of the estate right after the wedding, and then repeatedly for the ensuing weeks. Their marriage never had a chance, and they grow apart in the silence. It's very tragic."

"Well, that sounds pretty simple. Get the job, then convince Susanna to tell her fiancé what's going on. Then the story should flow as it does in the original version, right?"

"Right," she said. And don't get raped, she thought, or killed, or get anyone else raped or killed, or fired, or poison the whole house, or start any land wars, or get leprosy...

Long-pampered nerves beneath her skin seared ablaze and her stomach twisted on itself, while Rossini's overture swelled through its final cadence, coming to a dismal close.

ACT I
SCULLERY SEAMSTRESS SEEKING SOPRANO

Chapter Ten

~~~
✿
~~~

Gaspar pulled on the reins as the wagon entered the Count's estate.

Blossoming trees flanked both sides of the lane, their branches running together, wild and unhindered by pruning. The deep brown stems crisscrossed, weaving in and out of one another, making it hard to see where one ended and the next began and reaching clear out and above the lane to form a bountiful canopy. Among the long glossy leaves, heavy bunches of orange, red, and yellow berries, swollen to the size of ping-pong balls, bobbed suspended in lush bouquets. Panicles of white lacy blooms burst between the berries like gentle snow. A cotton candy scent wafted from up beneath the wagon wheels where crushed red fruits carpeted the path.

"What are these?" she asked.

"Strawberry trees. Perfect time of year for them too. They bloom the same time they harvest. You've never seen them? Surely you have these in Boston, don't you?"

"I have never seen anything so lovely. Can you eat the fruit?"

"Can, but only when bright red, and before the birds get it. I know the Count has a bit harvested to make a spirit for drinking, but some he sells in town or serves at his table. Truth is, you can't harvest them fast enough. See how there's so much have fallen. I think he keeps them more for their beauty. Rich men like beauty."

"Surely beauty is evident to everyone, isn't it? What on earth are you laughing about? This is very serious, Gaspar. Very serious and terrifying. There's a sick man ruling these lands, and I'm going to work in his house. Going to make a fool of myself every time I open my mouth and say anything. Do they burn witches at the stake in eighteenth-century Spain?"

"No, no. Nonsense. That good head on your shoulders will get you through. You'll be fine."

The trees fell back, and the great estate of Count Almaviva climbed into view. So unnaturally white and pristine amidst the greenery, it caught the morning sunlight with a radiance. The mighty manor dwarfed every other building Elizabeth had seen here so far. Four stories of sculptures, glass, railings, and terraces towered, like a mountainous wedding cake. It sat peacefully nestled amid endless meandering acres of manicured shrubs and shining pools. Elizabeth gasped at the sight, and her mind burst with a familiar declamation.

"Cruda Sorte!" Cruel Fate!

Unbidden music exploded into her ears. Orchestral swells and the straightforward declamation of a mezzo-soprano in full chest voice.

Elizabeth remembered the voice well. It was junior Rene Bobeck singing the entrance aria from Rossini's *L'Italiana in Algeri* at the production the college had mounted four years ago.

It had taken every skill in Elizabeth's arsenal to get Rene onto the tiny stage. An oppressive terror had dominated the young mezzo in the months leading up to opening night, and Elizabeth felt like a psychotherapist, standing backstage in the foggy darkness. She peered towards the light as Rene stepped out from behind the plank of plywood painted to look like a wrecked ship. The mezzo's skirts swished around her ankles, and her thick stage makeup held to her face like clay. It was opening night for Rene.

Elizabeth and Gaspar passed a row of shrubberies sheared to perfection. The warm sun made the greens greener, and the blue sky seemed to crystalize above this place of order and decadence. She looked down to avert her eyes from the mighty house, but as the horse clip-clopped past a long rectangular pool, the smooth waters mirrored an upside-down image of the mansion steadily growing larger. Its gables, arched windows and balconets reached out to her with menacing rippled fingers.

"Questo è il premio di mia fe!" This is the first day of my fate.

Rossini's mezzo heroine in his opera was Isabella, a woman thrown into a world that was not her own, shipwrecked during the overture onto the shore of savages, without rights, without family or recourse, abandoned and alone.

The house towered over her as Gaspar steered toward the eastern wing, the gravel beneath the wheels rustling like a percussion section before a guillotine climax. Bees danced in colorful blooms of rose bushes, buzzing out their part with the apprehension of an impending sting.

"Non v'è orror, terror, né affanno pari a quell ch'io provo in me." No horror, terror or anguish exists compared to that which I now suffer.

Well, Rossini's Isabella wasn't quite alone. She did have Taddeo, and Rene had Elizabeth and Elizabeth did have Gaspar, so she really wasn't totally alone, and that would surely have been the worst thing, wouldn't it? To be alone through it all.

Rossini's opera was a comedy. Only a truly male insensitivity could intend it as such. What could be funny about abandonment? About loss of rights? About the natural vulnerable state of being a woman in a male-dominated reality? This was no comedy. *Shame on Rossini!*

They passed into the building's shadow, and Rene's voice reverberated back into clarity. Elizabeth hid in the wings, with only a stage manager too wrapped up in light cues to notice her. The reduced orchestra of only ten strings and a couple woodwinds played the accompaniment in a variety of keys. The house only seated three hundred, and due to a lack of air conditioning, half the seats were empty.

The Count's massive estate was a testimony to vanity and opulence with dozens of rooms for only two people. Two people and all their shiny things inside a mansion with two giant wings that reached out like a claw to pinch anyone who got too close.

"Io mi trovo in tal periglio." I find myself in such danger.

Elizabeth gave in to her curiosity and gaped up at the sprawling fortress. Like anyone might, she tried in vain to enter those portals, to perceive what lay behind the rows of arched windows, all stacked up like tidy chorus girls standing on four risers.

She clutched her father's book to her chest, feeling small and naked, shivering with the terror of the beauty around her. It reached out, its seductive talons, touching her through every sense, strangling her. She wished herself back to the disorganized and highly unprofessional stage of Gaspar's farm.

"Da chi spero, O Dio consiglio?" From who, oh God, can I hope for counsel?

Just keep singing, Rene. Keep breathing. One phrase at a time. Remember the story. Remember who you are tonight. It was opening night for Isabella.

At the midpoint of the mansion, above what Elizabeth assumed was the main entrance, the house protruded forward in a four-story outcropping of stone. The center of the edifice, flanked by four tall pillars, was a concave cutout holding a statue of a man on a horse. The beast's front hooves perpetually pawed at the air while the man's arm remained frozen aloft, his sword brandished against the invisible onslaught. A man ever vigilant, ever powerful, ever locked in an invisible siege of life. The Count.

Gaspar drove towards a dirt path around the east wing to a back entrance where the ground pitched downwards towards the service door. A handful of other, smaller, and unglamorous structures stood behind the house, out of view of the main road.

"What are those buildings for?"

"The dependencies. Where most of the real work gets done. Let's see, there's the wash house, and attached to that is the spinning room. There's the salt house and the smoke house together in that building there. Over that hill you'll find the gardener's work shed on one side and the stables will be on the other. Beyond them is the blacksmith. Here on your right is the necessary for the family and their guests, if they like. The servants' convenience is next to the wash house."

The necessary. Even the richest of the rich didn't have flushable toilets. The family outhouse was octagonal and made of red bricks. It had small trap doors at its base for collecting the waste. Elizabeth's stomach curdled.

"Chi conforto mi darà?" Who will give me comfort?

On this side of the manor, the beauty was not so all-encompassing. Stacks of barrels and crates lined one wall, while horses, white linens hanging out to dry, and a small entourage of peasant ladies crowded the other.

The women looked up at the approaching wagon and their stares seemed to follow Elizabeth all the way down the ramp while Isabella and Rene wailed through Rossini's wild **cantabile** unbidden in her inner ear.

Elizabeth closed her eyes and endeavored to force Rene to skip to the cabaletta. With its more buoyant music and perky phrases, Isabella finds her resolve and decides she is a modern Italian woman who can handle anything life throws at her. Elizabeth wanted to hear that part of the aria; she needed that part of the aria.

But just as the orchestra started the introductory chords, the stage faded from her grasp, Rene's young voice dissipated back into foggy echoes and the memory melted away, leaving only the bees about their business, and the rocks grinding under the wagon wheels as Gaspar pulled gently on the reins.

They had arrived at the home of Count Almaviva. It was opening night.

Chapter Eleven

※◈※

Murmurs passed through the gaggle of women.

"Who are they?" Elizabeth asked.

"They're your competition. If I heard about the job, be sure everyone else has too."

"Gaspar. I don't stand a chance against any one of those women."

"Perhaps not, but worth a try. Just do your best."

A matronly woman in more sophisticated skirts stepped out of the house and inspected the candidates.

"That's her," said Gaspar. "You'd better go and join them. Go on."

"I can't do this."

"Sure you can. That house there is nothing, just another rotten tooth." He took her hand and helped her step off the wagon. "I'll be waiting here. If it doesn't work, we'll go home and think of something else."

Elizabeth climbed down and joined the gaggle while Gaspar moved his wagon alongside the back of the house to another service door.

The matronly woman didn't say a word as she walked around the young ladies, inspecting each girl like furniture. Her gait was like her shape, rather lumpy. Still, she bore an air of authority, despite being barely five feet tall. Her chin maintained a strong parallel relationship with the ground, while her eyes moved up and down over the girls. Her dark-red hair had some feathers of white streaked through her tightly fastened bun, but her skin was like smooth cream, without a flaw on it, though, like the rest of her, slightly pudgy.

She stopped at Elizabeth as though waiting. "Who are you?"

"I'm Elizabeth."

"Who are you?" the woman asked again.

"Oh, of course. I'm sorry. I am Dona Elizabeth."

A flutter of chuckles passed through the applicants. *Oh hell.* Gaspar had made her memorize a short series of Spanish names, but she had hoped not to have to recite it so quickly and with such a tremor in her hands.

"I mean, I am Senorita Elizabeth Marta Lopez Montilla." She ended the final syllable with triumph and relief. "I am here with my uncle, Don Gaspar. Who makes the cheese?" She gestured to Gaspar waiting in his wagon.

The woman glanced over her shoulder at Gaspar and then eyed Elizabeth up and down again with one raised eyebrow before inspecting the recruits one more time in renewed silence.

"All right," she said, choosing. "You, you two, you, you and," she hesitated for a moment with her finger reluctantly kept aloft while glancing over her shoulder again at Gaspar, who smiled and gave a friendly nod, "and cheese girl."

Elizabeth sighed, amazed by what the reputation of good cheese can do. "You six come inside. The rest of you can go."

Elizabeth and the other five candidates followed the woman through the service entrance into a large mud room where cool lanterns, aprons, and tools hung on the walls. They passed through a long, narrow corridor that moved lengthwise through the center of the house, shooting off into various workrooms where servants engaged in tasks from chopping food to polishing leathers. She heard chatter in some of the rooms, some hammering and pounding' and smelled something astringent, however, as they passed four cramped staircases and one large dining room, the six candidates did not converse between themselves. At length they turned left into a small windowless office.

"There. Line up against that wall," the woman said. "I am Dona Marcellina,"—Elizabeth had to hold back a gasp—"and we only need one girl. So, five of you will leave today disappointed. The last girl who held this position had to be let go because she found herself in a maternal situation. I assume I don't need to emphasize to you that such behavior on these premises will not be tolerated. Now, you will each tell me your abilities and experience."

The girl on the opposite end of the line began describing her qualifications. Elizabeth didn't understand half of what she said. She still didn't even know what position she was applying for, and now knew beyond any doubt that this whole venture was hopeless.

By the time it came her turn, she was fighting off both tears and laughter. She had a mental vision of Reggie doing interviews for her position back at the college, since she would undoubtedly never get back home from eighteenth-century Spain. She imagined Reggie stifling chuckles as young, desperate pianists told of their experience and background. Some bachelor's in music from somewhere or other, a list of teachers, half of them well-known and not worth anything, and the other half decent technicians, but then he would put them on the bench, tell them to sight-read and expect them to follow the stick like it was one of their own limbs.

She could get that job. That was her job. Why did Reggie want her to go away?

Here in the Count's basement, the other girls were far more qualified than her for just about anything in this century. She didn't understand half of what they were saying and wished she had Google or some other search engine on hand to look this stuff up. Every now and then, the other candidates would utter a word she understood, like laundry or baking. She shuddered at the word scullery. It sounded too much like skull and made her think of pirates and *Hamlet. Skull.*

It came her turn, and Elizabeth stuttered more than anything. She knew enough to say something about sewing and perhaps overelaborated on the few skills she had learned from Gaspar, but her list was still much shorter than the others. When she finished, Dona Marcellina stared on at her in silence while the other girls snickered.

At great, agonizing length, Dona Marcellina's countenance reshaped itself to total disgust as she inhaled to pronounce "Well, it's very obvious that—"

A knock at the door interrupted and a young woman's voice came from the doorway behind her. "Excuse me, Aunt, but it's very important."

Marcellina rolled her eyes and trod out of the room. The six girls could hear scattered tidbits of the conversation taking place just outside the door, Marcellina's voice direct and shrill, the young housemaid's softer and indistinguishable.

"What? Which one?... Are you sure?... Well, how can you know that?... Did you get a good look?... One more time, are you absolutely sure?... Ay!" Marcellina cried out as one injured to her soul. The door opened again, and she stood before Elizabeth with a long windy snort. "Very well," she said. "Cheese girl. If you can start right now, you have the job. The rest of you may go."

After the necessary gasps of incredulity, the five other girls left with tight-lipped glares. When the door closed, Dona Marcellina leaned against it.

"Wait. I don't understand," Elizabeth said. "You've got to be joking."

"Do you want the job or don't you?"

"But I'm horribly underqualified! Surely any one of those girls could have been a better choice. What on earth could have ever—"

Marcellina raised a hand and turned back to the door. A young servant girl stepped inside.

"May I present my niece," Marcellina said. "Amada, this is Elizabeth. I believe you have already met."

Amada was young, probably only fifteen years old, with light-brown hair and caramel skin, but indeed familiar. Elizabeth had met this girl before.

"Yes, Aunt," said Amada, "that's her. I'm sure of it."

The last time Elizabeth saw this face, she had just whacked a would-be-rapist on the back of the head with a fallen branch. Amada was the very first person Elizabeth had met after arriving in Spain, when she could barely walk for lack of shoes.

"If you think this will incur you any further favors, you are wrong," Marcellina said. "Your actions on behalf of my niece have bought you an opportunity to prove yourself in this house. But I can't protect you beyond this. Amada will take responsibility for training you, and you will be on your own from here forth, with no special treatment. I can just as easily put the word out and get those other girls back here tomorrow morning."

"Yes. Yes of course. I understand completely," Elizabeth said. "I will do my best not to let you down. I promise."

With a grunt and another puff of air through her dragon-like nostrils, Marcellina waved them off. "Amada, see that she gets her uniform and show her to her quarters. Start working with her right away. We want the upstairs rooms all cleaned before the weekend, and there's laundry on Monday."

Amada gently grabbed Elizabeth's arm and guided her out of the office. "Come on now. You don't want her to change her mind, do you? I'll show you to your quarters. Do you have any personal items?"

Elizabeth and Amada went out tell Gaspar the news and retrieve her sack. She tried not to cry as he headed off, promising to return in one week's time.

"This is a good time to get started here," Amada said, leading Elizabeth through a myriad of passageways that seemed too cramped, too dark, and built with too many squeaky planks. "The family is away on holiday for the last week and won't be back for another. That means a lot less cooking and best of all, a lot less laundering."

"Laundering? Is that what I've been hired to do?"

Amada laughed "*Pobresita*! You don't even know what you were applying for?"

"I'm afraid not. We just heard about a position last night and decided to give it a try." Elizabeth and Amada both had to duck as a tall man dressed in livery passed, lifting a tray of small silver containers over their heads.

"Well, you're a housemaid now, and we go by seniority here, so you're the lowest rank until someone else gets sent off."

"What does that mean?"

"Mostly it means everyone is going to talk down to you and treat you like dirt. But it does also mean you get stuck in the scullery most days and the rest of the time you'll never knowing exactly what you'll be doing, from cleaning the hearths and latrines, to running messages between the kitchen and the staff."

"You sound like you speak from experience."

"Until today, I was the lowest rank. So, I like you for a lot of reasons. Here's the ladies' quarters." Amada led her up a narrow winding staircase that creaked on every step. Together they passed several doors until reaching the top, which was hot and musty. "You'll share with me, right in here."

They entered a room of absurdly restricted space. Not only did the two tiny beds, one nightstand and two small dressers barely leave any floor space on which to stand, but the ceiling angled downward towards the one tiny window at the back, such that neither girl could stand up straight except by the dressers and the door.

"Goodness. Well, it's snug, I guess."

"Don't worry, you won't spend much time up here. Just drop your things on your bed. We've got to get you some proper uniforms. Those clothes are a bit too fancy for the latrines and scullery, I think."

Oh, that word again.

"Scullery. You know I'm from another country. What does that mean exactly?"

"Another country?" Amada seemed suddenly very excited about Elizabeth as she led her back down the stairs. "What country are you from? France? Italy? What brought you here?"

"A book, actually."

Amada looked disappointed. "Oh. Well, my aunt runs a pretty sensible ship. No girl is condemned to the same position every single day. That way we're all trained in different duties if someone gets sick or has to leave suddenly."

"And scullery?"

"You'll be scullery four days a week. I'll still have to do one day, and so will Sancha. But I'll be training you on. Mondays are laundry and we all chip in on that. Fridays and Sundays you'll be trained as a housemaid and kitchen maid. First week though, you're in the scullery since that's your main position."

"That sounds like a lot to learn."

"It is, and I'll tell you right now, Cook gets her aprons in a ruffle every time we have to train a new girl. I don't know why she complains so much. It's not your fault that you're new."

"And scullery..."

"*Pobresita.* You really don't know anything, do you?"

Amada led her into a small basement room lined with closets. Something resembling an ancestor of the ironing board stood in the center of the room. A woman in a bonnet sat beneath a small rectangular window, silently stitching a massive rose-colored gown. Most of the woman lay hidden beneath waves of silk and lace as her hands managed their meticulous needlepoint. She looked up and smiled at the girls.

"That's Beatriz. She doesn't talk much."

Amada opened a closet. "Now let's see about your uniform. You'll need a new stay, I'm guessing. There are a couple of nice shifts in here." She held one to her nose and took a perfunctory sniff. "Not bad. Do you need another? You'll be getting everything dirty in that scullery, you know. Probably best to have one on hand to air out during the day. It gets maddeningly hot down there."

"Um, I guess I—"

"You'll need some new stockings with the Count's coat of arms on them. Hate wearing them. Can you believe we have to? Better get you two pairs. You'll find them in that draw to the left of the sink."

Elizabeth went in search of stockings. "Um, about that scullery."

"It's a big stone oven that you live in from first light until after everyone else has gone to bed, and you do whatever Cook needs. And she won't ever be nice about it. Don't expect that. Cook isn't nice about anything. Soon enough, someone else will come in and you'll be down to once a week, like me and Sancha, and I've only been here six months, so you can survive that long. Anyone can. You know, some ladies in other manors live their entire lives in that little stone room, scrubbing and chopping and not saying a decent word to another human being for months. Sort of like Beatriz here, only dirty, hot, and endless. Here's a pocket bag, do you think you'll need two?"

"I—"

"Probably not, since you'll be in the skull. But we'll get you one anyway, and here's a new petticoat, and a pair of outer ones. Do yourself a favor and just tie that back every morning when you start. It gets so wet down there you have to spend your sleeping hours laundering, just in case some of the family should see you out and about. Honestly, I've wondered why we even need the thing? No one sees us down there. Here's a pair of aprons, those will have to be laundered no matter what."

"So, I wash the dishes?"

"Scrub the pots and clean all the non-breakables, tend and clean the kitchen fires, scrub the kitchen and skull floors, but mostly you do the prep work for Cook, and it's never done fast enough. Oh, and she hates for the scullery maids to be seen in the kitchen. Remember that. You've got to get there in the morning before her and get things running, or you'll be in for it."

"But how can I possibly do all the prep work without—"

"She sends in kitchen maids to get everything from you. Believe me, you'll be grateful for having to run around less. Then at night you have to keep the scullery clean. Oh, here's a neckerchief and a bonnet, and that should be it."

"So, I prep the food? Like peel carrots and chop onions?"

"Pluck the fowl, scale the fish, you know, that sort of thing."

"Pluck? Scale? I think I will call it the skull. Just to keep my spirits up."

Amada sighed. "Look, I'll ask Aunt to let me work with you the first day or two. And after that, anything comes along, you find me. You'll be fine. You can do anything."

"How can you say that? You don't know me at all."

"You can whack the Count on the back of the head with a stick. You're one step short of a Roman Goddess. Scullery's no problem, it's just hard work. Trust me. Now let's get you back upstairs and dressed. No doubt Aunt's already hearing it from Cook."

"Wait." Elizabeth grabbed Amada's arm despite the loads of petticoats in hers. "That man that attacked you, that was the Count?"

"He went off to Cadiz next day, so I don't know what he thinks happened. Probably that he got the best of me and passed out. That's how I'll play it anyway, all broken and spoiled like. That'll end it, Aunt says. They like to think they broke you in, like you're one of their horses. Listen, I'm sorry I ran off like that. I was very—"

"Don't worry about it," Elizabeth said as they left. "If you can get me through that scullery, then we're even."

Elizabeth was greatly disappointed to learn that the Count did not supply his staff with footwear, and she would have to fulfill her duties in the awkward wobbling discomfort of the tiny pointy heels she had inherited from that motherless book.

Arms laden with petticoats, they ascended the four winding flights back to the girls' quarters. In the narrow passage, a door ahead opened, and a man stepped softly out. He wore untucked shirtsleeves, no shoes, and an open waistcoat over tan breeches. A long brown leather satchel hung draped across his chest and a coat over his arm. Tall black boots dangled in the hand beneath. He was of medium height with butterscotch hair pulled back in a tail.

"Hey, what're you doing up here?" Amada asked, and her voice wavered.

He pulled the door gently closed without concern.

When Elizabeth saw his face, something in her abdomen clutched with so foreign and sudden a sensation that it paralyzed her. Amada stopped frozen too, and the man approached.

Warm. Warmth was all Elizabeth could think, the sole thought in her mind. Warmth. He was a young man, probably younger than herself, with honey-colored eyes. Like golden shackles, they locked onto Elizabeth with a terrifying confidence. He moved closer with a careless gait, and the clutch in her abdomen swirled. Her breathing accelerated.

Despite his magnetic attraction, an old disfiguring scar ran down his face, from his left temple to his chin, perhaps from a sword. It protruded outwards from his cheek, deforming mildly the left side of his face. Elizabeth studied it without blinking. She wanted to reach out and touch it, for though it was horrible, it did not abate the swirling inside her.

He ignored Amada's question and passed dangerously close to them. Amada looked away, but Elizabeth could not break her eyes from him.

"Who's this?" he asked. His voice was supple and melodic.

Amada continued staring at the ground as though she were somehow bowing to a nobleman. "New housemaid."

"New housemaid," he said, and Elizabeth felt her body run with a dizzy lull. She had never felt so utterly vulnerable. She wondered if he could sense it. He affected her so consummately that her suddenly absent intellect assumed he held the controls. Condemning judgements, even rational thought speedily evaporated. She thought nothing but surrender to a desire that had apparently lain in decades of hibernation. If he had decided to take her right there on that hallway floor, he could have.

"Well, nice to meet you, new housemaid." He smiled and passed so close she could feel his breath. "I guess we'll see you in the scullery." When he finally turned away, Elizabeth stood trembling, her arms embracing the petticoats. Her eyes lingered where he disappeared. She wanted to stand there staring after him, willing him to come back.

Amada grabbed her arm and yanked her into their room.

"Come on!" she said. "That's one to watch out for, Aunt says. Says he has bedroom eyes. I don't know but whenever I see him, I get shivers and can't talk so much. He frightens me more than the Count does."

"Why is that?"

"Because the Count has to take you by force. Has to drag you out somewhere and pin you down. This one. He just looks at you like he already has you, you know?"

"Yes. Who is he?"

"His name is Aleix, but Aunt calls him Don Juan. I know what you're thinking, but trust me, if Aunt says stay away, you should. She says he has the ear of the Count too. Only been here six months but walks around like he runs the place. If he gets a hankering to get rid of you, you're gone. A girl can lose herself, her whole life, to one like that in an instant."

Yes, in an instant, Elizabeth thought.

Chapter Twelve

E lizabeth entered the scullery ten minutes later and fell into the burden of physical labor for the next eight hours. Since the family was out of town, the meal preparations were minimal. Cook ordered all the pots and utensils sent down for a deep scrubbing, and Elizabeth spent four hours scratching her hands through greasy water, wishing to her depth for some Dawn dish soap and a Brillo pad.

She never actually saw her supervisor. Cook, who she suspected was female, shouted orders at her through a twelve-inch hole in the wall that connected to the kitchen. Elizabeth felt so detached from that massive, wonderful-smelling space just outside her cell that she imagined it another world. If it wasn't for Amada checking in on her every fifteen minutes, she might have fallen into the delusion she was in some kind of labor camp.

Back home at the college, she had often said to her students, "You pay me for these," and pointed to her ears. "You can't hear what it all sounds like outside of your head."

Her words came back to her with disquieting clarity. For the first time in her life, she saw that music itself was not really her job. She got into people's heads, into their hearts. For hours every day, she pried them open and found their vulnerabilities. Music was the tool with which she would guide each young person to look inward and then spread themselves across the score and the stage. She was an interpreter of the human spirit, and she missed it. Locked in this dimly lit stone room with her pots and aching shoulders, she felt isolated and empty.

When that first day was over, every muscle ached. Well after dark, as she finished up, muffled bursts of laughter and clinking echoed from the servants dining room down the hall. She wondered if Aleix was there, relaxing with the others.

Smelling of sweat and grease, and worn out to her core, she started spontaneously crying on the scullery stoop.

On the second day, Amada shook her awake before the sun, and strapped her into the stay. They descended together into the cool, dark kitchens where Amada said something about lighting the fires, then handed her a pair of small items and disappeared to fetch the milk and eggs. While Elizabeth glanced uselessly between the hearth, the rock and the strange U-shaped piece of metal in her hand, a grounds man came in with two short, fat dogs that immediately settled on a straw crate near the hearth. Above them, what could only be described as an overgrown hamster wheel hung attached to the wall. A thin chain hooked on its outer rim ran all the way to the turnspit in the hearth.

And that's how they made rotisserie chicken in eighteenth-century Spain.

Elizabeth silently set the metal U and rock down on the cold, stone hearth and tiptoed back to her scullery. A large, ominous container of water sat on one of her counters. In it, seven black eels swam contentedly in horrific slimy swirls.

Amada returned with the eggs and three recently beheaded chickens. Plucking their feathers made Elizabeth cry, and then she threw up from the smell, but at least Amada took control of the eel problem, and when Cook started screaming about the fire, Amada just rolled her eyes and said, "*Probesita!* You need to say when you don't know how to do something."

Elizabeth wanted to tell her that she didn't know how to deal with the eels, and that she would never know how to deal with the eels, and if it came down to her and the eels, she might just start the fire and throw herself in it before touching an eel on purpose.

Amada grew as important as a limb. She regularly checked in between her own duties to quickly pull her apron back and demonstrate some terrible new chore before Cook spouted a slew of Spanish profanities from the other side of the hole. Once, Cook was so angry, a pair of chicken legs came flying back through the opening, hitting Elizabeth in the face. She surrendered to tears again and thought about running back to Gaspar's peaceful and disorderly farm, where her few pathetic skills were at least appreciated.

By the third day it was the silence that bothered her. Music was so easily accessible back home. Radios, iPhones, and stereo systems gave one an unlimited access to any life accompaniment from any century. She yearned for the bell-like tones of her Baldwin piano and wondered if she would ever hear the rich sonorous blend of an orchestra again. This scullery job would be more bearable if she could turn on a little '80s music, or wallow in some Bach. One time she tried singing to herself softly, but after only seven bars of Gershwin, Cook began hollering through the hole with only her bony nose and pointed chin showing. Elizabeth closed her eyes and imagined green skin and a tall black hat.

At the end of the third day, Elizabeth slumped onto a stone step and started crying, not even having the strength to make it up the stairs to her room. She wondered if anyone would notice if she just slept here in her little smelly cell and wore the same clothes the next day. How much would she have to stink for someone to complain? And who would complain? The chickens? They'd lost their heads before they even got there.

"It's not as bad as all that, is it?"

Elizabeth jumped up. Aleix stood in the doorway. Terror seized her at how quickly her sexuality could leap into action, despite her exhaustion. The brown leather satchel hung across his torso like a medal of honor. Important men carried important things in their satchels.

Before she could summon the will to respond, a shrill voice peeled through the passageway behind him. "What are you doing here?"

Aleix turned to allow Dona Marcellina past.

"You don't have any business in here."

"I was just concerned," he said. "She seemed upset."

Elizabeth tried wiping her eyes before Marcellina could see.

"I'm fine," she said, her voice raspy and ineffectual.

"I'm sure we're all very grateful for your concern, Aleix. Now get out of my scullery and keep your head about your own duties."

Aleix bowed lightly and left.

"All right," Marcellina said. "Your three days are up now. Tomorrow you'll have the first half of the day off and then two more in here before you can train another position."

"Thank you," Elizabeth said, again wiping away reluctant tears. "I'm not ungrateful for the job."

"You think you're the first girl to get sunk by the scullery? I started in one of these myself. Besides, I saw your pretty hands when you arrived, and I hear you calling for my niece all day. Have a fall from station, did you?"

"Something like that."

"Well, you work hard. I can't deny that, and despite Cook's complaints, which I get anyway, you've shown yourself capable." Marcellina lifted a knobby hand to one of the stone walls and stroked it pensively. "Many ladies have passed their entire lives in this room. You don't have to worry about that. I've got a rotating system in this house. Three days a week you'll learn a new position, and things will get easier."

Elizabeth found this woman compelling. The Marcellina in Mozart's opera was a sort of comic jab at spinsters. The proverbial "bad guy" of the first two acts, she plays the jealous rival, threatening the happiness of Susanna and Figaro. In Elizabeth's book, the head Housemaid had received a similar introduction.

◈

Susanna would not give herself to the Count freely and Figaro's constant flirtations, winking, giggling, and chasing one another around the estate like teenagers only riled the Count's fury onward. In his zeal to re-establish his Droit du Seigneur, he resolved to stall, postpone, and avoid the subject of Figaro's wedding all together. But this could only work for so long of course. Two hot blooded younglings like Susanna and Figaro were not easily put off.

It was only when the spinster Housemaid, Marcellina, appealed to him, that the winds turned in his favor. Marcellina, frumpy and bony at the same time, with white streaks in her hair and a musty smell about her, was far beyond the age of fruitful marriage possibilities.

But she had, it seemed, a contract signed by Figaro almost ten years before. The contract bound Figaro into marriage unless he could repay a loan by a certain date. It was like finding a pot of gold. The Count could influence the ruling in either party's favor, and so long as Susanna was being obstinate, he could postpone Figaro's marriage indefinitely, or even force his manservant to marry the spinster wretch. It was marvelously convenient.

◈

Elizabeth had always felt a little bad for Marcellina. Susanna shamelessly mocked her insecurities by flaunting her beauty and youth and Figaro's preference for them. But this woman was not insecure or petty at all.

"You're much nicer than in the opera."

"The opera?" Marcellina's eyes widened. "You used to be in the opera, did you?"

"Not exactly. But, while we're talking about opera, I wonder if I can spare us both some difficulty and just sort of skip to the end of the third act."

"You know, you don't always make much sense."

"Figaro. You can't marry him."

Marcellina gasped, clutched her sternum. Her previously cool and compassionate eyes sizzled to a sneer, and her posture rose to tower above Elizabeth like a velociraptor readying for the kill. "How dare you," she said with such spit that Elizabeth had to shake the sudden Jurassic image from her mind.

"No, wait. You don't understand."

"I'll tell you what I don't understand," Marcellina said. "What makes you think you have the right to intrude on my private affairs? How dare you even voice your opinion to me, you little hussy!"

"You misunderstand. You can't marry Figaro because there's something you don't know—"

"What I don't know is where a scullery maid learned such insolence."

"Wait. You're overreacting. I'm trying to help—"

"One more word out of you and you're out, you understand?" Marcellina crossed to a shelf and snatched a pail and well-worn brush. "Now scrub these stones."

"But I just finished for the night."

"We can't have rodents coming in here after the smell. This place is a disgrace. You'll stay and scrub until there's nothing left beneath your feet but the stone, and you'll do that at the end of all of your shifts here. You'll do the same in the kitchen tonight and twice a week."

Marcellina tossed the pail clanging at Elizabeth's feet. She spun around on her black heels and stormed down the hall to her office, where her door slammed with a furious crash.

Elizabeth was too tired to cry. She just carried the pail out to the water pump in a stupor, resigned to her fate. Fifteen minutes later she was on her hands and knees scrubbing with what little breath she had left, when Marcellina returned and towered over her.

"Scrub harder," she said. "You have to get rid of all the grime or this place will rot along with you in it."

Elizabeth started over, her tears mixing with the pail water.

"Get on your knees," Marcia Stuporio had said. "Get on your knees and sing it again."

Marcia had been speaking to Avina Cloud, a third-year soprano who had a glorious nightingale voice and the full diva ego to go with it. On the day of this particular master class, Avina was sporting a long, black skirt with a slit that rose to the top of her right thigh. Her four-inch heels had pointy toes, and her sleeveless, ruffled top covered just enough of her torso to accentuate her lovely curves. A cut-crystal necklace reflected the stage lights back onto all the surrounding walls.

"I'm—sorry?" Avina had asked.

Masterclasses, though infrequent at the college, honored a singer with an opportunity. If chosen to perform, she would receive personal coaching from a well-known artist. But of course, the school always wanted to showcase singers with the most potential, so Avina sang for everyone.

"Get on your knees and sing it again," Marcia, the guest prof repeated. "I know it's embarrassing in here. I'm sorry to ask you to do it, but you've got a lot of upper torso tension that's inhibiting your abdominal support. You won't really bloom on that high note until you let go of all that. So, on your knees."

"On the floor?"

"Yes, on the floor. Just trust me on this."

Avina moved her skirt aside and looked down, as though the floor beneath her feet was the only floor in the room.

Slowly she descended, chiffon, crystals et al., down, down,

down in awkward spurts and jangles, until she was on all fours. It was deliciously humiliating. Murmurs passed among the students, along with a few amused snorts.

"You mean like this?" Avina asked, trying to pull her slit closed over her exposed thigh.

"Yes, sorry about your skirt. Now sing it again, keeping your arms strong beneath you. Take it from the start of the cabaletta."

Elizabeth began playing Verdi's masterpiece on the piano, and at first Avina sang with a muffled, nasal tone, barely audible.

"Sing!" called out Marcia. "You've got to really sing it now. Don't **mark**!"

Avina raised her voice and put some power behind it. She sang in this oddly demeaning position, as though her torso became an empty chamber of vibrations, and she reached deeply for each breath, producing a sound that would cut over an orchestra in a three-thousand seat hall without a microphone. The runs and climaxes of *Sempre Libera* tore through the space with a raging fury.

When finished, the young soprano sat back on her heels.

"You see," Marcia said, "sometimes, to go high, we must first go low."

Later that night, Amada found Elizabeth sleeping against a scullery wall, a snarky grin on her face and a greasy scrub brush dangling from her hand.

Elizabeth awoke to the silence of a sleeping house. It was so dark she could barely see, but she roused herself dreamily from the bed. She didn't bother putting her shoes on but left the tiny attic bedroom wearing only her loose shift. The air was warm, and she wanted to remember freedom for a few moments. Freedom from irrational controlling superiors, freedom from unending back-breaking work, freedom from solitude. Her bare toes made not a sound as she moved over the cool floors and down the winding stairs.

In the servants' hall, she wandered aimlessly through the dark workrooms, studying the tools and chores of others whose faces were in darkness to her day and night. The kitchen looked so tidy and cozy in its silent state, like a reproduction in a museum, complete with hanging pots, big sinks, and a hearth that appeared in the darkness like a black hole.

She found the back door and unbolted it. Her feet stepped outside onto the gravel. She wouldn't mind the pain.

She meandered through the gardens under the moonlight and the cool damp grass felt wonderful between her toes. The cool cotton of her loose shift tickled her shins. She stood a long time in the center of a grassy plot looking up at the stars with no one to answer to, no one to order her here or there, not even stiff pointy-heeled shoes or a stay to force her back into form.

An inner impulse sent her wandering towards the stables at the eastern end of the house. The smell of sawdust and horses reached out to greet her, reminding her of the secure comfort of Gaspar's barn with all that hay.

The barn door squealed when she nudged it open, amplified by the night's silence. She stood there, in the entrance, like a specter of the moon, a goddess of her own choosing. Horses stomped their hooves or snorted in objection as she wafted past. In the center of the alley, an enormous pile of hay beckoned. She meant to throw herself down and roll like a child until covered with straw.

From behind a shadowed pillar, Aleix stepped out. He wore what he had the first time she met him in the servants' quarters, the white shirtsleeves, billowing around him in luscious waves. Without his satchel, there was an air of nakedness, since she had only ever seen him with it strapped across his chest.

He did not appear surprised to see her. Stepping forward, he pulled her to him. Her body trembled at the feel of him through the thin shift, so close and strong. He held a power so maddening that it opened her insides and called him to her. She felt his warmth, and she dug her fingers into him as he guided her willing body down to the hay.

"Hey! Come on, sleepyhead!" Aleix hit her on the back of the head. "Wake up, you nut! Or you'll miss all your free time and breakfast to boot. Now get up!"

Aleix faded away, and Amada stood above her, fully dressed, her hands on her hips. The bedroom was light, and the window was open.

Elizabeth sat up. "What time is it?"

"Past waking, if that's what you're asking. I knew you were up late, but I never thought you'd sleep this long. You've only got two more hours before Aunt wants everyone cleaning the sheets. It's laundry day. So, you'd better get up and enjoy your freedom before it's over."

The next minutes spanned in a blur, between the sweet song calling her back to pleasure unrestrained and Amada conveying a chain of information so horrible she couldn't digest it. "I don't know what you said to Aunt, but I've never seen her so mad."

"Dona Marcellina?"

"Who else do you think? What's gotten into you, girl? Aunt says I don't have to do scullery duty after this morning and you're back in there until the end of the month. That's three full weeks without a break."

"Wait—why?"

"How should I know? She's never made anyone do that before. She's just mad. What the heck did you say to her?"

"Oh. I tried to skip acts."

"What? *Pobresita*. Now hold still so I can get this thing tightened." Amada yanked on Elizabeth's stay, forcing it tighter and tighter around her waist, re-confining her, caging her in.

"Stop!" Elizabeth pulled away, and Amada dropped the laces.

"That's tight enough. It's asphyxiating." Elizabeth took the laces and loosened them. "I can dress myself."

"Well, you don't have to get all bent about it. I was just trying to help." Amada grabbed her apron and swept out. Elizabeth wanted to collapse back on the bed and cry, but she had a hard time bending over in the stay. *How do sopranos sing in these stupid things?*

Downstairs, a small breakfast had been left out for her in the servants' hall. She ate, but did not see Amada or Marcellina. Other servants passed through without acknowledging her existence.

She wanted to use her remaining free time to explore the house and grounds, which she had never done outside of her disturbingly erotic dreams. Slipping into the sunshine felt like stepping into a hot shower. About twenty yards from the house, the vinegary smell of the skull abated, and she waltzed along, enraptured with at least a temporary olfactory freedom. No one could tell her what to smell.

Inside each dependency, some laborers smiled or glanced up from their work and nodded, while others frowned at the uninvited intrusion. She resolved that no matter how terrible the next weeks would be, she would smile at everyone who peeked inside her labor tomb. Not that anyone ever did. She would smile at Cook. Even though she'd probably get screamed at.

Even the discomfort of her shoes annoyed her less as she passed over gravel, grasses, and dirt. She strolled down a long lane of orange trees and sat on a hillside picking wildflowers near some oblivious sheep. She visited the actual stables, which looked nothing like the ones in her dream. When she stepped inside with curious trepidation, only a few lonely mares and a shoveling stable boy noticed her.

In the gardens, a world of man-made beauty beckoned. Sculpted shrubs around a tall obelisk opened at a Chinese bridge spanning a rocky brook. She crossed it to a carved grotto shrine where a Madonna looked down on Elizabeth from a pedestal so bejeweled, it dwarfed even the Mother of God.

A series of shouts from the main house echoed through the gardens, and Elizabeth realized she was wasting precious time. Most of Mozart's opera would take place inside the house, mostly in the Countess's chambers on the second floor, and once the family returned, a scullery maid would certainly not be able to sneak above stairs. Perhaps getting a layout of the house now could help her later on.

Back in the servants' corridor, she found a spiral staircase she had never used and climbed to the second floor. She gently pushed the door ajar. Any servants wandering about their duties would certainly object to her presence above stairs.

It was another world, above the stairs. Beyond the servants' door, a salon with high, carved ceilings felt so cavernous compared to her small skull and bedroom. Long heavy drapes of blue velvet tapered into bronze fixtures around tall arched windows. Polished parquet floors set in a triangular pattern lay beneath an enormous Persian carpet. And a sculpture of a tall, slender bird with green eyes stood on a wrought iron table, frozen in an eternal parade of self-appreciation. Opposite the windows, a balcony overlooked the main entrance, where a crystal chandelier hovered inches away from curious fingertips.

She tried to imagine people filling this space, drinking and laughing and showing off an impressive variety of fabrics and embroideries. Elizabeth grinned at the thought. Just like the singers, after the show, these too would take off their costumes and go to sleep in their undergarments.

When she heard a housemaid coming up the stairs behind her, Elizabeth scurried guiltily down the far eastern side of the house. Ducking through a door, she found herself in what could only be the Countess's chambers. Three rooms linked together, all decorated with hand-painted Chinese wallpaper, Persian carpets, carved mahogany tables and bookshelves laden with glass decanters and silver brushes.

The middle room was where the Countess dressed. Three closets lined a curved inner wall, each with a gilded golden frame and a fleur-de-lis molding. A large red armoire with mirrored doors caught Elizabeth's eye. How strange that girl in the mirror looked to her, with a dirty face, tangled web of hair, and curves busting out atop the stay, almost to perversion.

Mirrors seemed to be everywhere back home, inviting vanity checks at every pit stop, bedroom and store window. Here, her appearance was as irrelevant as the sun passing between horizons while she scrubbed away in her tiny stone room.

The Countess's blue bed reached towards the high ceiling with four tall posts. Carved birds sat perched atop each one, regarding Elizabeth with silent disdain. Beneath them, the bed looked so much fuller and softer than her cramped and flattened one upstairs.

Beyond the bedroom was a small private room for a "water closet." Though decorated in porcelain and copper, it was horrifically primitive. *Without running water, it stank, no matter whose bathroom you visited in eighteenth-century Spain,* she thought.

Leaving the Countess's rooms, she wandered through other suites, a game room, an ornate dining room, and two parlors, each with a portrait of the Master and Mistress. After a while, it all started to look the same: gildings, moldings, cut crystal, tapestries, and so on.

In the western wing, a long narrow room led out into the main hallway. It had a hidden servants' entrance and a back door with a staircase that led directly outdoors. Compared to the rest of the house, this room was much simpler. A pair of black leather benches sat quietly at the center and tall closets veneered in exotic wood extended along both sides. Inside their glass paneled doors, rows of rifles, pistols, and swords stood tall on display, like art in a museum.

"What are you doing in my domain, little scullery maid?"

Aleix leaned against the door frame, a long, thin rifle in his hands. His brown leather satchel hung across him, and she wondered how he crept up so quietly behind her on the wooden floors. Her body seized up when he stepped inside and moved closer. There was a grace about his movements, a calmness in his voice that gave her the unsettling feeling he was always in control. She could not take her eyes from his teasing smirk, nor the mysterious scar that ran down his face. *For crying out loud Elizabeth, say something. Move yourself.* This was absurdity at its height. For goodness' sake. She was no woman of ancient dominated cultures. She was from the twenty-first century, a product of suffragettes, the sexual revolution, women's rights. Thousands of women had fought, labored, and marched so that she could know independence. She was not an animal; she could control this warm, spinning sensation within her. She could put a subject and verb together in five different languages. She could play Bellini and Rachmaninoff. She could interpret great poetry, follow an orchestral score—

"My name is Elizabeth!"

Aleix's eyes glistened. "Elizabeth," he said, and the sound of him pronouncing her name delighted her. "Elizabeth." He seemed to be thinking about it, as though it was somehow optional. "And what do they call you, then?"

"What do you mean? They call me Elizabeth."

"Surely you don't say all that every time. Do they call you Liz? Or Lizzy?" He began circling her, taking his eyes away to inspect the large weapon in his hands. "Or Eliza, or just maybe Liza?"

"Elizabeth. They call me Elizabeth."

"How about Beth? Or Betty? Elise? No, not Elise. Elsa? Lisbeth?"

"Just Elizabeth."

"Or... Elly." He stopped walking. "Elly. That's it. I'll call you Elly." He slung the weapon over his shoulder and stood grinning, his other hand tucked inside his waistband.

When he took another step, Elizabeth turned and ran, her skirts swooshing back and forth as the sound of his laughter echoed between the rows of ageless artillery.

Chapter Thirteen

S he ran.

She didn't know why she was running, but she sped down the long hallway, hearing her own childish footsteps resound through the pillars and vases. Maybe she could return to Gaspar's farm and live out her days in that safe place. Maybe she could run to the sea and find a boat to take her back home to join General Washington in the revolution. Maybe she could just run until her feet burned with blisters.

At the main entrance, she reached for the ornate brass handle, but stopped. Something called her attention, beckoned her subconscious. A pair of large double doors on her left opened off the foyer into a long and bright room. Polished marble lined every wall, hearth, and corner, as though the whole space had been carved out of a mountain and transported to the Count's estate. Tall, slender windows filled the room with glistening light from the front side of the house.

There was only one lonely item here, standing on three legs at the center of the room. Elizabeth's heart leaped. She lifted her skirts and dashed across the sprawling floor, reaching for it with anxious trepidation, just in case it was some mirage, a final joke from this realm of her insanity. She eased around and sat on the bench with guilty pleasure, like a criminal on the throne when the King is away.

It was smaller of course, a fortepiano with only five **octaves** instead of the customary eight she was used to. The keys were miscolored, whites turned black and blacks a deep brown. Even as she dangled her fingers above them, she knew they would make a quirky, unfamiliar sound. This archival ancestor of the piano she knew was built with leather hammers on thin, harpsichordian strings. Whatever twangs might erupt would only have a light wooden casing to resound off and little to no sustain. But it would be music. Sweet, wonderful music, ringing like church bells on Christmas morning.

She pressed a few keys gently down. Sound, precious, pitched sound rang through the hall. Like an addict escaped from rehab, she sank erotically into Chopin's Nocturne in E-flat. What drizzled forth probably sounded strange, with buzzy low notes, tinkling highs and an overall shallow resonance. Eventually she'd have to recompose or drop some notes, but to Elizabeth, suddenly aware of her deprivation, the sound was more beautiful than a mighty orchestra in a perfectly constructed hall.

She drowned in the pleasure, like her loins had wanted to drown in Aleix. For a few sacred moments, she passed beyond time and literature, forgetting what page of what story she was in. So deep was the trance that when a voice interrupted her, she jumped in shock, and sucked her hands off the keys, launching into an awkward case of hiccups.

"Who are you, and what are you doing in here?"

Elizabeth rose, backing up, the bench tipping behind her. "I'm so sorry." Her skirts caught the bench's leg and she stumbled, toppling backward clumsily draped atop the seat.

The man stood at the door in servant liveries, carrying a small trunk, while behind him, servants passed in and out of the front door hurriedly. The man had thick black hair pulled back in a tail, lively brown eyes and deep, sensuous, baritone voice.

"Don't," said another voice from behind him. "Please, don't make her stop."

The man stepped aside.

A woman stood like a statue in the doorway, dressed to the highest degree. Layers of grey-blue satin shimmered across her bodice and skirts with long, sweeping ivory lace at the elbows and just below the knee. Every inch of her skirt curved into some ornamental ruffle, braid, pleat, or cinch. Fabric tumbled in mystical waves, gathered around her hips in a polonaise that protruded so far to each side, she would have to turn sideways to pass through a doorway.

Her hair stood atop her head, almost defying gravity in a bulbous tower of sculpted curls. Her wide-brimmed grey hat was adorned with a blue appliqué on its upturned front and a bouquet of white feathers gushing from behind.

"Tell me," the woman asked. "What was that music you were playing? Who is the composer?"

"That was Chopin, Madame," Elizabeth said, wondering whether Chopin's parents had been conceived yet.

"Chopin? I've never heard of this composer. Where is he from?"

"Poland. He's Polish." Elizabeth racked her brain to remember if Poland was a country in 1778.

"Polish?" said the Countess. "So, this is what comes out of the Convocation?"

Elizabeth made a silent promise to take some European history courses.

"Please," the Countess said, "play it again for me. And Figaro, don't let anyone in. Shut the door and keep them out. Just for a moment."

Figaro!

Elizabeth got control of her hiccups while Figaro stepped out and softly shut the doors against the sudden bustle of servants filling the entryway at the arrival of the Count's carriages.

The Countess Almaviva crossed to one of the tall windows

and gazed through the glass with melancholic eyes. Underneath all her refinery, she was a simple beauty. A porcelain face, powdered and rouged with a flawless oval shape. Her mournful introduction in the second act of Mozart's opera had been moved forward by the unearthly powers of Chopin. "I don't care who you are," she said, "or why you are playing my fortepiano. I just want you to play it again. Please."

"I'm sorry, Madame. This instrument is very different from what I am used to, and I don't know the piece so well. I will have to rewrite some of the—"

The Countess's head turned atop her lovely and elegant neck, the massive wig and hat hardly displaying a tremor. She had an almost mystical way of speaking without words. Merely by silence and the smallest purse of her colored lips, she could indicate the absurdity of a question and thereby imply its answer.

The Countess didn't care if Elizabeth had to play some wrong notes.

Elizabeth lifted the bench back up, sat down, and prayed her memory would not fail her. It did not. The notes came easily, and while her fingers sped across the runs, which probably sounded ridiculous without the **sustain pedal**, the Countess only stared through the window, her breaths slow and trancelike, as though willing herself to somehow be transported through the thick glass panes to a realm of peace far from this gilded palace.

When the Nocturne ended, the harmonies dissolved into the walls, and Elizabeth sat with her fingers hanging over the keyboard. Gradually, the sounds from the corridor invaded the reverie as the servants struggled to haul in trunks and shouted orders back and forth.

"Thank you," said the Countess. "Now, if you please, tell me, who are you?"

"I'm newly hired in your household. My name is Elizabeth. I've been working in the scullery while you've been away, Madame."

"The scullery?"

"Yes, Madame."

"Where did you learn to play so beautifully?"

"Oh, I studied for a long time. Went to school."

"Went to school?"

"I mean, I had private tutors."

"And now you work in a scullery?"

"It's a long story, Madame."

"Those hands should be put to no such abuse. You play directly to the heart. I wonder, do you know any more by this Chopin? Perhaps something joyful?"

"Joyful? I believe so, Madame. I could play something for you, but I will have to recompose a little. I might trip on the—"

Once again, the Countess's head and all its refinery turned ever so slightly towards Elizabeth, and with neither sarcasm nor frustration, she spoke wordless and simple truths with her eyes and the slightly concaved shape of her cheeks.

The Countess did not care if Elizabeth made mistakes.

Elizabeth sat down again. *Something joyful.* She felt like a child released into the backyard after weeks of rain. She played.

At the first statement of the main theme, the Countess spun around in her ruffles and lace, crossing to the entrance and opening the ballroom doors, so the ringing tones of the Grand Waltz Brilliante could pour into the foyer.

The bustle of unpacking slowed to a stunned stall. Servants paused, dropping their loads, ignoring distant shouts. They stopped to listen, to surrender to the distraction, to waltz, to dream. The empty ballroom filled with misty imaginings spinning across the floor, more alive than any gathering of satin and jewels. A pair of young servants giggled as they tried to mark the steps, and the Countess laughed, holding her hands together over her bosom as though in prayer.

Elizabeth pounded the keys. Joy. Yes of course, sneaky, naughty, wonderful joy.

At some point, Marcellina appeared, and Amada, hovering with the others along the sides of the room. No one pointed out that work had stopped, or the impropriety of the new scullery maid. No one allowed such a horrible thought. Elizabeth held them all captive, her hands occasionally stumbling as she reworked passages too wide for Mozart's keyboard. No one noticed the dropped notes. No one left the fog for any pedantic criticism.

Elizabeth fell into the final climax, and just as she reworked the tremors onto the poor amputated keyboard, Aleix himself rushed in, not nearly so calm as usual. His chest heaved forth, as though he had been chasing something. He fixated on her, half bent over, gulping at the dancing air, while his satchel swung back and forth beneath him like a pendulum.

Oh Chopin, you naughty imp. You have seduced us all.

When it was over, she again suspended her hands above the keys, as though holding the strings of a puppet before the eyes of children.

At last, the cast had arrived. Finally come to the stage, all lined up for a company bow at the curtain call. Figaro, the tall handsome one with the dark hair and strong legs. Susanna, no doubt the petite maiden with the bouncy brown curls. The Countess grinning ear to ear, and lastly the Count, not so tall as Figaro, but a slim figure, well draped in travel coat, riding crop in hand, and an intelligent face that caught her off guard.

The spell dissipated at the entrance of the dogs. Someone had, in their hypnotic stupor, left the front door ajar, and now four huffing spaniels scampered across the marble floors, scratching the polish, sniffing the drapes, and generally yapping and panting with great enthusiasm.

"Who the hell is that?" the Count asked, while three servants rushed to control the animals before they convened on the fortepiano.

"She's the new scullery maid," the Countess answered. "Marcellina hired her while we were away."

"Scullery maid? Why is she playing my fortepiano?"

"Because I asked her to. It's my fault, dear. Please don't be angry."

The Count regarded his wife with a raised eyebrow and a relenting shrug before turning on his shiny black-boot and strutting out.

Servants began moving again. The Countess followed her husband but stopped at the door to mutter something to Marcellina. Amada hugged Susanna, and the two girls whispered to each other. Only Aleix remained, breathing heavily, as though he'd been running, and transfixed on Elizabeth with an unnerving fidelity.

Marcellina stepped between them. "You had better learn your place or you're going to be thrown out as fast as you got here. Don't think I won't do it for any half decent reason."

"I'm sorry," Elizabeth said. "You're right. I shouldn't have touched it. I just haven't played in so long and I couldn't help myself. I thought it wouldn't do any harm, since no one was here."

"Well, they came back early."

"Why?"

"That is not your concern, or even your place to ask," Marcellina snapped before swooshing her big black bustle out the door.

Of course, she was right. But how on earth was Elizabeth going to fix this plot, when she couldn't even ask any questions about the main characters?

Chapter Fourteen

❧❧❧

Elizabeth followed Marcellina back downstairs where the servants gathered in the dining room. So many people to serve so few. Marcellina began spouting orders with such fierceness that spit flew from her lips, landing on the closest unfortunate soul.

Due to the early return of the family, only a handful of housemaids would do the laundry, while Elizabeth was immediately deported back to the skull.

Figaro bounced through the door, and one could literally feel the air lighten or at least the humidity drop.

"Hello, everyone. So sorry to have thrown you all off like this, showing up early, but we all know that once the man makes up his mind, eh?"

Muffled snickers passed through the cramped and stuffy room. Elizabeth wondered why humanity took so long to come up with deodorant. Didn't anyone else notice the smell?

Figaro doled out orders in a cheery manner, making everything sound much more doable. Marcellina stood nearby with adoring eyes, her bosom uncharacteristically perky.

Susanna sat demurely in a chair by the door, her hands tightly folded on her lap, eyes on the floor. She looked concerned, not happy like a newly engaged girl should. The somber appearance of the show's notoriously cocky leading soprano struck Elizabeth as odd. Perhaps the Count had already made his advances, and after her rebuffs had decided to pack everyone up and return home in an act of fury.

So, it had begun.

In the opera, Susanna would tell Figaro about the Count's advances, and they would work through it together. But for some reason she had not told Figaro yet. That was blatantly obvious from the Major-Domo's cheerful demeanor and carefree posturing. Men! How could he not see that something was wrong with the girl?

"What's wrong?"

The question had been asked without prompt, or previous acquaintance. He was so handsome, Elizabeth assumed he was talking to someone else. Naturally, she had forced her eyes back to her morbid pile of Music Theory homework.

Undeterred, the boy sat right beside her at the table, dropping his bag with a clunk on the stone floor. He leaned in over her chordal analysis like he was making a pass at it. Why anyone would willingly get that close to a bit of theory homework was beyond even her love of music.

Elizabeth sat back, not sure how to react. They were the only two people at the table, and the nearest student lay snoring on a sofa a good fifteen feet away.

"Ah," he said, "theory got you down? Hey, don't forget when you cross the street, C-sharp, or you might B-flat."

The student lounge resounded with an echoing silence.

"You don't seem yourself today," he said.

"I'm sorry, do we know each other?"

"Don't you remember me? I'm the guy who spent all last

semester checking you out in Dr. Harvey's early music history class."

"Dr. Harvey's—weren't there like eighty people in that class?"

"You do remember! Anyway, it's time I finally got the guts to introduce myself." He extended a hand. "No, no, let me. You're Elizabeth, a piano major. You frequent the salad bar, unless it's international night. You study with Roberts, and you're a second year. You live off campus and ride your bike to school."

"Are you some kind of stalker? Should I call security?"

"Oh, I'd love that! I've always thought I'd make a great stalker. And yes, I probably was stalking a little, but lost my nerve for nine whole months until I saw you brooding just now. You looked so miserable. I thought, how could I do worse than that?"

"Well, all this theory," she glanced back at her chordal analysis. "Sometimes I have to ask what's the point. Can't I just play my pretty songs?"

"We've all asked that. But we plebes must assume that the academic powers have some great educational goal in mind. Damn them."

"You know, if I were nitpicking, I'd point out that you never actually said hello."

"Oh, how rude of me. Hello, it's very nice to meet you, miserable nitpicker. I'm Reggie."

"I'm Elizabeth."

Back in the land of eighteenth-century Spanish delusions, Elizabeth found herself returned to her tiny stone prison, with a freshly embroiled Cook casting orders through the hole in the wall. Her disembodied superior had somehow still not been present at the servants' gathering. Or had she been present, and was just so unrecognizable?

Servants rushed back and forth outside her door, frantic to

catch up with the unexpected arrival of the family. Elizabeth felt herself slipping back into invisibility as she regarded the mounds of potatoes she had to peel with a tiny dull knife, and the ominous looking pile of fish that had appeared on one of her counters.

Only Figaro stopped by her door amid the chaos. Not for long, just to say hello and introduce himself and apologize for being so short when he first met her, and oh welcome to the house and let me know if there's anything at all I can help you with, and "you don't know how to prep a fish? What a relief; there's something you don't know how to do. Let me show you. Just take a nice sharp knife—oh that's dull as cotton weed. Let me have that —now you just put the blade right in the vein here and cut it almost to under the chin, then opening him up like so, pull out all these slimy bits, well it's not like playing the fortepiano. You'll have to cut this bit out, don't worry, he won't mind, sleep right through it. Now take the back of the knife, although with this dull monster that doesn't change much. Bring it to your basin over here, hold the tail, and start flicking off the scales. Flick, flick, flick! Can't be gentle about it, just whack at it. Think about someone you hate. Oh sorry, did I get you? Not in the eyes? Sorry, I really do hate that fellow. Now you'll cut under his little fin here, see? This will be much easier when I've got these sharpened for you. Then just grab the head and twist the whole thing off like this. Now, if you'll just teach me to play piano, I believe we'll have an even trade."

Elizabeth found herself laughing. "You really are just like in the opera."

Figaro seemed to expand and heighten. "I always knew someone would write an opera about me someday!"

And with that he was gone, leaving her with five more fish to filet, in a hot, stone room that suddenly reeked of charm. No wonder Marcellina wanted to marry him. Everyone should want to marry him. Was there anything the man couldn't do? Back home, he would probably fix the plumbing, change the oil on the car, and update the computer all before lunch. Elizabeth went back to her fish with a smile. She would have a talk with Susanna before the day was done.

☙❦☙

A few hours later, her fingers bloodied from peeling and chopping, her arms itching with fish scales and her feet throbbing inside her pointy-heeled shoes, Elizabeth slipped out to the necessary. Another great indignity of eighteenth-century living. If she only fixed the plot of this story for the sake of returning to the land of flushable toilets and running hot water, that would be sufficient.

After lifting her layers of skirts to an embarrassing height and holding her breath for the stench, she opened the door into fresh air with gratitude. Perhaps she could slip quickly into the house and find Susanna.

Beatriz, the silent seamstress from the basement, leaned against the warm stone wall of the necessary, waiting. She was shorter than her perceived posture while hidden under the mounds of hems and bustles. Today, she did not smile gently at Elizabeth, but dazed off with dark-circled eyes, her face pale and moist. Trembling hands clutched a shawl around her shoulders.

"Beatriz, are you sick?" Elizabeth reached a hand for the woman's forehead, but Beatriz swept it away.

"I'm fine."

"No, you're not. You're ill. You need to go to bed."

"The Count needs his riding clothes mended. I'll just be a minute."

"What? Nonsense," Elizabeth said. "You can't keep working like this."

But Beatriz waved her off and climbed past into the necessary. "Please don't tell anyone. I can't lose this position."

"Beatriz, they can't fire you for being sick." Again, Elizabeth caught herself too late. Of course, they can fire her for being sick. They can fire her for being a woman, for having a pimple, for slurring her R's or slurping her soup. This was eighteenth-century Spain, and a fever was more than enough to get a person evicted permanently.

Elizabeth started back towards the scullery in a daze. She had to get out of this place. Gaspar was right, she didn't belong here. No one belonged here. She would go speak with Susanna right now, forget the consequences with Cook, and get this whole plot straightened out so that stupid magical book would transport her back to the land of running water, women's rights, and labor unions.

As she headed back inside, she met a stroke of good fortune. Susanna stood just outside, near the water pump, a basket of clothes under one arm. She was conversing with Aleix in quiet, solemn tones. Their conversation seemed so intimate to Elizabeth, that it felt completely wrong to intrude. She hadn't thought of that. How would the opera's heroine react to being interrupted by a complete stranger and told that she was completely mishandling her relationship with her future husband? No one appreciates that kind of intrusion in the best of scenarios.

But what could Aleix have been saying to her? The armorer and the Countess's chambermaid? Susanna did look concerned as she listened intently to him. Elizabeth thought, perhaps she should interrupt. Perhaps the poor girl might welcome an interruption. That's it. She should interrupt.

Just then, Beatriz passed, leaning against the door frame, her clammy hands trembling beneath her ineffective shawl. She wobbled, almost falling off the stoop.

Elizabeth stepped up and put an arm around her. "All right, that's enough. You are going to bed, and I'll have Cook send down some hot fluids."

"No. I can't. Please, you mustn't tell anyone."

"Well, what about Marcellina?" Elizabeth said. "She drives me crazy, but surely someone else can do the mending for you for a few days."

"I'm the only seamstress. They would have to hire out."

"The only seamstress in an eighteenth-century house! I find that hard to believe."

"The Count is very particular. Now, with the family back—please, just let me be." Beatriz tried to push her away, but she lacked any strength.

"Job or no job," Elizabeth said, "you have to go to bed. Now where is your room?"

Elizabeth hobbled with the woman down the stairs to a tiny, sad room, so well-hidden behind the wardrobe that the door blended in with the closets. She laid Beatriz in the bed, took off her shoes, and covered her up.

When she returned to the kitchen, she found a pair of scrambling kitchen maids.

"Where's Cook?" she asked.

"Gone to town last minute. Needed to pick up an order."

Elizabeth set about boiling a pot of water. She snagged a few of the used tea sacs, and even located some honey before sneaking back down to Beatriz's bedside table with stern warnings to drink and rest.

When she returned, both Susanna and Aleix had disappeared.

Inside the house, the familiar hollering of her superior had returned, so she ducked back into the scullery. She would have to speak with Susanna after her duties were done for the day.

But Elizabeth's shift didn't end until long after dark, when the family had been fed, and all the other servants were again lounging in the meeting room. Elizabeth sank to all fours and began scrubbing the stone floors. She hadn't talked to another person in hours and felt exhaustion down to her bones. She longed to stretch out in her thin, uncomfortable bed and luxuriate in the pleasure denied to no financial bracket...sleep.

But no. Sleep could wait until she found Susanna. She would find that chambermaid and set this right tonight.

Marcellina appeared, towering. It was remarkable how the woman could sense whenever Elizabeth was on all fours.

"That petticoat needs to be laundered. Now that the family is here, you'll have to make a better show of your appearance. When you're done, go downstairs and get a clean one for tomorrow."

Amada stepped in behind her, and gasped. "*Pobresita*! Are you still here? Let me help and we'll get this done together." Amada grabbed a second brush and got down on the floor with Elizabeth. Marcellina grunted and swished away. Fifteen more minutes and they had the floors, and the scullery put to bed for the night.

Finally finished with work, more exhausted than she had ever known, Elizabeth waddled out of her pen just as the other servants were saying their goodnights. She thanked Amada and trudged off down the hallway to see if Susanna had been chatting with the rest.

No luck. So, she made her way back downstairs to the wardrobe to find the new petticoat.

In the dim light of a pathetic candle, she found Beatriz back in her chair, shivering madly and fumbling with a useless needle. Tears dripped down her cheeks onto the Count's riding pants.

"All right," Elizabeth said. "What is it? This?" She lifted the pants off Beatriz's knees. "And that jacket? Now stop that crying and give it to me. Beatriz, don't be a pill. I promise, I'm not so bad with a needle. I'll take care of it. Now back to bed."

"No, last spring, the Count, he let go—"

"Beatriz, you have to trust someone, don't you? You can't go through your life, day in and day out, in this sewing stupor and never rely on anyone. Now go back to bed."

Beatriz obediently trudged out and Elizabeth heard the pathetic squeaking of her tiny bed as she sank into repose.

She collapsed into Beatriz's chair. It seemed she wasn't going anywhere. Her inability to locate and have a simple conversation with the one soprano who spends more time on stage than any other character in this show was becoming downright laughable.

Elizabeth awoke in great discomfort. Falling asleep at all had been a small miracle, sitting in a stiff wooden chair, holding a needle in her hand and wearing the stay. Even so, the sleep felt wonderful, though her neck bore the brunt of it.

A sensation had stirred her. A feeling of being watched.

Aleix sat in a chair opposite her, reclining in his shirtsleeves and vest, watching her with curious eyes, as though inspecting her while she slept. His legs were stretched out and crossed at the ankles and his brown satchel hung draped over the post of his chair.

Elizabeth sat up. "Hello." A pin from the Count's riding pants pricked her. "Ouch! What are you doing here?"

"It's nearly two o'clock in the morning. I might ask you the same question."

This wasn't another embarrassing dream. She was alone with this man late at night in the isolated basement. She pulled her pricked finger from her mouth, shook it off, then began hunting for her needle and thread.

"I'm just helping out, that's all," she said.

He raised a doubtful eyebrow.

"Do you think I have some ulterior motive? I'd much rather be upstairs in my bed."

His features softened and he turned towards the blackened window. The dim, flickering candlelight made his scar protrude with a grotesque shadow. What was it she found so magnetic about this man? He relaxed so easily in the exact same chair she sat so stiffly in, not a care in the world. Like lounging in one of those fancy movie theaters back home, watching the world with disinterest and a big soda in his cup holder.

"You don't need to be afraid of me, you know," he said.

"I'm not afraid of you."

"Yes, you are. I'm not good at first impressions. I like to think it's the scar, it sets people off. But I don't think that's it with you. I mean, the scar doesn't bother you."

She shook her head.

"I looked in on your patient," he said. "She's sleeping, and we probably should let her."

"She was afraid she'd lose her position."

"Well, that's not completely unfounded, but I'll take care of it."

"You must have some influence. I understood you've only been here six months."

"I move around a lot."

"But you must know something valuable to be so trusted by our Count."

"You'd be surprised what I know."

Elizabeth was pleased that she was able to converse in a mildly adult manner again. "Well, if it's so late, and you know so much, why are you awake? Why aren't you in bed somewhere?"

"Somewhere? I often have difficulty sleeping. A lot, actually."

Elizabeth finally located her needle, still dangling on the thread where she had dropped it. She found her seam and her hands resumed the metronomic dance of the stitches. "Difficulty sleeping," she said. "They say that's from a guilty conscience, don't they?"

For goodness' sake! Why on earth did she say that? *Who says things like that?* She didn't even remember thinking it before it was out of her mouth. Did she ever say stupid things like that around Reggie?

"So, what's your major then?" Reggie and she had nestled around a tiny corner table at Java's Cafe.

"Well, that's an odd question. I'm a music major. Aren't you?"

Reggie shook his head. "Nope."

"Well, you knew about the music theory, and you were taking

music history, so I assumed you were a musician." A barista deposited a pair of frothy drinks on their table.

"Oh, you should be right," said Reggie. "I was a music major for a bit, but no more."

"Then, what is your major?"

"Today? Let's see, I think I'm still graphic design, but only until the paperwork goes through. So maybe by Friday I'll have a better answer for you."

"Wait, how many majors have you had?"

He cocked his head and squinted his eyes as though doing complex calculations in the air above their table. "Seven—or no, eighteen. Yes, eighteen."

Elizabeth laughed and the table wobbled, jiggling their frothies. "Wait. You're not joking. You've had eighteen majors? What year does that make you? Not a perpetual freshman, I hope?"

"Oh no. I'm beyond years now. Have been for a long time. They don't even have a word for someone who's been here as long as I have. It's kind of embarrassing, for the admins, I mean. I'm the guy who outlives everybody at the retirement home. Others graduate and move on, but I just keep turning up every fall. Eventually, I think they'll get sick of me and invent some new major just to make me go."

"How long have you been a student here?"

"Eight years?"

"Eight years! But you could have three degrees by now."

"I know, isn't it a tragedy? They should write a play about me. Something Greek with a multi-syllable name that everyone has to sound out three times."

Elizabeth caught herself laughing again and she realized how unfamiliar it felt, like she was with an old relative she hadn't seen in years. "Well, how are you affording this?"

"Oh, there's plenty of money. Mummy's on the board, and she's so pleased I got through high school without drugs or STDs that she still writes the checks. Bless her. She does believe that someday I'll find it, whatever my *it* is."

"It?"

"You see," said Reggie, "I'm not willing to settle. I keep seeing bits of it here and there, and I follow the trail. Take some classes. Convince myself I've found it, and then after a few months or weeks even, realize that wasn't *it*, and go looking somewhere else."

"What was your major when you started?"

"Oh, back when I was a wee lad, you mean?" He said with an Irish accent. "What they let me in on? Double Degree of English Lit and Drama, with a minor in French."

"And what happened to that?"

"Cognitive Science. Almost killed myself after three lectures. Poor mummy would have been so sad. So, I switched to something else. Full Drama was next, I think."

"You could have just switched to another science class."

"Maybe, but I was good on the stage, and I just loved the use of language. But not for life. Nope, that wasn't it."

"*It*. Aren't you afraid you'll never find it?"

He shook his head. "I'll find it."

"Isn't it possible you're just lazy? Perpetually avoiding real life, hanging on as a student?"

Reggie raised an eyebrow over his frothy. "Figuring out your path in life isn't so easy, you know. So many people are stuck forever in jobs they hate, wishing they could do something else day in and day out, just to pay the bills."

"So, you're afraid."

Reggie set down his drink. "Now hold on. I know I'm not the customary student, but I've got a direction. I'm going somewhere with all this. I just need a little faith."

"You need a catechism and a bull whip," Elizabeth said too loudly. "Wait, no. I'm sorry. I don't know why I said that. I don't think those things. Really, I don't come out of my practice room very often."

"Yes, I know. E wing, third floor. You prefer the grand at the end of the hall, but you'll settle for the spinet near the elevator."

"Goodness, you really are a stalker."

"Admirer."

"Well," she said, "the truth is I'm the one stuck with a ball and chain. I've never thought of anything but my piano for as long as I can remember. Six years old when I started. Couldn't even reach the pedals."

Reggie sat back and crossed his legs. His brown eyes sparkled on her before wandering out the window to where the back-packed students trudged past on the rainy sidewalk. "You know," he said, "I think you might just like me."

In eighteenth-century Spain, Aleix smiled too, strangely amused with her. "A guilty conscience?" he said. "Well, then you must have a pretty clear one. You can doze off anywhere, it seems. Stone floor of the scullery or stiff-backed chair."

It didn't surprise Elizabeth that the Count's estate would be a buzzing rumor mill. What was surprising was that Aleix had asked about her.

Somewhere in the darkness behind Beatriz's door, the seamstress launched into a brief coughing fit that passed before Elizabeth could even stir to respond.

"That music you played today in the ballroom," he said. "It was very beautiful."

"Oh, that wasn't so much me as Chopin. The composer. I'm still just a servant."

"A scullery maid is a servant. The Countess picks what clothing to wear, but it doesn't really affect anyone. You pick which composer to play and wake people up. Everybody standing there, frozen in the ballroom. Not even aware that they had stopped. It was incredible."

"You didn't stop," Elizabeth said. "Seemed rather flustered and out of breath."

"I heard something in your playing that I haven't heard for a long time."

"Oh? What's that?"

"Hope."

Elizabeth's hands froze mid-stitch, the thread taut between her fingers and the fabric. "Hope? What a strange thing to say."

"Really? What is it that makes you play then, if not hope?"

"I don't know. I guess it makes me happy."

"No. That's not it. Then it wouldn't stop everyone. Are you? Happy?"

"Well, right now, working in the skull and staying up after hours to do this, that's hardly a question. But on a normal day, I would say that I am extremely...content." She proudly nodded.

"Content?" He laughed. "What is that?"

Elizabeth felt foolish. He had a point. What was content anyway? Suddenly, sitting here in this basement, with an epic of problems to solve, the word *content* seemed vulgar. Somewhere between crassness and outright insensitivity. *Content.* If it was a color, it would be gray. If it was a flavor, it would be soggy oats. And if it was a sound, it would be the steady drop of water from a leaky pipe, slowly driving an inmate insane. *Content.*

Her posture had straightened, and her neck tensed up. She still held the needle poised in her right hand and felt overcome by an irrational desire to drive it deep into her own leg. Perhaps that would wake her up from this unending operatic nightmare.

"I'm sure there's something you do well," she said, shaking off the urge. "Doesn't everyone have—"

"No. They don't."

"Oh, come on. You must have something."

"I survive," he said, his head falling backward onto his chair. "That's what I do. That's what the rest of us do."

"Well." Elizabeth turned the pants back out and inspected her work. "I doubt Marcellina will allow me anywhere near that ballroom now that the family is back." She bit off her thread and returned the needle to its cushion on the window ledge. "I'm done here," she said, shaking out the pants. "So, I think I'll finally go to bed, in an actual bed this time."

She passed him with only a mild trepidation and said, "Goodnight."

He muttered the same, but to her surprise did not stir from his chair, though she listened for his movements all the way up the servants' staircase, wobbling on the tiny pointy heels of her impractical shoes.

Chapter Fifteen

Waking the next morning felt like climbing out of a deep, dark well.

"Where were you last night?" Amada asked, throwing clothes at her. "I woke up late and you weren't here. I was worried."

"I'm sorry. There was something I had to do."

"Well, I hope it was worth it because you're a full day in the skull today, and Aunt's even madder, if that's possible. She says you're in for the next three days straight. I think if she could, she'd have fired you over that music scene yesterday."

Elizabeth allowed her torso to be tugged and pinned into the stay.

"But," Amada continued, "that music you played, it sure was pretty. Made me want to dance around. Who'd have thought you could play so beautiful like that?"

"I had to be good at something, didn't I? I'm certainly no good in the skull. Not without you."

"You're doing fine. Here, put this cap on and tidy up your hair. I just wonder if you'll be able to out-stay Aunt's rage."

Elizabeth realized that in her stupor she had allowed Amada to put her stay on her before she put on her boots. Now she

would have the impossible task of bending over to lace them up. "Amada, did your aunt fire the girl who was here before me?"

Amada's eyes fell and she lowered her voice. "Yes, but she had to do it. The Count wanted her gone before he got back from Cadiz."

"Was she your friend?"

Amada nodded. "Roommate, too."

"Did she go home to her family?"

Amada shrugged. "She didn't have any family that she ever spoke of."

"But she was sent away because she was with child?"

Amada grabbed her own cap and apron. "It's better not to talk about these things. Anyway, we've got to go. You don't want to rile Cook."

Elizabeth felt a familiar longing for a world where one could talk about these things.

She barely saw sunlight the next three days. Her sleep deprivation lingered unsatisfied, loitering in the shadows throughout each afternoon like a hangover that would not abate. Each night, she returned to Beatriz's domain to find a new mound of clothing tossed in a heap with instructions scratched on scraps of paper. Surely everyone in this house could sew, so why did everything have to be dumped on this poor woman? For that matter, why did it all have to be dumped on Elizabeth?

Aleix did not reappear during her sewing seances, though she dozed off occasionally, hoping she would wake to find him sitting across from her, his feet crossed at the ankle, his fingers intertwined.

Cook was merciless during those three days. Her customary outrages poured through the little stone window at a newly heightened pitch, occasionally warbling with fury while Elizabeth scaled fish, plucked chickens, and scoured the unending line of pots. When the same pot appeared on her counter five times in one day, she wondered if someone had a bet going to see how many times she would scrub it before throwing a fit.

Her fingers grew waterlogged and split open at the tips. The backs of her hands itched incessantly. Her feet throbbed from standing on the precarious tiny heels of her boots, so she frequently sat down on the stoop, just to peel a carrot. From the knotted hair beneath her cap, a drop of sweat would occasionally roll down her temple and neck. Most of all, she longed to rip the stupid stay off so badly, she considered using her little knife to do the job.

At the end of the third day, she no longer wished for anyone to enter the skull and attempt intelligent conversation. Instead, she muttered to herself as she hauled a crate of potato and carrot peelings out back. Wobbling through the servants' hallway, numb to anything but the desire to sleep, she felt something bowl into her with the force of a speeding bus. She toppled sideways and the peelings flew out of the crate, dispersing into the vortex. As she slipped to the floor and caught her breath, all the colorful peels fell like snowflakes on her head and skirts and the stones around her.

The person who had barreled into her (for she quickly concluded it was not a bus) neither stopped to assist nor offered any apology. She never even saw his face in the blur of his escape, and only knew it to be a man by the flapping of his coattails as he sped guiltily across the back lot.

"Hey! Watch out there!" a familiar voice shouted. "Come back here this instant and apologize!" Figaro offered her a hand. When she saw the mess of peelings scattered across the floor and walls, she gave in to her God-given right to be emotional.

"Oh now, don't do that. No one's ever cried in this passage-way, and we're not going to break the tradition today."

"Gaspar!"

At the sight of Gaspar's familiar silhouette in the doorway, Elizabeth descended into an abyss of self-pity with the full fury of female chemistry, sobs coming convulsively, and new salty tears trickling down her peel-laden cheeks.

"Well, what a state to find you in! What's all this?"

"Oh, just that damn page boy," Figaro said. "Came careening through here like a bull. You're all right, aren't you? No broken bones?"

Elizabeth continued to sob in a very satisfying manner.

"Well, that's a relief then," Figaro said. "Wouldn't want those musical fingers of yours getting hurt. No harm done then, just these peelings. I'll just pick these few out of your hair here, and oh, look at that, one landed on your nose. I won't get them for you, but I do believe some strayed down further, in that general direction as well. Now don't you worry about this mess. I'll send someone to come pick all this up. You just have a sit down. Get some fresh air and sunshine. Don't let that stupid page throw you off."

"The Count's page, you mean?" Gaspar asked. "Why on earth did he plow her over like that? Did you have some words with him, Elizabeth?"

"I've never even seen the boy!"

"Oh, that brat," Figaro said. "He's on fire because he got caught where he shouldn't and now the Count's sent him away."

"Wait. Come again?" Elizabeth said, pausing her wallowing. "The Count sent him away? But he's supposed to enlist him in the regiment. And that's not supposed to happen until the end of the first act!"

Figaro froze, a small collection of wilted peelings stuffed between his palms. Gaspar stepped forward and put a gentle arm around her shoulders.

"All right, come on now, little niece. Must have gotten a bump on the head. Let's go for a nice stroll, maybe stop at the pump and get a drink of water. Wash yourself off a bit." He led Elizabeth out the door and swiped some remaining peelings from her matted hair.

Elizabeth was still trembling and whimpering when they reached the pump. Gaspar sat her down on a stone wall and handed her a cup of cool water. "You've got to be careful, Elizabeth," he said. "Can't keep referring to everyone like pieces on an opera set. They lock people up for less than that."

"But they are! None of this is real."

"Am I real?"

"Of course, you are. Of course, you are real to me. You know that. You don't understand. This whole thing is completely impossible. I'm stuck in that tiny room from dawn till dusk every day, hardly any human contact for hours on end, doing a chain of chores that don't matter to anyone. Then at night I'm sewing for a seamstress who isn't even on the cast list."

"Then why are you helping her?"

"Because I'm an idiot. I'm so tired, I want to cry all the time. I can't feel my poor fingers, or my feet in these horrible shoes. I smell wretched and I'm certain there is new life growing beneath this stay. I haven't had a shower in—I can't even remember. How long have I been here? I can't remember how long I've been here. What day is it? Did I miss Mass?"

"Went together last week, and we'll go again tomorrow. I'll come back and make sure, just so you don't lose yourself. And I don't smell anything bad about you, either."

"Well, the people upstairs don't smell, do they? I can't even go upstairs to interfere or get involved in anyway. How am I supposed to fix this plot? I can't even ask about the leading characters without getting shot down by my employer, who despises me. She's hoping I'll quit or turn up dead one afternoon. I haven't done a darn thing to fix this plot. Susanna still hasn't told Figaro anything, and I can't just walk up to her in the hallway and bring it up, you know? 'Hello, you don't know me, but I'd like to give you some marriage advice.' I tried being direct with Marcellina, and look where that got me."

"Just have to be patient, I guess."

"Patient? Didn't you hear? The plot is progressing without me! How many potatoes am I going to have to peel before I can have one decent conversation with the leading lady and get this thing turned around? This is taking forever."

"Well, how long did it take in the opera?"

"About two and a half hours."

Gaspar laughed. "Perhaps you're going at this the wrong way. What does the book say you should be doing? Does it give you any guidance? Perhaps you've affected things already. Or there might be tiny details, clues you could be employing. Maybe a passageway that Susanna likes to use, or a particular subject you could use to start up a conversation. Are there really no helpful details at all?"

Elizabeth stopped flailing about. She scrunched her eyebrows into a distinct scowl.

"What?" he asked. "What have I said?"

"That's a very good idea. I should have thought of it. I admit, it hadn't occurred to me to pick the book up again since I got here."

He laughed, which was so nice to see, even at her expense.

"Now sit down here," he said, patting the stone wall next to him. "We're in this together. Remember, you're never alone."

"Oh, Gaspar."

Elizabeth told him about playing the fortepiano and how dull the instrument sounded compared with her Baldwin back home. She told him about enchanting everyone, and how much she missed her job, her students, music that hadn't even been written yet, instruments that hadn't finished evolving.

"And you think you haven't accomplished anything since you've been here? Elizabeth, you want to go home."

"Yes, I do want to go, Gaspar. I really do. You're right. It's not the plot that's changed. It's me, isn't it?"

They sat together in the sunshine for a few minutes. The warmth felt so good on her skin, Elizabeth couldn't have enjoyed it more in a poolside lounger.

"Can't dictate the pace of things," Gaspar said. "No matter how tired we might get. A girl may want to get married, but if she marries in haste, might marry the wrong fellow. Even the Count up there in his chambers, or out on the battlefield, if he wants to be successful, he has to sit back and let time do its job."

"You mean I don't get to set the tempo?"

She had said that to someone else once. *Who was it?* Something about setting tempos and Reggie in the shadows. Oh yes, it was during a production week at the college.

"Well, you're not the conductor, are you?" McDanials had responded with an offensive snap.

"No, of course not," Elizabeth had pleaded, "but these singers, they're still just students. For many of them, this will be their first time on the stage with an orchestra. They've all trained and studied for months, practicing at much slower tempos. They'll be nervous, not to mention what this will do to their breathing. Dorabella's aria is moving so fast she can barely catch a breath, and—"

"Listen Miss—what was it again?" the Maestro said, cutting her off.

"Kirtenpepper. But you can call me—"

"Kirtenpepper? Really? Is that German? Are you even full-time faculty at this point?"

"Well, no, not yet, but we're hopeful that the opera program will—"

"The opera program? Miss Kirtenpep, you do not have an opera program. This, *all* of this, is just a huge financial experiment that started because your director back there, hiding away in the shadows, has a mother with strings attached to every finger. So, before you get the nerve to step up to my podium and tell me how to do my job, I would remind you that this is not a music school. This is a football school. This building, the music building, exists merely to support the marching band and all its related duties."

McDanials was a bent man with a long thin neck and red whiskers always in need of trimming. His grey eyes hid behind thick glasses that were perpetually slipping off a perspiring nose. He made no pretense of trying to hide his voice, and only raised it with each ensuing epithet. His words rang throughout the performance hall with perfect reverberation, even to the back rows where Reggie sat steaming in the shadows.

This production of Mozart's *Cosi Fan Tutte* was the first for which Reggie and Elizabeth had tried to assemble an orchestra. Until now, the piano had accompanied all performances. When they first put the word out, various string players had eagerly jumped at the opportunity to play in a **pit**. Scholarship-laden, band-playing winds had to be dragged in with bribes and promises of extra credits. After assembling the bare minimum, Reggie and Elizabeth had approached the only viable conductor on the campus. McDanials had refused outright. It wasn't in his contract; he was already over extended. How much was he going to get paid in addition to his salary? A Mozart score was a tremendous amount of work.

He would have no part in it.

Elizabeth had left the conductor's studio dejected. But Reggie had just bounced down to the Music Office on the third floor, whistling all the way, and made a quick call to mummy. Thirty-six hours later, the first orchestral production of the opera program was off and running. But having a resentful conductor is like having a resentful chiropractor. It might work, but it's going to hurt like hell.

McDanials was still diatribing when Elizabeth snapped back to the rehearsal.

"You and Mr. Greene have asked me to conduct this...production, and against my better judgement I agreed. So, like it or not, I am holding the stick, and you, along with all these," a wave of a limpid hand, "singers, will have to leave the tempos to me."

"But you're not being reasonable. This isn't the marching band."

"Perhaps you would prefer to do my job, Miss Kirtenpiper?"

McDanials held his baton pointing towards the ceiling, like a middle finger. He stood, gesturing for her to take the podium.

Elizabeth shriveled. "No. I couldn't possibly. I'm just a coach."

She slunk back to her keyboard in the corner. It wasn't a real orchestra pit, just the floor in front of the stage where Reggie had pulled up the first two rows of seats. But it felt like a pit. A deep dark pit from which she could see her poor asphyxiating students. Their wide eyes pleaded with her, while the orchestra flew through a Mozart's trio, surely one of the most beautiful things ever composed. She would swear he was taking such inhuman tempos to make the whole thing get over faster.

"I don't get to set the tempo," she said to Gaspar.

"Have a little faith. You're starting ripples. Sure thing. And whatever force brought you here hasn't left you stranded. You're not alone, remember?"

"Are you going to get me upstairs, Gaspar?"

"Not me, Elizabeth. I just make the cheese."

Chapter Sixteen

❧❧❧

That night, Elizabeth found Beatriz sitting in her chair, wide-eyed and full color with not a stitch to be sewn. She smiled up at Elizabeth. "Where did you learn to stitch up a stomacher like that?"

"Opera class."

Elizabeth pulled herself up the stairs, feeling heavy and barely lucid. As she peeled off her clothes, she tried to rouse herself. She wanted to take Gaspar's advice and dive into her father's book. But when she fell onto her stiff, lumpy bedding, it felt like the softest most pleasurable nest, and she curled into a fetal ball, quickly slipping into deep, dreamless sleep.

In the morning, Amada gave her a tongue lashing for letting the candle burn down, but at least she'd finally had a full night's sleep. She dressed and headed down to the dungeon for another day of wasted labors.

As she passed the kitchen, Marcellina stepped out. "You're not going to the skull this morning, cheese girl."

"I'm not?" Someone rudely knocked into Elizabeth's shoulder, and she turned to see Amada's familiar frame scurry off down the passageway.

"Amada? What's wrong?"

Marcellina lifted a hand. "Leave her. You're called to duties elsewhere."

"What do you mean?"

"The Countess has requested your presence in her chambers."

"Me? But I'm just a scullery maid."

"Not anymore. Though mind you, with your tongue and attitude, I don't expect you'll last long in either post. Now get downstairs and change into something cleaner. You can't go up there looking like that."

Elizabeth returned to the wardrobe basement, where Beatriz fitted her into a new dress minus any aprons and hair caps. A small crescent pillow was added under her skirts, hanging just above her posterior. She remembered how maniacal the girls at the college always were about rounded posteriors and how in any other generation, skinny-minnies weren't the rage. Finally, the stay. Either the darn things were slowly driving her insane, or this stay was even stiffer than her scullery one.

Marcellina escorted her back up through the winding passages and knocked lightly three times on the Countess's door.

While they waited, Elizabeth heard grunting and muttered orders from the center hallway, as if someone was hauling a heavy load.

The Countess's door opened and at last, she found herself face to face with the opera's leading lady.

"Ah," said Susanna. "The Countess is very excited to see you. Wait here."

Marcellina nudged Elizabeth in the back with a knuckle and they stepped into the sitting room. She stood fixed to her spot, listening to the mutterings from the dressing room and the ever-approaching grunts from out in the hallway. Once, she tried to ask what was going on, but Marcellina cut her off with a crisp "*sssht!*"

The Countess's chambers had high ceilings and a myriad of carefully placed mirrors. Fixtures strewn with crystals and shining metallic surfaces, like silver hair pieces, doorknobs, pitchers and frames, caught fragments of light. The whole room gleamed in startling contrast to the dim scullery. It felt like stepping from behind a **tormentor** curtain out onto the stage. The black **fourth wall** loomed ahead, spraying her reluctant, squinting eyes.

The Countess entered, turning sideways to maneuver her satin and lace skirts through her own bedroom door. Her tall white wig swirled far above her face in a patterned maze.

"Welcome, Elizabeth. I am so glad you will be joining us."

"Joining you?"

Another crisp "*sssht!*" from Marcellina, and a fingernail jabbed between her shoulder blades.

"Come here and let me see your hands," the Countess said.

A nudge in the small of her back and Elizabeth tripped forward, holding out her scratched and waterlogged hands.

"Just as I thought. We cannot have this. This is a crime to everything decent. From now on, you will assist my chambermaid Susanna in her duties, and you will play for me."

Elizabeth realized she was holding her breath. "Play for you, Madame?" she asked, in such a tight whisper, even she had trouble hearing it.

Someone knocked on the open door, and four sweaty men bowed lightly to their Mistress.

"Put it over there by the window," said the Countess, "so she has enough light."

The men passed Elizabeth, carrying the main body of the fortepiano, turned sideways to gingerly process through the dressing chamber door. They laid the instrument on the floor and began assembling the legs and pedals while the Countess continued.

"I've convinced my husband to move the instrument up to my chambers. Susanna will show you how to keep yourself, and you can participate in any duties she needs help with, so long as we don't do any further damage to your poor hands."

"Madame, I hardly know what to say. I mean, thank you.

Thank you very much. It would be an honor to play for you. How often will you be needing my services?"

Once again, The Countess Almaviva turned her head ever so slightly, and assumed such an impassive expression that she spoke the obvious without saying a word.

She would be needing Elizabeth every day.

"But during what part of the day?"

The Countess would be able to request Elizabeth's services at any time she so desired.

Elizabeth wondered if Marcellina's poking would leave a scar.

"Madame, this is all so very gracious. I'm overwhelmed. I don't know what to say."

"You don't have to say anything," Marcellina snapped. "Just keep to yourself and do your job."

"Don't worry about music," the Countess said. "I will have Basilio give you access to our library, and my husband can order whatever else you might wish to learn."

It was too good to be true. A promotion, directly into the room in the house where most of the second act takes place.

"So," Elizabeth said, and Marcellina grunted, "then you'll be hiring a new scullery maid?"

"You're not to worry about that anymore," said the Countess. "Marcellina will fill in with other housemaids."

So that was it. Amada's promotion would be revoked, and she would be sent back to the skull indefinitely. The bright light in the Countess's chambers seemed to suddenly grow dim from a swiftly descending curtain.

All she had to do was fix this stupid mixed-up plot, and she could go home to her Keds and her bicycle and her comfortable bed. She could use an electric toothbrush and toothpaste with fluoride. All she had to do was get into this room, and get a conversation started with Susanna, and then she could go home to the land of Rachmaninoff and Mendelssohn while eating dark chocolate and sipping red wine in a big basin of soapy hot water. Just to hear the lovely dulcet ringing of a real piano, her ears ached, pined, the desire manifesting to her like an absent limb. She wasn't whole without it.

But Amada.

"I'm sorry, Madame," she said, "but I cannot accept your offer."

Silence descended on the room like a **subito piano**. Marcellina ceased her prodding. Susanna stopped mid-stride, a massive gown of yellow satins in her arms, and the men paused their mutters. Even the decapitated fortepiano seemed to turn towards Elizabeth and gape with dismay. Time itself began to slow steadily down like a huge unrelenting **ritardando** with a giant fermata suspended perpetually above everyone's head.

"Forgive me, Madame," Elizabeth said, her voice suddenly an echo somewhere outside of her pounding head. "I do appreciate this kindness. It's just, the girl who'll replace me was so relieved to be out of the skull, and she has helped me so much. I would have drowned without her."

The stillness lingered, unaffected by Elizabeth's speech, such that she wondered if she had actually spoken, or only imagined it. She wished Marcellina would jab her in the back again.

The Countess rose. She seemed to levitate underneath all those skirts, floating across the Persian carpet towards Elizabeth. She smelled like orange blossoms.

"You would rather go back to the scullery than work here in my chambers?"

"Had I not so carelessly strayed into your ballroom and allowed myself to play on your lovely instrument, then you wouldn't even know I exist, Madame. Anyway, this girl I was speaking of, I happen to know that recently, she suffered a betrayal by someone she should have been able to trust. I don't want her to lose faith all together. I can't be the one who does that. I just can't. I'm so sorry. Really I am so very—"

The Countess Almaviva wanted Elizabeth to stop talking.

Elizabeth thought she heard an echo remnant of her voice slipping through the open door and floating down the long, paneled corridor. The Countess turned away, her skirts swiveling as she floated back towards the veranda doors.

Elizabeth took this as a sign to leave, and Marcellina did not try to stop her. She made a pitiful curtsey, stepped backwards, and after passing through the door, scuttled off down the dim corridor, out of the light and back towards the basement of fish scales and peelings. Or perhaps she should head up the stairs to her room and pack. She would probably lose her job for this. Would Gaspar take her back after doing something so foolish? She stood for a long time at the door of the stairs, wondering which way to go.

"Well cheese girl, you're a masterpiece." Marcellina stood in the corridor behind her. "The Countess bids me to ask if you would accept a half-day in the skull and half in her chambers."

Elizabeth squealed and lifted her skirts. She dashed back down the hall and popped her head in the sitting room with carefree impudence.

"Madame, if you please, don't put the fortepiano directly in front of the window. As lovely as that might be, the sunlight is no good for the instrument. We'll be tuning it every hour." Then she uttered about a half dozen 'thank you's' before Marcellina's cold clench swung her back out the door. She practically skipped down the hall.

"You'll be changing your wardrobe twice a day."

"Leading sopranos have to do it in seconds."

"You'll have to scrub those precious hands of yours before you go near it. Get under the nails."

"To the very bone!"

"And you'd better learn to keep your mouth shut. No eavesdropping or spreading gossip."

At the basement landing, Elizabeth burst into the passageway, spinning around and almost knocking over a housemaid.

"You're ridiculous," Marcellina said. "I guarantee, this will soon blow up. It's absurd."

"Isn't it? You should tell Amada. I don't want to play the

hero. I wonder if I can remember any Bach. Or Beethoven. Oh, a Beethoven Sonata!"

Marcellina stood stiffly contemplating Elizabeth, the burgeoning wrinkles on her face like cold wax, her eyebrows unevenly twisted. When she spoke, only her lips moved. "I can't figure whether you're superior, stupid, or just a lunatic."

◌⟡◌

Marcellina gave Elizabeth the morning off to gather music and prepare for her duties upstairs.

Elizabeth slipped back to the attic and spent a few hours re-reading her father's book, only now heeding every detail, every nuance. She was right that most of the first act had already proceeded without her. It still veered off in an ugly direction so long as Susanna did not confide in her fiancé about the Count's advances. According to the text, her employer had already gotten her alone in the house three times and tried to have his way with her. For some reason, he was determined not to force himself on her. He wanted her to submit to him.

What is wrong with men?

"Elizabeth!" Reggie's voice rose above the rush of students on Belar Street. He was late, as usual, but when he swept up and planted a kiss on her, Elizabeth only knew that familiar sensation of falling. That was what love was. It wasn't some tidal wave of emotions, or some tyrant controlling one's ability to behave in a decent manner. Love was knowing when you fall, you'll be caught.

"All right, I have a surprise," he said, pulling away. He took her hand and pulled her into one of the college's athletic buildings. They weaved through the first-floor corridors, navigating

146

hordes of backpacked students hunched over at the end of a long day.

Elizabeth felt herself giggling as he pulled her along. They ascended a flight of stairs and turned sharply down a darker hallway to a set of double doors with small rectangular windows.

"Okay," he said. "Here we are." He pulled the door open, and she stepped inside with giddy hesitation. "Well? What do you think?"

"Well, I...what is this?"

Floor to ceiling mirrors covered the longest wall, and a row of wooden folding chairs lined the back. Young college kids sat staring at cell phones, but a few over-dressed and well-perfumed senior citizens also sat chatting quietly. Water bottles and tossed apparel lay scattered on the floor.

"Oh good, they haven't started yet," Reggie said. "We're still in time to make a good first impression. Here, let me get your coat."

"Wait, Reggie, what is this?"

"It's for a credit. You'll get a credit," Reggie said. "And it will be lots of fun."

"I'm sure it will," she said. "It's just—"

A slender, middle-aged man in form-fitting black pants and a shimmery grey shirt swept into the center of the floor. He projected his voice easily with a mild Spanish accent.

"Welcome to Ballroom Basics for beginners. My name is Enrico."

"A dance class? That's the surprise?"

"*Shh*. It's for a credit. You can fill an elective."

"But I can't dance. Reggie. I've never taken a step in my life."

"Neither have I. That's why we're here."

A woman made an entrance, her arms extended to full breadth. She touched the end of Enrico's hand, and moved in a long flowing circle around him, smiling at every corner of the room. She wore tall thin heels, stretchy capris, and a flowing pink shirt that dropped below her hips in ruffles. Bubbly silver earrings dangled from her lobes, catching the lights.

"This," Enrico said, "is my lovely partner, Fantine."

Some people applauded. Elizabeth wondered why.

Reggie pulled off Elizabeth's coat and bag and tossed them in a chair. He slipped his arm around her waist and took her hand. Damn, the man was warm.

Enrico called out, "We begin with the waltz!" Somewhere in the universe, someone hit the play button on a stereo system, and a string orchestra began playing some Johann Strauss.

"Reggie, I don't think I can do this."

Enrico and Fantine circled around the dance floor and the students countered away. Enrico twirled his partner like a human yo-yo.

"No, I definitely can't do this."

"Sure, you can. They're pros. We take some classes, and soon we'll look just like them."

"You could send me to the Magic Kingdom to study with Cinderella for six years and I will never look like that."

"The waltz basic step is very easy," Enrico began. "The women will follow Fantine, and the men will stand behind and follow me."

Reggie gave Elizabeth a nudge and scampered away behind Enrico. Elizabeth tried to get her bearings but found herself sinking into the hypnotic pull of Fantine's bulbous earrings.

"My feet, darling! My feet!" Fantine hissed.

A minute of clumsy footwork later, Enrico spoke again. "All right, now find your partner. Gentlemen, you hold your lady like so, and ladies, like this. Very slowly now, always counting, *One, two, three, one, two, three, one, two, three...*"

Elizabeth stepped on Reggie's toes on four, seven, and twelve.

"I can't do this."

He pulled her close and kissed her.

"All right, I can keep trying. But tell me why we're doing this, at least."

"I thought it would be fun, and it's something I really should get some experience with in my field."

"In your field?" She stepped on his toe again. "Sorry! Wait. What do you mean? Are you changing majors again?"

"They are allowing me to create my own. But this time I know it's right. I've finally found it."

They barged headlong into a small elderly couple.

"So sorry!"

"Well, that's something," Elizabeth said when they straightened back up. "So?"

"I'm going back towards the arts. I'm going to direct operas."

Elizabeth found the Count's library and the sheet music available to her. A sad lot: Scarlatti, Corelli, Purcell, and some Rameau, plus a slew of forgotten composers. There were a couple pieces by Handel, but not a shred of Bach. She could probably only play a tiny bit of Bach from memory. She certainly found nothing so glamorous as Mozart, Hayden, or Beethoven. She wondered if she could request the Classical composers yet. Could one order music from Vienna and Germany to be sent to Spain? How comprehensive was this imaginary world she found herself in? Did Mozart, or some poetic version of him, exist right now, on the other side of Europe?

She hadn't even thought of that. Goodness, she could forsake this whole plot and go meet Mozart. Poor, starving, impoverished Mozart. All right, so she wouldn't do that, couldn't afford it, probably would have to prostitute herself to get there, and would have to cross France right before the Revolution. *No, no, no.* She definitely didn't want to be anywhere near France for the next fifteen years. And besides, everyone knew Mozart was a brat.

But this raised a serious question. *Could* she abandon her story? Could she just cease to play in this plot line and leave

Susanna and Figaro to their doom? Or did a massive perilous cliff exist just beyond the invisible borders of *Marriage of Figaro*? Like some old episode of the *Twilight Zone*, would any road not significant to the story melt away into drippy watercolors? Or was there a whole world here? An entire universe differing from her own only in the slight irregularity of an improbable opera plot, where people with Italian names all speak perfect English as they languish forever in a country called Spain? The culture clash alone was enough to make one dizzy. How Spanish was this Spain after all? Did Count Almaviva visit the bull fights? Did the whole crew traipse into Seville for the Holy Week extravaganza? Elizabeth winced, visualizing the Count in any public ritual of penance.

Or did this whole place cease to exist once she fixed the plot and went home? Her heart sank. Gaspar, Amada, Aleix. These were not characters in an opera plot. Surely, they had the right to continue their own stories once the tale of Figaro and Count Almaviva was told.

When she reread her father's book, as Gaspar had suggested, she didn't learn anything that might help her approach Susanna to breach the uniquely personal subject of her relationship with her fiancé, or how to subvert the advances of her inappropriate employer. That, Elizabeth decided, she would have to trust to ripples.

But the book did present something alarming. A new character had appeared on its pages, inexplicably inserting herself into the story of Figaro, Susanna, and the Almaviva's. A character invented by no Mozart, Da Ponte, or Beaumarchais from neither opera nor play, but present nonetheless, stepping onto the stage to her own accompaniment. Originally just hired to replace the scullery maid, she was soon promoted to the Countess's personal musician, a young lady with a moral backbone and a tendency to say foolish things, playing music that spellbound both servant and master. Her name was Elizabeth, and she had a fascination with an armorer named Aleix.

INTERMISSION

ACT II
HOW THINGS HAPPEN IN A
COMIC OPERA

Chapter Seventeen

"I've always thought a ribbon was like a relationship," Elizabeth said. "One should be honest with their beloved, even if it might result in a clash. That blue may relate well to your dress, but the yellow is not quite the right shade as the appliques. It's like they don't belong together. When things belong together, they complement each other, they trust each other. They have to, or really what have they got but a future of deceit?"

The Countess and Susanna stared with unblinking eyes while Elizabeth's words resounded through the high ceilings and crown moldings of the dressing room.

I've always thought a ribbon was like a relationship.

It had taken five full days to get her first interaction with the leading ladies of *Figaro*. Five days of waking early and running to the skull to endure Cook's eighteenth-century obscenities through the hole in the wall. Five days of dashing upstairs to change and appear calm and cool at the Countess's chamber door. Five days of playing music on demand, and doing whatever remedial chores Susanna concocted, from polishing shoes to cleaning the Countess's chamber pot. Five days of listening to mumbled conversations, trying to eavesdrop between cadences and then chasing Susanna down the corridor at the end of her shift, only to find that the confounded girl had disappeared through some passageway.

Damn, the woman was slippery. But that was true to the opera. Mozart's Susanna covered one disaster after another in the first twenty minutes of the show. Elizabeth should have known she would have difficulty worming her way into an acquaintance.

At least in the scullery, Cook's rantings made Elizabeth feel alive. Sitting at the fortepiano in the Countess's chambers, Elizabeth felt like a painting on the wall. One might appreciate it, but never stop to think, 'Perhaps I should say hello to my painting once in a while, ask how its morning is going, offer it a cup of tea or maybe just talk to it about my cheating husband...'

It was like she wasn't there at all.

George Kirtenpepper sat across the dining room table, patiently slurping his soup. After his wife's funeral, he had moved his customary seat from the end of the table to the middle. This was not so close as a more convenient corner, where one could easily reach out and touch another, or lean a head on an available arm, or just nudge a neighboring water glass when reaching for the salt.

Strangely though, despite sitting across from Elizabeth, their eyes never met. Eleven-year-olds don't necessarily notice that kind of thing, but Elizabeth watched her father intently, hoping. She didn't want to miss it. Anything, in case it happened.

Her father generally looked up two or three times during the meal. In the first few months after her mother's death, Elizabeth had been foolish enough to look down all the time. Even during meals. So now, he had probably given up, thinking that's what she would always do.

"How is your soup?" he asked. *First time looking up.*

"It's fine. Thanks." She cursed herself for not thinking of some more creative answer.

"We'll get some pizza tomorrow," he said, then his eyes returned to the open book next to his plate. "How does that sound?"

Six months ago, they would resort to pizza when everyone was too tired to cook. It was the paper-plate, no-dishes-to-clean, sit-on-the-sofas-making-fun-of-one-another meal.

He looked up from his book, his eyes half hidden behind the top rim of his glasses. *Second time.*

"Pizza's good." Why couldn't she think of anything to say? Anything?

Eyes gone again, finding their place, weaving through endless lines of words, trying to construe some meaning from it, trying to better oneself.

"How was school?" No eyes.

"Fine. We had a test in Math."

That's not what she wanted to say. She wanted to talk about Holly Ember, who had called her a music geek in front of Allen Laraine at lunch. She wanted to know if her dad thought she was a music geek, and if boys liked music geeks and if she should stay away from Holly or from all boys and hide herself in a closet where no one could find her.

"That's nice. Did you do all right?"

"I think so. We don't get the grades until Monday."

"I'm sure you did fine."

Elizabeth put her fork down and watched him read. How long could she stare before he felt her eyes? How long could they sit in silence before she went crazy? She couldn't remember what bread smelled like. It used to fill the house, the smell of bread. He had hired a house cleaner a few weeks ago. Whenever she came, every room smelled like lemon.

Elizabeth pushed her chair back with a scrape. She rose and strode through the wide, pillared archway into the front living room. With a yank, the piano bench emerged, and she plopped herself down. Her fingers set about the "William Tell Overture," starting somewhere about three minutes in, so she could really feel herself plunking down on the tremors. She played louder and louder, winding herself up, shaking the walls, disturbing the family of birds that had settled in the chimney. She could feel the vibrations in her hands, her feet, her head.

The small porcelain figures on top of the upright started dancing in a jittery gallop towards the edge. Her pounding wailed on, skipping past the pianissimos like they weren't there, ignoring them, digging deeper and deeper into the keys, her ponytail flinging back and forth behind her until—

Crash!

Elizabeth jumped up.

On the floor beside the upright, the shards of the statue lay scattered across the wooden beams. Her mother had bought it at a garage sale, and Elizabeth had paid no heed to it before. Just a silly scene of a boy and girl from some other century, where clothes were always flowing and breasts always hanging half out. They sat on a stone wall, their hands reaching perpetually for each other, while around them, the flowers bent over in an invisible porcelain wind. Her mother had said that it wasn't just a statue. It was someone's story.

And now Elizabeth had ruined it.

When she peeked around the corner at the dining room table, her father had gone. All that remained of him were a few drips of soup on the table, for someone to wipe up.

On Elizabeth's first day in her new eighteenth-century position, Marcellina escorted her to the Countess's chambers. Despite their history, she felt like a teenager being dropped off by a protective parent. Once Marcellina finished sneering at Susanna and took her leave, the Countess requested some calming music, preferably by "that Polish person."

The fortepiano had been set close to the sitting room doorway so the Countess could fully enjoy the music from either room. This middle room was obviously for dressing. Several doors opened to inlaid closets for gowns, shoes, stockings, and hats. A dressing table stood opposite a pair of stiff chairs, and tall mirrors framed in gold flanked both sides of the room.

The third, innermost room was the Countess's bedroom, but the Countess did not spend much time there.

Elizabeth played on and off for three hours. On her first break, Susanna asked her to fold and hang clothing. When she finished, she took out the Count's scores and played some very bland early Classical music. An hour later, she ran a pair of dresses down to Beatriz, and when she returned, she tried a Mendelssohn piece she had learned in high school.

Susanna took her in a closet to clean shoes. She showed her how, in not nearly so dashing a manner as her fiancé. "Take that rag and this oil and rub it all over these boots and those shoes, then buff until they shine." Funny how the delivery affected the lesson. Elizabeth would rather learn to scale fish than polish shoes.

After the shoes, Elizabeth played some Debussy, just to test the waters with her new Mistress. She received no complaints and began to wonder if she could bust out some Bartok on this poor instrument before someone noticed the downfall of Western tonal harmony.

Sometimes they called her upstairs first thing in the morning, at other times in the afternoon. And when the Countess was out, she had the pleasure of Cook, the hole in the wall, the fish scales, and chipped fingers. Some mornings she would play for a few hours, then back to the skull, only to return upstairs in the evening. She never knew day to day what her schedule would be since it was entirely dependent on the Countess's activities.

Any lapses in Elizabeth's musical memory did not cause a

problem in her new position. The Countess was so fascinated with every piece she played, she would ask its name and jot it down in a little notebook on her dressing stand. Elizabeth pulled everything she could from her memory, even some early preschool learning pieces. Some music, of course was completely out of the question. Most Chopin she could accommodate, but Liszt was just impossible. She played the accompaniment parts to her favorite opera arias, but without a singer, they really didn't make much sense. She did take out accompaniments of Schubert and Schumann Lieder which she had played so many times at the school for lessons. Somehow without the voice, Schubert was still lovely. One time, she played some of Mozart's *Figaro* score, but after only thirty or so bars, the Countess called out from her boudoir to stop playing that piece right away; it didn't suit her tastes. So much for *Figaro*.

Elizabeth was being wickedly manipulative. She had no sustain pedal, and the fortepiano was barely touch sensitive, with no ring to the tone, only harmonic flow and tang. But her audience of course had never heard anything like it, since it wouldn't be composed for fifty to a hundred years in the future. It was a violation really, introducing harmonics to ears that had never heard them before.

Meanwhile, the opera plot crawled. Scenes that happened directly adjacent in the opera fell one, two, or three days apart, as though the whole thing stretched out over the course of a month. And there was a necessary chronology that she couldn't avoid. Until Susanna confided in her fiancé about the Count's advances, she certainly couldn't confide in the Countess either.

No matter how uplifting the change from downstairs to up, from off stage to on, from skull to boudoir, five days felt like an eternity in which Elizabeth kept wondering if this was still Mozart or she had somehow shifted into an eternal **Wagnerian** melodrama.

Then suddenly, on day six, the Countess turned from her dressing table, holding up a potential hair ribbon in each hand and asked, "Elizabeth, what do you think?"

Startled, Elizabeth held her hands over an unresolved domi-
nant chord and cleared her throat. "I beg your pardon?"

"Do you like the blue or the yellow better?"

The Countess had almost finished dressing, a feat that took
nearly an hour every morning. Elizabeth had to think fast. This
opportunity might not arise again. This could be her only chance
to affect some change, to redirect the story, to get out of Spain and
go home.

"I've always thought a ribbon was like a relationship..."

"Do you," asked the Countess, a deflated ribbon hanging in
each hand, "make a moral quandary out of everything?"

"I've found profound depth in a pile of hay."

The Countess did not wish to hear the long story about the hay.

"Well then Susanna, please use the honest ribbon."

❦

Elizabeth left her shift that night in moderate despair. It was time
to face the facts; she was never going to see Ibuprofen again.
Whatever her father, or this book, had thrown her into was
beyond her ability to control.

After the ribbon fiasco, she spent the rest of the afternoon
playing minor keys, movements from the **Mozart *Requiem*,** The
Albinoni and Barber *Adagio*'s, a piano reduction of the fourth
movement of Tchaikovsky's *Pathetique*, Bach's "Come Sweet
Death," Purcell's "When I Am Laid in Earth," and every scene
Verdi wrote involving a dead soprano. By dinner time, she had so
lulled the suite into such a state of manic melancholy that all three
women, each with an intimate secret to hide, were contemplating
the great waste of their lives.

Only when Marcellina's stretched scowl appeared at the suite
door like a welcome breeze did the ladies realize how hypnotized
they were into a darkness of the soul. Marcellina announced
dinner, but no one was very hungry.

Elizabeth shut up the fortepiano and trudged toward the

door. The door of her future. The door opening into the dark corridor of the Count's perverse house, where the law still stood with men who would be sexual tyrants over their women. What was Mozart thinking, writing a comedy about something so vile? Elizabeth shuddered. If Mozart and Beaumarchais had lived in the 21st Century, they never would have gotten an agent to read their score.

"Did you mean that?"

Elizabeth gasped and jumped against a wall.

"Oh, I'm so sorry!" Susanna said, stepping out from behind a statue of a Toreador.

"For goodness' sake, you gave me a heart attack! I thought you were the Count come to finish the job."

"Finish the job?" Susanna's eyes glowed, even in the dim light.

"Surely you know you're not the only girl who's been accosted."

"Of course," she said. "I should have guessed that. I don't know why I didn't. How did you know about—"

"Never mind that now. What did you ask me just now? Did I mean what?"

"What you said about honesty and trust in a relationship, and something about ribbons."

Elizabeth straightened. "Of course, I meant it. What's the point of being in a relationship, if you can't trust your partner with your fears and concerns? Really, that's not a relationship at all. It's just some kind of game. Is that really what you want, Susanna?"

"Of course not."

"Well then, what are you waiting for? Go tell Figaro everything."

"But he might think that I—"

"That you what? Prefer the Count's sexual advances to Figaro's honest ones? Really, if you think so little of Figaro, you shouldn't marry him at all."

"You're right," Susanna said. "Of course, you're right." She stomped her right foot on the marble, and somewhere in the recesses of Elizabeth's mind, the *Aida* triumphal march began playing. "I do need to tell Figaro! I don't know why I didn't see it before. I guess I listened to some bad advice."

"Well, take some good advice. Go tell him everything, and don't spare him any details."

"That's exactly what I should have done as soon as we got back. I'll go do it tonight. Thank you, Elizabeth. You are a bit strange sometimes, but a good egg. I was wrong to avoid you." Susanna took off down the corridor, her long brown curls bouncing in the candlelight.

Avoid me?

Despite that curious mystery, Elizabeth skipped up the stairs to bed. Just like that, it was over. Right when she had been on the brink of despair, she had done it with a ribbon. Figaro and Susanna would now team up to defeat the Count's disgusting plans and engage the help of the Countess. All would be back on track with the original plot, and Elizabeth would hopefully be on her way home. Done. Check. Print it. Roll the credits!

Amada was downstairs helping with dinner, so Elizabeth had the room to herself. She undressed gleefully and dove into bed with the book in hand. *How would this work?* Probably, she would return home the same way she had come.

She stood a candle on the nightstand and covered herself with the blanket, feeling a little nervous. The last time she had transported through the book, she had thrown up. And—

Elizabeth had a terrible thought. What if, instead of going back home, she ended up in some new operatic nightmare? Like *Traviata*, or *Otello*? *Oh Lord, please don't let it be Wagner.* Anything but Wagner. Magic Rings, Mermaids and all those Norse Gods in Valhell-a. Even eighteenth-century Spain would be better than that.

But then she wondered if the French Revolution ever made it near Seville. Would she have to endure the Reign of Terror?

She opened the book. The inscription had changed again.

"Read Carefully" and "Stick to Your Story" had now become "You Are Not Alone."

"What does that mean?"

Was that a reference to Gaspar? Or perhaps it was her father's spirit, somehow watching her through the pages of this literary medium. *You are not alone.* Elizabeth shivered to think she could be holding some talisman between herself and the afterlife. Perhaps the new inscription was a reference to God himself. She definitely liked that better. Maybe God, who could create a universe, could also create other worlds beyond our understanding, where mangled opera plots got resolved. That was much better than a talisman to the dead.

Elizabeth turned some pages and found where it had veered from the Mozart. She began reading, but nothing happened. No fireflies, no shifting universe, no quantum leaps, and no nausea.

Well, maybe she had to read the whole thing to the end. So, she snuggled herself back into her thin pillow and began skimming. Tired, and probably still a little depressed from all the mournful music, she drifted off to sleep.

"You're incredible. Do you know that?"

Reggie lay on his back beneath the old, six-foot baby grand in the band hall. The room was unusually tranquil, as all the nearby practice rooms had been abandoned for the night. They had not bothered to turn the lights on when they came in, hand in hand, dancing a bit on the cool linoleum floor before he asked her to play.

The piano was an abused instrument, under-tuned and poorly maintained, banged heartlessly at band and chorus rehearsals with scars of chipped paint and more than a few fractured keys.

"What should I play?" she asked, lifting the fall board.

"I don't know. Something wonderful," said Reggie.

"Something, quiet and calming, or something bombastic and terrifying?"

"Could you do that, Lizzy? Play something bombastic and terrifying?"

She sat down and thought about it for a moment, then lifted her hands,

"Wait!" Reggie dove under the piano. On the floor near her feet, he lay his head and closed his eyes.

"What are you doing?" she asked.

"I'm appreciating." He folded his hands on his belly and smiled sweetly, as though dreaming. "Now terrify me."

She chose "August" by Tchaikovsky, not the most terrifying perhaps, but it was a terror she could understand, one with a story, and she dug in for the ride. The horses on a dark road in a dark storm, bringing a dark message, only pausing for a moment to remember love between the icy blasts. The final chords resounded like church bells through a mountain valley, and they both listened to the last reverberations fade.

Without thinking, she let her fingers fall into Mendelssohn's "Songs Without Words." She wound in and out of the simple melodies and arpeggios like stringing vines of roses over him, so sweet that perhaps, he could smell them if he never opened his eyes. Then bees would come, and hummingbirds would sip at the buds, and sunshine, from where, who could tell? But crystal, glorious sunshine on green places where water ran. And they ran too, Reggie and she, along the white foamy rushes, past the thick of summer and the bitter smells of the earth and sky.

When the double bar line came, as bar lines always do, she did not play again. That's when he asked her.

"You're incredible. Do you know that?" She heard him shuffle around a bit until his eyes popped up near her knees. "Do you?"

"Please stop. I know you love me."

"I do love you, Lizzy, but that's not why I'm saying it."

"I just play the piano. Lots of people can do it."

"Not like you. Lots of people take lessons or go to music school. But they can't do what you do. You play a piece once and you remember it forever. Or you just hear a piece a few times, then you sit down at a keyboard and work it out in your fingers. It's amazing. Surely your teachers have told you that you're extraordinary. If not, they're jealous. Jealous and afraid that they won't be able to teach you anything." His eyes disappeared again beneath the piano. "I mean, why do you play, Lizzy? When you play, something inside me moves. Something I didn't know was there. Is that why you do it? Is that why you play?"

She left her bench and sunk to the floor beside him, where she rested her head on his shoulder and shut her eyes.

Why do you play, Lizzy?

The Count's house was silent with night's darkness, and her candle had been extinguished by Amada, who lay sleeping. Elizabeth felt a tinge of sadness that she would not see Amada again, and even considered waiting until she could tell Gaspar all was well before returning home. But tomorrow she had a long morning in the skull, and even evaporating into the pages of a magical book offered a more pleasant foray than that. So she lit the candle, pulled herself up, and lifted the cover. After the opening, with trips to Cadiz, and lengthy descriptions of the Count's exploits, she found the relevant paragraphs.

Chapter Eighteen

Figaro sank into a highly uncharacteristic state of woe. His beautiful Susanna did not love him anymore. It didn't take a great scholar to see that, and Figaro had been reading the sighs and glances of women as far back as he could remember. Whole days had come and gone since Susanna had sent a glance in his direction. In fact, since they had returned from Cadiz, she had withdrawn into herself somehow, as though mourning.

It didn't make sense. Everything had transpired splendidly. Figaro approached the Count for his approval of the marriage and received more than that: a dowry for Susanna, private rooms in the main house, and even assurances to nullify that ridiculous contract with the old hag. Rooms, a dowry, Marcellina squelched, and the most perfect bride in all the world. Along with a wonderful job in a beautiful house in Spain, what else could a fellow wish for?

Then, the very next morning, nothing. No sparkles, no flirtations, no innocent smiles hidden where only he could see. And no explanations.

She grew more distant every day, lost to him, and no amount of cheering, cajoling, or conspiring could jar her back into his arms. A few times, he caught her off-guard about her duties and not expecting him. She would catch a glimpse of him hiding behind a pillar, stealing a precious peek, and her lips spread so lusciously into that warm, coy smile that completely melted him. But then, as though she remembered something, it would fade back to the timid grin or tilted head and apologetic shrug, waving him away and returning to her chores.

She didn't love him anymore. That was obvious. But what had he done? Was it something he had said, some insensitive remark intended as a jibe perhaps? But no, he couldn't imagine that of Susanna. Why, it was her impenetrable fortitude that he so cherished. She would not, could not be easily offended. On the other hand, he was new at this sincerity business, and perhaps he had gone too far on some off-hand joke, perhaps her vulnerability towards him made her more easily offended...These arguments went round and round in his head all through his miserable workday. He began to wish himself away from this place, from the Count's employ, and especially from her. He couldn't bear it, to feel her withdraw like this, yet to know she was so near when he had been so close to utter happiness.

How quickly could he evacuate the Count's estate? That evening. He could easily vanish back to the itinerant life on the streets. Wasn't that, after all, what he was meant for? He was Figaro! What was he thinking, taking a steady position? Taking a wife?

Standing at attendance with a silver water pitcher while the Count and Countess slurped their soup, he realized he didn't belong in this house at all. The nomadic lifestyle was his custom. He never should have left it. Mentally, he mapped out his retreat from all things committed and stable. Why, in just a minute or two, he could pack up and go, back to the life of the streets, free from tyranny of woman, tyranny of employer, tyranny of—

Something in the hallway caught his eye. A tiny glisten so surprising, he nearly dropped the silver water pitcher. Muttering some excuse, he bowed and swept out of the room.

"Listen, weasel," she said, her eyes aglow, "Are you too tired to walk tonight?"

"Never."

"By the obelisk, after you're done, I'll be waiting."

As she disappeared down the corridor, his feet stirred to life, bouncing a little jig. He returned to the Count's table. What nonsense had he been thinking? One doesn't retreat from a rare jewel for a life with the swine.

The evening was dark, but the stars danced across the heavens when he found her by the obelisk, just as she had promised. Even as he approached the tall dark spear of stone, he saw her outline rise from the shadows and run to him.

"I'm so sorry," she said, holding him close. "I've had something on my mind, and I should have told you. I should have told you right away, but I was afraid."

He kissed her and led her to a small bench. "Tell me now."

She spoke with trepidation, her voice wavering in and out of courage. No sooner had she begun, than all became clear. Fury fired through his veins. The Count, his lord and Master, his friend and accomplice, would proposition his own bride-to-be? Naturally, it was too hard to accept. Perhaps she had led him on, flirted with him foolishly, unknowingly.

Figaro rose, stepping away, but she continued, describing how the Count had accosted her in Cadiz on two occasions, gotten her alone, and she had forcefully refused his advances and slipped away from him.

Figaro regarded his petulant, fearless girl. Even in this darkness he could see her tremble. Sitting down, he wrapped her closely to himself and a silence engulfed them.

"But the dowry?" he said.

"An enticement."

"And Marcellina?"

"A threat."

Figaro straightened. "What? You mean—"

"If I refuse him, he will lean in her favor. You will have to marry her."

"This is a lascivious bribery!"

"It's his Droit Du Seigneur," Susanna said, her frankness returning the natural colors to her voice.

"But he himself abolished that privilege!" Figaro rose and marched around in a circle, kicking at the gravel and spitting out nonsensical syllables. *"He thinks he can win with me? He's a fool. You know what we should do?"*

"You should leave this estate immediately." The unfamiliar voice had spoken from the shadows, startling them both.

"Who goes there?" Figaro said, but the face hid beneath a black hood and cape.

"The Count has plans far more diabolical than you have imagined. If your fiancée does not concede to his desires soon, he will take her by force."

"I will kill him! And I'll kill you for intruding in these private affairs!" Figaro lunged at the dark figure, but the flip and swish of a sword cut through the moonlight with a menacing sparkle.

"I only came here to warn you. You will not persuade him, and if you do not leave this place at once, you will regret it for the rest of your lives. You must depart quickly, tonight. Leave no trace. Give no notice, for he will follow you. So strong is his desire for her, that he will hunt you down and make your lives a ruin wherever you hide."

The man melted into the blackened shrubs behind the obelisk. Figaro stepped forward to pursue, but Susanna held him back.

Stunned and furious, Figaro fell back on the stool. *"We should go,"* he said. *"Tonight."*

They agreed to meet back at the obelisk in one hour.
Pack only the barest of necessities,
carry not too much,
only the clothes they had on their backs,
sneak off into the woods,

where they would pass the night out together.

The next morning, when they awoke, a band of gypsies swiftly murdered them both and left their naked bodies to the birds of prey in an open field.

"WHAT?" Elizabeth closed the book and shot up in her bed.

Amada stirred and grumbled. Elizabeth wrapped the blanket around her shoulders, leaped across the room crashing into the door.

"What are you doing?" Amada whined.

"Nothing," said Elizabeth, wincing at a stubbed toe. "Nothing, just going to the necessary. Go back to sleep. Sorry, I tripped, that's all."

Elizabeth fumbled with the door handle and finally clambered into the hallway. She felt her way along the wall to Susanna's door. A dim light shone, but the room was empty. In her haste, Susanna had forgotten to extinguish the candle.

"Dammit!" Elizabeth darted back out into the hallway, feeling her way to the spiral staircase. Her hands clutched at the walls as she stumbled down the three flights of stairs in the pitch dark. She ran through the servants' passage and out the back door where tiny sharp stones stabbed her feet.

Where to go? Perhaps the encounter hadn't even taken place yet. She hurried to the blackened gardens, managing her way by moonlight through a jungle of shadows she had only explored once. Repeatedly she cried out whenever her foot landed on a stray branch or slammed into an ill-placed rock.

When at last she limped up to the obelisk, it loomed tall and sinister, pointing into the night sky. She heard no trace of them. What could she do? She had to find them. She should return to the house and wake people up. Wake up the staff. Wake...the Count? But how would they explain themselves? How would she explain herself? How would this strange turn of events further complicate Mozart's plot? No, she couldn't involve any main characters.

But at this hour, who would be awake?

Elizabeth darted off through the gardens back towards the dependencies. Which one was it? There was the laundry, and next to that the leather craftsman's shop, then the private stables, the pottery kilns, and on the other side of that was a building she had never entered or visited, the men's quarters. When she reached the stoop, her courage failed her. Should she just barge in and start knocking on random doors? She might wake up some ruthless rogue. Heck, the dark figure in the hooded cloak might just be dozing beyond that door. But the longer she waited, the further Figaro and Susanna got from the estate. She reached for the door, but it opened suddenly and a tall man in his night-shirt, peered down on her with half-sleeping eyes over his flickering candle. He was so tall and angular that Elizabeth had to crane her neck to look up at him. A momentary glaze filled his features, as though she had appeared as a wonderful dream, but it quickly melted into disappointment, and he shrugged. "He's not here," he said, with a grumble and pushed past her towards the necessary.

"Who's not here?" she asked.

"Aleix," he said over his shoulder. "Try the stables. He goes there when he can't sleep."

She recognized the man from the servants' hall. He sometimes carried deliveries into the skull and dropped them on the floor for her attention, but they had never spoken before, and she didn't even know his name. "How did you know I was looking for Aleix?"

"You all are," he said, then slammed the necessary door behind him.

Elizabeth sped off towards the stables, her feet screaming. She stepped inside the dark structure, smelled the horses and the hay, and again hardened herself against the stabs and prickles on her feet.

Aleix's tall frame stood in shadow between her and the far

door, stroking the temple of a placid animal. When he saw her, dressed only in her shift, her shawl almost completely fallen, her breathing accelerated, he strode towards her, but she stepped back and raised a hand.

"I need your help," she said. "Two people have gone missing, run away into the night, and they will be in grave danger if I don't find them and bring them back. But I don't know these parts, and I don't know how to find someone, and—"

"You're not wearing any clothes."

"Right. I'm sorry about that, but this is all very sudden, and very important. Will you help me? Please? They will die if we don't find them."

"They will die? How do you know that?"

"I can't explain that. I'm just asking you to help. I came looking for you because I knew you'd be awake."

As though she had said nothing, he pulled her to him and kissed her, engaging a fire of desire she really didn't want to ignore. When he let go, she stumbled back.

"Who are these people?" he said.

Elizabeth considered not telling him, but if she was going to ask his help, she had better have some names, and anyway he'd find out soon enough. "Figaro and Susanna."

"Figgy and Suzy? Why on earth would they run off in the middle of the night?"

"They're engaged. It hasn't been announced yet because the Count hasn't formally given permission, but I can explain the details to you as we go. Please, there isn't any time."

His jaw jutted forward, and he bit his lower lip. Obviously, he wasn't used to the women who came to see him having any expectations beyond a roll in the hay. He released a frustrated sigh and looked off over her shoulder. "Stay right there," he said, and disappeared into a tack room between the stalls. A black and white gelding tilted a perky ear at her, and she felt a strange need to lift and close her shawl.

Aleix reappeared, his satchel draped across his shoulder. "Put these on." He threw her a pair of tattered men's pants, like Gaspar wore on the farm. "Use this to hold them up." He tossed a leather guiding rein.

While she dressed, he put a harness on the horse he had been stroking and led it to a stoop.

"Where are they headed?" he asked.

"I don't know."

"You don't know?"

"Well, no. I thought maybe you could guess at that since you know the territory better."

"The territory?" He snickered. "Hold these." He passed her the reins and disappeared again into the tack room. The horse undoubtedly sensed her trepidation and stomped an arrogant hoof. She heard a puff, and the light in the tack room went dark. He returned and quickly slid up onto the horse. Then he reached down his hand.

"Wait," she said. "You don't expect me to go with you?"

"Well, I'm certainly not going without you."

"But I've never, I mean I don't know how, and aren't you supposed to put a saddle on these things? I mean, is this safe? I haven't even got any shoes on. What if I fall off? What if—"

"You'll survive," he said, reaching towards her. "Now get on."

Her hand crept toward his timidly, and he reached past her wrist to pull her up onto the horse with one even tug. She flailed around behind him, trying to get her legs around the horse and scooch herself up.

"I don't know about this," she said, suddenly realizing how high horses stood from the ground. "I mean, I'm not sure I—"

"Do you want to save them or not?"

"I was kind of hoping you would do that."

He laughed, then kicked the horse and flipped the reins. The animal bolted beneath them and Elizabeth flung her arms around Aleix's ribs, clinging to him as she madly bounced up and down through the whirling night air.

She clenched her eyes shut and kept them so for several minutes until the animal stopped galloping.

"If they're trying to escape quickly, they'll work their way through the beggars' forest to the main road towards Palma," Aleix said. He pulled up at the edge of a dark mass of trees that stretched as far as her eyes could see. "It would be difficult to navigate the woods at night, but Figaro could probably manage."

"How do you know they're heading towards Palma?"

"I don't," he said. "But I seem to remember Susanna has some family or something in Granada, and that would be in the right direction. Unless they're foolish enough to try tramping over the mountains. But if that's the case, you'll have to get someone else to save their lives."

"Wait. Are you saying we're going in there?" Elizabeth scanned the long line of trees. In the night darkness, they looked like a black wall of Mordor. "We won't be able to see anything!"

"Our eyes will adjust, but the horse also knows the terrain. The woods path is one of the routes we take to the regiment. He's done it many times, night and day." The horse pulled back on the reins and turned his head, which to Elizabeth looked like he was disagreeing with Aleix.

"We're going to trust a horse?"

"You'd better hold on. This will be bumpy."

Elizabeth squeezed her eyes shut again and hid her face in Aleix's back. He kicked the horse, called out and whipped on the reins.

Elizabeth clenched her fingers into his shirt, praying it wouldn't rip apart. Flopping up and down, surprised by every turn, and brushing past branches and insects, she felt like a flimsy piece of fabric in a hurricane. She still remembered her long frightening night on the forest floor and shivered to think what might happen if the horse fell, or tripped, or they ran into a tree. In fact, while they bumped along though the cool whipping darkness, a hundred horrific scenarios passed through her panic-driven mind, none of them involving Figaro, Susanna, or the murderous gypsies.

How she longed for something simple and mundane: her little corner studio with the vending machines on the other end of the hall. Shelves of opera scores, piano scores, diction books, and her quiet little apartment on a third floor with two fire escapes and four locks on the door. How wonderful it had been to spend ten, twelve, fourteen hours a day sitting at a piano, creating art that would have no greater lasting effect than the very moment in which she played it. To come and go and never be known or seen. How simple and perfect and wonderful her life was!

"Wait, what did you say?" Reggie held his fork in mid-air as though someone had hit the pause button on his meal. He raised his eyebrows over the dinner she had cooked for him in her father's kitchen. "You're kidding right? You can't be serious."

"What's wrong with being a teacher?"

"It's just the way you say it. 'Lizzy, why don't you do the concerto competition? Lizzy, why aren't you applying to Juilliard or Eastman?' 'Oh, I don't know. I'm not very interested in any of that. I think I might like to maybe, someday, perhaps, possibly teach some piano lessons'...?"

"We don't all have to be international stars. I'm just not cut out for that kind of thing."

"Teach where? Here at the college?"

"Oh, no. Just, you know, from my home, I guess."

"You mean little kids and retirees?"

"Or maybe accompany some high school program. Maybe. What's wrong with that?"

"For one thing, there's a whole world between international star and Marian the Librarian. You don't have to be Horowitz, but you could do so much more."

"Not really."

He threw his fork down and wiped his hands with his napkin so thoroughly, it reminded her of Pilate washing his hands before the Crucifixion.

"Listen," she said, "I know what you're saying, but those things can't happen without me getting on a stage. I'm just not cut out for it, Reggie. I get nervous and my hands start shaking. I don't want all those people looking at me. Have you ever tried it? It's terrifying."

"It's wonderful."

"I'd have to invest in drugs."

He didn't move.

"Reggie, your stew is growing cold. Look, I don't need all the things you need. Stepping out of student life and starting your own program at the school. Founder and producer."

"Don't forget director, lighting technician, and props-master."

"Props? Surely the theater department can—"

Reggie shook his head. "Don't get me started." He reached for his wine. "And coach and accompanist." His eyes slithered over the glass as he took a big gulp.

Elizabeth paused, her fork suspended in a chunk of beef. "Accompanist and coach? Reggie, you can't play the piano."

"No," he said. "But I need someone, and the department won't force anyone's hand or even give them credit. A student can't do it. There's no student at this college who could pull it off, even if I could get them the credits. Accompanying requires more than just hitting all the right notes. It's a skill. They have to sense where the singer is going next, feel their breaths, guide them dynamically, but never cover them. You know what I mean?"

"I'm sure I don't."

"It's ridiculous. I've got funding. I can pay someone. But then who's good enough to read a million opera scores and learn all those languages?"

"Languages?"

"Opera, of course, they'd have to be able to translate Italian, German, French, Russian—"

"Punjabi?"

"Possibly. I'd have to look it up. But really, we'd probably just start with Italian. Do that for a couple years to get going. With a start-up program, you really don't want to stray too far past spaghetti opera. Probably Mozart and Rossini, even though it might get screechy. Then try something French or German for a couple years, hopefully by then up to three productions a year."

"Three a year!"

"One in the fall, a small one-act in the winter and then a larger Spring production. And of course, a summer scenes program."

"You've thought all this out."

"I'm obsessed," he crooned. "But the fact is, I'm on my own. And I can't do it all on my own."

"One-man opera?"

"Apparently no. It's like I need someone who loves learning music, but never really wants to perform it. Just sort of sit in the wings and get everyone else ready to go on stage." He forked a few potatoes and carrots, still talking with a cheek full of mush. "Someone with all the passion, the talent, the drive, but none of the vanity. A truly humble soul, a martyr really for the cause, the great cause."

"Love of art and music and all that?"

"Exactly."

"I'll do it."

"Oh darling, I hadn't even thought of you."

"You're a terrible fake, Reggie."

"It keeps working for me."

"Indeed. Now eat your mush and crow, or we'll be late to that Italian class you signed me up for. Trip to Rome, my eye."

"Whoa, hold up there." Aleix pulled on the reins. The horse stomped in protest, breathless. "What's that?" He pointed to a distant glow of light between the trees.

Elizabeth smelled burning embers. "A camp? Could that be them?"

"Unlikely, if they're trying to make speed. But Susanna might have gotten tired."

"What if it's some gypsies who'll kill us and leave our remains for birds of prey?"

Elizabeth felt him turn and give her a questioning glance, though she couldn't see it.

"Well, if that's the case, you have nothing to worry about. Gypsies generally kill very quickly and without any mess. They're just after your clothes."

"I haven't got any."

"Then maybe they'll keep you as a sex slave."

"Aleix! What do we do?"

"We approach quietly, and you stop shouting every time I make a joke. Relax. I won't let anything happen to you."

"Did you bring a weapon?"

Aleix dismounted, leaving her alone on the horse. He wrapped the rein around a branch and pulled an ancient pistol from his satchel. "It's a flintlock. Pathetic things, but enough to scare the locals. I'm going to creep up for a closer look. You stay here and try not to make any noise."

"What if you don't come back?"

"Whether I want to or not," he said. "I always come back."

Elizabeth didn't find his cryptic words consoling as he disappeared into the darkness. Chills went up her spine, and the horse puffed through its nostrils impatiently beneath her. She held tightly onto the mane and tried not to listen to the clicks and occasional coos around her. Dark sinister forms gathered in the air, rising from unseen places with long prickly fingers and black sludge dripping from toothless mouths.

In another time and place, these insane images wouldn't

have taunted her. But in this eighteenth century delusional forest, every episode of *Twilight Zone, Star Trek* and *The X-Files* burst suddenly to life while hungry velociraptors studied her through the darkness. She felt things crawling on her back, tickling her face. What was taking so long? Did he leave her alone here? What was she thinking, trusting Aleix, who she hardly knew? Perhaps he was negotiating the sale with the gypsies right now. Irrationality took over and she gripped the reins, unwinding them from the tree branch. She kicked the horse's flank just as Aleix stepped out of the trees and grabbed the harness.

"You won't last long if you don't learn to take orders."

"I thought you had left me," she admitted. "Who is it? Is it them? Figaro and Susanna?"

"No. It's just one man set up alone. I recognize him, a merchant at the estate. He's harmless, but what he's doing out here is a mystery." Aleix led the horse on foot. "We should approach him. He might have seen them and can point us in the right direction."

The heavy hooves thumped on the forest floor, occasionally snapping branches and pushing past shrubberies.

Aleix called out, "Hello!"

"Who goes there?" the man replied, a black shadow rising quickly in alarm.

Elizabeth gasped. "Gaspar?" Coming into the light, she slid off the horse onto the forest floor, remembering too late her bare feet. "Gaspar, what are you doing out here in the woods all alone?"

"I might ask you the same now. Who is this with you?"

"Gaspar, this is Aleix. He is the Count's armorer, and he's helping me find Susanna and Figaro. They've run off. Have you heard anyone pass this way?"

"I have not."

"Wait," Aleix said. "Don't you deliver the cheese? How do you two know each other?"

Gaspar raised an eyebrow. "I don't deliver the cheese. I make the cheese."

"Aleix, Gaspar is my...uncle."

"Your uncle?"

"Gaspar, what are you doing out here in the woods so late?"

"Oh, just sitting out by a fire. Enjoying the night." There was a tension about him that she had never sensed before. "But what're you two hoping to find out here in the dark?" he asked. "Seems a fool's errand. Should wait until morning. Elizabeth, perhaps you should stay with me. I'll pack up here and take you back myself."

"That isn't necessary," Aleix said.

"No Gaspar, really," she said.

"You always call your Uncle by his first name?"

"I—look, we just have to find Figaro and Susanna tonight, or the whole book will be thrown off, permanently."

"You told him?" Aleix seemed to be getting angrier, but Elizabeth couldn't understand why.

"I—"

"Is there any reason she shouldn't confide in her uncle? I suspect she'd be safer than to trust the likes of you. What did you say your name was?"

Aleix stepped up to Gaspar and peered down. He started laughing. "Forgive me, but you are both so entertaining and you don't know it. Listen, Senõr Cheese, Uncle, or whatever you are. I'm only here because your, ah, niece asked for my help. I'd gladly drop her with you, but you don't seem to have any method of transport, and she was very adamant we find this couple before they do themselves in."

"Actually, they get murdered by gypsies," Elizabeth said.

"Dead is dead. But please, by all means, if you can find them faster, you are welcome to take up the chase and leave me in peace." Aleix mounted the horse.

"Please, Gas—Uncle, Aleix is just helping me. I'm fine. And we should get moving if we're to find them. But if you come across them, do your best to convince them to return home." She took Aleix's arm and remounted the horse. "I'll see you soon, I hope."

"Take care, Elizabeth," Gaspar said, as they trotted back into the shadows.

"I will!"

Aleix whipped the reins and kicked the horse. Again, they were off on another bumpy chase through the blackness and horrific imaginations for many minutes until the horse stepped out onto a long dirt road lit by the moon. "We'll wait here," he said. "I'm betting we passed them in the woods, and if I'm right, they want to get to this road before daylight." He dismounted and helped her off. Her feet met with soft grass and dirt.

"Aleix, thank you for doing this for me. For them, I mean."

"Charming Uncle of yours. What do you suppose he was doing back there?"

"I don't know. Camping, like he said."

"You're going to have to be less naïve."

"You think he was up to some ill business? I can tell you, he is one of the most honest men I've ever met. I trust him completely."

"Your Uncle, you mean? Fine. I don't know if he was up to some 'ill business,' but he was hiding something. That's certain."

"Well, I'm very grateful for your help tonight. No matter what happens. You could have said no."

"I'll find some way for you to make it up to me."

"That's what I'm afraid of. I didn't really think any of this through. I just knew you'd be awake and that you could do the job."

"I thought you said you weren't afraid of me, Elly?"

"Please don't call me that."

They heard voices and rustling in the underbrush. Aleix raised a finger and two shadowy figures stepped out from the trees.

"Looks like you're up," whispered Aleix.

"Oh, Aleix!" Elizabeth cried. "You did it! I knew you could do it! It's them! Figaro! Susanna!" The couple froze. "Don't be on guard," she cried. "It's me, Elizabeth. We've come all this way to find you both, and we did it!"

Figaro spoke out. "Who's there? Elizabeth who?"

"The scullery maid. You know, can play the piano but can't scale a fish?" Elizabeth stepped forward and threw her arms around Susanna. "Listen, you must stop this nonsense right away and return to the Count's estate."

"We can't do that," Figaro said. "You don't understand what's going on."

"Actually, Elizabeth does know," Susanna said.

"Beloved, is there anyone you did not tell before you told me?"

"Listen," Elizabeth interrupted, "you two can deal with all that later. Right now, you have to get back and fight this thing out. Figaro, what's gotten into you? This isn't like you, running off in the middle of the night. You can handle the Count."

"He's become a bit of a violent man," said Figaro. "I was afraid for Susanna. I can't protect her all the time."

"He doesn't want her by force," Elizabeth said. "His pride's too deep. And honestly, this whole thing can be settled in a matter of hours, or maybe days if we assume we're not in an opera anymore. But this running off, it's not the way. Come on, Figaro, where's your courage? Your audacity? Your gameness! Surely you haven't forgotten who you are, with all this bowing and scraping. Come on man!" Elizabeth began singing on the moonlit dirt road, chanting at the top of her lungs "*Se- vuol- bal-la-re,- Signor- Contino!*"

"Contino?"

"Yes, yes! You know, **Se- vuol- ball-are,- Signor- Contino-!** You know it!" She danced a gleeful little jig around them both, "*il chitarrino le suonerò, sì!*"

"I don't speak Italian," said Figaro.

Elizabeth laughed. "That's okay, I don't speak Spanish."

"All right," said Aleix, "I think that's enough of that. You have to forgive her, she had a long day and just took her very first late-night forest romp."

"It was horrible!" Elizabeth began singing in German. "*Wer reitet so spät durch Nacht und Wind? Es ist der Vater mit seinem Kind!*"

"Okay," Aleix grabbed her arm. "Time to get you home and into bed." He nudged her back towards the horse.

"Whose bed?" she said, overcome with a desire to giggle.

"Your bed, Elly, your bed."

"But wait," said Figaro, "What are we supposed to do?"

"Come home and have a little faith in yourselves, darn it," said Elizabeth, spinning back around. "Susanna, first thing in the morning, you confide in the Countess about the Count's advances. Tell her everything. She's miserable in her marriage and could use some help cornering the louse. And Figaro, you march all over the estate announcing the news of your engagement. Have the servants bring some public tribute to the Count to honor him. You'll think of something. Anything is better than this."

"What about Marcellina?"

"I already tried to jump that plot point, and look where it got me!"

Aleix had dragged her to a protruding patch of stones and lined the horse up.

"Go back by the road," he said. "It will be longer, but I'll send a carriage for you as soon as we're home. You'll get back before sunrise."

"We will," said Susanna. "And we won't run away again. Thank you, Elizabeth."

"When you feel any doubt, just start singing! Remember, *Se-vuol- ball-are,- Signor- Contino-!*"

Aleix mounted the horse, pulling Elizabeth up behind him. All the way home, she leaned on his warm, strong back in a state of hungover delight.

Chapter Nineteen

The next morning, Susanna told her mistress everything. She waited until The Countess had fully dressed and finished with her meal, then cleared away the dishes, tidied up the dressing table, and simply dropped it out in the open while her Mistress finished a note. The Countess's pen froze stiff in her hand, her eyes fixed on the page.

"Tell me," she said at length, laying down the pen. "I want to know everything."

"I promise you, Madame, I have related everything to you as it's happened so far."

"So he, my husband, tried to seduce you?"

"Oh no! He wouldn't deign to stoop so low for a mere servant, Madame."

"Then to force himself on you?"

"Neither that, Madame. No. Let's say he proposed a financial agreement."

The Countess rose and stepped away, hiding her face from both light of window and horror of mirror. Her left hand clutched at the hinge of a closet door. "To buy you?"

"In a manner of speaking, yes."

"And what, that is, how much did he offer in return for your, your—"

"He threatened to lean in favor of Marcellina and force Figaro to marry her."

"So, it was bribery."

"I suppose you can look at it that way."

"I knew. I knew he was unfaithful. But to hear it...Forgive me. I'm not surprised. I'm not."

"Madame, I don't believe, I mean, I think he does still love you."

"He ignores me. Like an urn in his gallery."

"He's just—"

"A man? So, one day soon Figaro will be bored with you too?"

"Forgive me, Madame. I've spoken disrespectfully."

"No," said the Countess. "It's not your fault."

"Did I do the right thing by telling you? We tried to leave last night, to run away, but we thought you should know."

"Does anyone else know? My husband bribing servants to sleep with him? My shame and disgrace? Who knows about this?"

"Well..."

"Of course. Everyone knows. Even the little page boy?"

"I'm afraid he was hiding in the room when The Count made the proposition clear to me."

"The scoundrel!"

"I'm actually one of the lucky ones. Last month before you left for Cadiz there was an incident, I don't know the details, but rumor is he tried to force himself—"

"Stop. Oh, Susanna. None of this is as it should be."

A ll of this is exactly as it should be, Elizabeth thought, shutting the book with a contented snap.

It was a beautiful morning. Outside the tiny window of her bedroom, every stone and blade of grass seemed to glisten in the Spanish sun. The skull smelled like vinegar and fish, a lovely smell, because that's what a scullery should smell like. Birds were singing somewhere else. Marcellina was in a foul mood, and Cook was worse. Elizabeth set about peeling and scrubbing, washing and rewashing, scaling, feathering, absorbing the morning's tirade through the tiny hole in the crusted wall of the stifling room in the dim quarters at the very bottom of the tiny winding staircase.

At some point, Figaro bounced in and thanked her for chasing them down and straightening them out and oh, by the way, he and Susanna were engaged, in case she didn't know, pending the approval of the Count, of course, and would she like to come upstairs in a bit and sing a song to our Lord and Master as he publicly presents the bridal veil to sweet Susanna in honor of his abolishment of a particular indecent custom?

Ah charming, clever Figaro. Of course, she would be delighted to participate in the ceremony in which all the servants would join hands and pressure the Count to do the right thing. A ceremony which should have taken place in the first act, before the Count sent Cherubino away, but this was all such good news, all part of Mozart's score, Da Ponte's libretto and Beaumarchais's play. The Countess's heart is breaking, the Count is abusing his privilege, the servants are struggling to attain integrity, and it's another sunny day in southern Spain.

Elizabeth didn't remember getting home the night before. She didn't think it was possible to fall asleep on a horse, but she had wafted in and out, the way one does on a bus or airplane, until some dark hour when Aleix had helped her off.

Drooping, she plodded away from him without even a good night. He grabbed her shoulders and turned her about face. Giddy with exhaustion, she fell against him and tipped her lips upwards, but he stepped aside.

"That way." He pointed toward the servants' entrance. "I assume you can find your room once you're in the house."

"Yes, yes, I'll be fine. Good night."

Or something like that.

About noon, Figaro marched through the servants' halls shouting and waving a lace veil in the air like a banner. Susanna moved with him, smiling coyly and passing out flowers.

"Elizabeth! You are coming, aren't you?" Susanna asked, passing the scullery door.

Elizabeth wiped her hands on her greasy apron. "Where are we going?"

"The ballroom. The new fortepiano just arrived, so it's a good time to catch him with an audience."

"Good for you! Of course, I wouldn't miss it."

"Here, take some of these." Susanna passed her a small bunch of wildflowers. "We'll throw them at his feet and make a good show of it."

"Nothing like a little public praise for doing the right thing," said a footman as he passed by and grabbed a handful of flowers.

Elizabeth followed them out the back door and along the path to the front of the house. Everyone whispered and giggled, a general aura of excitement about the troupe de coup. Figaro reached the large front doors, then stepped up and began booming some patriotic song, or perhaps it was military, or maybe a drinking song. Elizabeth tried to mumble along and look like she knew what they were singing. They all sang out so loudly, so vehemently, as though they could force their will on the Count with a peaceful protest. As though hundreds of years of feudal practices could be forgotten with a promise and a song.

The servants entered the ballroom and spread out along the walls, singing and waving their flowers. They each bowed to the bewildered Count, who stood stunned in the center of his polished floor, watching the spectacle with an outraged smile.

The Countess was already there, demurely floating in the background.

"What's all this? What's going on here?" the Count asked when the singing ended.

"Merely a show of honor and appreciation," said Figaro, like a speaker at a rally. "Your broadmindedness and great love for your bride has shown respect and mercy for all of us."

The Count was not an unattractive man. He wore well-fitting clothes and stood above average height with a slender frame. His face was still youthful, and he had a nice head of thick black hair above two deep brown eyes. One could argue that he was the better looking of the two rivals for Susanna's virginity. Had Elizabeth not seen his aggressive tendencies in action, she might have doubted them possible. There was refinement and grace in his movements, a comfortable ease in his mannerisms, and subtle sophistication in his speech.

"I am grateful, my friends," the Count said, "for your demonstrations of honor. But please dispense with any such tributes and praise. When I chose to abolish the unjust right from my estates, I merely restored duty and nature to their place..."

An image of Amada running through the woods flashed in Elizabeth's mind. Politics were the essence of deception in any generation. He leads the world with one hand visible, and the other on the table of his own corruption. One could honestly transport the man back to the twenty-first century, hold a campaign slogan under his picture, and he'd probably win, even though he didn't know what a cell phone was.

The Count would now promise to host the wedding but request a delay for some flimsy reason. Unable to endure it, Elizabeth slipped between staff and disappeared into the crowd. She passed aprons stained with every hue and drenched in scents both aromatic and sour, scents of manure, wood chippings, iron and char, dusty roads, animals, smoke, grease, and bread.

Outside the ballroom, she tiptoed away down the corridor to the far west wing. She found Aleix alone in his armory, quietly assembling a gun with a disturbingly long muzzle. The room seemed dark despite the morning cheer that captivated the estate around him. His satchel lay crumpled in a heap at his feet.

"Aren't you joining the others?" she asked.

As though he had been expecting her, he did not look up from his task. "Not my thing really."

"Artifice and deception?"

"No, the other thing."

"Figaro and Susanna? You don't think they're well suited? Or perhaps you have your eye on the chambermaid yourself?"

He raised an eyebrow. "I don't ascribe to the whole philosophy, if you must know."

"Surely you don't mean love. You don't believe in love?"

He assembled the parts of the large weapon with graceful ease. "Does that bother you?"

Elizabeth sank onto a bench between two closets full of tools for killing people. "Well, I should believe in romantic love," she said. "Without it, I wouldn't have a job. I mean, how many operas would exist?" She snickered, but he did not join her. "I guess if I'm being honest, I probably don't believe in it either."

"If that's true, then you'd be the first woman I've ever heard admit so." With a satisfying click, he pushed the weapon together.

"Well, let's be real. True love. Romantic love, that the poets languish away for. An all-powerful force, transcending explanation to deposit itself into people and incite voluntary insanity. I mean, if you study the great works of romantic literature and art, it's responsible for more tragedies than the plague. No, I like having all my acumen. I'd rather live in a world where it's a hoax."

"Aren't you afraid you'll miss out on something wonderful?" he asked.

"I'm not sure it is something wonderful. Just look at our leading couple. Isn't it love that has brought them to this humiliation? Or our Countess stashed away like some collectible. Wasn't it love that brought her here?"

"So, they say. More like security. Or a desire for progeny. In the end, it's just as selfish as everything else."

"I wouldn't go that far," said Elizabeth. "Love is selfish? Have you ever encountered it? Personally?"

He shook his head. "Then I'd be in there with all the other believers, wouldn't I?"

Cheers erupted from the gathering down the hall, followed by a new hymn of laud to their Lord and Equivocator.

"Listen," she said. "I want to thank you for last night. I really threw you into that, and you proved yourself a hero."

He began work on another weapon from a pile of parts resting on a piece of linen.

"I was in trouble," Elizabeth continued, "well, they were in trouble, and you just trusted me, jumped on a horse, rode through the woods like you had some stake in it all. I don't think I've ever seen anyone act so, so—"

"Foolishly?"

"Faithfully."

"Oh, don't curse me with that."

"Well, you trusted me, and I'm grateful. You see, when I get nervous, I say stupid things that can be...insensitive."

"Insensitive?" Now he laughed out loud, his series of giant guffaws echoing so much it reminded her of the laughter sound-tracks on a sitcom. "Insensitive," he repeated as he rose and returned the weapon to its closet. "Well, I don't mind insensitive, as long as it's honest." He shut the door and stowed the key in a pocket. "Now you'd better get back to your little cell, hadn't you?"

"Oh!" Elizabeth jumped up. "Yes of course, Cook will be planning to use my limbs for an entrée, but, for what it's worth, thank you."

"Do you trust me now?" he said.

"Enough to ride alone with you half-naked on a horse through the woods at night?"

"That was necessity."

"Not really. I could have chosen to let them die. For a minute I thought I would when you asked me to get on that horse."

Elizabeth scurried off through the corridors and slipped into the servants, east stairway. She wound her way down on her tiny, pointed heels, hoping to sneak back into the scullery before anyone noticed she wasn't with the group. As she passed her superior's open doorway, a pair of conversing voices caught her attention.

"Figaro, that arrogant clown," a man said.

"Oh, honestly, Doctor Bartolo," Marcellina's voice replied.

"I predict one day that loaf will hang for his insolence."

Elizabeth assumed Marcellina was laughing, but it sounded oddly similar to her groan.

"And you for your professional indignity," Marcellina said. "Your patients might just die on the table in front of you while you go through their purses. Imagine you, married to the Countess Rosina." She laughed again. "What could you have been thinking?"

"Well for starters, she wasn't the Countess then, and you know it."

"But she had some very lovely...purses."

"Is this why you demanded I come all this way today? To open old wounds with mockery?"

"Well, if anyone has the right, it's me. You were jilted by Rosina, but I, good Doctor Bartolo, I was jilted by—"

"All right that's enough. Tell me you didn't summon me to bring that old subject to flame again. Get back to it. Is something wrong with your employer, the Count?"

"No more than any other jealous rake."

"Jealous rake?" A chair screeched as someone pulled it across the floor inside the office. "Now this is some news worth traveling for. Tell me, our Count is miserable?"

"Miserable, no. Bored with his wife, yes. Vain, yes. Moving on to other interests...yes."

Elizabeth heard a pair of hands clap and the high-pitched squeal of a man's **falsetto** voice. "Hooray!" cried Doctor Bartolo. "I am avenged in their mutual misery."

"And not only them, but the arrogant clown who assisted them."

"Figaro? Oh, now bitter prune of yester-years, now you have my ears. Tell me a means to his misery, and I am at your service."

"Truly? If you would only do your duty and fulfill the promise you made to me so many years ago, I would not be reduced to such—"

"Woman!"

"Very well," Marcellina continued, "if you will not honor your word and do the right thing in marrying me, the least you can do is help me to marry someone else."

"Figaro? Oh, nothing would delight me more than to saddle that clout with your ancient remains, but he would never have you."

"Indeed, he has set his eyes on Susanna, the Countess's chambermaid. They're engaged and with a generous dowry gift from our Count. However, our Lord and Master has a thirst for the bride. She's not the first, of course, and won't be the last, as I'm sure you'll be delighted to know. But in this case, I think it has more to do with Figaro than the girl. Only she won't submit, despite constant pressure from Basilio and threats from the Count himself."

"Basilio? Mighty calamities of Venus. Is that serpent slithering around these corridors now too? Well, this Susanna girl sounds a fool," Bartolo said with a sneer. At least Elizabeth felt a sneer, but she could have heard it from the way he was employing his nasal pharynx in the lengthening of the "u" vowel.

"You waiting for Mz. Kirtenpepper?"

Elizabeth didn't know who had said that. She remembered this conversation in cold detail, but that voice she could never place. It was absurd. By this point in her career, she had become a virtual master at voices, identifying every nuance of timber, each individual character, guiding each young sound to its most expressive potential.

But this voice, this sound with no face that coolly said, "You waiting for Mz. Kirtenpepper?" would forever fade into an echoing corridor in her memory.

"Yeah. Coaching," another male responded.

Now, that voice she recognized. Of course, she did. She had a five o'clock coaching scheduled with Mark Turner, a senior aspiring tenor. Aspiring, because who could really claim to be a tenor as an undergraduate? Anyway, that was Mark Turner.

"Too bad about her, huh?" The mystery voice again. Elizabeth stopped, paralyzed, hidden mere inches around a corner with a steaming cup of coffee in her right hand.

Too bad about her? Too bad about who?

"Who, Mz. Kirtenpepper? What do you mean?" Mark said.

Elizabeth had stepped out a few minutes earlier. Her four o'clock student had stood her up, so she'd fallen into a stupor playing some Bach and then made a last-minute run for coffee. In the faculty lounge, Maureen Steadman, the voice department chair, had launched into a useless conversation about why juries should have to be memorized, even if this wasn't a five-star music school, and it never would be unless they had higher expectations on the undergraduates, and yes, what did you mean by that? *What's too bad about her?*

"Oh, you know, about her and Mr. Greene."

Mark, no doubt, was sitting on the wooden bench just outside her studio door, his posture abysmally slouched after a long day of classes, a backpack of scores tossed carelessly on the floor near his feet.

The mystery voice always hung somewhere floating in the space above him.

What about her and Mr. Greene?

"Aren't they a thing?" Mark asked.

"Maybe not."

"Wow. I thought they'd been together forever."

"Maybe too long, looks like."

Elizabeth felt her stomach lurch. A few drops of coffee spilled to the floor.

"Why? Did something happen?"

"Maybe. Jan Wade and Shay saw Mr. Greene Saturday night."

Saw Mr. Greene... what? Bobsledding? Tap dancing? What?

"Wait. They saw him with someone else?"

Of course, it was someone else. Why would he even take tap dancing lessons?

"I guess so, yeah."

"Wow. Who?"

"They didn't say. Maybe there's some understanding or, maybe, they just split up or something."

Or something? What the hell was something?

The faceless voice threw out a nonchalant, "Hey, I gotta go. Later," and dissolved forever.

She should have stepped around that corner and given them both a tongue lashing. Slandering other people, spreading gossip. How dare they chit-chat so lightly about other people's private affairs, like some celebrity headlines?

But she stepped back. Once. And then again. Carefully, nonsensically, she set the coffee cup on the ground in the corridor. When the elevator opened, two beautiful college girls stepped out, pushing their hair back behind their ears, whispering nothings to each other and passing her as though she were a statue made of cool, lifeless stone. A statue that had always been standing frozen at that music school, with a cup of hot coffee at her feet, balancing between forward and backward in that hallway.

She slipped onto the elevator and pushed a button. The car was maddeningly silent. When the door opened, she floated ghost-like through the darkened corridors of post-rush academia. At the end of a dim hallway, her trembling hands pulled out her keys and opened a vacant music classroom. She didn't bother with the light as she passed the whiteboards and cluster of half-desks. At the long black grand, she laid her fingers across the keys.

What to play?

Her mind suddenly seemed a library of vacant, echoing shelves, the memory of her fingertips a dementia-laden legacy. Empty, all gone, torched in a fire, swept away by a Kansas wind. There was nothing to play.

Where were they all? Debussy? Brahms? Chopin? Or perhaps some opera. Puccini surely, or Verdi, of course, Verdi...But what? How did that one aria from Aida go? She couldn't even remember the triumphal march, so overused on advertisements and popular culture. Even a toddler could recognize that one.

How about the Lucia mad scene?

What was wrong with her hands? Why couldn't she make them move? Not a single note of music would reveal itself to her numb fingertips. She held them, hanging mute over the keys, waiting for the music to return. A tingling sensation marched steadily past her wrists and up her forearms. Surely there was something accessible to her. Something she could pound away on. Some Tchaikovsky or Vaughan Williams or some pent-up twentieth-century composer who could let the fire burn away. The numbness crept past her elbows towards her shoulders. Wasn't there anything left? Something written by some long-dead man who never knew her name? *Where were they?*

It was cold in here. Someone had turned off the heat. The numbness reached her neck and continued upwards, making her jaw tremble. *What about some Bach?* Something complex and intertwining on itself, self-absorbed in its simplistic beauty, so vainly mathematical in its order. Beauty wasn't necessary, only sound was necessary, just sound. Sound to fill the vacancies, the wide-open places, the air around her, the room, the campus, the city. Shatter the windows and peel out across the cornfields. Fill it all up and wake it all up. Wake them all up.

The numbness sank past her throat and embedded itself between her hollow breasts.

In Count Almaviva's basement, more than two hundred years earlier, Elizabeth stood transfixed to her spot, while Doctor Bartolo and Marcellina bantered about other people's stories.

"She's sly, Susanna, but she is no fool. You know, Doctor, your ward Rosina was stolen out from underneath you because you underestimated her. Married to your rival right in your own salon. And here you sit, still unmarried and belligerent. I wonder with all that, you've never once considered things from a woman's perspective."

"Please, don't enlighten me."

"A woman may be seduced by pleasure, but she must never be seduced away from her wiles. Susanna is not worthy of Figaro, but not because she isn't clever. No, she's put the Count and Basilio off for a while now, still going about her business in her chipper way."

Elizabeth heard a chair push back and Marcellina's heels clunk across the wooden floor. A drawer opened, and something paper came out.

"I have a contract," Marcellina said, "signed by Figaro. He owes me money."

"How much?"

"Enough. If he could not repay by a certain time, he promised to marry me."

"That's ridiculous."

"Happy marriages have been built on less," said Marcellina. "And now, with Susanna refusing the Count's advances, and your own testimony on my behalf—"

"It's brilliant."

Elizabeth leaned a little too heavily on the wall outside the doorway and it released an unfortunate creak. The office fell silent, and she slipped around the corner out of sight as Marcellina plod across the floor and shut her door. Elizabeth didn't need to hear any more to know everything was still on track. She would have gladly walked away just then had a voice not suddenly whispered two inches from her earlobe.

"Eavesdropping, are we?"

Elizabeth jumped and gasped.

"Oh, pardon me," said the nasal voice. "Did I *startle* you?"

A rhetorical question. The man had crept behind her with the stealth of a python, carefully navigating both board and shoe so as to not release a single crick. He hovered so close upon her that she could feel his warm, vinegary breath on her neck.

"No," she said, stepping back. "I mean, I'm fine."

The man's long angular nose had such a hump atop it, she couldn't dispel the word "dromedary" from her thoughts. So profound was the comparison that she quickly flashed back to a sixth-grade vocabulary class and her indignation at being forced to learn words she would have absolutely no use for. Yet here she was, all these years later, in eighteenth-century Spain, summoning all her will not to say it aloud while it looped endlessly through her mind. *Dromedary. Dromedary. Dromedary.* She held her lips between her teeth.

The man's narrow black eyes matched the rest of him, from his pointy-toed shoes to the black cap on his greasy head. He scanned her like a copy machine, up, up, up and down, down, down. When he grinned, the corners of his lips stretched almost outside his cheeks towards his ears, making a grotesque display of joy.

"I wonder what one could be doing all alone here, so conveniently placed just outside the offices? Hmmm?" he said, with a smile that might inspire small woodland creatures to kill themselves. He stood straight and raised a scrawny black eyebrow. "I don't know you. Who are you, little quip?"

"Uh, I'm Elizabeth, the new scullery maid. Little quip."

The narrow eyes widened, popping so far open that Elizabeth feared they would topple out of his head to the floor like two glossy marbles.

"I know who you are," he hissed. "You're the little witch who's after my job."

"For the last time, I am not a witch." An assertion profoundly ironic, considering the ghoulish appearance of her accuser.

"I know a witch when I see one, you little vixen, harlot, harpy, quip. Sure, sure, give the old man a few days of the high life in Cadiz. Fool him into thinking he's made some permanent impression,"

Elizabeth suspected this man would shrivel up if left on a beach for more than a minute.

"Then, almost as soon as they return, send him away. Get him out of the way, off to Madrid to fetch some new and interesting scores for Madama. What's wrong with the music we have now? Oh, it's not enough, we need more, new and exciting scores from far-away composers whose names are so irrelevant they can't even be found in the best libraries."

Or they haven't been born yet.

"Showpan!"

"Chopin."

"Debyussee."

"Dromedary."

Elizabeth cupped her mouth with her hand.

"And while I'm away, you traipse out of your little dungeon up to my turf to put on a conniving show for everyone. The new little prodigy."

"Actually, I think that probably happened before you left."

"Shut up, little runt! You have taken on the wrong enemy."

"Enemy?" Elizabeth had an epiphany. "Basilio! You're Basilio."

"DON Basilio, little harpy, backstabber, cretin, necromancer, conjurer, vixen. Little quip."

"You already said some of those."

Basilio leaned into a real hunch, the tip of his camel coming perilously close. "You listen to me. Whatever it is you are up to, whatever scheme you are working, I will find it out, you understand? And I will wreak misery down upon you."

He snapped his fingers right between their noses, then spun on his heel and swept away, his black cape rippling down the hall behind him.

Elizabeth recalled reading about the hooded figure in the gardens who had appeared so mysteriously and sent the leading couple to their doom in the middle of the night. Could that have been Basilio? Anything was possible. He certainly wore enough black. But a sword? That character? Elizabeth couldn't imagine anyone trusting that man with a butter knife.

Chapter Twenty

S ervants began trickling back from the rally. They picked up
loads and tools and dispersed to their various stations.

Elizabeth was about to turn back for the scullery when
Amada appeared. "You're excused from skull. Requested
upstairs."

"Oh, I'm so sorry. I'm sure you were looking forward to—"

Amada held up gentle palm. "*Oye!*" she said. "You don't ever
need to apologize to me for anything, ever again. Aunt told me
what you did, or almost didn't do. I think she might have even
softened a little towards you, too."

"Well, there's an argument for miracles. But listen, since
you're in such a generous mood, I wonder if you might answer a
few questions for me before you start up again?"

They followed the flow back down the passageway towards
the scullery.

"Amada, you once told me that the girl who held my position
before I arrived was a friend of yours."

"Frescura, yes."

"And they dismissed her for being pregnant. Is that right?"

Amada's eyes bulged out, and she glanced over Elizabeth's
shoulder towards the passageway.

"Oh, for goodness' sake Amada, it's not a bad word."

"We shouldn't say such things. It's a scandal!"

"It's not a scandal. It's a word. And it's not even a bad word. Pregnant. Pregnant. Pregnant."

"Hush up, you loon!"

Loon, witch. Gaspar was right, a twenty-first-century woman would not survive long in eighteenth-century Spain.

Amada pulled her to the back wall, away from the passageway door. "Someone will hear you."

"All right, fine. She was in a *situation*. Can you shed any light on who might have been the, I mean who might have gotten her in that situation?"

"Not really. Manuel was very fine on her. He used to work with the blacksmith, but he had some problem with his eyes, I think. He works in the stables now. He would have treated her well, but when Aleix came along, she wouldn't hear talk of anyone else."

"Aleix? The armorer?

"Who else?"

"Was she friendly with him?"

"Well, everyone wanted to be. At first. She talked about him a lot, but most of the girls did. Anyway, who cares who it might have been? What difference does it make?"

Elizabeth felt her eyes roll backwards into her head. "Never mind. Apparently, it doesn't make any difference in eighteenth-century Spain."

✦

Figaro bounced back and forth across the blue and gold Persian carpet in the Countess's greeting room. "How do we proceed now?"

Seated at the fortepiano, Elizabeth let her fingers stray over some delicate Schumann while trying to eavesdrop. Between the pacing, the Countess facing the opposite direction, Susanna running in and out of the room, and occasional flirtations, she only caught snippets here and there. Nevertheless, it was easy to see that the discussion was undoubtedly veering far from the literary scripts of both **Beaumarchais's play and Da Ponte's libretto**.

"He'll stall as long as possible. He's very stubborn." The Countess and all her refinery sat poised in a gilded armchair near the hearth. "You won't bend him."

"Bend him, Madame? I want to twist him so he thinks he's lost his wits."

Then Elizabeth heard something about twisting throats...

"Dearest," Susanna said, "You shouldn't even suggest such things, at least not in the presence of—"

Mumble, mumble, mumble...

"Good heavens, Figaro! What are you suggesting?" That was the Countess.

"We can't approach him," Susanna said. "He'll just deny it and settle with Marcellina."

"Ay!"

A spattering of phrases she could only assume were Spanish curse words.

"We *could* hunt down some of the girls he's seduced."

"Figgy, who is going to admit to that?"

"I'm not sure I can take much more of this," the Countess said, her fan fluttering wildly at her neck.

Mutter, mutter, mutter...mumble, mumble...

"He would only assume any threat came from me, my dear," Figaro again. "Then he'd promptly have me sent away or permanently damaged. Wait, how about we invite some dignitaries..."

Mumble, mumble.

Elizabeth played as softly as she could.

"...with the Duchess of Ayora?"

"Where is Ayora? Is that even in Spain?"

"Sweetest heart, it doesn't matter where she is from, as long as we can contrive..."

Then suddenly the Countess, "That would raise a terrible scandal!"

In and out they weaved their wretched little plots, further and further from the original, each idea and suggestion more bizarre than the last.

"What about his financial dealings? Everyone has some under the table activities."

"This may surprise you, despite my present situation, but I don't want my husband going to prison, or losing our estate. And honestly, Figaro, can you swear your financial dealings are perfectly pure? What about that Marcellina contract?"

Mutter, mutter, mumble, mumble...grumble, grumble... curse, curse...

"Wait," Countess again. "What if we dressed up one of the sewing models and set it aflame in the gardens?"

Now what were they talking about? Burning effigies? Elizabeth couldn't help but notice that these characters bore the same unde- pendability as their lord and master. The Count was indeed a more violent man in this version of the tale, but Figaro was less clever, Susanna less courageous, and the Countess seemed to have no *vipera* at all. Reality had somehow put a damper on their strongest traits. Or perhaps it was the other way around, and the opera's comedy had just accentuated them. Now that she thought about it, the only character who stood up to their theatrical coun- terpart was the mischievous music teacher, Basilio. Oh, she shouldn't have thought of that, *darnit!*

Dromedary, dromedary, dromedary...

"Figaro, exactly what authorities are you talking about? My husband *is* the authorities."

"A fact you might have considered when you decided to marry him, Madame."

"Figgy!"

Elizabeth found her fingers slipping unconsciously into the midway point of Liszt's *Hungarian Rhapsody No. 2* as more frag- ments of the demented conversation flew past her.

"...not one for violence and when it came to it, I don't think I could do it. At heart I'm an artist, not a soldier."

"But we could get him into a position where he will have to allow the wedding."

Oh Liszt, take me away.

"I know a man, well a gypsy of sorts, who can induce certain enchantments..."

"Perhaps we should bring it straight to his confessor. Can't he do something?"

"My darling, your naïve nature only draws me to you..."

The conversation took a gradual rise in dynamics, making it easier for Elizabeth to eavesdrop without interrupting her *Rhapsody.*

"You mean bribe him?"

"I would never stoop to his level. No. I want to shame him."

"Publicly?" asked the Countess. "Is that necessary? Wouldn't bribery be better?"

"That's the point of shaming, Madame," said Figaro. "It's where everyone can see it."

"Why not expose him to all the staff?" Susanna again. Getting more level-headed by the measure.

"Why stop there?" An inflamed Figaro.

Seriously people, Gilbert and Sullivan could have worked it out in less time.

The Countess rose and fluttered herself furiously with a fan. "Madrid? You mean raise the whole scandal politically? Figaro, you must realize he is the first landowner to even consider dissolving his feudal right."

"And he won't be the last, Madame! Why not warn all future phonies of the perils of challenging the lower classes?"

Elizabeth considered what she really knew about camels. They can go days without water, and they had some kind of presence at the manger scene. She knew some distant relatives, the llama probably, spelled with two *L*'s of course. That never came from an opera. What about the alpaca? Had she ever seen an alpaca?

Perhaps it was just another word for llama, like dromedary was another word for a camel with one hump. Thinking about the word llama was like thinking about the word vacuum with two *U*'s. *How did they clean all these carpets in eighteenth-century Spain?*

"But you're talking about a general uprising!"

Elizabeth had no idea who was speaking as the flags began to wave in descent from opera comique into cannon fire at the rise of the lower class in Spain, a full year before France even got started. How long would she have to sit here and play this ridiculous instrument with only five octaves and no sustain pedal, and sleep on a bed that brought more kinks than rest, and get screamed at through a portal by a faceless cook with a butcher knife?

"Why not? They're doing it in America right now, aren't they?"

"Revolution!"

"All right, that's quite enough." Elizabeth slammed her fingers down on Liszt. "What's the matter with you people? Have you forgotten who you are? We're not starting a revolution here. This isn't *Norma* or *Aida*, it's *Figaro*. Now, first thing tomorrow, Figaro, you send for the page boy to come back, secretly. How quickly could you get him back here?"

"I don't know, maybe—"

"Good enough. We set the farce for two nights from now, right after the page is secretly ensconced at the estate."

"But he was sent away," Susanna said.

"You know," Elizabeth continued, "if this turns into Verdi, you'll probably regret it. Cute little sopranos like you don't last more than three acts. Just go get him. Have the Countess write him a note, saying she wants to discuss his dismissal with her husband together. She is his Godmother. Now, sometime between now and then, Susanna will find a coy, seductive way to invite our Count to the gardens after dark—"

"I'll never allow it!"

"Put down the sword, Figgy. During the afternoon, you will

send the page in here to dress him in Susanna's clothes, and at the appointed time, our benefactor will court the page unknowingly, and you'll all step in and catch him in the act. Shame, embarrassment, pardons, wedding bells, and they all live happily until the sequel."

"I don't know if I like involving that young man in all this."

"We have no choice, Madame," Elizabeth said. "If we're going to get through the Act II finale, we need all the comprimarios exactly where they're supposed to be. Okay, all clear? No revolutions in Spain, voodoo dolls or burning effigies. Now, if you don't mind, I'm going back to the scullery to calm my nerves."

Chapter Twenty-One

The scullery maid and part time pianist retired early that night, exhausted in a variety of ways. She had worked two shifts in the skull, burdened by the discovery of the impotency above stairs. Apparently, the main characters of her melodrama were not complying with the script. Oh, the little details of character showed through when they were about their duties, scaling a fish, combing some hair, or keeping a humble pianist in her place. But where were the real theater-worthy traits that made one fall in love with them, pay for a ticket and watch them year after year? In reality, the little musical scullery maid found them all so normal, so devastatingly human, that they were almost useless, even to themselves.

What an absurd idea, thought the little scullery-pianist while scrubbing her pot. At least the cook on the other side of that wall didn't need an accompanist to tell her how to run her own story. So why should Figaro, the Countess and Susanna? And what if the little scullery-pianist had never opened this ridiculous book and slipped into its enchanted pages? Would the Count have had his way with little Amada in the woods? Would Cherubino have made it back for the Second Act? Would Figaro have started revolutions in Spain?

The page boy was not so easily summoned as Figaro had assumed. Already returned home to a sick mother and struggling father, the little Cherub had to remain caring for siblings and tending farm until health was restored. It took almost a week for the page boy to respond to his Godmother's summons. By that time, the Count had received a call from the court in Madrid. When Cherubino arrived at the estate, the Lord and Master had already galloped away, leaving Susanna and the Countess to wallow in the sad, lethargic melodies of a despairing and melancholic scullery-pianist.

Elizabeth resented that last bit. She was frustrated, not despairing, except perhaps for a decent pair of shoes.

In the scullery maid's desperation to move things forward, she decided to do something progressive, take charge, plunge headlong into the fray rather than just labor away her days, while everyone else got their theatrical acts together.

She might have taken the opportunity to explore the estate. Now wouldn't that have been a nice idea? Perhaps learn some new trades, make some new acquaintances, better herself by embracing a new culture? She could have immersed herself in the opportunity of the day, stretched beyond the peelings and bar lines of the scullery-pianist life. There was so much opportunity, if only she could have seen it.

Who was writing this thing? She was a woman in eighteenth-century Spain. Her *opportunities* consisted of being cast out, impregnated, or burnt for being a witch. All right, maybe not the burning part, but in a couple years she could get her head cut off if she accidentally strayed over the border.

Even little scullery-pianists must learn to read a map, unfold the instruction manual, or ahem, follow the score? It's a free trip to Spain, after all. She might consider experimenting with some of the local cuisine or visiting Roman ruins. There are so many varieties of floral species in this part of the world. How about sampling some historical Spanish cuisine?

She could have Mexican ten feet from her front door in Wichita.

The world is not always so grim as she would paint it. Had she really needed for anything during her adventure? Had everything not been supplied on demand? Perhaps little scullery-pianists should be more grateful for assistance rendered. Some appreciation might be just the thing for her bellyaching.

Now here was media brainwashing at its finest. She had been stranded, alone in the woods, starving. And what about that hooded figure in the dark? She might as well read fortune cookies.

Stubbornness, whining, and self-pity fired up the scullery-pianist's own version of theatrical heresy. She made up her mind to try again, skipping to Act III by giving Marcellina the full story. If the Housemaid would not hear her arguments civilly, then perhaps she would accept them in writing.

Shame. Shame! Little scullery-pianist, sneaking around the Countess's dressing table, stealing ink and paper to quickly pen a note, unsigned of course, (how original!). Explain to Marcellina why she can never marry Figaro.

The little scullery-pianist proudly folded her nice little note and left it on the Housemaid's desk. Surely, even without Figaro there to prove it, just suggesting the idea to Marcellina might be enough.

However, during the night, the nice little note mysteriously disappeared from the Housemaid's desk, and Marcellina never got it.

"Oh, come on!" Elizabeth sat up in her bed.

Where oh where did her little note go? Oh, where oh where could it be? Oh wait, that's not from an opera.

"Now that's just downright offensive. Look, I'm not the author of this story. I didn't write up all this nonsense. I'm fine with dropping them all off a bridge. Let them start a revolution. I don't even want to be here."

Amada rolled over in her bed and groaned. "*Pobresita!* Who are you yelling at?"

"No one," said Elizabeth. "I'm sorry, just go back to sleep."

"Blow out that candle."

"I will." Then with a hiss towards the pages, Elizabeth slammed the book shut and tossed it on the floor. "And there is no such thing as a scullery-pianist!"

She threw off her covers, then wrapped a shawl over her shoulders and snatched up the candle.

The spiral staircase creaked beneath her bare feet as she crept to the basement where the shadows of her own candle gave her a terrible fright. Thomas Edison could not be born too soon.

Marcellina's office door stood ajar. She peeked inside and gasped. The note *had* vanished. Something in the dark hallway knocked, and footsteps padded down the servants' passage.

"Who's there?" she called out, then dove for the office door. The footsteps quickened, and cool night air streamed towards her as someone opened the back door. A figure stood on the threshold, a shadow with no real shape but a hooded cloak.

"Who is that? Who are you?"

With her heart pounding in her chest, she plunged forward, but he fled like a dusty breeze across the back lot, sweeping off into the shadows of the garden. Despite her many faults, she was not so foolish as to pursue him alone, barefoot and nearly naked. Yes, that might have been moderately imprudent, no matter how many scrapes she had under her fingernails from peeling carrots with a tiny, dull knife.

Back in her bedroom, Elizabeth folded the pages of the book together again, resigning to stay put in Act II until further notice. Her father's book was at least right about one thing: she was not alone.

⁂

The next day, almost ten days after her rant in the Countess's chambers, Elizabeth awoke to a morning of freedom. She should have gone to Mass. It was Sunday, and when the Count was present, all servants must attend. But no one would notice her absence. What was the point, she figured, except to mark another week in this baffle? She didn't understand the mumbling at the front of the chapel anyway. It wasn't real. None of this was real.

So, she had five hours to spend however she wanted. There were things to do, items she needed, but she had no idea how to get them. She decided to take a long stroll into the village and see if she could find something so simple as a hairbrush, or some baking soda. She hadn't brushed her teeth properly in weeks now, and the image of Gaspar's dental decay still brought shivers. Surely, she could invent something similar to dental floss.

She walked around the side of the estate, intending to cross through the grove of strawberry trees she had passed with Gaspar on her first day. As she rounded the western wing, Aleix appeared, leading a large brown and white horse with a loose rein. He tipped his head and Elizabeth wondered how he cleaned his teeth.

"Off on another adventure?" he asked.

"Hardly. Just going to the village to get some things."

"Like that?" He laughed. "You'll get blisters walking so far in those shoes. Can't you wait until the livery wagon on Tuesday?"

"The livery wagon?"

"Brings staff into the village twice a week. But perhaps you've been in the scullery."

"It feels like I've always been there."

"Well," he said, "you're in luck. I can take you on Ferdy here."

Elizabeth caught her breath and swallowed. She regarded the tall beast with appropriate respect. Despite having ridden madly through a dark forest, she still dreaded the idea of being so dependent on its whims. "Thank you, but—"

"You're not still afraid? After last week? That's absurd."

"No. No, it's not absurd. Not when you think how large he is compared to me, and how, you know, alive."

"Let me get this straight. You can play endless chains of unbroken notes for the Countess without a heart flutter, but you're afraid to get on a horse? You really are a neophyte. How do you intend to survive? Come on, give me your hand; let's get over this right now. I'll teach you how to ride. Then you'll ride yourself into the village."

"Oh, I don't know." Elizabeth stepped back and regarded his extended hand as though it were a marriage proposal.

"What are you afraid of?" he said. "He won't hurt you."

"He could throw me."

Aleix laughed. "He won't throw you. I promise. Last week you trusted me with much worse than this."

"It's not you I'm worried about."

He reached out and grabbed her hand. "Well, that's your mistake. Now come over here on this stone wall."

Elizabeth allowed him to pull her along. His hand was warm, and though he took hers without permission, she felt a comfort in his strength. For a few moments, things got a little blurry, and before she could find her voice again, she was seated atop the beast, her skirts spread beneath her legs, and Aleix behind her. When the horse moved a few inches, she gasped and sunk her fingers into the mane.

"Hey," Aleix said, grabbing the reins. "Calm down. He can sense your fear."

"Precisely why I never should have gotten up here. Why did he start moving?"

"He was shifting his weight. They do that, especially when two big people get on top of them."

"Is he angry? Maybe he doesn't like having two people on his back. Maybe we're hurting him."

Aleix took some comical pleasure from her concerns. "He's fine. We're just going to walk around the grounds a bit, nice and slow. Then we'll go back to the stables and ride solo into town."

"Ride solo? I don't think I can do that. I'd better get off."

Aleix clicked softly, and the horse started forward. Elizabeth felt her hips rock back and forth with the animal's tread.

"It's okay," Aleix whispered into her left ear. She felt the warmth of him all up her back, his arms around her a welcome assurance as they clip-clopped over gravel and grass, so far below. "You're a character I can't fathom," Aleix said after a few minutes.

"You're not accustomed to fear?"

"You're the only woman I've seen mount the horse astride."

"Astride?"

"Generally, a woman rides with her legs off to one side. But both times, you immediately assumed the position. Not that there's anything wrong with it, but you might get some glares."

Of course, she should ride side-saddle. What was she thinking? "Well, I guess fear can be a safety precaution. The other night, I wasn't thinking—"

"Oh, you were thinking. You were just focused on finding those two in the woods."

Elizabeth hadn't considered that. She had just jumped on and ridden through the dark woods with a man she hardly knew.

"Yes, yes I did do that. And in the end, everything, I mean, I was just—"

"Drunk."

"I was going to say fine."

"You were drunk. If a person can get drunk on courage." Aleix raised the hand holding the reins. "All right, I think you're ready to pick this up a bit now."

The horse began trotting, and Elizabeth lost all sense of romance as she bobbled up and down clumsily, clinging to the mane, her insides curdling. Gratefully, they soon arrived at the stables. Aleix dismounted and helped Elizabeth down. "I'll take Ferdy in. He's a big fellow and can be stubborn."

"In?"

"Into the village. You didn't think I'd send you off unaccompanied on your first ride?"

"Actually, I'm not sure I've got time to go to the village today. Perhaps we can try another day."

As Aleix lead a smaller horse from its stall, Elizabeth continued. "You know, now that I think of it, if I'm late this evening I could get in trouble, and the village is a way off. To be honest, I probably wouldn't have made it past the strawberry trees anyway. I probably just wanted to see those and was using the village as an excuse to make the hike."

Aleix slung a saddle onto her horse and began to fasten the straps. "This is Barbarina. She's small and easily lead."

"Barbarina? Seriously? Wow. Some, comprimarios really got downgraded."

Aleix tightened the saddle straps, then reached for Elizabeth.

"Listen, I really can survive with what I've got. I'll probably never need to go to the village, actually."

"What are you afraid of?"

"Nothing," she said, her voice suddenly pale and opaque.

For a moment, his eyebrows scrunched slightly, the rein still dangling in his right hand, the horse beside him shaking the flies off his mane. Suddenly, he let the reign drop, slipped his arm around her waist, and pulled her to him. He pressed his mouth to hers firmly, as his other hand slipped wonderfully behind her neck.

Spirals widened and amplified within her, sweet, candied, red-ripened strawberries hanging in lush verdant bunches from long green vines under a hot Spanish sun, the dusty road beneath them slipping quickly away. She reached her hands up to take them from the branches, to devour them. To drown in them.

"You know," Reggie had said, carefully placing his score down on the piano. "Don't you? You know."

She didn't know what to say. She felt stuck in the middle of a long hollow archway, not sure which was forward or back.

"Lizzy, you've been avoiding me for two days. You're too straightforward. You can't pull this iceberg thing off."

Elizabeth lifted her hands.

"Don't you dare touch that piano. Oh man, you can't even look at me? Look, I didn't want to have this conversation now. Certainly not here in the middle of a rehearsal."

"So, you did want to have it then?" she said, her eyes still fixed on the undulating patterns of black and white on her keyboard. "I mean, you were going to have it eventually. You weren't going to let me go on thinking everything was wonderful between us forever. The whole student body seems to know, but you were going to let me know eventually, right?"

"Lizzy."

Words came spewing out without thought. "When, I wonder? When were you going to have this conversation? Next term? When you'd had enough time to find a new pianist? Maybe just wait until the production was over? Was that when you were going to tell me? Would that have been a more convenient time to bring it up? Or perhaps after you'd left the country with her?"

"Lizzy, you don't under—all right, all right. I deserve that, you're right. I've behaved like a jerk. I'm a scoundrel. A rascal, a heel, a worm. But there's something you don't know. Something I have never dared to tell you. Something I never dared to even tell myself."

"Don't forget asshole, Reggie. It won't make you any less of one, but let's not forget it."

He lowered himself onto the bench. "I know you don't

understand. You won't, but I am sorry. Lizzy, I'd rather cut off my right arm than hurt you."

She felt herself crumpling, like a piece of aluminum foil collapsing into crusted wrinkles, tighter and tighter inside a menacing fist.

"Then why did you?" she said, or maybe she didn't. She'd never be sure. She squeezed her eyes to halt the forming rush, but sobs came, reluctantly jerking from her. She couldn't look at him. Not ever again. She couldn't look at anyone ever again.

Chattering students were returning from break. She ran from the band room, hiding her face as best she could, and tripping over her own feet.

Then why did you Reggie? Why did you?

Back in Spain, Aleix's lips tasted suddenly sour, his warmth overwhelming, wet with perspiration and rough with years of labor. She pushed him away and wondered for the first time where the scar on his face had come from.

"I'm sorry," she said. "I'm just not, I don't want, I'm so sorry."

She ran.

ACT III
A BARITONE, A TENOR AND A MEZZO WALK INTO A CLOSET...

Chapter Twenty-Two

The Act II Finale was upon Elizabeth before she realized it. That afternoon, Susanna managed to covertly get the page boy up into the Countess's chambers. While the leading women giggled and cooed over the little adolescent brat, Elizabeth rolled her eyes recalling him barreling through the servants' passage.

Cherubino was about fourteen, and true to the opera score, a shameless flirt with Susanna, and incapable of communicating in an intelligent manner in the presence of The Countess.

Susanna pulled out the song he had written, and the Countess requested Elizabeth to accompany. To her surprise, the music was neither Mozart, nor any original composition, but rather a simple melody, possibly by Handel. She couldn't put her finger on exactly what, but the little scoundrel was a plagiarizer anyway. That was enough to fuel her dislike of him, without watching him dance around google-eyeing his Mistress and pinching Susanna.

As in the opera, the plan was to dress the little runt up like a girl and then trick the Count into wooing him in the dark gardens where the rest of the cast would jump in and tsk-tsk, bring the Count to his climactic moment of shame. With the Count away for a few weeks, this was a perfect time to safely dress Cherubino and practice for the little garden charade in the fourth act. Of course, even in the opera, the garden scene never went according to plan. In fact, while the familiar Act II scene played itself out in the Countess's chambers, Elizabeth, momentarily panicked. *The Count is supposed to interrupt this scene. How could they progress with the Count and Figaro off in distant Madrid?*

But, since the rest of this plot had crawled along like winter in February, perhaps the second act had its own mind-numbing pace that would stretch into two weeks of absurdity. She knew better by now than to interfere, so she watched them dress Cherubino up like a girl, admitting a small amount of pleasure when they squeezed him into the stay.

Now that she thought about it, why couldn't they just skip the whole Act II Finale nonsense all together? It really was a much ado about nothing. A lot of villains parading around making threats and heroes squabbling over trivial details and accusations. Nothing really comes of the chaos. They could probably just do without it and skip to the end. What a relief that would be. But in any case, with the Count halfway across Spain, the Finale couldn't happen as it did in the opera, so Elizabeth relaxed, playing some Mozart as these silly characters engaged in their coy flirtations.

Until someone knocked at the door.

"Who is it?" called the Countess.

"Your most gracious servant, Madame. Don Basilio, Master of Music. As always at your shervice."

"What's he doing here?" Susanna whispered.

The Countess shrugged. "Basilio, do we have an appointment this afternoon?"

"Oh no Madame, but I have something very important I need to discuss with you, right away." His voice sounded higher than Elizabeth remembered, and as though he were speaking with his mouth so close to the door that his lips had gotten stuck on the molding.

"Well, I'm engaged at present. Come back later this afternoon, if you don't mind."

"Oh, but I do mind, Madame, and so will you, when you hear what I have to tell you. I am sure you are engaged in slomething at the present moment. Very sure. Something very interesting. I have little doubt that I am interrupting Madame's...acspivities?"

"What's gotten up his cuffs?" Susanna said with a scowl.

"Who knows? But I'll get rid of him quickly."

"What about Cherubino? We can't let Basilio know he's here."

"Why not hide him in a closet?" Elizabeth said, rising from the keyboard.

"Good idea. Cherubino, hurry now. Susanna, take these shirtsleeves and this vest. Hush now, he'll hear. All right, Elizabeth, let him in."

Elizabeth did a cursory inspection of the greeting room and opened the chamber door. Basilio stood so close to its wooden fibers that he nearly fell through. He reeked of liquor, but still managed to summon a loathing glare.

"Oh," he said. "I should have known it was you, little quip. Though I wouldn't run it past you. I wouldn't run it past you in the least to be assisting in more than, sall we shay, extramusical activities. Hymnnn?" A long branchlike arm extended from his cloak and shunned her to the side as he stepped past. "Move out of my way. Madamea? Where is your Mistress, quip?"

"I'm here, Basilio." The Countess Rosina appeared at the door of her dressing room. "What is it that cannot wait?"

"Oh, Missssstresss!" he cooed with a slippery smile. He crossed the Persian carpet, his feet making two slight detours en route to the Countess, where he bowed and snatched up her hand to sneeze on it.

"Basilio!" she said. "You're drunk! What on earth could have compelled you to come here in this state? I insist that you leave at once."

Basilio sighed, or perhaps it was a long-drawn-out whimper. "No. Not yet." He stumbled past her into the dressing room.

"What are you doing, coming in here like that?" Susanna said, wagging a finger. "You get out of here right now."

"Just the three of you?" he said. "How disappointing. Unless of course they are all hiding." Basilio scurried through the room like a black spirit, launching into an inspection of all crevices and corners.

"Who is hiding? What are you talking about?" The Countess said. "I'm telling you to get out of here at once. Elizabeth, open the veranda doors before we all suffocate."

"Aha! So, it is true!" Basilio pulled aside the veranda drapes, revealing a small collection of rifles, strapped together with a brown leather belt.

The women gasped.

"You *are* planning to murder the Count and take over his estate. A coup! A coup! You and your secret lover!"

"You drunkard," said Susanna. "How dare you make such an accusation! You probably planted those weapons yourself!"

"I, sweet Susanna, have never laid a finger upon a weapon. My hands were made for more, m-musical activities. And in any case, I did not invent such a tale but only came here to confirm it was in fact a lay, I mean a lie." He made something of a shrinkage in the general direction of the Countess.

Of course, at that precise moment, Cherubino in the closet had some kind of unfortunate tumble, and what sounded like the Pamplona Running of the Bulls fell crashing behind the previously ignored door.

Basilio's eyes popped open, and he sucked in a self-indulgent gasp and strode in a very uneven line towards the offending closet. "He's in there now, isn't he? Your lover, Madame? Hiding in the closet. Oh, what fabulous treachery."

"Hush up, you fool!"

"What on earth were all three of you ladies doing in here with him all this time, while our Lord and Master is away on affairs of State? Hymnnnnn?" This time the hymn sounded a bit melancholic, as though Basilio were disappointed at not receiving an invitation.

"Get away from there, you drunken idiot!" Susanna howled and blocked the closet with her tiny body.

Just then, a **melittologic** miracle happened. As Basilio hovered threateningly over the chambermaid, a small black bee buzzed past his nose, did a double take, made a U-turn, and returned to alight with obvious delight on the most perfect of perches.

Basilio, solid as stone, regarded the intruder with crossed eyes. "Get it off me," he hissed. "The last time one of these things bit me, my arm swelled up twice its size for a fortnight!"

"You mean you're allergic?" Elizabeth asked, using every mental power to stifle the vision of his nose swelling to a colossus. Nevertheless, the question "Are you allergic" was as foreign here as Maestro Basilio was to Greek mythology. Susanna, the Countess, and the bee-laden nose all turned quizzically in her direction. Could she say anything right in eighteenth-century Spain?

"It's an expression, I mean," she said, "for when someone can't tolerate something. They get very sick, like eating a peanut, or crustaceans. Never mind. Here Basilio, I'll get it off you." Elizabeth waved her hand in an aggressive shoo, but the bee remained blissfully affixed, preening itself contentedly and no doubt drawing up blueprints for some permanent lodgings or a summer home, perhaps.

"Let me try something else," she said lifting a pamphlet from the Countess's dressing table. Sensing the hour to depart, the bee leaped up to call the realtor and make an offer. It spun gleefully around Basilio's spirit-scented head in a happy frolic. Basilio stepped backwards, swatting this way and that, in a wild dance between man and bee, both determined on their goal. At length, he tripped on a footstool and fell over the divan, crashing into a shelving unit. Atop the shelf, a large urn wobbled precariously into a threatening totter. Elizabeth and Susanna both jumped forward to stop the inevitable, but neither could catch the urn in its graceful, slow-motion nosedive for Basilio's greasy head. It impacted directly on his skull, scattering clay fragments across both divan and music teacher.

Naturally, the bee landed back on the hump and began bathing itself.

"Is he dead?" whispered Susanna.

"Well, he certainly isn't *supposed* to be!" Elizabeth said. Actually, now that she thought about it, Basilio was the one character who could probably just disappear completely without affecting the plot at all. *What a wretched thing to think!* "Well," she said, "we should at least get the bee off him. If that nose swells up, he'll asphyxiate. Susanna, pass me that pamphlet again."

The bee climbed aboard her pamphlet, and she carried him back to the veranda.

"Oh, my goodness, the scandal," said the Countess. "And all that nonsense about murdering my husband! Where did all that come from?"

"And those guns," Elizabeth said glancing back at the weapons, "so carefully set out of place."

"But what do we do now?" Susanna asked. "We can't just leave him there."

"Perhaps we should check his heartbeat or see if he's still breathing."

"Right. Yes of course."

But no one moved. And most conveniently, there was a knock at the door.

Elizabeth leaped past the fortepiano into the greeting room, where she slipped on a throw rug and careened headlong into a crystal candelabra that crashed to the floor with a multitude of jingles and clangs. She quickly pulled herself up and limped frantically, slamming into the door, just as someone tried pushing it open.

"What the hell?" said the male voice from the other side.

Elizabeth locked the door and straightened her corset. "Who is it?"

"What on earth is going on in there?" The voice of Dr. Bartolo boomed from the hallway outside. "It sounds like a herd of elephants."

"Oh, no problem," Elizabeth said. "I just slipped on my way to lock the door and knocked my head. I mean a candelabra with an urn. I mean, when I fell on the bee. I'm fine, though. We're all fine."

"I've come to see the Countess."

"Oh, I didn't want to embarrass her, I mean you. Our Mistress is trying on some new mutinies—music teachers— mantillas! So, they sent me to lock the door, but I tripped, or slipped rather on the—"

"You already said that. Who is this? Listen, it's very important I see her right now. Mantillas, those are headdresses, aren't they?"

Susanna began miming something from the dressing room doorway where she stood perched with the Countess. To Elizabeth, it looked like she was doing semaphore with a dolphin strapped around her hips.

"Oh, oh!" Elizabeth said. "I mean, of course. She's trying on some dresses with her new mantillas."

Susanna and the Countess nodded approval, their curls bobbing atop their heads.

"Well, it's vital that I speak to her immediately," said Bartolo. "So, I'll wait until she has something on, but do hurry up. I haven't got all day."

Elizabeth winced. The Countess grimaced. Susanna rolled her eyes and slouched her shoulders, which seemed impossible in that corset. The three women skittered back into the dressing room.

"What do we do?" Susanna said.

"The scandal alone will destroy me," said the Countess. "Bartolo is still bitter about being thwarted. If he finds Basilio in here like this, he'll spread some horrible rumor."

"Well, we can't let him in here," Elizabeth said, but another knock at the door made them jump.

"I haven't got all day," Bartolo bellowed. "I'm supposed to see the magistrate at four. Just tell her to throw something on, for crying in the night!"

"He won't leave me alone," said the Countess.

"What do we do?"

"We do the same thing we did with Cherubino," said Susanna. "We put Basilio in one of the other closets."

The Countess gasped. "A dead body in one of my closets!"

"We don't know that he's dead yet, and anyway, you're going to have to help us," Elizabeth said. "Something tells me he's made of mortar and brick."

Elizabeth and Susanna shuffled quickly about moving furniture, opening the closet door, and clearing a place between shoes, hats, and ribbons. Elizabeth bent over and picked up Basilio's feet. Susanna grabbed one of his hands.

They looked up.

The Countess was not going to drag a dead Basilio into her closet.

Another curt series of knocks at the door.

"We're working on it!" Elizabeth shouted. "Oh, come on Rosina, remember your *vipera*. *Ma se me toccano, sarò una vipera, sarò!* Remember? He can't have taken all that away from you. You're still Rosina under all that powder and hair. Dig deep, woman. *E cento trappole!* **Prima di cedere farò giocar!**"

The Countess stood frozen in her layers of satin and lace, her breasts heaving up and down in waves of regulated precision behind the ruffles at the top of her stay. Gradually, recollection swept across her features like white mist on a silent sea. Ever so slightly her left eyebrow angled upwards and her unnaturally colored lips pursed. With a mighty gust, the sea wind rose, and the Countess Rosina lifted her skirts and stepped forward to take the drunken corpse-arm in her dainty, polished hands.

With a satisfying click, Susanna shut the closet door and dropped the key in her cleavage. Elizabeth helped tidy the dressing table, while Susanna swept the urn fragments behind the divan.

"For the love of olives, what is taking so long in there?" Bartolo hollered.

"All right," said the Countess. "I think we've done it. Elizabeth, please play something calming. Susanna, let him in."

Susanna's tiny feet traipsed back through the greeting room, and she opened the door.

"It's about time! I'm supposed to meet the magistrate at four, you know."

"We're sorry to have kept you waiting," Susanna said.

Bartolo stormed past, tramping carelessly into the changing room. Elizabeth played some soft Chopin, and the Countess lay draped across her divan, her skirts concealing any remnants of the urn.

Elizabeth had never actually seen Bartolo. He stood as tall as Gaspar, but thicker than cheese in the middle, with a strange turned-out gait that made Elizabeth think of ballet classes. He wore a fine dark green suit that bore not a single snare or stain on the inlaid damask fabrics, all of it lined with a subtle bronze embroidery. He had a fat neck beneath his white cravat, and his skin was so un-sunned that his round face matched the white wig atop his head. An unfortunate perspiration problem leaked through his face powder, causing white blotches in his skin, and a brown ring around his cravat.

Dr. Bartolo carried a sizable wooden box in his arms, which he dropped thoughtlessly on the table. "Your papers, Madame, as requested." He plopped onto a chair and retrieved a handkerchief. "I assume we are free to communicate in front of your staff. Do you trust them?"

The Countess trusted her staff implicitly.

Dr. Bartolo wiped his hands with the kerchief. "When I got your summons, I immediately knew where to look. And yes, I would be most delighted to assist your efforts in any way possible."

"Dr. Barto—"

"No need to apologize my dear," he continued. "Let us not

have harsh words between us. You were very young, and I was most foolish. We both made mistakes, but we can now let that go, as we begin our relationship anew. Let us agree to never speak of it."

"Good Doctor," said the Countess, "I'm not sure what you mean by all this. What is in that box?"

The Doctor smiled and lifted a triumphant finger into the air. "The documents you requested. Of course, I would never have been able to access them with His Dominance in town, but I must admit, this whole scheme is so well thought out on your part. You really are a vixen, aren't you?"

"Good Doctor. Am I to understand that you have stolen documents from my husband's offices?"

"I'm sure you'll find all his financial information in here, plus contracts, correspondences, anything you'll need to hold against him in court."

"In court?"

"There will have to be a lengthy legal battle, but we can easily win, with my testimony and yours, along with this little box."

The Countess sat up, her back forming a curious tilt of her sternum. "Dr. Bartolo, what are you talking about?"

"The letter you sent me, Madame." Bartolo rose stiffly and crossed to her, where with some awkwardness he fell to one knee. "I received it this morning, and immediately knew it all to be true. You have long regretted your decision to marry that rat, and plagued by loneliness and despair, have returned to me, your wretchedly-wronged guardian, to assist you and reunite." He reached for her hand with a sweaty palm and held her fingers towards his lips. "I accept your apologies, Madame, all of them, and I am with you as you enact this righteous war on tyranny."

The Countess pulled her hand away. "Apologies? War? Doctor, you forget yourself," she said, rising. "I have no idea what correspondences you have been getting, but I certainly did not send you any note, nor do I have plans to denounce my husband, or betray him. I am shocked that you would believe such dribble, but even more disgusted that you would consider this behavior acceptable on your part. I'm afraid you've been the victim of a jest, Doctor. From whom, I cannot guess, but shame on you, sir. Shame on you for thinking such horrible things of me. Now take that box back to wherever you got it, before anyone else knows of your foolishness."

Elizabeth had long since stopped playing. Her hands rested on the silent keys. Susanna held her lace and needle frozen on her lap.

"You, didn't send me the note?" Bartolo asked.

"Most certainly not. Now I must ask that you leave at once. You are very fortunate that my husband is not here right now."

"Fortunate indeed!" Bartolo clumsily rose to his feet, his fat face reddening. "You think I don't know your hand? You are all playing me for a fool? You think you can have one more round of fun on the old doctor?" The finger he had previously raised in triumph now wagged above his head like a flimsy sword. "Mark my words. I myself will put that note in the hands of the Count on his return, and you will see the flames of outrage and humiliation cast back upon you, Madame. He will have you thrown out to the wolves!"

"And I will tell him how you brought that forged document to my chambers along with his personal documents and financial papers, which you yourself testified in front of my ladies that you stole with the intent to overthrow him."

"You rake!" the doctor bellowed, slamming his hand down upon the Countess's toiletries table with an unfortunate whack. The whole structure wobbled onto two legs, propelling a canister up from its silver throne and dispersing white powder evenly across the Doctor's nice, green suit. "The devil!" he said, coughing. "Look what you've done! I can't meet the magistrate like this. Woman! Are you set out to destroy me in any way you can?"

"Well, actually," Elizabeth began, "that whole 'trying to force her to marry you' thing in the first opera, locking her inside and monitoring her like a prisoner—"

"Elizabeth!" *The Countess was not pleased.*

The be-powdered Bartolo frantically slapped his waistcoat and pants, further impounding the grit.

"Dr. Bartolo, it's obvious that someone has played a terrible ruse on you, and I'm sorry for that," the Countess said. "But it was most certainly not me. Now you must leave at once and return that box to my husband's offices before it is discovered missing, or you will have much more explaining to do than the state of your clothing."

"To hell with your box! I've got to meet the magistrate at four, and I can't do it looking like this. I won't leave this room until you get me some respectable garments."

"What?" Susanna said. "We don't have anything in the house that would fit you."

"Well, I'm not leaving looking like this, and that's final." The Doctor flipped up the wings of his tailcoat and plopped down decidedly on a gold satin ottoman.

"Perhaps Beatriz can do something with them," Elizabeth suggested, "your clothes, I mean."

"Yes," said Susanna. "she's a real genius when it comes to fabrics. We could bring the suit down to her and ask her to clean the powders out. You could wait up here until she's done. What do you think, Mistress?"

The Countess subtly tilted her head in the direction of her two closets, both presently occupied.

An unspoken conversation passed between the three ladies. A dialogue of head tilts, shoulder nudges and every underemployed facial muscle.

"We can't put him in there!"

"What about the other two closets?"

"Well, it's not like he's going to fit into one of these dresses."

"Don't be ridiculous. The stench alone."

"The what?"

"Can we please make a decision? Someone is going to be discovered eventually."

"We still have another closet."

"Oh, what's to become of us?"

The ladies' eyes widened and narrowed, stretched, and dug furrows that might cause signs of early aging. The Doctor turned back and forth between them, always just missing the last repartee, until he grabbed his right shoulder, yelping in pain.

"Confound you harpies. I've twisted my neck!"

The Countess spoke at last. "Very well. Doctor, you may step inside a closet and take off your clothes—"

"Not that closet!" All three women jumped forward.

"That closet there," said Susanna. "Go in and take off your suit and I'll run it down to Beatriz."

"Meanwhile, why don't you tell me where you got this box, and I'll return it safely to its home," said the Countess Rosina, "before anyone notices it has gone missing."

The Doctor took off his jacket and waistcoat while explaining exactly where she should return the box. Susanna packed the Doctor into the third and final closet and he passed out his pants. "Hurry up. Four o'clock, remember."

Susanna rolled her eyes and folded the pants up without even looking for a clock. "Madame, what is going on here? First Basilio gets a crazy message, then Bartolo?"

"Someone is certainly out to frame me," said the Countess.

"Well, it could be worse," Susanna said.

"Forgive me," Elizabeth said, "how could it be worse than a dead Basilio, a naked Bartolo, and a cross-dressed Cherubino?"

"The Count? Imagine if he walked in right now, with all of them testifying to the Mistress's treachery. It's a good thing he's on the other side of Spain."

"Good point. Of course, you're right. But on that note, we'd better get going. I'll bring these clothes down to Beatriz and drop the guns at the armory on my way. Susanna, can you return the box to the Count's offices?"

"Yes, of course."

"Madame, you should stay here, just in case anyone wanders in."

"But should we leave her alone?" Susanna asked. "I mean, someone is out to get her. What if something else happens while we're gone?"

"Susanna, we've got to get all this evidence out of here. This stuff is crazy."

"Oh go, go!" said the Countess. "I can take care of myself. I've got them all locked away, and none of them want to be caught in their present situation. Just go quickly."

"Mistress," Susanna said, "perhaps you should look around a bit. Make sure there aren't any other surprises hiding under the bed."

"Good thinking. I'll do a thorough search."

The Countess's courage and audacity had appeared. So, there were three men locked in her closets. That wasn't anything a coloratura-slinging soprano couldn't handle. Her voice was suddenly more candid with a hint of playfulness. Her eyes not blinking off some dusty anxiety, but bright and piercing past lights and orchestra. Her posture ebbed and flowed with fullness of life, making her draperies so much more appropriate. No more moaning and sighing, no more woeful abused and neglected, but returned had Rosina to her own stage, afire, a *vipera*.

Susanna grabbed the document box. Elizabeth stuffed Bartolo's clothes under one arm and hugged up the rifles in the other, and they all headed for the chamber door. What a sight they must have made, the scullery-pianist laden with powdery clothes and rifles, the chambermaid barely able to hold up the big mahogany box, and their lace and satin-covered Mistress glowing at the ridiculous prospect of being left alone with three imbecilic men stuffed in her closets.

"And for goodness, sake, Madame," Elizabeth said, "lock that door behind us!"

⚜

Waddling under her load towards the servants' stairs, Elizabeth finally had a chance to consider what had just happened. Someone had obviously gotten Basilio drunk and filled his head with all that nonsense. Unless of course in this more violent version of Beaumarchais's story, the Countess was indeed plotting to mount a revolution and murder her husband. Elizabeth considered that possibility as she clunked down the small winding staircase. She would stop on the first floor to rid herself of the guns. Oh, she hoped Aleix wasn't in the armory. She certainly wasn't looking forward to seeing him again after her behavior in the stables. In fact, she wouldn't mind if she could wrap this whole plot up and go home without ever seeing Aleix the armorer again.

When she finally managed to bumble her way around the steps, she found the first-floor door open, and the familiar, friendly face of Figaro greeted her. "Elizabeth! My goodness, what on earth are you doing with all those guns? And whose clothing is this? Looks like that just needs a good whacking out in the sunshine."

"Oh, Figaro," she said with relief. "Yes, it's all a very long story, but would you please be a dear and take these awful things back to the armory? I suspect Aleix is missing some weapons. Please don't ask. Your charming fiancée will fill you in later. And I'll just run these clothes down to Beatriz for—"

Elizabeth froze, her throat suddenly constricted in such a clench that she could neither take air in, nor release it. She was computing some internal error, some horrific thought that was so brutal, so troublesome that her own mind was hiding it from her grasp. It flitted around from room to room while she tried to grasp its tail, to take a hold of it and get a solid look at its eyes and ruffle its whiskers. She held herself frozen in this stance as in a sort of hopeful prayer, unbreathing, wishing that time around her would also stand still, slow down for a moment while she figured it out, solved the equation, understood the problem, resolved the cadence to something far worse than any Mozart opera.

Then all at once, her thoughts unraveled themselves like the final cadence of a Bach fugue. "Figaro. You're in Madrid right now. You're not here."

"Oh, that's no worry. Everything's all right. Turns out the summons to Madrid was all a big hoax, or a mistake. I'm still not sure which, but we weren't expected, and no sooner had we arrived than the Count received a message from home. Not sure about what, but it must have been serious because he sped off ahead before we even had a chance to pack properly."

Elizabeth squealed through her constricted throat. Her feet scrambled beneath her, slipping on the tiny, pointy heels of her stupid, impractical boots. She stumbled down the first three steps, bruising her shins and knees while the stack of rifles scattered on the floor, Bartolo's clothing a tangled mess between them. She felt like one of those cartoon characters whose legs start spinning five seconds before they move. "The Count. He's returned?"

"Yes," Figaro said. "Are you okay? Do you need help with anything?"

"The Countess! I've got to go."

At last, her feet remembered how to climb, and she whipped up the stairs pulling the very walls around her. When she arrived breathless on the second floor, a man was shouting. Elizabeth ran through the gallery and caught herself up at the corner, where she found the Count pounding on his wife's door. Seeing Elizabeth, he dropped his shoulders and stepped back, gripping his fists behind him. She smiled at her master, trying to control her rushing breath, and strolled forward nonchalantly, her sweaty hands cupped together. "Welcome home, sir. I'm just here for my shift to start."

"Your shift?"

"Yes sir. I play for the Countess on the fortepiano?"

The Count's dark brown eyes rolled slightly at the recollection of Elizabeth's job. "Oh yes. Don't you need some sheet music for that?"

"Sometimes sir, but mostly I just play from memory."

"You must have quite a musical memory. I've never been able to play anything unless I had the music right in front of me."

Elizabeth had forgotten that the Count could play the fortepiano. Of course he could, if the previous opera had transpired as written. She found it difficult to imagine this man, who seemed all tyranny and deceit, making something so trivial and human as beautiful music. She shook the visions of this from her mind.

"Well," he continued, "perhaps you'll do a better job than me at opening this door."

"Are you sure she's in there, sir? Perhaps she and Susanna went out for an afternoon stroll. Have you checked the gardens?"

The Countess's voice rang out from beyond the door, "I'm sorry, I'm not well at the moment."

"I'm sure." He knocked again. "Madame, it is your husband. Now open this door."

"Madame, it's Elizabeth. Now we're worried. Perhaps you should let us in, and we can assist you in some way."

"Oh... all right."

The door unlocked and smoothly swung open, the Countess hanging on its side. The Count swept past her into the greeting room where he did a cursory check, then passed immediately into the dressing room.

"Mistress," said Elizabeth, "Are you ill?"

The Countess hung on the door for support. "I don't know," she said. "I just feel so dizzy and tired. I wouldn't have gotten up from the divan but for you, dearest."

The Count tromped through the dressing room into the bedroom, his boot heels resounding on the floors.

"Oh, Mistress," Elizabeth said, "you're burning up!"

"Am I?" She allowed Elizabeth to assist her to the nearest chair. "I don't feel hot. In fact, I feel a bit cold. Is there a chill in here?" She sank down amidst her satins and laces, lightly stroking her neck with a trembling finger, her head a teetering top of unfocused motion. "Where is my husband? Did I hear his sweet voice? Or only imagine it?"

"I am here," the Count said from the dressing room doorway, where he stood looming between deception and chaos. "Are you not well, my dear?"

"I am fine, I'm sure. Just a blast of heat. Perhaps I got too much sun yesterday, that's all."

The Count approached his wife, dropping to a knee, and Elizabeth stepped away. "Perhaps Madame would prefer if I did not play my shift this afternoon? Would the silence be better for you?"

"Oh no," the dying Countess replied. "You're playing always makes me feel better. Please stay and let me hear some of that wonderful Polish man's work."

The Countess waved a foggy hand towards the fortepiano and smiled dimly. Elizabeth took her seat at the instrument, playing a light nocturne while the Count raised a hand to his wife's forehead. The Countess took the hand to her breast. "I'm so glad it is you," she said. "I thought you were in Madrid for a fortnight. Is everything all right?"

The Count seemed to be melting under her wiles, his posture relenting, his eyes softening. He focused unabashedly on her, his ears no longer listening for invaders in the closets. The sudden sincerity of concern struck Elizabeth to her core. Damn the bastard. He was a proud, violent, power-hungry pervert who ought to be hog-tied and hung out to dry. But here he was, brought to his knees before the Countess Rosina, frightened.

Elizabeth wasn't so ignorant of everything in eighteen-century Spain. She may occasionally forget about medical terminology or dental floss, but she knew what a fever meant. It meant you might die. So, in one sense she was awestruck by the Countess's sudden *vipera* to call on such a powerful card. The fear did seem to stir some humanity in the man, a tender concern that Elizabeth could not deny.

The chamber door opened, and Susanna slipped inside. Seeing the Count on his knees, she gasped a high-pitched sort of squawk, then immediately covered her mouth with a dainty white hand and fluttered through the room.

"Susanna," the Count said, rising to his feet. "I'm sorry if I frightened you." His voice was too sweet, like caramel on a hot fudge sundae. "I was called back to Seville earlier than expected."

Susanna curtseyed demurely. "Welcome home, sir."

The Count's eyes followed her like a creepy portrait, the rest of him still, his nose and tail pointedly fixed on the prey.

Elizabeth felt her stomach lurch. She wanted to throw up, or at least to get up and throw this primitive excuse for an instrument over the veranda. All this pretense of beauty and loveliness. Playing this music in the middle of all these lies. *Was this why she played?* To make the disgusting seem more acceptable?

She thought back to her conversation in the armory with Aleix. She had told him she didn't believe in romantic love, and he had accepted that without question. Agreed with her. And here was the proof acting itself out in front of her fortepiano. *This is what love looks like*. She always knew it. Always suspected it. The best one could hope for came down to a landowner lusting after his wife's chambermaid, and plying all levels of deceit to violate her, while his wife feigned a fever, calling on whatever tenderness might remain from the prequel to draw his concern away from the three idiots hiding in her closets. Elizabeth's hands had wandered into the military rhythms of a John Phillip Sousa march. She cursed under her breath and flipped back into some Schumann.

"Well, my lady," said the Count, "perhaps you should take to bed and get some rest. I know Dr. Bartolo is due here this afternoon. I will be sure to send him up to check on you."

"That would be very nice."

He offered her an arm. "Shall I help you to your bed?"

"Oh no, darling, Susanna will help me. Thank you though. I'll send word when I'm feeling better."

The Count bowed to excuse himself and turned to leave. Right as he reached for the door handle, closet number one reverberated with an explosion of pubescent sinus pressure, mucus and gruff. "Haaah- chewwwwww!"

Elizabeth jumped up and pulled a handkerchief from between her breasts. She blew into it, shaking her head and clearing her throat in as manly a voice as she could muster. "Oh," she said, "I am so sorry." She padded her eyes with the kerchief. "My goodness, that was horrible. Please excuse me, sir."

The Count seemed mollified but skeptical. Elizabeth cursed herself. Now she was in on it: all the deceptions, the lies. But even if she wanted the Act II Finale to work its way out, this was not the time. The Count needed to suspect Cherubino in one closet. Not three closets full of dead, naked, drunk, cross-dressed men.

"Well, my lady," he said, "if you are ill, I suggest an infection in your chambers. You might consider a healthier staff." He lifted a doubtful eyebrow towards Elizabeth. "Perhaps you should ask Basilio to play for you."

"Basilio?" the Countess said, rising to her feet.

Naturally, at that moment, summoned from beyond the grave at the mention of his name in a moment of off-hand flattery, Don Basilio let erupt a drunken belch of such magnitude, its echo bounced in sonorous perfection through the lofty ceilings, crown moldings and crystal chandeliers. Even Elizabeth had difficulty imagining which closet it came from.

The Count spun around to see dainty little Susanna, all corset and curls, lift a dainty little hand to her dainty little lips and smile. "Excuse me."

"Madame, your servants seem to be suffering from maladies of the throat."

"Whatever do you mean, dear?"

"I mean, they all sound like men. Like drunk men."

"What a terrible thing to say. Don't you girls mind him at all. He's always rude when he's been traveling. Now come help me, dear."

The Count relinquished his position between the three closets. Behind him, Susanna and Elizabeth's eyes met helplessly across the great expanse of dressing room. He gave his arm to his wife, and together they passed through. The Countess leaned on him lightly, her free hand dabbing at her forehead, and just as they crossed the center mark of the great, blue, Persian rug...

Door number three, behind which the good Dr. Bartolo no doubt sat quivering in his shirtsleeves, and perhaps driven to a nervous digestion by the horrific knowledge of his predicament, released an unusually long, bubblingly pungent, and distinctly male sound of his own.

That is, he let go a bean blower.

He cracked the slitters.

He deflated the eggy doorknob.

He threw some flapper flames?

He fumigated the fragrant fuzzy, hailed the Emperor Crush, did the one-gun salute, quacked the ozone layer, roasted the jockey-burner ka-boom, squeaked one out, stepped on a duck... Oh what the heck.

He farted.

The Count's eyes shot up at the closet doors and he released his wife.

Susanna looked at the Countess.

Elizabeth looked at the Countess.

The Count looked at the Countess.

Inside his closet, a trembling Bartolo probably wiped a bead of sweat from his forehead as he peered through the keyhole to look at the Countess.

Two robins on the veranda stopped their gleeful chirping and craned their heads through the open door to look at the Countess.

It was a beautiful day in Seville. Hardly a cloud in the sky, and a soft tickling breeze tripped across every nose with hints of citrus, sawdust and dark green leaves warming in the sun. Basilio's bee returned and buzzed merrily through the room, passing each character, swerving in and out, looking for some legendary facial perch on which to place all one's pollinated hopes and dreams.

Buzz... buzz... buzz...

Disappointed, he made a final spin and shook his stinger at the sad lot of real estate before departing back to the sunlight.

"Madame, you have a man in your closet."

"All right," said the Countess. "Yes. There is a man in the closet."

"And when I arrived in your chambers, you were alone in here with him. Your musician met me at the door, and Susanna came in after I arrived."

"If you will just remain calm," she said, straightening the lace draperies that hung from her sleeves, "I can give you a perfectly reasonable explanation."

The Count strode towards door number two and yanked on the doorknob. He stepped back and gestured. "Unlock this door at once."

"You suspect me, when I am not guilty."

"My suspicions are only now confirmed, for it was due to this matter that I have left Madrid in such haste. This!" The Count pulled a paper from his coat sleeve. "Was put into my hands in Madrid. A brief but stunningly accurate portrait of betrayal."

The Countess gasped. "You dare accuse me?"

Elizabeth sat back on her piano bench and watched the disgusting disparity of eighteenth-century marriage play itself out. The Count was fine with taking every servant girl he could to his bed, but even the suspicion of infidelity in his wife, and it's an opera.

"I see you are suddenly restored to health. Now open that closet."

"Who sent you that note?" the Countess asked. "Who dared to malign my name in this manner? You show me that man's face, and I will gladly open that closet for you."

"I don't need more testimony," said Count Almaviva. "But if it will speed this along, then see for yourself." The Count threw the paper down at his wife's feet and strode back to the closet door, shaking on the handle again. "Come out of there, you coward. Hiding in a closet. Is this the best you could do, Madame?"

Susanna stepped forward and lifted the note to her mistress's hands. The Countess unfolded it and read aloud.

"My good sir, I feel it is my duty to inform you of the impending destruction of all you hold dear. Indeed, you must leave Madrid at once and return to Seville before it is too late. There you will uncover scandals not only of marital infidelity, but an even larger plot to condemn you, possibly involving bloodshed."

The Countess flipped the page over. "But this isn't even signed," she said. "You have no idea what scoundrel penned this nonsense."

The unsigned notes were apparently getting together while everyone slept and covertly populating a paper universe.

"Exactly what I had thought Madame," returned the Count, "until I arrived here to find the truth of it."

"Until you arrived? You mean, until you jumped on your horse and let the dust fly behind you as you galloped back here to condemn me."

"For the last time, open this door."

"Before I do, I will tell you who is in that closet, and you sir, will owe me an apology."

The Count kicked at the door, vibrating its fibers against the hinges. A whimpered moan emanated from within.

"I highly doubt that," said the Count.

"The man in my closet is none other than your own Major-Domo."

Elizabeth perked up. *There was some Mozart in that.*

"Figaro," the Count laughed. "Figaro, who was behind me all the way back from Madrid, somehow bested me here and made it up the stairs before me to hide away in your closet?"

"He was eager, naturally, to see his fiancée. Where else would he go looking for her?"

"But she was not here when I arrived."

"You mean when you came pounding on my door with rage

in your voice, after your gallop back from Madrid? Naturally, realizing he had arrived here before you, and that you were already, in such a state of fury, he panicked and jumped into the closet."

That was actually pretty good.

"Madame, that's insane."

"Is it? Can you state that you hopped off your horse and climbed the steps so directly, stopping not even at the necessary? Not even to have a drink, or wash your face? Indeed, there is no dust upon you. That's not your riding jacket at all."

Well, that was just stupendously impressive.

"Very well," he said through clenched teeth, "if that's Figaro in there, and your story is true, Figaro speak up. Reveal yourself."

"He's frightened."

"Figaro isn't afraid of anything."

"You barged in, flapped an accusatory note in my face, kicked the door..."

The Count stepped closer to his wife, and her eyes wandered to her skirts, which she straightened with trembling hands.

My gosh woman, don't look down now. Eye contact! Eye contact!

"Figaro!" The Count called out. "I demand that you speak up at once."

"Figaro, don't you dare," said the Countess. "Let him stew in his jealous rage. It seems to please him so much. Anonymous notes. Wasn't it another such note that sent you out to Madrid in the first place? How many tales are you going to fall victim to? Destroy your home? Your marriage? Your reputation? When will enough be enough?"

"When you open that closet door, Madame."

"I don't have the key," she said. "He is Figaro, after all. He pulled it out of the lock as he ran in there."

Elizabeth caught herself grinning.

"Then I will go to the basement to retrieve the master," said the Count, "and perhaps we'll run into Figaro on the way and he'll tell me all about it." The Count grabbed his wife's elbow.

"We?"

"I can't have you helping him out. I'll lock the chamber doors from the outside and *Figaro* will be trapped here until we all return with the closet key." The Count wagged a finger at Susanna. "You're coming too, and you, piano girl. No doubt, one of you has that damn key tucked into your corset and will release him as soon as I'm gone."

"Now my servants are plotting against you," said the Countess. "Do you hear yourself? If you can't stop this, you won't need a mutiny in your ranks. You will surely destroy yourself."

"We shall see, Madame."

Elizabeth rose and followed the Count as he dragged his wife back through the greeting room where he reached for the door-knob but stopped.

"Wait a moment. What is this?" He bent over and lifted an axe.

"What is that?" said the Countess.

"It's an axe," the Count said, considering it.

"An axe? Susanna?"

Susanna shook a doubly perplexed head. "I have no idea, Madame."

"Wait, what?" cried Elizabeth, pushing Susanna aside to get a glimpse of the thing. "There are no *axes in Figaro!*"

"No matter," said the Count, releasing his wife's arm. "It seems we don't need to go to the basement. If you will not open that closet door, I will break it down myself."

The Count swept past the ladies and stomped back into the dressing room, axe in hand. The Countess and Susanna followed him, but Elizabeth stayed back.

Arguing commenced. Elizabeth imagined the Countess throwing herself in front of the closet door, probably confessing about Cherubino, maybe even Bartolo or Basilio, but eventually the Count would have no part of it and just chop his jealous way through to kill whichever unfortunate man he found on the other side.

She sank into a chair and let the arguing blend into clouds of sound. *Where, in the name of countertenors, had that axe come from?* Had it been there all along and she had just never noticed an oddly placed axe leaning quietly against the Countess's chamber wall? She had already passed through that door three times today. And she hadn't seen it once?

Perhaps Basilio had carried it in. Or Bartolo. Surely, they would have noticed Basilio carrying an axe into the Countess's chambers. Not something one lets slide into the subconscious. *Oh, there's old Basilio, the music master, carrying his axe again.*

Grinding, maybe. Carrying, no.

Things were escalating in the dressing room, but what could she do? If she tried to interfere, goodness knows what could happen. Someone might just pre-invent nuclear power and blow up the whole country. Or they might discover Dr. Bartolo smoking weed and doing yoga in that closet. If axes were randomly appearing in the universe, what else could she realistically do? With such nonsensical events destined to plague the pages of this literary nightmare, what was the point of even trying?

"All I'm saying is that we should reconsider the repertoire for the scenes program."

Elizabeth remembered the scene well. They were in the music department President's office. It was a nice-sized room, filled with passed down furniture and the smell of industrial air freshener. An American flag stood beside a wall of framed marching bands parading around various stadiums across the country, all tightly fitted in the school's blue and yellows.

McDanials had caused this scene with the phrase, "Reconsider the repertoire for the scenes program."

Elizabeth thought Reggie should have caved. Give the man an

olive branch every now and then. The poor guy detested the whole opera venture, everyone knew that. He only did it because he was forced to. Didn't want to lose tenure. Why not let him win one every now and then? For the band. Was it really this big of a deal?

But there Reggie sat, uncharacteristically red in the face, slouched low in his chair, his arms crossed.

"Perhaps," said the President of the Music School, "we should start at the beginning. Jim, why don't you tell Mr. Greene and Ms. Kirtenpepper what you told me yesterday."

Yesterday must have been when the fireworks hit their grand finale. McDanials had been groaning for the last week, and Reggie had snapped four times in rehearsals already, but until this moment, Elizabeth didn't even know what the war was all about or why they had included her, an accompanist and coach. She certainly didn't have any administrative power, but then as the opera program was still in its infantile years, neither did Reggie. He had probably called her for support, although they didn't talk much these days.

She wanted to open a window.

"It's pretty simple," McDanials began, looking back and forth between herself and the President, as though Reggie was on trial. "This University, as you know, has recently suffered two tragedies. Two of our students have taken their own lives. We may never be able to fully comprehend why. All across the country, this is happening. Young kids, killing themselves in high school, college, for what? And what's more, everyone knows it's contagious. Once one kid does it, others follow. Studies have proven this, Jack. I'm not making it up."

"Oh yes, yes, of course," said the President, lifting his head from the required bow when referencing a tragedy. "Of course, Jim, we've all gotten the memos, but neither of these kids were in the music department."

"Yes," said McDanials, "but we have a responsibility to protect our kids."

"Protect them?" Reggie spurted out. "Protect them from what? From opera?"

"From certain subject matters, yes. All I'm suggesting is that we limit our choices to more comical pieces for a while."

Hardly suggesting when we're all called to the President's office at four o'clock on a Friday afternoon.

"Comical pieces?" Reggie said. "You've got to be kidding."

"No, I am not, Mr. Greene," snapped McDanials. "A woman jumping off a building is hardly a subject for these kids to be immersing themselves in right now."

"You're talking about one of the greatest masterpieces of all time. Surely, we can't start censuring Puccini."

"It's not just *Tosca*," continued McDanials. "It's all of them. Aida buried alive. Butterfly stabbing herself. These stories are disturbing. You've got at least six of them on this upcoming scenes program. They are totally inappropriate, and, frankly, dangerous."

"Dangerous opera, Jim?" said the President.

"In this climate, making the kids bury themselves day and night in these scores could be dangerous, yes. Things could happen. And I wouldn't be surprised if the school were held accountable."

Reggie covered his face with his hands and shook his head. "Held accountable? Jack, tell me you're not listening to this."

All three men in the room had looked at her expectantly. Whether they needed an outsider opinion, or they wanted a female viewpoint, she couldn't tell. Unfortunately, she couldn't think of anything to say, and only sat there mutely, her mouth slightly ajar, like a place holder in the conversation.

"Well now, Reggie," the President said at length. "I can see why Jim is concerned."

"Of course you can," said Reggie, "Of course, we're all concerned now that he threatened financial losses."

"Reggie!" Elizabeth finally said something.

Reggie shot up from his seat. "Well, isn't that why we're even listening to this? How many kids do we have at this college? Twelve thousand? And how many of them do you think have ever even seen an opera? Maybe, just maybe, if we'd stop selling the whole life-should-be-easy, incessant happy endings, princesses and white horses and happily ever afters, the kids wouldn't feel so alone. Alone with stress and failures and looking for some happy-answer-all narcotic. They're so threatened by their own lives. Before we go full censorship, maybe we should consider these stories are about them, about their own lives."

"All the more reason we shouldn't be putting such self-destructive ideas in their heads."

"Look," Reggie said. "what's *Aida* about really? It's a love triangle that came to no good. You think the kids don't relate to that? Or misplaced faith, what about that? Like *Butterfly*. For crying out loud, haven't any of you ever trusted someone who used you?"

Elizabeth stiffened, but Reggie didn't look at her. He hadn't cut his bangs in a long time. They hung over his darkened eyes. He also needed a shampoo.

Reggie continued. "Or even just pure down-to-earth manipulative evil like that *Tosca* scene you're so riled up about. We raise our kids with all this happy-happy, and then we send them into the world expecting perfection. But when it doesn't happen, they think they've failed somehow. There's a reason all these stories live on year after year, centuries later. The kids need them. We need them. If taking them away is the direction this school is going, then you win, Jim. You can have your stinking band room back. We might as well have them sing nursery rhymes."

❦

A half an hour later, the tower bell across the quad tolled the end of the school week. A wave of sweet cacophony rose up to the President's open window, chipper voices hiking to dorms and meals, full of weekend plans.

Elizabeth stood on the grass and watched a red squirrel dodge the clumps of backpackers, this way and that, up the tower steps onto a low stone parapet, where it squatted down and nibbled away at something as temporary as a nut.

"Lizzy!"

Reggie ran towards her, passing students bowed towards cell phones, weaving in and out, just like the squirrel, his greasy bangs bouncing in the wind, his left arm carrying his satchel of scores.

She waited for him.

"I wanted to thank you," he said catching his breath. "Thank you for coming to that."

"I didn't do much."

"Oh, but you did. That stare you gave was just the ticket."

"Reggie, I didn't do anything."

"Well, we won. And what a relief. I think if we had to teach them all new music, we really would have some tragedies." He was still getting his breath back. "Old McDonald has always been against the program. That's what that was about, no altruism lost on him."

"Indeed."

"Listen, Lizzy. How, are you? I mean, are you all right and everything?"

"I'm not a Verdi heroine, Reggie. I'm not going to lose my mind."

"Oh damn, I was kind of hoping...sorry. Too early to be joking. Listen, I should have told you. Long ago. I should have let you in. Trusted you with it. I was just scared, I guess. It's hard to explain. I'm just so sorry."

"You don't need to apologize anymore."

"I can't stand that I hurt you."

"What do you want me to say? I love you. I will always love you."

A pair of perfumed teenage girls passed them, chattering in loud, colorful tones.

"Oh Lizzy. Can't you just, I don't know, admire me?"

"It's Elizabeth."

Behind him, across the expanse of quad, the President's office window reflected the orange light of a setting sun. Like some triumphant courtroom scene had taken place, she felt elated. Though it was so far away, she could see herself clearly in that shining window. Some deeply satisfying personal reflection had been uncovered in that meeting, in that office, through that small arched, shining portal.

The answer was through the window.

How sopranos die.

In *Madame Butterfly*, Cio-Cio San tearfully says goodbye to her son with a fury of high notes and then stabs herself. *Carmen* is also stabbed, but by a jealous lover. *Norma* gets burnt alive. *Aida* gets buried alive. In *La Traviata*, Violetta sacrifices her ailing health for her lover. *Rigoletto*'s Gilda sacrifices herself to assassination for a false lover, and *Lucia* kills her bridegroom, then sings a whole lot of crazy talk before sinking into a broken-heart sort of end. And so it goes throughout history, these and other great sopranos suffering every known method of mortal sacrifice up to and including the ever-strange incident of *Manon Lescaut* dying of thirst in the deserts of Louisiana...

Martyrdom is the undisputed fate of treble clef singers. Butterfly, Lucia, Carmen, Gilda. Rather than sit back and let anyone else declare their destiny, they would all pay the ultimate price. No soprano among them sacrificed the smallest **cadenza** or fermata to the tyrannical enemy, be it father, brother, lover, husband, or conductor. Noble heroes all in an unending battle for women's rights and freedom. More to be honored than the bravest of soldiers. Vulnerable in body, but not in spirit. Incorruptible by life or fear. Each a triumph of humanity.

But still, rising a length above them all, the reigning queen of opera's most morbid stories, the role model for soprano self-sacrifice, the most legendary of heroines, stood the femme fatale of all opera, the resolute, the steadfast, the ever-unwavering diva of them all, *Tosca*.

Floria Tosca. The opera diva playing an opera diva. When the hour of her great cadence came, this soprano stepped proudly into the light. No sorrow, no remorse, no regret, no hesitation bore her down. She simply stabbed the bastard and left his cooling baritone corpse on the stage floor. Then, after watching her lover get assassinated (opera's casualties also contain a healthy list of dead tenors), she hit a dazzling high note and jumped off the parapet of the Castle Saint Angelo, plummeting through her final moments in a wild twist of velvet and sequins, her rhinestone tiara adhering doggedly to her large, synthetic wig.

Tosca jumped.

Vissi d'arte, vissi d'amore. I lived for art, I lived for love.

"Why do you play, Elizabeth?"

Elizabeth sat in the Countess's waiting room, deeply buried in her reflections of heroines and tragedies, while the *Figaro* tragedy played out in the next room with distant tympanic rumbles. Once again, they couldn't help themselves.

Non feci mai male ad anima viva! I never caused harm to a living soul...

Elizabeth Kirtenpepper had not sought out the lights of the stage. Music was a harmless artform. There was something saintly about being an artist, slaving away in solitude hour after hour, polishing up something so temporal that it's forgotten as soon as the applause ends and the ushers begin picking up programs from the auditorium floor.

Just beyond the door of the Countess's dressing chamber, the bright light of a Spanish afternoon poured in through the veranda doors. If this plot had not taken so many bizarre and unfortunate twists, the pageboy Cherubino would have jumped off that very balcony to escape the Count's wrath.

So, the window was the way.

Con man furtiva quante miserie conobbi aiutai. With a furtive hand, so many troubles I aided.

Elizabeth rose and pressed down her skirts. Merciless destiny had been absurdly bequeathed to her, a mere servant, a comprimario, a part of the fixtures. Like Tosca, she would have to be unflinching. She must stand up for the true plot. She must be willing to sacrifice, like all those golden-haloed sopranos.

Sempre con fè sincera la mia preghiera. Always with sincere faith my prayer rose.

She thought about saying a prayer, but it felt so ridiculous. All that sanctimonious parade was as real as this whole convoluted, operatic nightmare. Look where it had all gotten her. To this. Her final crossing into the unknown.

The Count hollered on and on like a blaring bugle, the Countess and Susanna pleading woodwinds with breaking reeds. Elizabeth slipped through the main stage scene, creeping behind the principles. They did not even see her as she floated trancelike to the window.

Diedi il canto agli astri, al ciel, che ne ridean più belli. I gave my singing to the stars, to heaven, shining more beautifully.

Did they even feel the warm Spanish breeze sweep in when she stepped outside and peered over the stone railing?

Cherubino jumped off of this?

Another absurdity. This wasn't like leaping off the high dive at the local recreation center, which of course she had never done. This was towering, sky-scraping. This was alpine. Even by contemporary architectural standards, this was one hell of a flight of stairs. Elizabeth cursed all those high ceilings on the first floor that gave the ballroom such great acoustics and Aleix's armory those tall storage closets.

And where was the nice soft garden of flowers Cherubio was supposed to land on? Nothing lay beneath this balcony but empty crates and scattered rocks.

Back in the Countess's dressing room, the argument surged forward like an impending tsunami. Soon the Count would lift his axe and chop an impenetrable divide in both his closet and his marriage. It was time for Elizabeth to do what she came to do. It had fallen to her. This was the cadenza. This was the high note.

Nell'ora del dolore, perché, In my hour of sorrow, why...

"No!" a man's voice cried out, and a figure appeared just beyond the courtyard, running and waving his arms. "What are you doing?" he shouted.

It was Aleix, speeding towards the house as if to stop some catastrophe. In his haste, he had even neglected to don his customary satchel. He stopped beneath her veranda, waving at someone. "It's real!" he shouted. "It's all real!" He disappeared into the servants' entrance.

Elizabeth knew better than to hope for a fairy-tale rescue. A soprano does not get rescued by a hero. Quite the contrary, tenors and baritones are usually the cause of her demise. Even as she thought this, the fury of the Count's jealousy (a baritone) raged on behind her. The Countess's pleading tones murmured somewhere beyond.

Perhaps this wouldn't be so devastating. Perhaps Elizabeth would finally wake up back at home, in a pristine hospital bed, or even on her father's bedroom floor, with nothing more to worry about than a nice little bump on the head.

She lifted a leg over the railing and felt the warm white stone beneath her skirts. Her heart pounded unharnessed as she slid her other leg over, feeling the height of her perch with a dizzying terror.

Perché, Signore, perché me ne rimuneri così? Why, Lord why do you repay me so?

The ground below ebbed and swayed as she shimmied herself closer and closer to the edge. Just a few more inches...

A loud crash from inside startled her. *Had the Count finally swung his axe?*

Elizabeth woke from her reverie, twisting back toward the dressing room, letting go of her precarious sense of balance as her torso turned beneath her. She slipped off the final inches of the railing and fell, screaming and grasping a balustrade. Her hands, wet with perspiration, clutched at the pillar while her legs danced beneath her skirts, reaching for the earth.

Heavy pounding from inside the chambers, or was it her heart again? She heard voices, orders shouted. Her fingers slid further around the balustrade, losing their final grasp of the pillar, releasing her body to the full power of gravity's clench just as a strong, warm clutch snatched her wrist, and she was part of something else besides falling, she was part of someone else, hanging arm to arm, linked to earth above and below. Aleix leaned over the railing and reached for her other hand. "Help me!" he hollered over his shoulder.

The Count appeared, and together they grabbed at her arms, her shoulders, the stay, her hips, pulling her back over the railing, to collapse safely on the veranda landing.

The men caught their breath. Aleix must have flown up the servant stairs to catch her in time. He leaned against the veranda door, gulping breaths. "What the hell were you thinking?"

"I'm sorry," she said. "I don't know what got into me."

"What on earth were you doing out on that railing?" the Count asked.

"I was frightened. You were so angry, and you had that axe."

"You weren't frightened," Aleix said. "You are just a very stubborn woman."

Elizabeth wondered if anyone had ever told Tosca she was stubborn.

Aleix grabbed her arm and pulled her back into the dressing room, where they found themselves face to face with mischievous triumph. Susanna and the Countess preened, glowing, with a perplexed and winded Figaro standing before an open closet door. The naked Doctor was nowhere to be seen.

"Figaro?" said the Count, stepping forward. "Then it was you in the closet after all?"

"Forgive me sir, but you were very angry."

Figaro could handle this. He was such a clever man. He and

the Countess, and Susanna, could cover the rest of this. Elizabeth's ploy of distraction had triumphed. The scene was saved. The opera on track again. Harmony in Mozart and the universe. Sopranos had again united in defiance of tyranny, and in this peaceful knowledge, Elizabeth Kirtenpepper blacked out.

ACT IV
NONE OF THIS HAPPENED IN THE OPERA

Chapter Twenty-Three

S he was somewhere wonderful. A delightfully soft experience, so pleasant and inviting that at first, she mistook herself. She had indeed slipped off that balustrade and had now returned, all in one piece, to the century where mattresses existed. Mattresses with down covers and silken sheets and deep feather pillows all framed by tall posts and a canopy, a lovely carved mahogany canopy, draped in blue satin and velvet.

No. This wasn't the twenty-first century. It was just a comfortable bed.

She tried to sit up, but a gentle hand stopped her.

"There now, no rush about it," said the Countess softly. "You are all right. Everything is quite all right, thanks to you."

Elizabeth lay back into the fluffy wonder behind her head. "What about the Count?"

"Gone, but satiated." The Countess padded Elizabeth's forehead with a cool damp rag.

"And the men in the—?"

"Also gone. After you fainted, Aleix brought you in here, and the Count and Figaro spun stories in and around one another until things got dizzy and my husband was about to explode. Then, just before he did, Marcellina trod in, accompanied by a clothed and furious Bartolo. He wasn't kidding; the magistrate is already here today, and they both demanded that my husband hear her case. They all left in a whirlwind, then Cherubino and Basilio stumbled out a couple minutes later."

"So Basilio wasn't dead?"

"No," she laughed, "but we managed to get rid of him anyway."

Elizabeth sat up and regarded the Countess's chambers that she had at first so envied for all their opulence. She suddenly wanted to get up and out of the seductively comfortable bed. She'd rather sleep a thousand nights on her flattened horsehair and straw two floors above than spend one night in all that these chambers entailed. "How long have I been out?"

"Just under a half an hour, but I wasn't going to wake you, not after what you did."

"What I did?" Elizabeth recalled something involving a balcony, and two strong hands pulling her up, and there was a soprano somewhere too... "Oh yes, that."

The Countess put down her cloth and poured a glass of water from a nearby pitcher. "You jumped off a balcony to distract the room away from those closets. You risked yourself to save me." The Countess passed her the glass. "I've never known such fidelity. Why on earth would you risk so much for me?"

"I don't know," said Elizabeth. She took a sip. "It had to be done."

"That doesn't mean anyone would do it. Why did you?"

"I told you, I don't know. It was all I could think of."

"Well, I'm grateful, but..."

Elizabeth rose and straightened her skirts. She moved back into the dressing room, inspecting each closet for herself.

"As grateful as I am," the Countess continued, "you shouldn't have done it. You oughtn't to just jump to your own death for someone, least of all someone you hardly know."

"There are many ways to leap to one's death, much worse than jumping from a veranda."

"Much worse, Elizabeth?"

"Like marrying the wrong person. It's a slower death, but it'll still kill you." Outside the closet that had once held the cross-dressed Cherubino, Elizabeth found the small axe, leaning forgotten against the wall. "He had an axe," she said. "He was going to chop down the door."

"And then he would have found Bartolo."

"And he would have killed him."

"You don't know that. He is my husband, after all. He's not a murderer. I think I know him better than that."

"Well, I don't!" Elizabeth turned on her Mistress. "I don't know that I can believe a man who can so separate his sexuality from his character. What kind of a man does that? Is that even a man? Who struts around making conquests of women, using sex like some trophy? Is that all it is, then? Just like changing the oil on the car? Or winning some card game? Maybe it is. Maybe that's all it's ever been, and it's me that's got it all wrong. Maybe I'm the fool, and opera is dead."

"I'm not sure I understand you, Elizabeth. But I know my husband. You must believe me. He isn't a tyrant."

"Or a rapist?"

"Or a rapist. He's just forgotten himself. We both have." The Countess's white and silver wig had misplaced a pair of curls during the fray, and they hung now, dangling freely across her temple and beneath an ear. How heavy that wig must be. It must weigh five pounds at least. Elizabeth imagined the subtle neck injuries one would incur, carrying that around all day long.

"I'm sorry," Elizabeth said. "I guess I'm feeling a—wait, what did you say when I woke up? Something about Marcellina?"

"Only that she's finally going to get her case heard."

"For her marriage contract with Figaro?"

"Yes. My husband is hearing her defense."

"You mean it's happening today?"

"Right now, in the public throne room."

Elizabeth dropped the axe on the Persian carpet. "That can't happen now! That's in Act III. For crying in the night, we just closed up the Act II Finale. Can't a girl have a little intermission?" Elizabeth ran into the greeting chamber and stopped. "Where is the throne room? I don't even know."

"Are you going to jump off another balcony, Elizabeth?"

☙❧

Elizabeth followed the Countess through the main corridor to the large central staircase and then down to the far eastern wing of the house. The room was huge. On the east wall, a long red canopy poured out from a mighty golden crown hovering above the Count's seat. The canopy was pulled back by a pair of brass lions that held the fabric in their jaws before it tumbled to the polished wooden floor. Two free-standing candelabras flanked the tapestries on each side of the Count's platform. A large coat of arms made with a colorful inlaid stonework hung mounted on each side wall.

Officials in starched black robes and stiff white collars sat before the Count. Beside them, Marcellina and Bartolo stood, bursting with triumph.

A cluster of servants whispered between themselves at the back of the hall.

Elizabeth sidled up to Susanna. "What's going on? Where's Figaro?"

Susanna shook her head. "No one knows. He just disappeared after leaving the Countess's chambers."

Someone hammered at the front, and a nasal voice with a stutter called for order. Elizabeth remembered the character of Curzio inserted in Mozart's third act for comic flare. It was almost impossible to cut the speech impediment from the score, but standing here in this very real courtroom, none of the opera's issues felt comical. It suddenly felt absurd to her that so much of what was considered funny to previous generations was really just cruelty at another, socially vulnerable person's expense.

"But surely they can't proceed without Figaro here," she said to Susanna.

"They already have."

Women with no sexual rights, public mockery of handicaps, abuse of the lower classes—was there justice anywhere in eighteenth-century Spain?

"No, no, this can't happen without Figaro here!"

"Order!" Don Curzio's voice hollered back. "Silence, or we will c-clear the room."

"No!" Elizabeth shouted back. "I will not be silent! This hearing cannot take place without Figaro. It's unjust." As though she had just announced she had leprosy, the cluster of servants spread away from her.

Marcellina turned on Elizabeth with a glare. Bartolo raised a doubting eyebrow, and the Count rose from his ancient throne.

"Who is that? Who speaks there?" called Curzio.

"It is my wife's private musician," the Count said, "Please don't pay her any heed. A little while ago, she demonstrated her instability by attempting to jump from my wife's veranda. She has no business in this case. Guards, remove that woman from the property."

Two men approached Elizabeth from behind, but she ducked forward and ran to the judge. "That's not true! I have vital information that both parties will need to hear," she said as strong arms grabbed hold of her and began to drag her out. "What is audacious is this trial proceeding without the main defendant, or anyone here to stand up and speak for him."

"Young lady, his f-fiancée stated his case. But there is no argument. The c-court finds in favor of the plaintiff, Marcellina. Figaro must marry her, ac-cording to the terms of their agreed c-contract, and he must marry her today."

Elizabeth felt herself torn between two rages. This poor man's speech impediment would be a source of mockery in opera houses across the globe for the next four centuries despite the therapies and awareness that would develop in a maturing civilized society.

For him, she could do nothing. But she could at least stand up to the injustice of this despicable plot. "No!" she cried as the two men dragged her further from the proceedings. Momentarily fighting her way free, she turned to Marcellina. "He cannot marry you, Marcellina!"

"Shut up, you little hussy!" hissed her superior.

The men grabbed her again, fingers digging into her arms. She felt their weight and slipped off the delicate balance ever holding her atop the tiny, pointed heels of her shoes. She grappled to get her footing back, but the heels kept slipping on the smooth floors. "You don't understand. You can never marry him!"

The courtroom gasped again.

The Count rose and waved a hand. "Remove her, please."

"No," a female voice said, and a hush swept through the courtroom. "Unhand that girl, right now."

Elizabeth felt the tight grip of the fingers around her arms loosen. The crowd divided and separated like choreographed dancers around the large skirts of the Countess Almaviva.

"Take your hands off my chamber maid," she said in a voice so deep, Elizabeth suddenly understood why she was often cast as a mezzo in the prequel. "She has testimony that could be relevant to this case. Since Figaro is not here, it is only fair that she be allowed to speak."

Marcellina rolled her eyes and wagged a flurried hand through the air. "It's nonsense! I hardly know that girl. Everyone knows she's a lunatic, always talking about opera. The only reason we've even kept her on until now was—"

Yes, that's right. Why have you kept me on all this time?

The Countess stood like impenetrable wooden roots had planted her to her spot. "She will not now, nor at any future date, be removed from this property."

"What can she poss—"

The Count raised a hand and stepped down from his platform. The courtroom grew starkly silent. The Countess let him come to her, every last step, waiting with apparent disregard for his scrutiny and an almost imperceptible grin spread thinly across the Count's lips.

"Let her speak," he said at last, and the room erupted anew with whispers, mumblings, and more banging from the front.

Elizabeth shook the men off, then straightened her skirts and stepped forward. She would keep it simple. Respectful. Skip the prelude and go right for the main theme of the thing.

"Marcellina," she said, "you cannot marry Figaro, for one very good reason."

Chapter Twenty-Four

Find Figaro.

It was the final act of Puccini's Turandot.

Nessun Dorma.

"None shall sleep until he is found," the Count had ordered, and though the sun was still high in an afternoon sky, the kitchens were empty and the workstations abandoned. The hallways of the great house carried only echoes of the few servants too old or frail to search the grounds. These few quiet souls now shook tiny tremors in the crystals and china as they sifted through every inch, every corner, every closet.

Where was he? The man, the legend, that singular anomaly of human dignity and today, the groom.

Find Figaro.

Workshops were ransacked, storage bins inspected, piles of hay moved from one spot to another. Nothing. None had seen him. No one had any clues. Just an unspoken assumption of innocence that stood as a written testimony to the man's character. No gossip bubbled carelessly between the searchers. No one wondered if perhaps Figaro had jilted his Susanna. Not a soul considered whether he had fled in an act of cowardice from the forced marriage to Marcellina.

Nessun Dorma. Find Figaro.

"Get the dogs out," the Count ordered. Even the Countess donned her night cape and strode through the gardens and orchards, peeking between hedges and topiaries. So many places a man could hide away.

"People don't just disappear," the Count had said to the general assembly of his staff gathered in the throne room. "Especially not this person. Take a handful of men and go into the village. Another group should take to the woods, interrogate anyone you cross. Visit the gypsy camps, offer financial reward from my pocket. We will find our Major Domo, whether any ill-will has befallen him or not."

And so, they dispersed like scattering ants. Find Figaro.

They had to find him. If they did not find him, the Count could only assume that the little scullery-pianist was inventing the whole story, and he would side with Marcellina. But then of course, if they did not find Figaro, none of that would matter anyway. Marcellina wouldn't marry Figaro, and neither would Susanna. No one can marry a man who's disappeared.

Find Figaro. Uncover every hole, knock on all the doors, and follow every trail. Find Figaro, or this opera might never end...

See! The gloomy night is bare
From the Heavens the immense vault undresses
Like a widow finally removing her brown cloth;
Who among the gypsies ornaments the days?
The ladies!

"Wait, what?" Elizabeth fumbled through the remaining blank pages in the book with a frantic horror. "That can't be all. There must be more. What good is quoting Verdi? I need to find Figaro. Figaro, not Verdi! Oh, you worthless, barren piece of trash!"

Elizabeth slung the book at the wall across from her bed, where it smashed open with a satisfying crunch and toppled to the floor. She would let it sit in its huddle of disarray. She hoped it would just wither away in self-loathing, slowly decomposing in dust and cobwebs for eternity. That would show it.

"Find Figaro. No kidding." She left the room and slammed the door.

In the cool hallway, Elizabeth felt alone and isolated. Wasn't it enough, all she had learned to do? Scaling fish and peeling carrots and scrubbing pots? She had come this far, all the way to Act III, despite vengeful housemaids, drunken music masters, and axes that materialized out of thin air. Had she held anything back? Had she not given herself completely to the task? Playing music on demand like some kind of pianistic jukebox and taking endless orders from a faceless cook through a smoky hole? Had she not even been willing to sacrifice herself for the story? Stood upon the parapet of destiny with the greatest of sopranos and offered her own plunge for the good of the plot? Had she not done all of this and more? So why should the book so villainously turn on her now, stealing away the leading man without reason, and hiding him from his most crucial scene, with nothing but some random mockery from a Verdi chorus?

Maybe she shouldn't do anything. Just let the book do its thing while she retired back in the shadows where she belonged. Who was to say this version of Figaro had to end with a wedding and the repentance of the Count? Perhaps Figaro and Susanna were supposed to be eaten by those gypsies. Or the Count was supposed to chop down that closet door and shoot Bartolo's head off.

After all, it wasn't her story. If Elizabeth Kirtenpepper couldn't find her way home by redirecting the story back upon itself over and over, perhaps she should just stop trying, and get comfortable. Get used to her new life in the skull and playing for the Countess. Who cared if axes fell in *Marriage of Figaro*? She wasn't worthy of even a tiny piece of information regarding the location of the leading man. She wasn't in the cast. She wasn't a stage manager.

She was no one.

A yearning stirred within her, a new desire creeping up with a furious salty wave. She felt a fool for standing on the outskirts of her own life. Never jumping in the tide, never playing with the undercurrents and splashing in the insanity. What was life without risks? She only took risks for others: Amada, Figaro, Susanna, the Countess. *What about risks for Elizabeth?*

Her feet began to move, carrying her down the narrow, darkened hallway, passing rooms and doors. Down the creaky spiral steps, down, down, down.

When she stepped out of the Count's house, the sun was beginning to set in Seville, orange streaks cutting across the graying sky.

Elizabeth moved like a spirit through the warm air, her skin alive in the intoxicating heat of late afternoon. She moved faster as she went, trying to escape any pursuant doubt. Out of the courtyard, through the garden of hedges and past the long reflecting pool. She lifted her skirts and began to run. Over the crest of the wide grassy hill bordered by low stone walls to the tall and inviting stables with their earthy smells and wild inhabitants. Where the hay lay.

No calculations. No delusions. She expected only pleasure. Wonderful, pulsating, agonizing pleasure. Pleasure no longer sitting on the side wondering. Pleasure like a pool she would swim in, not wading up to her ankles, but fully submerged.

The stables just ahead, the smell of straw and horses blowing lightly to her, calling her in. She approached, swimming down the hill, faster and faster through the hot, spicy air. As though expecting her, Aleix stepped into the doorway and their eyes met.

"Elizabeth?"

Aleix had said nothing. Perhaps she had not heard it. She kept moving.

"Elizabeth," the voice called again. It came from behind with annoying impudence.

Her feet slowed.

"Elizabeth!" The voice rumbled closer, almost frantic.

Running, feet padding on the dry earth and breaths heaving. She stopped.

"Elizabeth, I've been calling you," said Gaspar, coming to her, panting. He followed her steady eyes to the man standing in the barn. "What are you doing here?"

"I might ask you the same question," she said. "What are you doing here?"

"Heard about Figaro. Assume he's not supposed to be missing, then? This didn't happen in your version?"

"My version?" Elizabeth spun on Gaspar. "None of this is my version. None of this happened in the opera."

"So, things aren't going well." Gaspar's eyes shifted back towards Aleix again. "What else has happened?"

"What hasn't happened? First, there's some hooded figure running around at night disrupting the plot every time I've got a hold of it. Then three insane men get locked in closets, and finally this axe, I mean an actual wood-chopping thing, you understand?"

"Yes, know what an axe is."

"It just appeared. Right there in the Countess's chambers. There were thirty-six feet of prop tables during this show, but never a single axe on any of them!"

Aleix sank back into the darkness of the dusty barn and Elizabeth sighed. The sun now lined up for its descent, sending long thin shadows sprawling across the grasses.

"Weren't at Mass this past week," Gaspar said. "Was concerned."

"You've been very kind to me, Gaspar, but you're not my conscience."

"You're right. Only, you had made such a point about it."

"Well, I don't see the point anymore, what with magically appearing axes, and uncomfortable beds and scrubbing pots and floors. What does any of it matter?"

A cool breeze wafted between them, tousling Elizabeth's hair. She raised a hand to push it back and realized she hadn't even looked in a mirror before coming here. She looked down at her hands, half browned with dirt and torn with a thousand tiny nicks.

"Elizabeth," Gaspar said, "have I lost your trust?"

"What? No. I don't know. Susanna says her Figaro would never abandon her. The Countess says her husband has just 'forgotten himself' and you say you want to help me, but...Maybe I shouldn't trust anyone. Maybe that's what keeps getting me into trouble, expecting people to behave like people."

The shouts of the search echoed through awakening crickets and lilting swallows. From beyond the dark barn door, a horse whined a loud, vain complaint.

"Gaspar, what were you doing in those woods that night?"

"What night?"

"The night we went looking for Figaro and Susanna. What were you doing out there all alone, when you wouldn't even let me go in search of a dentist or the barber because it would have been too dangerous? I only know one person in eighteenth-century Spain outside of this score, and he shows up right after a dark-hooded figure sends the leads off to their deaths."

"Oh, Elizabeth, life isn't an opera."

He turned away and moved slowly across the glen, his head bent, his hat in his fingers. Without really deciding to, Elizabeth followed him.

Beneath the shelter of a towering oak, he leaned against a stone wall, whose members, probably laid by some Moor, would still be standing here in Elizabeth's twenty-first century. The great oak's branches reached over and above them like a thatch roof with the few remaining splinters of daylight peeking between its thick darkening foliage.

"You have to believe in something," Gaspar said. "Can't get on without believing in something. Why else do you play all that beautiful music then? Scrubbing pots isn't enough for you now. Not content to stay here in Spain any longer. You've got something inside you. That's why you play your music. That's why.

Now, I don't know much about this story you're fixing. Don't know much about opera. But whoever you're trying to punish by going in that barn back there, one thing I do know for certain, only thing going to get hurt, is you."

The cries of the searchers wafted again across the hillside.

"Guess I'd be more help with the search now. You have a head on you, Elizabeth. Can't help that. Just the way it is. You have a head on you." He put on his hat and left her alone under the oak.

The cool onset of night framed Gaspar's graying silhouette as he climbed the hill and disappeared through the opening in the wall. In the newly fallen night, it felt like he was stepping over a precipice into the eternal darkness.

Find Figaro.

Chapter Twenty-Five

⚜

To be lost in the dark was much worse than being lost in the light. *Is he here? No, not there. Have we looked here? Looked there already. Maybe look again.*

Find Figaro.

Elizabeth knew what she must do. Return to her room and pick her father's book up off the huddled mess on the floor. In effect, she would apologize.

At the crest of the hill, she met Basilio carrying a pair of lanterns in each hand. "Oh, hello little vixenette," he cooed. "This is quite a delicious pickle you've gotten yourself into, isn't it, quip? Find Figaro. Run, run quick as you can, can't catch me, I'm the gingerbread man. Find him and what? You become a little hero? A little she-wolf? A little beetle-nibbler? So convenient for you that he has disappeared, isn't it?"

"What are you talking about? I want to find Figaro as much as you do."

"Oh no, little harpy-katydid. No, no, no. I assure you, I want to find Figaro far more than you do, because if we find him, then your little tale will be debunked and you, little locust-eater, you will be sent out on your snippy little derriere. Goodbye little lammergeier, goodbye to you and all your twisted teeny scheming."

"I'm not scheming. Figaro is Marcellina's son."

"Yes, yes little dribblet, I know, and there's that birthmark to prove it. What a wonderful story you will make when this is all over. Do enjoy your last night here. Even the Countess cannot get you out of this coffin-hole. I am off to join in the futile search. Good nighty-night, little quip." He brushed past, nearly knocking her to the ground before disappearing behind the blackened hedges.

Elizabeth made a mental note to look up the word "quip" as soon as she returned to the twenty-first century.

She found her way back to the main house where a matronly figure stood shadowed in the servants' entrance, hugging herself in a tattered shawl. Elizabeth stiffened for a scolding.

"Look, it's true," Elizabeth said. "I swear to you, I'm not making it up. He is your son."

To her surprise, Marcellina did not bite her head off or snatch at her with any bony appendages. A placid voice in the dark simply said, "I know."

An evening breeze blew between them, and the scents of Cook's un-eaten feast wafted through the door behind her.

"I've always known somehow," she said. "That's why I was so drawn to him."

"Then, you're not angry with me anymore?"

"Angry?" Marcelina laughed softly. "I don't know how I could ever be angry again."

Somewhere, dogs barked furiously, and muffled shouts echoed through the gardens. Two men pushed past them through the doorway carrying shovels and more lanterns.

"You remember him then?"

"Do you think I forgot?"

"I just didn't expect you to be so accepting. You did cut me down awful when I tried to tell you."

"You can't understand. You don't think it will. Destroy you, I mean," Marcellina said, shaking her head. "You think you're just going to leave it on that doorstep and walk away, like it's some article of clothing and go back to your life. Wake up the next day the person you were before all this. Like it will be over. Left there on that step. Even today, I could paint that step, in clearest detail, every crack, what the night air smelled like around it, the weeds that framed it in the spring dew. It was just a moment in time, wasn't it?"

Long-restrained tears welled up and tripped down the matron's cheeks. "But then one day, some crazy cheese girl, scullery maid, tells you he's here. You just lost each other. And then, you just know."

"You know he's your son?"

"You know that you'll never be angry again." Marcellina wiped the tears away. "I have no idea how you came to all this information. I don't know if you're a gypsy, a witch, or an angel—"

"Or a leper." Elizabeth stepped forward and passed her hand-kerchief. "Dona Marcellina, there's something I really want to ask you. Before I came here, to work in the scullery, there was another housemaid who was sent away. Amada told me about her. You sent her away—"

"Because she was with child. That's the real rub, isn't it? I couldn't save them, could I? I couldn't even save myself when it came to it. But I had a slightly more understanding employer. I have no choice, cheese girl. I hate myself every time it happens. But what can I do?"

"Do you have any idea what happened to her? Did you follow up to see that she was okay?"

"If I did that for every one of them, I'd have to start an orphanage. I did what I could. Found a family that would take her in, feed her and keep her in exchange for labor. I keep my eyes open for such people when they come along."

"For labor?"

"Well, you don't expect anyone to take her in for free, do you?

Once or twice, I had to send a girl packing with nothing but her belly. At least I found Frescura a situation with a family. They're a rough lot, but she had enough of a head to survive them, I think."

"Frescura?" Elizabeth shook her head. The preceding weeks had been so full of awkwardness, strange occurrences, and encounters. She could hardly expect herself to remember everyone she had met, or every head that had bobbed silently passed the tiny doorway of her kitchen cell. "Is there anyone else on the estate with that name?"

"Not that I know of."

"But I'm sure I've heard it before. It rings in my head like a hammer."

"Well, I know everyone on the Count's staff inside and out. If you heard her name before, it wasn't—"

"Like a hammer!" Elizabeth shouted out suddenly, and Marcellina jumped. "Like a hammer! It rings in my head like a hammer, Marcellina. Like pounding on metal. It wasn't a random excerpt from Verdi, it was a clue. It was giving me a clue!"

"What are you saying, foolish girl? I take it back. You are a loon."

"Dona Marcellina, are there any anvils on the estate?"

"I'm almost afraid to ask this question, but—?"

"I don't need an anvil. It was a clue, don't you see?" Elizabeth began singing and stomping around the yard, calling out into the dark night. "*Chi del gitano i giorni abbella*?"

She returned to Marcellina and grabbed her by the shoulders. The matron stiffened as though no one had touched her in years, her eyes opening so wide that even in the darkness they caught some of the moon's light. "It wasn't mocking me," Elizabeth said. "It was helping me. Is there a blacksmith here on the property?"

"Well, of course, out past the stables. It's kept far from the house in case of fire, but it's been locked up for the last week because the wife just had a baby, and she's not in the best of—"

Elizabeth pulled her. "Come on, we've got to get there, quickly."

Marcellina balked. "No, we can't. He's very particular about his space. Won't let anyone touch anything. Work's starting to back up, though."

"The shop has been locked up? So, no one would go in there?" Elizabeth squealed and began spinning again.

"Not if they value their hands."

Elizabeth took up the matron in her arms and pulled her into a clumsy dance. "***All'opra!*** *all'opra! Dàgli, martella! Chi del gitano i giorni abbella?*"

They stumbled together across the dirt and pebbles, spinning into dizziness. Marcellina clutched fast in horrified terror until Elizabeth relented and crossed back to the door. "Come on, Momma. Grab a lantern and come with me. I know where your son is. I know how to find Figaro."

Together, they sped across the Count's property, past tall dark hedges that loomed like black fortresses. At a juncture, they careened headlong into another shadowy form wandering through the night.

"What the sickening devil? Who goes there, running like a lunatic?"

"Bartolo!" Elizabeth cried, "Come with us. We might need you."

"You? Oh, I should have known it was you, lunatic girl. Why on earth would I assist you? You've begun a most slanderous lie—"

"Oh, shut up, Bartolo," Marcellina said, dusting herself off. "It's no lie and you know it. Have you no shame, man? He is your son. Surely you don't expect to find another during this lifetime, do you? Or perhaps you've behaved so monstrously with so many women that you're hoping something better will show up with your bone structure and lack of moral decency."

"Anything would be better than this. That clown."

"Your son."

"Stop saying that! Someone might hear you."

"Oh, for crying out loud, Doctor," Marcellina said. "When will it be okay for the masses to discover you're as rotten as the rest of us?"

"I do not deny—"

"Just come with us, you idiot. I'm done being bullied by your kind. What is wrong with you? Like it or not, he's probably all that will be left of you after you're gone."

"Don't say that!"

"And while I'm at it, if it weren't for this girl, you'd have been decapitated in the Countess's bedchamber this afternoon. You should be bowing and scraping and rubbing your neck every time you see her. She jumped out a window to save you, did you know that, you weasel? For once in your miserable existence, do the right thing. Choose some dignity. Help save your son."

Marcellina pushed past his shadowed visage, and Bartolo reluctantly followed as they hurried forward on neatly woven paths past a rose garden with a tall figurine, its arrow ever pointing towards the stars, its sleek, stone corpus glistening silver in the moonlight. Behind them, a monotone chorus of voices approached, one with soloistic leadership.

"It's the Count," Bartolo said.

"Good," said Elizabeth. "Go tell him to bring everyone to the blacksmith's workshop."

Bartolo scurried off, and Elizabeth clutched Marcellina's wrist. Off again, through an opening of hedges to the crest of a wide sloping hill. At the bottom, the stables hovered tall and curiously unfamiliar, even though she had been there just a few minutes before. Halfway down, the Count and his entourage crossed to join them. "Have you found him?"

"Not exactly, but we know where he is," Marcellina answered with such unflinching confidence that Elizabeth momentarily questioned her interpretation of the Verdi libretto.

Elizabeth led them all past the stables, scurrying on the dirt road with the awkward tiny heels under her long skirts. She spared only a passing thought for what might have happened within these flimsy walls had Gaspar not come along.

The smith's shop was a long narrow building with three stubby chimneys poking towards the night sky. At the familiar smell of burning coal, Elizabeth stopped. "Marcellina, didn't you say the place has been locked up for the last week? Then why is one of the chimneys smoking?"

Marcellina tried the door, but the handle slipped between her fingers, dangling from its sole remaining screw. "It's broken," she said.

The Count stepped up and inspected it. "Bring the torches," he said.

A sound emerged from the impenetrable darkness beyond, a groan, stretched and thin.

"Figaro!" Marcellina jumped forward, pushing past Count, scullery-pianist, broken door, and darkness. "Where are you?"

Another groan, then something toppled to the ground with a metallic clang. Marcellina's skirts fluttered across the studio, navigating work benches and fire pits towards the back of the room. "He's here! Come and help me. Bring the light. Oh, God be thanked!"

The men followed her to the back where Figaro lay collapsed next to a pile of metal what-nots. A hot oven smoldered behind him. His hands were tightly bound to its black iron leg. Marcellina knelt beside him, and the great hero of opera and theater collapsed in his mother's arms with groans and labored breaths.

When she tried to unbind him, he winced. "My arm! Please, don't touch it."

Marcellina lifted the limb into the light.

"It's burned," Figaro said, reeling. "The bastard branded me!" With his other arm, he gestured to a branding iron, tossed astray on the floor.

Basilio picked it up. "Still warm." He passed it to the Count.

"Tell me what happened," said the Count.

"I don't know exactly. After leaving your wife's chambers this afternoon, I returned to your rooms to unpack when I found a note."

"What note? Who was it from?"

"I don't know. It was unsigned."

It occurred to Elizabeth that all of Seville's problems might be solved by some legal proclamation forbidding the future opening of anonymous notes.

"It said there was evidence to clear me of Marcellina's contract and I should come here. Since I knew you were on your way to the hearing, I came straightway. That's when the bugger knocked me on the head and dragged me inside."

"Did you get a look at the culprit?" asked the Count.

"He wore a dark cloak with a hood. His face was hidden."

"The same figure you met in the garden with Susanna?" Elizabeth asked.

"Possibly. I don't know for sure."

"Well, how do you know it was a man?" Basilio slithered. "Our little scullery maid seemed to know exactly how to find you when no one else could. Seems fairly obvious to assume that—"

"Her?" Figaro said coddling his scorched arm. "Not possible. The blighter knocked me out and carried me in here. He was bigger, too."

"Perhaps she was working with someone then. An **acccompalice** of sorts." Basilio snickered at the pun which only he got.

Everyone else turned an eye towards Elizabeth.

"Basilio has a point," said the Count. "How did you know where to find him?"

"I swear I had nothing to do with this."

"She had nothing to do with it," Marcellina piped in. "Don't listen to this idiot. He can't string anything together sensibly. She was in the Countess's chambers passed out before the hearing, and we all know that the Countess herself escorted her to the throne room. I don't know how this girl knew where to find my son, but anyone who tries to touch her will have to go through me first. So back off, fish face."

Basilio raised an eyebrow so far it almost touched his hairline.

"Your son, Madame?" said Figaro.

Elizabeth bent down and inspected the branding on his arm. "Count, whoever has done this was trying to hide the truth. The burn of your crest is conveniently placed. Figaro, is this where your birthmark was?"

"Yes, my only remaining link to my, wait—how did you know about that?"

"Never mind that. Before anyone says another word, Figaro, can you tell us what that birthmark on your arm looked like before you were burned?"

"I always said it looked a bit like a spatula."

Marcellina released a wretched wail as gushes began to flow. She held a stiffened and confused Figaro tightly to her bosom. "My precious boy!"

"Gently, gently now!" he cried out. "You can't imagine pain until you've felt something like that. I passed out from the shock. Those cursed things were not made for human skin."

"Indeed, it's already starting to blister," said the Count. "We'd better get you some treatment. Can you stand?"

"Can I stand? Wait. Everyone just...wait. Are you telling the truth? Are you truly—?"

"My poor, sweet boy," Marcellina said. "It seems that cheese girl was correct about a great many things. I cannot marry you, because I am the very poor, downtrodden soul that left you on a doorstep so long ago. My heart, my love, can you ever forgive your poor mother?"

Marcellina wept and wept, the tears and jerks of remorse coming so much easier now, with nothing to constrain them: no denials, no self-loathing, only the pure admission of imperfection. She held tightly to her son, who appeared dumbstruck by the revelation.

Elizabeth watched with disbelief as the hardened matriarch so abruptly softened. No one moved or tried to change the scene. Not even a light cue transpired in those frozen magical moments, as though a great fermata perched indefinitely over the score. Elizabeth had always felt this moment got plowed over too quickly in the comedic version of the tale.

"Mother?"

Figaro sat up and looked on the wretched weeping woman. He whispered it again, "Mother," in so quiet and tender an utterance that its effect rippled through every soul present. Despite the crowded and darkened room, the exhaustion and all the unanswered questions, not a sniffle followed that mighty whisper. For it was universally evident that their Major-Domo and friend, their hero and leading man, the star under the lights of center stage, Figaro, had never before used such a term on a human being. *Mother*.

"Can you stand, Figaro?"

"Mother," Figaro said again. "I could fly."

Chapter Twenty-Six

✦✦✦

On the hike back up the grassy hill, they met Susanna. Elizabeth didn't need to witness the discovery scene: Seeing Figaro with Marcellina, Susanna assumes he has shifted his affections and she flies into a tizzy. Marcellina explains all, and the two women who were once at each other's throats now embrace with familial affection.

Elizabeth climbed the servants' winding stairs to her quiet attic room. She felt an absurd need to apologize to a book. Holding her candle aloft, she did not see it on the floor. Amada must have come in and taken it from its crumbled mess. But it was not on the nightstand, or on Elizabeth's bed. Nor on the dresser.

"Where did you go?"

She searched the bed and its covers. She opened every drawer and rifled through the caps, stockings, and handkerchiefs. In a fluster of panic, she searched Amada's bed and all her things. Perhaps someone else had come into the room and put the book on the wrong side. Just as she was tearing up Amada's pillows and covers, the door creaked open, and a familiar voice startled her.

"*Oye!* What are you doing, girl?"

"Oh. Amada, I'm sorry, but I can't find my book. I thought

maybe someone had come in and moved it to your side. Did you see it by any chance?"

"You know I can't read. What would I want with your dumb book?"

"I don't mean to imply that you took it. It's just that I left it here on the floor, just about an hour ago."

"Well, you might take better care of your things." Amada began undressing. "Don't worry, someone probably came in and thought, 'What's that doing here?' and returned it to the Count's library."

"Yes, that's possible."

"It's been a day, hasn't it?" Amada said. "Here, help me with my stay."

"I really should try to find my book."

"*Probesita*! Don't you ever get tired? Playing and working all day, jumping out of windows, standing up in court, chasing down Figaro. You've got four hours in the skull tomorrow morning. Just go to bed and look for your dumb book tomorrow. You'd never find it in there tonight anyway without a dozen candles. All right, your turn."

Elizabeth turned around and submitted to the most pleasurable moment of her eighteenth-century days: the untying of the stay. Once she could adequately breathe again, she realized Amada was right. She should go to bed and look for her book in the morning.

"Wait," Amada said, bending down, "what's this?" She reached under the tiny nightstand between their beds and retrieved a single piece of folded paper. "It's not a book, but maybe it fell out and got tangled up in your bedding. Is it yours?"

Elizabeth opened the paper and caught her breath. This was not an anonymous note from a mystery figure. "It's from my father," she said. "It must have gotten dislodged when I threw the book against the wall."

"Is that why you're so worried about that book? Did it come

from your dad?" Amada crawled into her bed and Elizabeth sat down. "Is he gone, then? Your dad?"

"He got very sick and died without me there. I didn't even know."

"I'm sorry. I wish I'd known my father."

"Did he die before you were born?"

"No. I just never knew him. Crazy, isn't it? Sometimes I pretend he's buried in a crowd, you know? In the village or at one of the Count's big parties. All those people. Surely one of them is him, I think. I like to pick one out and imagine what it would be like if that was him."

"Oh, Amada."

"It's okay. Aunt takes good care of me. Sometimes, though, I wish I had anything, even a note like that. That would be nice. Just to have a note from him." Amada rolled over and curled under her covers.

Dear Elizabeth,

All post-mortem letters must begin with an apology. Isn't that the rule? Well, when you read this, you will either be relieved, or very angry at me. I hope I am wrong about both. But for either and all else, I am very sorry. Forgive me.

I found out about the cancer four months ago. It moved, as they predicted, very quickly. As I write this, I am in the final chapter of my story. There are still things to do. This letter is one of them.

Even knowing these are the last words you'll get from me, I'm not sure what to write here. I'm a reader, not a writer. That deficiency leaks into all aspects of my life. Just talking is a terrible form of writing. It's horribly risky. Choosing just the right words at the right time with the right inflection. It's always seemed to me that words are best chosen by other people, and I was only meant to read them.

Your mother, God rest her soul, understood this about me,

and loved me anyway. I never really forgave God for taking her. Still haven't. I guess we'll have it out soon now.

My point is, (have I already made it?), I don't blame you if you hate me. After Gwen died, I fell into my books, when I should have buried myself in you. That's why I decided not to tell you about the cancer. I hadn't bothered to share my life with you, so why should I burden you with my death? I hope I've done the right thing. I hope that I haven't bungled this up too.

But the books, the books are what I can leave you, Elly. Now there's a certainty one can really hold on to. The books are a reality. All things created are real, you know. Don't fool yourself into thinking that they are just words on a page. They are as alive as you and me, or at least as you will be when you're reading this. Never judge the value of any reality that you cannot fully comprehend. All uncertainties must be treated with appropriate reverence.

Oh no, I didn't want this to turn into another lecture. I'm sorry. You see? The words, the words...

Elizabeth, I know you will do wonderful things. And when the time comes, no matter what I've made you believe with my mistakes, choose love. It's worth everything. I hope you know that you were worth everything too.

Your Father,

George

As Elizabeth blew out the candle, climbed under her cover, and stared up into the darkness, she had an uneasy feeling, like she was forgetting something. She wished she hadn't thrown her father's book against the wall. She wished she'd gone to visit him more often. She wished she'd tried to understand him better.

Darkly haunted visions filled her dreams. Visions of her book growing feet, pressing down its wrinkles and marching out of her room forever.

When Elizabeth overslept, no one came to wake her. Not Amada, not a raging Marcellina, not even faceless Cook. She awoke naturally and jumped out of her bed to dress. The end of this thing was so close now. She had to find her book, make sure the cast didn't mess up their plans for the fourth act, and of course, she had to scrub, peel, and scale in the scullery for the next four hours. What time was it? *Why hadn't Amada woken her?*

When she reached the skull, she was still tying her aprons behind her as Amada stepped out to greet her. "Well *qué susto* girl, you slept later than even I could've imagined."

"What time is it? Did I miss my shift?"

"You missed the morning. But Aunt said no one was to wake you."

"Marcellina. I've got to talk to her. Where is she now?"

"They're all in the Countess's rooms getting ready. You know there's going to be a wedding today after all. Not only that, but a double wedding. Old nasty Doctor Bartolo has finally agreed to marry Aunt. I'm going to stand up for her."

"They're not planning the wedding. They're planning the Fourth Act. Oh, this is terrible! I need to be up there. They might start some new Asian land war or something. Amada, can you please stay in the skull a bit longer? I've got to get to the Countess's chambers. It's very important."

"*Guay.* Go play some of that sweet music."

"Thank you, thank you, Amada!"

Elizabeth flew back down the servants' hall and up the winding staircase to the second-floor landing. She didn't even knock on the Countess's door, but just barged in, panting nearly to hyperventilation. "Mistress!" she cried "Whatever it is you're planning, you mustn't—"

Figaro, Susanna, Marcellina, Bartolo, and the Countess all beheld her with statuesque stillness, such that she suddenly had the impression of walking into a historical wax museum. Only in this reenactment, everyone was suddenly interrupted by an out-of-order scullery maid who had no business intruding and displayed such appalling manners, so shocking that—

"Elizabeth," said the Countess, "are you all right? We thought you were taking the day off."

"I was? No. I couldn't possibly. I mean, thank you, Madame, but I really couldn't leave you at such a crucial time, I mean, I couldn't bear it if anything, if I could have helped with anything, and I was just sleeping away."

"Well," said Susanna "Madame was just telling us all of her plan to straighten the Count out for good. It's genius."

"For good?"

"Yes," said the Countess Rosina. "I have an idea."

"The guns, or the documents?"

"No, no, you've been listening to Basilio. I have a far more effective and harmless plan to catch my husband in the act of his own infidelity."

Elizabeth could barely endure to hear it. How would she talk them out of whatever ludicrous scheme they had concocted?

"Tonight, after the wedding, we will send the Count a note."

Oh no... "An anonymous note?"

"No. It will be written by Susanna. Offering to meet him in the gardens this evening at a specified time and bestow upon him the very favor he asks."

"I must object to this," Figaro piped in.

"Wait, Figaro, hush!" said Elizabeth. "Please Mistress, continue."

"Then I shall myself dress in Susanna's clothes and meet my husband in the darkness. I'll let him woo and seduce me before I reveal my identity to him."

Elizabeth stood in stunned wonder. "Forgive me, Mistress. I think I would like to retire after all. I have a wretched headache, and I'm not sure I should be up yet." She bowed lightly and stepped backwards. "I'm so sorry to have intruded."

"You could never intrude, Elizabeth. Are you sure you're

quite okay? You had a long and wild day yesterday. Perhaps you should return to your quarters."

"Yes, perhaps I should, Madame. Thank you. I'm sorry to have intruded. Excuse me."

Elizabeth stepped out and softly pulled the door shut. She passed through the grand corridor as though floating and again stood at the stair entrance, pondering which way to go. She could go down to the scullery and relieve Amada, but she wasn't really needed there. She wasn't needed anywhere, in fact. The Countess's plan was exactly how it happened in the opera.

❦

Her book was not in the library. She asked the staff who cleaned the collection, the women who shared her suite, Marcellina, Figaro, and even Basilio. No one had seen her book, and what would a little scullery-maid snibbet need a book for anyway?

Elizabeth wondered if Basilio had taken her book. Perhaps he was the mysterious character in the dark hood, foiling the plot at every opportunity. He certainly fit the bill for instability. But why? To gain favor with the Count? Hooded capes and stealth didn't seem his style. And burning off Figaro's birthmark? That was a little dark for someone so mortally terrified of bees.

Why would anyone want to ruin this plot anyway? Well, there was Bartolo. If the plot didn't resolve, he would get his revenge on Figaro. But was he strong enough to cart Figaro around? And clever enough to send them off into the woods that night?

For that matter, how about the Count himself? Perhaps he sent those men up to frame his wife and publicly humiliate her. It was possible. But Elizabeth couldn't shake the memory, as though from some perverted melodrama, of the Count kneeling at Rosina's feet, afraid she was ill, so sincerely concerned for her and genuinely surprised by everything that followed.

But none of this mattered anymore. The plot was moving

forward, and in just a few more hours, Elizabeth could hopefully return to the land of dish detergent and hair conditioner.

No.

It wasn't just about the conveniences.

Elizabeth missed her life. Her wonderful life of making music every day on a stunning instrument, while beautiful voices sang soul-searching music yet to be composed. It was time to go home where she belonged.

She just needed to find her book.

Chapter Twenty-Seven

❧❦❧

S taff and villagers packed into the Count's personal chapel to witness the betrothal of their favorite baritone. Elizabeth sat in the back, wishing for a decent sound system. Why she wished for that, she didn't know. She barely understood when everything was in English. Now she was in an odd version of eighteenth-century Spain where everyone spoke English, except of course the priest, who distantly mumbled in Latin. When she occasionally caught an odd phrase reverberating with some clarity off the stone walls and wooden rafters, she recognized it more from choral works than from anything in her own practice of Catholicism.

Still, the incense smelled the same. The candles flickered the same, and there was a regularity about the rituals. Most familiar though was the weighty sensation in her abdomen whenever she sat in church, like gravity had increased, pulling her down. Reggie was right. Why did she go to church every Sunday? It was like she had some debt to pay, or more likely, some debt to collect.

Elizabeth leaned between the shoulders of fellow servants to get a peek at the happy couples. For an instant she saw them at the front, Susanna's veil almost glowing in the blue and red light from a stained-glass window. They held hands and looked into each other's eyes, completely confident in their decision to trust one another. Elizabeth had to sneer at this perfect moment. If she remembered correctly, Figaro would spend the rest of the fourth act furiously chasing Susanna around the gardens, convinced she was cheating on him.

"He was his friend," Elizabeth said to her mother.

"What, honey?"

Elizabeth remembered the scene so well. They drove from Mass in the blue Toyota Corolla, her mother's car. Funny how a person could become associated with their chosen vehicle of transportation. Even today, whenever Elizabeth saw a Corolla, she had to stifle a momentary nonsensical excitement that her mother had returned, like she had been on a decade-long road trip and had forgotten to tell everyone, and here she was, back to pick Elizabeth up at school and take her home.

Elizabeth must have been much smaller, because in the memory the seat was bigger than she was, and the belt fell awkwardly across part of her neck. It had been an especially long service, dimly lit and thick with incense. Just when she thought she was going to tip over with sleepiness, somebody knelt down and started washing other people's feet. *Really? Couldn't everybody keep their shoes on and we could go home sooner?*

Elizabeth's father sat in the front seat, staring silently out the window as darkened Wichita sped past. Perhaps he had some profound experience during the lengthy service, but more likely, he just wanted to get back to his books.

"What did you say, Elly?" her mother asked again, and Elizabeth realized she'd been caught. She was too tired to get sucked into a meaningful conversation.

"That was a sleeper," she said.

"Oh, come on, it wasn't that bad. You could at least sing

along, you know. It wouldn't hurt either of you. But that's not what you said. You said something else."

Her mother had an instinctual radar for Elizabeth's intellectual sparks, hunting them down at the slightest whiff and relentlessly pestering until she could uncover some deeply meaningful idea that mattered to the world at large but to no one in particular.

"You said something about being friends. Did something happen at school?"

"No." Elizabeth's resistance would be pointless. Better to face the problem and get to bed sooner. "I said, 'He was his friend.'"

"Whose friend?"

"Judas. He was Jesus's friend. One of his best friends, right? And he betrayed him."

"Yes, but Judas didn't believe in him."

"That doesn't make any sense. How can you be someone's friend and not believe in them?"

"Oh, easily. Are all your friendships the same?"

"No. But I don't think anybody would send me off to be crucified."

"Well, maybe not crucified, but betrayal happens every day." Elizabeth had to admit she had seen betrayal for herself, at school, if she was being honest, even in the mirror. She watched the sedate features of her father's profile, staring stubbornly out the window as passing streetlights strobed across him. He paid them no heed, like he paid no heed to their conversation, adding nothing, saying nothing, thinking nothing, as though he weren't even there really, but somewhere else, another world perhaps, in a book somewhere, like this one.

"So," Elizabeth said, "everyone's a Judas. We can't trust anyone. Not even ourselves."

"Faith is not seasonal, Elizabeth. You can't just taste a little here and there whenever it's convenient. You either believe in something completely, or not at all."

"Praying, Princess?" Aleix's warm voice startled Elizabeth from her memories.

The ceremony had ended, and the chapel emptied. Elizabeth sat in her back pew watching a boy extinguish candles.

"Princess? You forget. I'm the lowliest of the staff, remember?"

"Not anymore," Aleix said. He removed his straw hat and sat down on the end of her pew. "You're untouchable. Figaro and Susanna love you. Bartolo owes you his head. Even Marcellina won't hear a bad word said about you."

"I did reunite her with her son. But I'm pretty sure Basilio still hates me."

"Is he real?"

"I've been trying to figure that out myself."

Aleix had a wonderful smile that, on its rare appearance, made him seem so utterly human. It lit up his face and made the long, thick scar dissolve into the natural folds of his cheeks.

"I owe you another thank you," she said.

"For catching you off the Countess's veranda? Or for something else?"

"Is there some other peril I've forgotten?"

"There was your courtroom scene."

"Were you there?"

"Everyone was. You certainly didn't need me then," he said. "And of course, you found Figaro. Didn't need me for that either. You're doing fine by yourself, Princess. So long as you don't decide to throw yourself off any more balconies."

"I promise I'll try to keep my feet on sturdy ground from here on. But it should be pointed out that none of the preceding plot points would have happened if you had not so graciously grabbed my wrist and pulled me up."

"You jumped to distract the Count and saved the day. It was insane. Like something you'd see in…"

"Don't say it."

He laughed again. "Then, why did you do that? I mean, why did you do any of it?"

"I don't know. It just seemed like the right thing to do."

"For who? Them?" Aleix nodded towards the front of the church, where a handful of stone caricatures silently watched their conversation with cold, lifeless eyes. "You believe in all this stuff?"

"What? Goodness, no. I don't believe in any of this."

"Then why were you sitting here all alone in the dark?"

Elizabeth saw herself as Aleix must see her, sitting in the Count's chapel, in her own solitary pew at the back, her shawl hugged around her shoulders. Funny how the pews felt the same whether it was eighteenth-century Spain or twenty-first century Kansas. She could close her eyes and imagine she sat in her own regular pew in St. Andrew's where she sat so often, saying nothing to anyone, dead or alive. At one time, Elizabeth's feet had swung carelessly over the cool linoleum floor while incense burned, songs were sung, and echoes of sermons passed by.

"I think it has something to do with my mother." Elizabeth curdled within. She hadn't meant to say that. She had never even thought that. But suddenly, sitting in this chapel with Aleix, it felt like the first piece of real honesty she had spoken in a long time.

"Your mother?"

"Yes. She couldn't play a note of music, and she couldn't tell Bach from Beethoven, but she made warm things in the kitchen and listened to my fears like they mattered. She talked about important things, and she taught me to do the one thing in this life she had mastered, even though I complained endlessly. It was like, by learning to sew a stitch properly, I had a piece of her."

"She died?"

Elizabeth nodded. "And now I do it on purpose, I guess. Have been for years, really. I just sit here and think about anything in the world: the laundry list, you know? Or my music, review my scores, go over my problems in my head, what to do with the rest of my day, how to avoid people I don't like."

A blast of cheers erupted from just beyond the chapel doors. Elizabeth jumped. "Goodness. What's going on out there?"

"Oh, the Count is promising to throw a festival for the couples. Food, fireworks, the whole thing."

"Fireworks? Oh yes, I seem to remember something about that."

Aleix lifted his satchel over his head and rested it on the pew. Elizabeth had to stop an instinctual desire to look away.

"So, I don't understand," he said. "You come to church, you sit here and think about anything in the world but your religion?"

"Yes, That's it. That's my religion. To will myself never to believe again."

"Then why come at all?"

"I don't know. I want to make sure it doesn't go unnoticed, I guess. What's so funny? That's a strange time to laugh. I've never told anyone that before."

"I'm sure you haven't. If you really didn't believe in any of this stuff, you wouldn't come at all. You can't ignore something and say, 'I don't believe in it' at the same time."

"You mean all this time I've just been proving I believe in God? No wonder you're laughing. Well, I could laugh at you too then."

"Me? Oh no. I couldn't care less about this place for anything but artifacts and some raw materials. Melt it all down and make something useful."

"Like weapons?"

"At least that's a reality with some usefulness," he said, his gaze drifting off through the chapel, perhaps evaluating the worth of all the precious metals.

"What about love?" Elizabeth said. "You said you don't believe in love. If that's still true, then why are you in here talking to me, instead of out there drinking it up and eating your fill? What are you on strike against, if nothing out there is real?"

Something wonderful and strangely familiar sang out just beyond the chapel doors. Man-made sounds, but organized, flute-like, then long and pulled thin, moving around carelessly from pitch to pitch. Elizabeth drew in a long slow breath to entrap the sounds within her very core. "What is that?" she whispered.

"The musicians. Surely you didn't think you're the only one around? They're here to play for the festivities."

"An orchestra?" Elizabeth jumped up and left her pew. She circled around towards the chapel door and put her ear to it. "Oh, how beautiful! I've never heard anything so wonderful. Listen, just listen to all the beautiful colors and harmonies. A real Mozartian orchestra. What will they play?"

"Just some dances. And I doubt it's an orchestra. The Count isn't that benevolent. Probably just a handful of locals."

The musicians finished tuning, then the sounds coalesced into a triumphant lilting melody, intertwining upon itself in simple repeating patterns. Elizabeth swayed to and fro with the lilting pulses, caught up in a rapture of momentary bliss.

"Do you dance, Elly?" Aleix rose from the pew and stepped toward her.

"It's Elizabeth. And a little. Do you?"

"Everyone dances where I'm from, but not like here."

"Forgive me, but it's hard to imagine you doing a—"

He was encroaching on her personal space, and she felt herself stiffen against a large stone pillar.

"It's hard to imagine me doing a what?"

"Oh, I don't know. Anything: a bourée, a gavotte, a rigaudon?"

"A rigaudon? Really? Can you close your eyes and see anyone doing a rigaudon? Do you even know what it looks like?" He moved in, so close that his warmth reached her skin, and her hands felt for the cool stone behind her.

"Well, maybe not that one, but perhaps a triple rhythm like a chaconne, a courante, a minuet." Elizabeth ransacked her wiles to understand why she was suddenly naming French dances. "Or there's, there's the compound duple rhythms, like the canarie, the forlana, or the gigue."

"The gigue? I could do a gigue." He wrapped her neck in a large, calloused hand, bent down, and kissed her cheek softly.

"No. No, I don't think you could do a gigue. It's very bouncy. Definitely not your style."

His kiss moved beneath her ear.

"But I bet you could learn an allemande. That's probably more suited to you. It only requires two people."

"That does sound more my style."

"Oh great, I'll teach you!" Elizabeth crumpled and ducked away from the pillar and his tickling kisses, wondering what the hell was wrong with her. "It's not so difficult; you can learn. Come, now you stand here, and I stand next to you, and we bow, or rather, you bow and I curtsey. Now we step right a little then left a little, like that, then you raise up your right arm and I turn like so. Now give me your other hand and we do two quick rosettes, up and over, well, oh my, not so graceful! You're a bit taller than I am. No, don't let go yet. Now your arm comes up here while the other goes behind my back. Like this, like you're framing me in a window. You are very tall."

"I feel like a pretzel."

"Well, it's funny you should say that. Did you know, in Switzerland, royal couples used a pretzel in their wedding ceremonies to seal the bond of matrimony, and that's where the expression 'tying the knot' came from?"

Was she talking about pretzels?

"Shall we go out?" she said. "Join the foolish rejoicing hordes of plebes? Sign in for all the hypocrisy and make our presence known on the dance floor?" She pulled on his arm, but he hesitated.

"Where did you learn to dance like this?" he asked.

"Opera class."

Chapter Twenty-Eight

E lizabeth skittered out of the chapel, pulling Aleix along behind her. Flowers had been strung together and draped between the trees and topiaries. Tables decorated with lace held spirits and colorful bowls of fruits. She could almost smell the joy in the air as she passed fellow servants and staff giddy with laughter, spinning and dancing in their fabrics of white, lavender, and cool misty pinks. As the musicians played on, everything felt brighter and cleaner to Elizabeth than anything she had seen so far in Spain.

She followed the orchestral sounds and stood spellbound next to the musicians, feeling like a child at an ice cream stand. Oh, how she missed music. Wishing to share that with Aleix, she only then realized his hand had somehow slipped from her fingers. He was gone.

She did a cursory search between the swirling fabrics, but only saw Marcellina and Bartolo seated together on a bench, accepting flowers and congratulations. The garden bustled with a massive gathering, not just of staff but also villagers coming to pay respects to the newly married Figaro, the beloved barber. Surely the word had spread far and wide of the celebrations, for it seemed to Elizabeth like a massive cast party of characters from opera high and low, all spinning, laughing, and toasting.

The whole atmosphere resounded with a hopeful faith, and that struck Elizabeth as odd. Faith in marriage? Faith in the future? Faith in love unending? Perhaps. But certainly, faith in joy itself, and despite her own misgivings about romantic love, she wanted to run and join them all, to dance and spin, to twirl her own skirts foolishly in the lengthening shadows of the day, to smile on everyone, even Cook. She wanted to find Cook and smile on her at last (Elizabeth assumed Cook was a she).

When someone brought her a mug, she drank. When a tray passed with strawberries, she indulged, and when a fellow servant she had never met asked her to dance, she danced. The shadows grew longer and thinner and the color of the sky faded from blue to gray. There was so much chatter, so much life that she could barely discern. She wondered if Gaspar was here somewhere, and a momentary blush of shame washed over her. She wanted to find him and apologize. Surely, he was here, but she had not seen him, and that was strange, for she was certain he would have come, laden with a circle of cheese for his friend.

As the darkness of evening finally settled in, the music slowed, and the newlywed couples took to the center of the grounds alone. Lanterns on stakes were lit around them, and the quartet danced a tender intertwining of arms and steps that reminded Elizabeth of a subtle and soft flamenco.

Elizabeth had never enjoyed a wedding as much as this one. Back home, she always felt so abysmally alone at weddings, but tonight she allowed wonder to fill her with questions. Would she marry one day? And would her wedding feel like this one? She would never dance with her father at her wedding. In fact, if he hadn't died, she probably never would have wanted to dance with him, tripping on her toes, smelling of cigars, and barely able to say anything to her. It would have annoyed her, the whole ridiculous thing.

A tall male figure walked out to the center, lightly holding a woman's hand. In the fall of evening, the Count and Countess looked only as distinguishable as their large formal attire. Together, the new sextet began a more formalized dance, like a minuet, constantly exchanging partners with one another, passing between, through and around in the flickering candlelight. The music changed, then more couples joined until the newlyweds were lost in the crowd. Only the Countess's skirts and the Count's tricorne hat marked them as different from the others. When the dancers multiplied, Master and Mistress both subtly eased out, her skirt to one side and his tricorne to the other.

The Count approached Elizabeth's bench and took a quiet seat beside her as though she were just another topiary. She wondered if he even knew she was there. He leaned over towards the posted candle and pulled a paper from the cuff of his sleeve, pricking himself with the pin that held it sealed.

Of course. Susanna must have passed him the note while they were dancing. Just like it should be. He would agree to meet her in the gardens and instead woo and seduce his own wife in the shadows.

If Elizabeth remembered correctly, the note was to be confirmed by returning the pin by way of...oh now, here was a pickle. The Count was supposed to send the pin back to Susanna with Figaro's cousin, Barbarina, but in this mockup, that poor girl stood stomping her hooves in the barn. How would the Count return the pin to Susanna with no Barbarina?

"I understand you used to play for the opera," the Count said suddenly. "Is that true?"

Elizabeth straightened. "Yes sir, that is true."

"What's the story there? I'm very curious what could have brought such a change in someone's line of work. Surely you don't prefer scrubbing pots to making music. Do you mind if I ask?"

"No, I don't mind. It's just difficult to explain. My father died."

The Count's silhouette turned on her, the large tricorne

blocking the candlelight from her face. "I'm sorry."

"No," Elizabeth said. "I mean he died, but that's not why I left the opera. I think the problem was that I forgot."

"You are a strange one. I don't know whether to send you to the bin, treat you like a scholar, or ascribe you a gypsy. But I doubt there's any sort of curse on you, since I've seen you at Mass almost every week."

"Yes. We've all been showing up at Mass, haven't we? But I don't mean that I forgot why I left opera. I mean, I forgot who I was."

"You mean you suffered a memory loss? I've heard about cases of that."

"No, that's not it. I'm trying to explain. Opera was just like a blanket. But it wasn't all of me. It was just..."

"It was just what?" The Count asked.

"It was just...enough."

Katie Baines, a junior mezzo soprano, sat like a defeated lily amidst the piles of theatrical carnage heaped around her. So chaotic and packed was the tiny costume room that with a quick scan, one might miss her completely, wedged on a small rickety chair between two stacks, her sad young face blended in with all the other things drooping, hanging, and languorous. Just another piece to be shredded, stitched, primped, and thrown aside.

There were piles of projects needing to be done, piles of projects dreaming of being done, and piles of projects waiting to be hung, pressed, and stored. Somehow, each costume would eventually work its way out of that merciless quagmire, but only one piece at a time, and always just before opening night.

Katie looked like she'd never leave. She had somehow arrived at such a low in her still infantile existence that she might just choose to stay here, another unnoticed scrap, dissolving into the fabric chaos. Let it all swallow her, so she could finish out her days as a mildewy thread on someone's corset, covered with human sweat and the drippings of stage makeup.

Elizabeth dropped a pile of pants on one of the heaps. Her help with costume alterations was one of many compromises made with the theater department to mount fully staged operas at the college. "Here you go, Meredith. All finished, I hope."

Hunched over a machine, just beyond a mountain of fourteenth-century leggings, sat the campus's main seamstress, Meredith. A living marvel, the woman perpetually completed impossible quantities of work, week after week with quiet precision.

"Oh good. Wait, nuh, nuh, put dem dere, over dere. Don't get my shows mixed up," Meredith said with fitting pins clenched in her front teeth.

Elizabeth removed the offensive pile of pants and turned to Katie. "Are you here for your fitting?"

Katie's look of despair could pass for a piece of twentieth-century artwork, like melting clocks, lost staircases, or a blur of limbs screaming on the end of a dock.

"She's next," Meredith said, grinding away on her machine. "Just give me two more minutes, hon."

"Is that your costume for *Romeo and Juliette*?" Elizabeth asked. "Oh, let me see!"

Katie lifted her eyes towards the opposite wall where Jessica, a soprano, preened between three mirrors in a thirteenth-century ball gown of light-blue satin. The empire-cut dress had puffs on the shoulders and a long full skirt adorned with lace appliques. Jessica looked so stunning that she glowed. An operatic icon. A descendant from every publicity shot of Maria Callas, Joan Sutherland, or Leontyne Price. Elizabeth sighed with delight. Seeing the girls in their costumes for the first time was always such a thrill.

"Oh, Jessica. You are breathtaking."

"Isn't she?" Meredith said, rising from her machine with a newly mended applique. "Let's just try this. Don't move, sweetheart, let me just pin this, and now give us a turn."

Jessica turned and cooed.

"Hold on," Meredith said, "I'd better take one more look at that hem. Don't want you breaking your neck on those risers."

Katie's eyes filled up with a gloss. Katie was not an operatic icon. Katie wore a pair of dark green tights topped off with puffy green satin shorts. Above this, she had on a green jacket buttoned up to the chin and a velvet cap on her red curly hair with a solitary, sad feather trying desperately to remain erect.

"Katie, are you all right?" Elizabeth heaved a towering pile of costumes off a chair and sat down. "What's wrong?"

Katie stared hopelessly at Jessica, who turned like a figurine on a music box raising a cocky eyebrow towards Katie. Oh, the wicked, competitive nature of sopranos.

When the seamstress dismissed Jessica, she lifted her skirts and swished past as a tear trickled down Katie's quivering chin.

"Oh, come on Katie," Elizabeth said. "You'll get to wear the pretty dresses someday."

It was a lie. Since most operatic heroines are written for sopranos, mezzos or middle-voiced female singers are perpetually condemned to smaller supporting roles.

"I'm a mezzo. All I get to play is little boys, witches, and maids."

"Now that's not true. Come on. What about Carmen?" There are a few exceptions to the mezzo fate of course, particularly if the mezzo can sing coloratura well enough to do Rossini, but Carmen is the only really famous mezzo to have great costumes and the soprano-esque death scene.

"I'll never play Carmen," Katie said between sobs. "I'm a lyric. I don't have any chest voice."

Elizabeth sighed and desperately tried to conceal any expression of tragedy from Katie. Here was the real opera. The girl was right. Without any chest voice to help project her low notes, she was fated to repeat the same roles over and over, eternally dressed as little boys, witches, and old hags. Always the supporting comprimario and never the star. Always carrying on the soprano's tea or her shoes, or whatever prop she needed to get through her next glorious high-note and ensuing death.

"And now you won't have any chest," said Meredith, stepping forward with a large strand of Ace bandages. "Stand up and open that jacket. I'll show you how to strap in your girls before putting on your costume."

Katie exploded into sobs, and Elizabeth didn't know what to tell her. Her dreams of tiaras and long, shiny synthetic wigs were fast crumbling. For no matter how hard she worked, Katie could never change her fate. She could never change what she was. She would have to learn to fall in love with something else. Something that she could be.

"Meredith, really," Elizabeth said. "A little sensitivity. Katie, listen. It's not so bad as all that. There are the Rossini heroines. And your chest voice will grow out in your twenties. Besides, think of all the fun things that mezzos get to do."

Katie wiped her eyes and Meredith passed her a Kleenex. "Like carry on props?"

"No. Did you know you get to be in a real sword fight in this show?"

"I do? I get to hold the sword? Not just sit on the side and watch the boys?"

"Heck no! If you don't get in a sword fight, we have no fight scene. It's in the score. We have a special fencing coach coming to rehearsal today to stage your fight scene."

"Really?" Katie blew her nose.

"Don't let Jessica get you down," said Elizabeth. "Listen, you can't spend your life trying to wear a size seven shoe if your foot is a size eight. You'll just ruin your feet. You've got to be who you are."

"I want a pretty dress."

"Well, at least you know what you want. Now stand up and unbutton so we can strap you down."

"Opera was safe," Elizabeth said to the Count. "But it wasn't my story."

The Count laughed at her. "And your story is working in my scullery."

"Right now, sir, my story is to help you with yours."

"You tried to jump out a window earlier today."

"To stop you from making a terrible mistake that would have permanently ruined your marriage."

"How dare you, you little strumpet!" He rose and ripped off the tricorne. "I should dismiss you for such insolence."

Elizabeth stood to face his towering darkness. "I am not afraid of you," she said, "and in your hand you are holding a pin that you want me to return to Susanna for you, to confirm your little tryst this evening. Well, I won't. I don't care if it's part of the plot. I don't care if this show never resolves."

"Susanna told you!"

"Oh, you are a piece of work. How arrogant does one have to be, to think you have some mysterious sophistication amongst your staff when you are forcing your way through every female on your property? You think we don't talk to one another just because the indiscretion involves our employer? You think we don't see things, like Susanna passing you that note during that dance just now? Do you really think us so plainly stupid as all that?"

"How dare you—"

The crowds stopped their chatter as Elizabeth's voice spread like an infection through the wedding festivities. The dancers slowed one by one, and the musicians wavered on perpetual chords, their violins perched atop curious shoulders, listening to the voice resounding through the shadows.

"How dare *you* sir. You remind me of every politician back home, wearing a public mask and hiding behind it with platitudes. You can't stop the marriage of Figaro now. You're too late. They are married under every law of land and God."

"I don't know what you're babbling on about, woman."

"Yes, I am a woman. In fact, how is that bump on your head? The one you woke up with in the woods when you chased down Amada? How do I know about that? I must be a witch."

The Count raised a guilty hand to the back of his head.

"I don't know what it will take to bring you to some sense of humility, or just humanity, in order to end this plot, but yesterday a friend reminded me that life isn't an opera. Even if this story ends like it does in the opera, you won't really change. You'll just go back to your lecherous leadership in a week or two."

"You would be wise to lower your voice, woman."

"I won't be a part of your scheming. I don't care whether I have to spend eternity in your scullery or fend for myself alone in the wilderness just because I won't pass that pin to your wife's chambermaid for you. I just realized I'd rather lose everything than lose myself. Find someone else to help you cheat on your wife."

He struck her.

She was on the ground, the left side of her face pulsating, her jaw and temple screaming with naked, raw pain. The Count shouted down at her in muffled echoes. She wanted to get up, to run away to her little studio and play something beautiful, but she was dizzy, and her head pounded. She suddenly understood the dissonance of every atonal piece of twentieth-century music she'd ever heard. The ugly, uncensored violence came to her with merciless clarity, a depiction of pain she had never really known in her comfortable life in Wichita, in her nice apartment with everything she needed and always some money to spare. It terrified her how quickly the pain seized her. This man, who was screaming at her, reaching down for her, grabbing her arm with an iron grip, saying something about impropriety and insolence, and learning a lesson. In the candle's light, she saw the shadow of his arm raise again, and she flinched.

But his hand did not come down. Someone stood between her and the Count's strike, a woman in servant's clothing.

"You will not strike this girl again sir," the woman said. "You will have to strike me first."

It was Beatriz, the seamstress from the catacombs. She had stepped between Elizabeth and the Count's fist.

"So be it."

"And me, sir," Amada said, stepping forward. "You'll have to hit me too."

Elizabeth felt herself nudged back by another swish of skirts. "Me as well." Marcellina, of all things.

"And me." Susanna.

"You can go ahead and %$# give me a good @#^$ whack too, then."

Elizabeth thought she was delusional, for that sounded like Cook. She tried to peek around the shoulders of the other women, but her head reacted with a stinging throb.

The men started stepping up. Figaro first, followed by servants and staff she had never met. One by one they stepped between her and the Count, wedging themselves in and nudging her further back, until a crowd stood between them.

Somewhere at the front, the Count faced his staff. When the last had placed themselves before him, a great silence passed, interrupted only by an occasional footstep, mosquito shooing, or pluck on a distant instrument watching from afar.

This was it. *The Count's repentance scene. This must be it.* The end of the opera had come, not through some pretend tryst in the gardens, but by Elizabeth herself standing up to him. Surely this was the mortification he needed to transform, to become a better man. Perhaps Elizabeth's courage had been all it really took to bring the man to his sense of dignity. Someone just had to stand up to him and tell him the truth...

"Then you can all leave my estate before the sun rises," the Count said. "All of you. And none will be given references. Now go back to your rooms and pack your things."

Before anyone could move, utter a word of protest, or even release a gasp of horror, the ground beneath them rocked as though from a mighty thrust, and behind the Count, his great house exploded into a massive tower of smoke and flame.

Chapter Twenty-Nine

E lizabeth ran.

"We're under attack!" someone hollered. "They've hit the armory!"

Servants and guests raced in a chaotic swarm of panic, darting between the darkened topiaries and holding useless hands over their heads. They careened into one another, searching for loved ones, while ash and smoke billowed into the night sky. Men shouted orders that were barely heard and less obeyed.

Elizabeth ran, her heart pounding so loudly she didn't know if the sound came from inside or out. The massive blast, the threat of debris falling randomly from the sky, the terrified cries of the Count's staff, it all gripped her with such a horror that she could only commit herself to that one thought. *Keep running.*

She reached a structure and felt along its walls for an opening, a place to hide. Pulling on a heavy handle, she slipped inside. In the new darkness, thick stone walls cooled the air and dampened the shouts and screams of the scene outside, sounds like nightmare echoes in a war zone. She huddled down in a corner, hugging her knees to her chest, waiting for a second explosion, a follow-up attack. But only the shouts remained.

She squeezed her eyes shut and willed herself home, where

everything made sense, where the only surprising element of her days was the unpredictability of weather. She tried to envision her second-floor apartment, sitting on her tiny sofa, her fingers wrapped around a warm ceramic mug. If she could just think it hard enough, imagine it fully, she could go home. Like Dorothy, who found her way without the Wizard's help. If she just clicked her heels together and wished for it, maybe she could get out of this horrible place, out of this horrible opera and go home. Home.

She opened her eyes. On a distant wall, a single lonely candle flickered within a red glass. How strange that she had found her way back to the chapel. She watched the tiny light jump up and down, casting gentle red waves on the sleeping sculptures, despite the chaos taking place just a few yards away outside.

What had happened? Were they under attack? She should go out and help them. Help round people up and stop the fire. They will want to make sure everyone is safe. They might even start looking for her or...the Countess. *Oh no!* What if the Countess was still in the house dressing for the tryst when the explosion took place? Hopefully not. Probably already in the gardens, waiting for her husband, and had already been found...

Something caught Elizabeth's attention, draped out of place over the last pew. She pulled herself up from her huddle and lifted her own shawl. *Of course.* She had left it here in her giddiness of the dance with Aleix.

As her eyes adjusted to the dark, she saw something else. A leather satchel with a long shoulder strap. Aleix had also left something behind during their dance. *What does he keep in this sack that's so important that he always has it with him?* It was probably just some sort of weapon, or maybe the keys to the armory closets. Yes, that must be it.

She looked over her shoulder, but of course no one was there.

She carried the satchel to the front of the sanctuary and stood within the glow of the sanctuary lamp. Feeling a little guilty but not enough to stop, she pulled back the satchel lip and peered inside. Too dark. Her hand reached in and grabbed something solid. Not a gun. A book.

It pleased her that Aleix carried a book everywhere. It reminded her of the simple safety of her father. What was he reading then? She held the book up to the light. Red threadbare covering, gold lettering on top, a capital "E."

She dropped it on the stone floor where it landed with a resounding smack. So Aleix had stolen her book.

A small paper fluttered downwards after it. She picked it up and held it in the light.

S,

> *Forgive me, but I must make a last-minute change for this evening's charade. After some wise counsel, I have decided that to meet in the gardens would be imprudent. Too many possible eyes. Instead, please rewrite our note and tell my husband to meet you on the roof of the west wing. There is a lovely, plateaued area up there, with plenty of chimneys and dark corners. I will set up a rendezvous spot for us that will enchant him completely. With the wedding going on, no one will be near there this evening. It will work for our venture much better. Please rewrite the note before giving it to my husband.*
>
> *Thank you,*
> *R-*

The chaos beyond the chapel doors continued with shouts and cries echoing through the darkness. There were no more explosions, but the house sporadically sputtered wildly, and whatever eighteenth-century attempts for containing fires were well underway.

But the Countess. *The Countess!*

Everyone would be looking for her. Elizabeth put the book back in the satchel and draped it across her shoulders. She stepped out into the night air and immediately felt the heat of the inferno blowing towards her. Darkened forms ran to and fro, shouting orders, passing buckets, carrying ladders.

Tongues of bright red and yellow flames licked out from every window on the east side of the house, smashing glass and stretching upwards into the night sky. Smoke billowed like a creature of hell. The curved structure had completely protected the west branch, but eventually the flames would spread through all the rooms and foundations. If the Countess was still dressing in her chambers, it was too late. But if she had finished or dressed somewhere else, then there was a chance she might be stranded on the roof of the west wing.

"Find her!" the Count's disembodied voice rang out above the chaos. No doubt Susanna or Figaro had already informed him of her location and...

Elizabeth held up the tiny note still clenched in her fist. The Countess's note had never made it to Susanna. Aleix was supposed to deliver it but got distracted in their dance, leaving his satchel with the note in the chapel. That meant that if the Countess was still alive, she was not in the gardens where everyone would be searching for her. She would be alone on the roof. And the only person who knew where she was...

Elizabeth let the note fall from her hand. Before her, the Count's mighty estate of finance and luxury billowed like a furious raging dragon.

A shadow passed, running with a ladder.

"Sir, wait! I know where—"

"Sorry miss, but I can't help you. We've got to find the Countess Rosina!"

"That's just it, I know where—"

But he disappeared into the night. Other shadows appeared, flowing in and out of her perception before she could grab hold of them. "I know where she is!" she screamed. "Someone listen to me!" Her cries blended into the chaos and the sounds of the house slowly crackling into oblivion mere yards away.

The fire remained temporarily contained in the east wing,

where servants ran in and out, carrying furniture and paintings. The servants' entrance sat ignored amidst it all, a small black rectangle, still clear of any sign of flames. That would not last. Soon they would blow westward, blocking any possible entrance and creating instability in the main structure.

Elizabeth lifted her skirts and ran for the door. Loose gravel scattered behind her as she dashed into the house, hoping against hope that she would find the Countess just beyond its blackened threshold.

❦

The servants' halls and the kitchen were still completely free of smoke and flame. Elizabeth headed for the servants' staircase, with which she had always accessed the Countess's quarters. She felt the door with her palm, then lifted a lantern from the wall and ascended carefully, feeling the second-floor door before opening it onto the great landing. Immediately her throat constricted in revolt. Smoke stung her nostrils, and she closed her flooding eyes, ducking down to the floor, grateful for the simple mantra pounded into every child— "stop, drop, and roll." She stopped and dropped to her back, convulsing. She could feel a draft blowing the smoke towards the center of the house from the eastern wing. She would have to crawl down the corridor to the far western stairs, which only began on this floor.

The heat sank upon her, and she wished to rip off her endless undergarments. Though she could not see it, she heard the fire roar in bellowing gusts down the eastern corridor. She stifled an urge to mourn her little harpsichord, sitting helpless in the Countess's quarters, crackling to pieces in the merciless flames like a helpless moth.

In a momentary clearing, she saw the mighty stone fireplace above her with two crossed swords hanging above, a reminder of her own impending death if she did not force herself to move.

She coughed again. What was she doing here? Why had she

314

come inside the house at all? This was not her story. This was not her problem. This didn't happen in the opera. Not even Puccini wrote anything like this. Why hadn't she just stuck to the plot and helped the Count deliver his dumb pin to Susanna for his little theatrical slap on the wrist?

The Countess was in trouble, and Elizabeth had nothing to do with that. She had not changed the location of the tryst. She had only found Aleix's satchel with her book and the strange note.

It suddenly occurred to Elizabeth that whatever she would encounter on the roof might be more than a frightened eighteenth-century soprano. Someone had convinced the Countess to move to the roof. Someone had stolen Elizabeth's book. Someone had caused an explosion that could have killed, and might still do so. Someone had kidnapped and branded Figaro, dropped an axe in the Countess's chambers, and frightened Figaro and Susanna off into a perilous night.

She remembered the dark hooded figure who had so cunningly intervened with previous plot points and easily thwarted any attempts at capture. Whoever it was, opera character, intervener, demon spirit, or baritone, he was to blame for all of this mayhem in the final act. He had changed the Countess's plans. He had somehow caused the explosion, and most assuredly, he was waiting for Elizabeth right now.

On the roof.

She pushed herself up on arms stiffened with terror. Still fighting the natural inclination to fall into fits of choking, she rose and dragged a wooden armchair close to the hearth. She climbed, rising into the smoke where the fumes assailed all her senses with intent to kill. She reached out as she closed her eyes from the sting. The heavy stones still felt cool beneath her fingers as she grappled around blindly, her head ducked beneath her armpit. At last, her fingers fastened around the sword's grip. Though heavy, it lifted easily from its wall-mounted perch, as though pre-set for her by some great composer, waiting patiently for its cue to come in the smoky darkness.

❧❦❧

Crossing to the western roof stair through the smoky corridor was foolish, so she returned to the servants' stair and shut the door behind her. Up, up, up she wound, feeling heavier with each step. Finding the third-floor landing less perilous with smoke, she stepped into the central parlor, relieved that she would not have to crawl to the west wing.

The long west corridor was a part of the house she had only frequented a few times. Most of the rooms would pass for high luxury in any century, each with its own fireplace. But Elizabeth still shivered at the idea of using anything but a flushable toilet for the rest of her life.

But maybe this was the rest of her life. This march alone down a darkened hallway, to a roof with no escape, an inferno that could not be stopped, and a villain with no face and no compunction. Perhaps this was her **double bar line**. The Conductor, the audience, the stage crew, and even the coaches stood now in the shadows, all holding their breath as they watched her, stick aloft, violin bows perpetually frozen just above their strings, lips whetted and ready for a great and devastating final cadenza.

At the far end of the hallway, she ascended the western servants' stair, arrived at a final door, and pushed her way out into the evening air.

The door sat embedded in a dormer on the far end of the western arm. Most of the flat roof was bordered with raked gables studded with chimneys. Flames crackled across the front courtyard from the western wing, thick with the smell of roasting house.

She followed the courtyard-side gable along the base of its rake, stepping cautiously, her sword pointed before her. Men's

316

voices rang out, arguing just beyond the wing's main chimney. She rounded the corner.

The Countess lay unconscious, dressed in Susanna's skirts, her hands bound.

On one side, an extended arm held a long thin blade. Gaspar. On the other side, with a primitive sort of pistol...

"Welcome, Elly," Aleix said. "You're right on time."

The Countess moaned and rolled her head.

"Elizabeth," Gaspar said. "You shouldn't have come. But knew you would. Knew you'd come."

"What's going on here?" she asked, stepping lightly now, her sword dragging on the roof floor.

"I just caught this villain in an abduction of our Mistress," Aleix explained. "He lured her up here and set fire to the house in an attempt to kill her, the coward."

"What?" said Gaspar. "That's not true. Was the other way around. I followed this braggart up here. Saw him poking around and knew he was up to no good. So, I waited here. Knew he'd be back. He abducted the Countess Rosina. He's your hooded figure who's been rewriting your plot all along."

"Elly, don't listen to him. He's trying to seduce you away from the truth. You mustn't believe this man."

"Elizabeth, I've never told you a lie."

"Nor have I. Have I ever once lied to you?"

"Don't listen to him," said Gaspar, waving his sword towards Aleix. "There's his black cape there. Only pulled it off right before you arrived."

Elizabeth bent and lifted the small mound of black fabric with her free hand, holding it aloft in the smoky night air.

"Elly," Aleix said, "That is not my cloak. It's his."

"I found your satchel," she said. "You left it in the chapel. I found the note from the Countess, and I found my missing book. Why was it in your satchel, Aleix?"

"Because he stole it from you, Elizabeth, in order to thwart your efforts at the plot," said Gaspar. "Think about it. Every time you fixed something, your book helped you to uncover his sabotage and bring things back on track. He had to get the book away from you in order to ruin your efforts to complete the story."

"Why would I want to do that?" Aleix asked. "He's the one with all the motive here, don't you see? I did find your book, but it wasn't in your room, it was in this man's cheese cart, while he was off misleading you into trusting him. He is not your friend, Elly. He's the one preventing you from finishing it. He's trying to ruin the plot so that you will never leave."

"Gaspar?"

Elizabeth tried to discern Gaspar's face through the wafting tufts of smoke, but he was in shadow. Both of them were, their faces veiled, leaving only their voices to plead their case. The fire raged beyond the crest of the gables. It cracked and moaned like an audience hidden in the darkness behind the stage lights.

"Elizabeth, don't let him into your head. How does he know about that book of yours then? Did you tell him about it too?"

"No, I didn't tell him."

"It doesn't take a witch doctor to know what that book is about when you start reading it," Aleix said. "I'm not an idiot, and neither are you. Don't you see? He lost his own family, his own pride killed them. He's trying to replace them with you. Make you into the daughter he killed."

"That's enough, you bastard!" Gaspar leaped forward. Aleix pulled the trigger, and a shot ripped through the night, searing past the fire and chaos of voices below. Elizabeth gasped, but Gaspar had tripped on the Countess's foot in his lunge and went flailing to the roof floor. Aleix dropped his empty pistol to the ground and swiped up the sword.

Gaspar rolled onto his back and brought a shadowed hand to his nose. Aleix stood towering above him, the sword in his hand. Elizabeth lifted her own blade, spread her feet out in a wider stance, bent her knees, lifted her back arm.

"Elly, surely you didn't believe him?"

"My name," she said, "is Elizabeth."

Aleix laughed. "Really? Are you going to fight me, Elly?"

"Elizabeth."

Aleix moved closer. She felt her feet sliding backwards along the roof. "You don't want to fight me."

On the ground, Gaspar grappled with something that scattered across the roof like marbles.

Undeterred, Aleix swung, and their blades met with a swift clang. She struck back and the blades twisted together in the blackness. His arm was stronger, and she could feel her blade give only a minimal theatrical resistance to his strikes. He was playing with her. She could see his eyes reflecting firelight, and the scar on his cheek seemed to protrude into a grotesque tentacled parasite as he lunged forward. She parried and stepped back again, swung, striking only air.

"Where did you learn to wield a blade?" he said. "Opera class?"

His features changed from amused to furious as he swung at Elizabeth with strength. She felt the vibrations shock her grasp beneath the knuckle guard. She clutched it with both hands and swung back at the night air wildly, forgetting anything she learned from the *Romeo* production.

Aleix inched her further and further from the Countess and Gaspar, his strikes becoming more and more heavy handed. "You have to make your choices in every story, Elly. You have to decide. It's them or you. Every story needs a villain, doesn't it? Someone has to push the plot along." In a quick twist, he sent her sword sprawling across the roof. "Didn't you learn that in your opera class?"

"Who are you?"

"Don't you know, Princess?" He pulled her to him. "I'm destiny." He pressed his lips to hers, but she pushed back.

"Stop doing that!"

"That's enough," Gaspar said, closer now.

Aleix stiffened and retracted his hands, dropping the sword. He stepped back. Gaspar held the pistol squarely to the back of

Aleix's neck. "Don't imagine you'd fancy a head full of lead. Put your hands where I can see them."

"There's nothing anyone can do now," Aleix said. "This story is far from over." Aleix turned suddenly and knocked Gaspar's hand with the back of his elbow. He grabbed and twisted it around, snatching the pistol back. He stepped to Elizabeth. "This," he said, wrenching his satchel off her, "belongs to me. Now, this part I know you'll understand. Making a big exit is part of the show, isn't it? You're clever enough to get off this roof by yourselves. You have to learn how to set yourself up carefully, Elly. Rule number one. Always find a convenient position. Being an armorer, in charge of the weapons, the gun powder." He took a few steps back. "Nobody really keeps track of you." He turned and ran towards the far western arm of the roof, disappearing into a gust of passing smoke.

"We can use the western servants' stair," Elizabeth said. "The fire is nowhere near it. We'll have to negotiate getting past the second floor."

"Come on, let's get the Countess." Gaspar and Elizabeth unbound the Countess and tried to wake her, but she only moaned.

"Come on, Rosina," Elizabeth said, slapping her softly. "We have to get off this roof!"

Suddenly another explosion erupted, shaking the very floor beneath them with a threatening tremor. Elizabeth and Gaspar steadied themselves and huddled together as a second fiery inferno stretched upwards into the night sky from the far western wing of the house. Debris and ash came tumbling down as they huddled close to the chimney.

"That bastard!" Gaspar said. "He's blown up our only way out!"

Chapter Thirty

E lizabeth collapsed against a chimney. She imagined its stone reaching through the roof beneath her, and the four floors of the Count's house, right to the very basement where Cook had made so many forbidden delicacies and Elizabeth had cleaned so many pots.

"Oh Gaspar, I'm so sorry to have dragged you into this. You shouldn't be here."

"Says who?" he replied. The Countess's head dropped onto his shoulder. "I stand by all my choices."

"You should be safe at home, on your lovely farm, making some wonderful cheese."

"I've made the cheese, Elizabeth. It aged without me. But I am curious. Tell me, how did you know?"

"You mean, how did I know who to trust? I just knew."

"Just knew? Something in that head of yours, then?"

"More like the heart." She smiled at him and the Countess rolled her head again, murmuring softly. Elizabeth hoped she didn't wake before the house collapsed beneath them. At least she could just dream her way into death.

"That spot," Gaspar said, "in those woods, where you and that scoundrel found me. That was where she died. My Mariella, I mean. They found her there, not so far from some decent shelter, but alone. She died there, having the baby by herself, probably screaming for me. But I never came. There were bloodstains for a long time. Maybe not, but looked like to me. Still does. I go, once a year, on the day she was found. Spend the whole day and night. Don't know why. Foolish, I guess. Can't do anything now to change it. Should've maybe told you up front. That spot...in those woods."

"Gaspar, please stop. I'm so sorry."

"Don't be sorry, Elizabeth. You made the right choice. Knew who to trust with your own heart, didn't you?"

"Well, almost," she said. "There was also this." Elizabeth got to her feet and crossed to Aleix's black cloak, still crumbled in a mound on the roof floor. She lifted it like a defense attorney in a courtroom scene. "You could never have traipsed around in this thing," she said. "It's far too long for you. You'd break your neck on those risers."

A small explosion erupted with fury from the eastern edges of the estate. The smoke piled in on them, and they both began coughing.

"Elizabeth, we should get off this roof."

"But how? All the stairs are blocked, and no one knows we're up here."

A voice broke through the rumbles of the flames, distantly calling from below. "Hello up there! Can you hear me? Is anyone up there?"

Gaspar gently set down the Countess, and they scrambled up the nearest gable to peek over. Sure enough, the distant, darkened figure of the Count, surrounded by some of his men, glowed in the firelight below them.

"We're here," Gaspar called, waving. "How did you know we were here?"

"Someone found a note on the lawn in my wife's hand. Then we heard the shot. Is the Countess with you?" the Count said.

"Yes, but she's unconscious."

"We're getting a ladder, but it only reaches the third-floor windows. If you can lower her down, we can send a man up to meet her."

Elizabeth sank back down the gable. "How on earth do we do that?"

"I may have a solution," said Gaspar. "Stay here and keep trying to wake her."

"Where are you going?"

"Brought something with me. Thought we might need it, just in case that rascal pulled something like this." Gaspar ran off into the smoky blackness.

"Come on, Mistress. You've got to wake up." Elizabeth pulled the Countess upright, holding her head and slapping her cheeks.

"Who's there?" the Countess moaned. "Susanna, is that you?"

"No Mistress, it's Elizabeth."

"Who? Oh, I have such a headache." She lifted a hand to the back of her head.

"Yes, I imagine you do. Do you remember anything, Madame? How you came to be up on this roof?"

"Yes, Aleix convinced me to come up here, but then, something hit me on the head."

"Aleix hit you on the head."

"What? Why would he do that?"

"I'm not sure, but I think it had something to do with me. It's difficult to explain, but right now, we have to get off this roof."

"I smell smoke. Is something burning?"

Gaspar returned, carrying a large load of thick rope. "Hid it behind a central chimney this morning when I knew he was planning something up here. Never know. Going up on a roof to meet a villain, always have a way to get down."

"Oh, Gaspar, you're a wonder!" Elizabeth said, inwardly disappointed he didn't have a fire escape or an elevator. Even a hot air balloon was more pleasing than a rope. "But how do you expect to get us down using that?"

The Countess got to her feet. "Gracious Merciful Lord! The house!"

"Yes, Madame, and we have to get you off of it."

The Count's voice rose up from the courtyard. "Rosina? Are you there? What's going on?"

Gaspar dropped the ropes, then scrambled up the rake and peered down below. "We're going to lower the Countess down. Get a man on that ladder."

"Lower me down?" the Countess said. "What are you talking about? Why don't we just use the—" Right on cue, the flames from the western explosion wafted above the gables in a steadily approaching heat that seared the hairs on their faces.

"Gaspar, what are you thinking?" Elizabeth asked.

"Excuse me, Madame." He wound the rope beneath the Countess's armpits and tied it in a knot. "We're going to lower you down to the third-floor windows where a man is waiting for you on a ladder. Just hold this knot here and keep your weight backwards."

"Wait," cried Elizabeth. "Gaspar, are you sure the two of us can sustain her weight?"

"Sure. Tie the rope around that chimney and wrap it around this one as a leverage point, then we'll release it gradually."

"Wait," said the Countess, "how will you two get down?"

"Same way, Madame. Once you're clear, I'll help Elizabeth down, and then use the same rope to rappel myself down to the ladder."

Gaspar ran to a nearby chimney. He wound the rope around it and a second anchor post and then his own back before gesturing for Elizabeth to join him.

"I don't think I can do this," the Countess said.

"Have to, Madame," said Gaspar. "No time to think on it. The longer you wait, the less time we'll have to get ourselves to safety. Now just climb up that gable and slide down the other end. It's only twenty or so feet until someone on the ladder can grab you."

"Elizabeth?"

"We've got you, Mistress. Now go, quickly."

The Countess lifted her skirts and kicked off her shoes. Unsteadily, she managed at length to reach the ridge of the gable, where she inched her legs over and shimmied down the other side. As soon as the Countess's fingertips disappeared over the crest of the gable, Elizabeth and Gaspar felt her weight pull on the ropes. Elizabeth was sure she wasn't helping much, but she engaged every muscle to maintain the pretense. All at once, the Countess's weight was upon them and they countered, their feet slipping on the roof, the rope inching its way around the chimney.

Through the waves of heat scorching their hands and faces, and the fibers of the rope cutting through their palms, past the constant rumble of the encroaching inferno and the sporadic unhappy cracks pealing out like lightning from surrendering beams and structures, beyond it all, Elizabeth could now and again make out just a phrase, a word, a cry of horror as it wandered upwards to her unpluggable ears.

"Too far...Come down! Move...Quickly!...Hold steady... Almost there...Careful!"

The taut rope vibrated in her hands, pulling like an angry fish on the line. She tried to imagine the scene beyond the gable and clenched her eyes shut against the onslaught of stinging smoke, focusing her mind on a single ringing thought: *hold on, hold on, hold on.*

Finally, the weight released, and the pressure relaxed.

"We'd better hold on for the rest," said Gaspar. "In case they lose her."

They held the rope in their burned hands, watching it stretch out before them to the crest of the gable. It flopped back and forth as the Countess descended the ladder unseen beyond the ridge.

A new explosion burst in the floors below, and Elizabeth steadied herself as the roof shook beneath her pointy boots. Beyond the gable ridge, glass shattered and a woman screamed.

Flames spewed outward into the air. A few seconds later, the rope in her hands went totally slack. She and Gaspar pulled it in together, gathering it with wild frenzied arms, but it ended too quickly with a charred nub cresting the gable to fall limp at their feet.

Gaspar stomped the smoking end of the rope with his boot. He climbed back to the top of the gable, but mighty flames rose and crested just beyond. Coughing and covering his eyes, he rolled back down to the roof floor.

"Gaspar!"

"That way is out for us —" he said. "The fire's beneath us."

A horrifying crack filled the night air. Elizabeth and Gaspar ran to the nearest chimney and watched as the far eastern arm of the Count's estate crumbled in on itself in a fiery blur, all his dishes, draperies, moldings, and papers collapsing into an impenetrable veil of blackness and flame.

At the western wing, fire now raged out the windows of all three floors, steadily creeping up beneath their very feet. Both arms of the house now converged with twin raging infernos towards the center, towards Elizabeth and Gaspar.

He grabbed the rope up and pulled Elizabeth. "It's good he set the flames at both ends. It buys us time. Fire probably hasn't even reached here yet. But will. All will come down soon enough. All but the chimneys."

He found a more central gable and climbed up, waving to the rescuers below. Elizabeth heard only muffles of their conversation: something about a broken ladder and the Countess.

Gaspar returned. "We have to get you down without the ladder. Come." He unwound the rope and wrapped it around a thin chimney near the edge of the roof.

"Wait, Gaspar, you can't lower me down all that way by yourself!"

"Indeed," he said. "Now take off that outer layer of skirt. Might be too much fabric between your legs."

Elizabeth obeyed. Gaspar tossed both ends of the rope down over the side of the house.

"Damn," he said. "Looks like you'll only get as far as the second-floor landing. But there's that trellis ledge there. Can work your way along that to a window. Get yourself inside and find a clear stairway."

"But what about the smoke? It had already filled most of the second floor when I came up."

"You'll stay low and manage it. But first you'll need something to break that window."

He strode off again into the darkness. She heard something clanking and found him hitting the top edge of a smaller chimney with the hilt of his sword.

"Gaspar, what are you doing?"

"Getting you a brick. Need something to keep it in. Your hands will be too busy. Find that cloak and see if you can tear a good bit of it off. We'll use the fabric to make a pouch and tie it around you, like a baby."

"I've never held a baby."

"You will, Elizabeth," he said, continuing to pound at the chimney. Small pieces of mortar loosened and crumbled. "Now, do as I say. The cloak. Go get the cloak."

Elizabeth ran back to the cloak and ripped a long stretch of the fabric free. When she returned, Gaspar was scraping the last of the mortar from the brick.

"Here it is, now tie it around your arm and neck in a pouch."

Gaspar pulled her right up to the edge of the roof between the gables where he'd tossed over the ropes. Elizabeth reeled at the height. "I'm going to push you around a bit," he said. "Now put yourself between these two ropes, that's it. One on each side, now we wrap them around like this." Gaspar wound the ropes around her back. "Now step over this. Now the other one. That's a girl. No gentleman's way to do this."

He reached between her legs with both ropes and pulled her

towards him to grab the ropes behind her, then thrust them into her right hand.

"Gaspar, I can't do this," she said.

"Sure. Hold the ropes here in your right hand. Wrap it once around your wrist, like this. Always leaning back, remember. Backwards with your weight and never look down. Pull your weight on the rope and hold it tight here now."

"Are you suggesting that I—?"

"Not suggesting."

"But I've never done anything like this."

"Nonsense. Nothing to it. One step at a time."

Elizabeth looked down at the Count's gardens spinning circles so far below. "I can't."

"Oh now, none of that. No one's ever cried on this roof, and we're not breaking the tradition tonight. When you get to the second-floor trellis, use the brick to break your way in."

"I—I can't."

"First step is the worst. After that, just one at a time, understand? One step at a time. Now turn yourself around. That's it. Got your ropes in your hand there? Good girl, now just lean back. Trust me. It's going to be okay. That's it. Lean, a little more. See? You're all right. Now just inch a little down with your foot there, over the edge. Leaning, whoa! Leaning back. There you go. Now release a little of the rope in your hands. I'm up here, the whole time. Got your back in case you release too much. Another step. That's it. See? Nothing to it. Release a little more, now. I've got you. There you go. Another step."

For the first time in all this opera mess, Elizabeth was grateful to be wearing the stay. She could feel the ropes cutting into her back as she released each new inch, but the thick stay protected her from the burn. The friction of the rope singed her wrist each time she released the pressure to drop another inch. One inch was all she could force her trembling hands to release. At first, she had no idea the vulnerability of her position when she released her grip on the rope and felt herself suddenly give way, slipping quickly down. Panicking, she grabbed a hold of it, searing her palm on the course fibers, so that each new inch was like rubbing sandpaper on a fresh burn.

She was suspended where no accompanist should be. This was no opera. This was no production or theater or circus. This was not entertainment.

This was death.

"One inch at a time, Elizabeth."

Until this moment, all terror in Elizabeth's delusions had been imaginary, springing from the threat of the unknown, the under-lived, the inexperienced. But now terror locked up within her, hanging backwards, too frozen to even glance at the distant ground below. The ground of safety. The wonderful earth. Why had she ever left it?

One inch, release then catch, feel the ropes shift around her back and through her skirts, then scooch down the wall of the Count's massive smoldering estate. Lean back, lean back, release some more, lean back while explosions and wafting smoke impelled her to do the ridiculous, to take her life in her hands, to lean backwards into the very gravity that wanted to suck her towards death.

"Keep going, Elizabeth," Gaspar called down from above. "Another couple inches. Let them go. That's it."

Move. Make yourself move with trembling hands and breaths barely taken. Move through the fear like swimming in a wild black sea, death below, death inside, death and darkness. Let go again, lean backwards, another few inches. Freeze up.

"You're doing great. Release it again. That's a girl, let it go a little."

Gaspar's voice charmed her into believing he was closer than reality. But her subconscious knew he was gradually getting further away, sinking into the abysmal darkness of this unending night.

"One step at a time. That's it. Now one more, and one more."

"One at a time, darling. That's all it takes. One at a time."

"It takes forever. How can you stand to do this all day long? Everything moves so slowly. It's so infuriating."

"But it's not impossible, my love."

Her mother lay in bed. She rarely got up anymore. Even bathroom trips required a lean on her father now. Elizabeth had to drag the big wingback chair from the fireplace right up to the side of the bed, so mother could see her stitches. She turned her head on the heap of pillows, her withering arm hanging off the mattress's edge. On the nightstand, the stately table clock ticked on softly, its black, needle hands a merciless metronomic pulse atop its fading golden face. Elizabeth didn't prick her fingers anymore. But she just couldn't stand it. It didn't make any sound, sewing the stupid thread in and out, in and out.

"Over and down, up and through. One stitch at a time. That's it." *Her mother's voice was so melodious, even in her descent, like an oboe, full of color and warmth.*

"One more inch, Elizabeth. Let it go a little more now," Gaspar's retreating voice said.

Elizabeth didn't want to finish that hem. She would never finish that hem. *Oh God, please don't finish that hem.*

"One small stitch at a time and you're there. You're there darling. You're there."

Her feet hit something, and she stabilized on the decorative stone railing that wrapped around the house at the base of the second-floor windows. Above her, Gaspar's tiny head leaned out past the chimney. She had reached the second floor. A large arched window was about twenty feet to her right. Its blackened panes offered no hint of flames broiling within. She inched her way along the ornamental railing, noting the rope in her hands had nearly reached its last frayed end.

An artificial veranda peeked out from the window, and she squeezed herself onto it, releasing the tension on the rope. She touched the window. Not hot. She cupped her hands to it but saw only blackness. She was too disoriented to even imagine what part of the house she was at.

Trembling, she reached inside the pouch for the brick and raised it up, giving the glass a pathetic smack. It barely chipped the surface. She took a deep breath and lifted it higher. The glass fractured and webbed a tiny bit. A third time she lifted her arm, but now the brick slipped from her sweating palm and fell careening to the ground. The ground where she was supposed to fall. Where she was destined to fall.

I am destiny.

How would she break the window without the brick? She peered down where the brick had fallen. She might survive the drop, but not without substantial broken bones, and more likely a broken neck. She banged on the glass with her fists, but her hands were not enough to make the final implosion.

"Gaspar," she whispered. "I've dropped the brick. I've dropped the brick."

"Lizzy..." Reggie this time. Soft and subtle, like a tenor singing Mozart. "I don't want you to go away. I just want you to go on."

Go on, Lizzy. Go on.

Shaking now, she climbed up on the railing and leaned back, away from the window. Swinging outward from the building, she jumped and let go. Her side slammed into the damnably strong Spanish glass. The web of cracks in the glass barely extended an inch in every direction. She remounted the railing, her head spinning with terror, and tried again. This time, when she jumped away and swung perilously up into the night air beyond the railing, she lifted her feet in front of her. When her ridiculous shoes with their clickety-clack heels hit the glass, the window relented at last, disintegrating around her as she passed through into the house.

She tumbled to the floor, rolling between the slackened ropes. Though she could smell smoke, it had not penetrated this room yet. She had to find the nearest stairway before the floors collapsed. She wrenched her skirts free of the rope.

The rope. *Why had it slackened and fallen with her? How would Gaspar get off the roof?* Still disoriented, she pulled herself up. In the darkness, she felt her way back to the window. Her foot slipped on the glass shatters and she crashed into a piece of furniture. Unable to find her footing, she stumbled, tripped again, and fell to the ground, hitting her head on something with a final ominous clunk.

Chapter Thirty-One

"It's time to go, Elly."

She was being lifted, carried. So much darkness. Throbbing in her head, better to not open her eyes. Doors opened. The smell of burning. Someone, a man, coughed but did not drop her.

Who was carrying her? He held her firmly, shielding her.

"Wait," she heard her own voice say, "Gaspar is still on the roof."

More coughing, then through another door, carrying her down, down. He was so close, but eternally far from her.

"Daddy, I'm so sorry. I should have understood."

"No more apologies now."

"Can we go, Dad? Can we go now with Mom?"

"Not today, Elly."

She sank back into the darkness, listening to the echoes of the voice fade away down dark and misty hallways.

When she climbed into consciousness, a man sat beside her, a tall shadow with a baritone voice.

"Elizabeth? Can you hear me? That's it, sit up now. Drink this. You've hit your head somehow."

"Figaro? Where am I?"

"We found you here in the gardens. You're safe."

"My father. He came to get me. Wait, is it over? Did Gaspar get down?" Her eyes scrunched closed against the pounding in her head, but in the distance, she could hear rumbles, shouts coming to her in waves of muffled chaos.

"I don't know," said Figaro. "We're not even sure how you got down."

"Someone carried me out. It must have been Gaspar, only—"

"Only what?"

Figaro helped her to her feet. Pain spiked through her head.

"No. It wasn't Gaspar," she said.

Both wings of the house had collapsed into a smoldering heap of ruin. Stone walls and chimneys made ghostly appearances between the billowing smoke as the flames converged on the center like two wild dragons.

"Gaspar! We have to help him!"

As though she had incanted the final phrase of a wicked curse, the remaining structure released a mighty crack and crumbled. Floors of moldings and tapestries, gildings and artwork, clothing, jewels, and guns, all disintegrating into dust with a lengthy morbid crash.

"Gaspar!"

Figaro held her back. "Elizabeth, no. You can't do anything for him now."

She collapsed onto Figaro and something in her chest struck against a string, pulling its shrill notes across a bridge of broken glass. She did not fight it, but screamed alongside it, tears both sour and salty. Her gut seized, her throat clenched like twisted wool, and her hands shook, though she held them to her bosom, like cuddling a tiny child.

She sat for a long time, rocking and weeping while faceless characters passed around her and the calm began to settle. A first cool breeze passed her cheeks, and Figaro reappeared and offered a hand to help her up. Amada came running and embraced her. Susanna, Marcellina, they all gathered around like she mattered.

Together they walked around the smoldering ruins in silence. On the front side of the house a large gathering stood in the growing light of dawn. They leaned on one another, or on rakes and shovels, exhausted from the night's labors, their heads bent, their lips silent.

"What's going on?" Elizabeth asked.

Her group joined the circle wordlessly. Elizabeth nudged her way between the statue-like attenders. At the center she found the Count, at last on his knees, the Countess Rosina laying unnaturally crooked across him. Her skirts were deflated and torn, her lovely white cheeks blackened with soot, a dark red gash glazed across her temple.

"But I don't understand," Elizabeth said. "We got her down. She got to the ladder."

Marcellina answered. "The flames escaped as they were climbing down. She lost her footing. The rope burned up so quickly..."

The Countess Rosina was dead. It was already difficult to imagine the stiffened, lifeless face, full of bloom just a few hours ago. The music had stopped. The graven silence of the servants, barely even shuffling or scratching their noses, signified a terrifying **cadence**.

"She was so beautiful," Elizabeth said, "and kind. So kind to me."

The Count, who had struck Elizabeth's face the previous evening, looked up, as though remembering who she was, who anyone was.

"She used to sing, you know," he said. "Before we married. You reminded her of that, I think. You and your music brought her back somehow. Reminded her we both had sung once. Earlier this evening I struck you, Senorita. I owe you an apology. In fact, I owe you more. That day in the woods with Amada, when you hit me on the head. You didn't stop me that day. You saved me. This is all my fault. All of it."

"No sir. Aleix, your armorer, has betrayed us all. He set the explosions and he has been behind all the treachery."

"Aleix may have started the fire, but I sent her up there. She was trying to teach me a lesson." He pulled his wife to him and dug his face into her hair, rocking her limp heaviness back and forth. He spoke softly through his weeping, words so intimate that Elizabeth couldn't bear to listen. She regarded her employer, whispering apologies to his dead Rosina, his back to the ashen remains of his mighty estate, as though he wasn't even aware it had burned down.

Slowly, with great delicacy, he rested his wife's head on his arm and pulled a hairpin from her wig. One by one he pulled each pin out, releasing their hold, until the mound of silver curls at last slipped off and dropped to the ash-covered ground.

❧

The sun seized the new day. Smoke poured away across the morning sky like a ghost wave rolling out to sea. It took with it the final chords of Mozart's score.

Villagers arrived to assist with the cleanup and the smoldering remains. The house looked like a skeleton, a hollow scattering of charred stone edifices. Only the chimneys and the front stone façade stood, solidly erect, whipped with black scars, but intact. The Count's statue survived as a terrible scorched reminder of the triumph of his vanity. His caricature sat unhindered, stiff and arrogant on the horse, his sword still raised, a mound of blackened soot crumbled at its feet.

That was odd. The stone façade protruded significantly from the front of the house, and the statue was embedded deeply in a stone alcove. How had such a hefty mound of ashes accumulated there? *And why was it moving?*

Elizabeth's steps quickened. Her heart skipped, and she lifted her skirts to run. "Someone is up there!" She pointed and waved, crying for attention. "Someone bring a ladder! He's behind the statue!"

Men started running, orders were shouted, a ladder was brought. Figaro ascended while Elizabeth waited, holding her breath. As the sun rose victorious into the full sky, the light shone brightly on the two male figures descending the ladder together.

There were hugs and tears, better tears, tears of joy. A villager brought over some food, and there was laughter and more tears.

"Why did you throw down the rope?" Elizabeth asked when a calm finally settled.

"I didn't," Gaspar said. "It ripped to shreds on that chimney. I just kept praying it would hold together long enough. Your swinging around down there tore through the final strands. It's a miracle you made it."

"A miracle *I* made it?"

"Well one man's miracle is another man's triumph, isn't it?"

"Oh dear. Let's see, if it's a miracle, a genuine miracle, then isn't it God who triumphs?"

"Well now, here's Elizabeth bringing God into the conversation?"

"I am," Elizabeth said. "Assuming God does exist and the miracle saved a soul."

"So, the definition of a miracle is not someone who climbed behind a statue to hide from a blaze, but someone whose soul is saved?"

"That depends on the statue."

"Oh, Elizabeth," Gaspar laughed. "I will miss you, very much."

"Why is that?"

"It's time for you to go home, I think. Your story is finished."

"I don't know," she said.

"Count's repented. Figaro's married. Isn't that the end of your opera?"

"Yes. But I've learned something. The most important story

isn't always on the stage," Elizabeth said. "In all of this, the only person I really cared about wasn't even on the cast list."

"You've fulfilled your contract by me just fine. Feel confident I've done so too. What else can we do? Go off to war?"

"No, it's nothing like that, it's just..."

Across what had once been the Count's front courtyard, peasants gathered around the rubble, hunting for remnants, metals, scraps, or shards that might be useful or valuable. Scavengers. Approximately where the armory once stood, a familiar face seemed to glow in the morning light. It was a young pregnant girl wandering through the wreckage with a satchel and a basket. A few yards ahead of her, a woman shouted obscenities in her general direction. Elizabeth instantly recognized the older woman as a character she would never forget: Laia, and her axe-carrying son Raymon, who had once thrown her off their cart for fear of being put in a comba.

"Gaspar, I know where I've heard the name Fescura before. Oh, it all makes sense now. Yes, of course. I kept trying to end the opera the way I remembered it. But it doesn't always work that way. We may not get the ending we want, but if we just keep going and have a little faith..."

"Elizabeth?"

"We might find a new beginning. Gaspar, come with me. Come." She rose and grabbed his arm, leading him across the courtyard.

"Hello?" Elizabeth approached the girl at a safe distance from Laia and family. "Do you remember me? Laia threw me off the cart when you were first taken from the Count's estate. Do you remember?"

The girl glanced with obvious trepidation in the direction of her new guardians.

"Listen," Elizabeth said. "Gaspar, this girl was released from the Count's employ for being pregnant. She has no family, and she was sent away with these awful people who will abuse her and her child until the day she dies. Frescura, this is Gaspar, and you should go home with him. He'll give you a home, and you'll all three be very happy." For some absurd reason, Elizabeth felt her throat constricting and her eyes welling nonsensically. "You can leave with him today. You don't ever have to go home with them again. You can trust him. Why don't you two just stay and talk a bit?"

Elizabeth stepped away and pretended to search through the rubble while the obviously awkward conversation ensued. After only a few moments, Gaspar smiled up at her and departed to take on Laia and Raymond. He would take care of it.

Frescura climbed over the rubble towards her. "Thank you," she said. "I don't know what to say. I've been so...afraid."

"You won't need to be afraid anymore. And he'll help you with the baby, you'll see. He'll love you both like you're his own."

"I found this over in the rubble," she said, reaching inside her satchel. "I thought, it must be very special, because it survived the fire. They scolded me for picking it up, but I thought, it must be special. I want you to have it. Remember, it survived a fire. Just like you."

Frescura pulled out an ash-covered book with a capital cursive E peeking out from behind the black soot. Elizabeth wondered how it had gotten into the rubble, because Aleix had taken it from her on the roof. Perhaps Aleix had not made it out of his own trap? Then his remains might very well soon be discovered beneath the debris. But either way, his days were numbered. The Count would soon hunt him down and have him strung up. He was after all, a murderer.

"Kind of odd, don't you think?" Frescura said. "That a book could survive all that?"

"Yes," Elizabeth said, taking the book. "Yes, it is very special. Thank you. Please tell Gaspar I said thank you, and I'll see him... tell him, I believe I'll see him again someday."

She found the chapel empty. Morning sunlight poured across the stone floors in mystical crystal colors.

Her mind swam with so many unanswered questions, especially about Aleix. Why would he do all those things to spoil Mozart's plot? It was of course now obvious that he had come to her room and stolen her book. But how had he known to convince Susanna not to confide in Figaro, or to steal the note from Marcellina's desk? Was it really the same alluring countenance that had branded Figaro's birthmark from his arm? The memory of what might have happened between them ran shivers through her, and she once again longed to return to her own story.

Her father's book had been well-beaten in the collapse, its binding no longer firm, the red cover shedding loose threads. She found the final pages.

It was what he had never expected: all his raging schemes destroyed by a cheesemaker and a pianist from Wichita. His wits confounded by an outcome pride could never have guessed. In the Countess's death, the plot had not been indefinitely postponed, but rather, through loss...humility had been born.

The Count had at last repented, so much so that he would amend his character to its very core. He would not remarry, but remain celibate the rest of his days, never again lording his position and good fortune over those beneath him. The new Count Almaviva loved with genuine sacrifice and fidelity, so that when Figaro's son was born, he would love him as his own, leaving him a generous inheritance and legacy.

As for the plot of the pianist's opera, it had resolved, despite all the armorer's futile machinations. Her mission accomplished, she could return home, and she did so in an unexpected manner.

Realizing his mistake, he ran frantically from his hiding place, dashing across courtyard and charred remains, despite the bounty on his head. He ran for the holy place where she sat, trying

in vain to stop the inevitable, again. Through the doors he burst, only seconds too late. Too late to stop her. Too late to stop anything.
Goodbye.

"Goodbye?" Elizabeth said aloud. "That's a strange way to end a book."

Behind her, the chapel doors burst open, and Aleix rushed in, his eyes wild, his voice crazed. "Elly, no!" he shouted, reaching for her, flying almost.

But she could barely see him through the fireflies that suddenly ascended past her eyes.

Chapter Thirty-Two

It was as though she had never been asleep. One second, she was in the chapel on the Count's estate with Aleix rushing towards her, and the next, exactly where she had always been, sitting in her mother's chair, in her father's room. Home.

She stood too quickly, and the room spun around her, sending her stomach into a whirling fury. She clutched the wingback chair and held her breath, squeezed her eyes shut and fought the urge to bend over and throw up.

"I'm home," she said as the swirling slowed and her insides calmed.

Everything was exactly as she had left it, the wonderful inviting smells of old books and stagnant cigars. She stumbled to her father's bed and fell upon it, pulling the sheets to her as the tears came.

Something knocked downstairs and she sat up. Hadn't Josh and Reggie left weeks before? Through the open window, the men's familiar voices rose up in muffled tones as they descended the front steps of the old Victorian and started down the sidewalk.

Elizabeth jumped from the bed and ran down the stairs. She pulled open the big front door and left it wide, taking off down the street. "Reggie! Reggie, wait!" She suddenly felt very giddy and bounded up, throwing her arms around his neck.

"Lizzy? We thought you were sleeping. Are you all right?"

"Yes! Yes, Reggie. I'm all right. That's why I had to come after you, after you both." She grabbed Josh's hand and held them both to her. "Listen, I have to tell you something. You once asked me why I play. I mean, why do I play piano. Do you remember? Anyway, I know why now. I know why, Reggie!"

"Why you play piano?"

"Because it's not enough to eat the cheese!"

"Are you sure you're all right?" Josh said. "Maybe we should get you back to bed."

"No," she held their hands tighter to her. "That's it, don't you see? I'm going to be all right."

"Of course, you are, Lizzy," Reggie said. "Of course, you are."

Chapter Thirty-Three

Three Months Later
Quip: noun. A witty remark.

E lizabeth stood in the doorway of her apartment. With all
the furniture packed away and carpets removed, the same
rooms that had once felt so comforting and safe suddenly seemed
sterile, small, and cold.

Reggie arrived behind her, panting. "That's everything,
isn't it?"

"Yes, just these two last boxes of books," she said, nodding
towards her feet. "Strange how different it feels without all one's
stuff."

"Well, your new place in Boston will feel just as comfy once
you move in, you'll see."

"It's not that. This place wasn't mine. And the next place
won't be either. We're like birds, you know? The nests we build in
the spring blow away every winter when we're gone. Everywhere
we go, we're temporary."

"You're not getting cold feet now? You sure you want to drive
all the way there by yourself?"

"Yes, yes. I'm fine. What else did I buy that car for?"

Reggie's face morphed into a palette of anxiety, and she touched his hand, inwardly wishing he was an eighteenth-century dairy farmer. "I'll be fine. I just need a minute."

"Well, take your time." He lifted the top box and headed out. "We'll be downstairs."

Every day since her return, Elizabeth wondered whether the whole Figaro episode had been real. Not a drop of the paint had faded from her memory. If she closed her eyes, she could still feel the Spanish sun beaming on her skin, hear Cook's hollering through the window, or smell the orange blossoms of the Countess's perfume. It wasn't like any dream she'd ever known, and whenever music, work or conversations paused for even a moment, she felt herself naturally slipping back again to the comfort of Gaspar's farm, the smell of the Count's stables, or even the warmth of Aleix's arms. But then she would shake herself off and restart the process of convincing herself it was all just a highly detailed dream.

Still, she couldn't erase them from her. Even just in the memory of them all: Gaspar, Amada, the Countess, her mother and father. Absence hadn't killed the joy. The joy that welled up within, unbidden, every time one of them passed through her thoughts, through her memories. It was a strange and wonderful joy at having known them all, having shared even the smallest fraction of life with them. She didn't need Gaspar to tell her this was the most real thing in all the world.

So, it couldn't have been a dream.

Anyway, besides that, there would always be the other thing.

She squatted down beside her final box of books and carefully lifted out her father's gift. Her hands trembled as she held it, caressing the torn red-thread cover, obsessively careful not to let it slip ajar, lest she accidentally glance on any words and vanish again, into a new reality. So many times since her return, she had studied the book, agonized with curiosity, but too wise to explore any further the strange new inscription beneath the soot of the Count's demolished estate.

Elizabeth, once inscribed in gold cursive across the cover, had been erased, and like herself before the adventure, she would never be quite the same. She had disappeared, and a new mystery had replaced her; but that was a story for another opera.

The Glossary of Notes

Acc-compalice: Elizabeth's official job description in the real world would be "coach and ACCOMPANIST." It's a bad pun. Terrible really. Even the author is embarrassed for Basilio. But how ironic that his little pun should be the first item in the glossary. Oh, good for you, Basilio. One for Basilio. There you go.

"All'opra!...": Lines from the famous "Anvil Chorus" in Verdi's opera *Il Trovatore*. "To work now! Turn the hammers upwards! Who brings beauty to the day of the gipsy?"

Beaumarchais's play and Da Ponte's libretto: The literary authors of Mozart's *Marriage of Figaro*. Beaumarchais wrote the play. Lorenzo Da Ponte wrote the libretto, or the words to the opera.

Cadence: From the Latin *cadentia*, meaning "a falling." A musical term referring to any melodic or harmonic progression giving a sense of resolution, finality, or stop.

Cadenza: A flashy improvised ornamental passage, sung in a free rhythmic style with major virtuosic displays, usually signaling the final moments of an aria, act or opera.

Cantabile: An Italian musical term referring to the first section in an 18th Century aria. The Cantabile was characterized by slower and more speech-like rhythms. The second section, the cabaletta was faster, and more melodic.

Chopin: Frédéric François Chopin (1810–1849), a Polish composer and pianist particularly remembered for his piano compositions.

Chordal Analysis: A step-by-step mathematical writeup of the harmonic structure of a piece of music, usually required in music theory classes.

Coloratura: Elaborate flourishes and ornamental additions to a vocal melody, particularly used in operatic or classical singing.

Comprimarios: Small supporting roles in an opera.

Damn Tooth (aka a musical epiphany): An author's excuse for a horrific run-on.

Double bar line: Two thick lines signifying the end of a piece of music.

Falsetto: A method of singing, most easily accessed in the male voice, to sing higher pitches by vibrating the ligamentous edges of the vocal cords. Think Frankie Valli.

Fermata: A symbol of musical notation resembling the top half of a circle with a dot inside. It is placed over a note (or chord) to indicate the note should be prolonged beyond the normal duration of its value.

Follow the stick: Follow the tempo set by the conductor.

Fourth wall: An invisible, imagined wall separating actors from audience.

Fresnel: A type of powerful stage light.

Mark: (v) A technique for sparing the voice during rehearsals by reducing volume and lowering some pitches an octave.

Melismatic: From *melisma*: An extended passage of musical notes sung on one syllable. Considered to be very ornamental, merely for beauty's sake, demonstrative of vocal skill.

Melittologic: Actually, it's not a word. The establishment just wanted to include an entry for something other than music. Melittology is a word. . .the study of bees.

Mozart Requiem ... dead soprano: A whole lot of depressing music.

Octave: A musical interval or acoustic range spanning the eight notes of a scale, or twelve consecutive chromatic tones, or half steps.

Piano Crook: An expression used to describe the bent or curved part of a grand piano where a singer can stand during performances and rehearsals so that the pianist can see them easily.

Pit: Short for orchestra pit. The sunken architectural structure directly in front of a stage in most theaters. Even without the lowered platform, the term "pit" can refer to any ensemble accompanying a live show.

"Prima di cedere farò giocar!": Lyrics from Rosina's most famous aria in the prequel opera, *The Barber of Seville*. "And I'll play a hundred traps, before I give in!"

Recitative: In opera, a rhythmically free style of composition intended to reflect the natural inflections of speech. Used mostly in operas and oratorios from the Classical period and earlier.

Ritardando: A deceleration of musical tempo or speed. A slowing down.

Score: In music notation, the printed manuscript of a musical work. As the accompanist, Elizabeth would be using a piano/vocal score or a piano reduction of the orchestral parts and voice parts.

"Se- vuol- balla-re...": Lyrics from Figaro's famous aria in the Mozart opera. Trans: "If you would dance, Signor Count, I'll play the guitar, yes."

Subito piano: Musical notation indicating an abrupt drop of volume.

Sotto voce: Spoken or sung in an intentionally quiet voice.

Soubrette: A soprano voice classification, often cast in lively, flirtatious roles.

Stravinsky: Igor Stravinsky, a Russian 20th century composer famous for non-tonal and somewhat chaotic sounding music.

Sustain Pedal: The most frequently used foot pedal on a modern piano. It allows any played notes to continue vibrating naturally until the pedal is released.

Tormentor: Stage term referring to the side curtains hung behind the main drape. Actors waiting to come on stage stand behind tormentors where the audience cannot see them.

Verdi and Puccini: Two of opera's greatest composers.

Vipera: The Italian word for viper. A reference to the prequel play/opera *The Barber of Seville*, in which Rosina (now the Countess) sings about being a viper when controlling men.

Wagnerian: Of or related to German composer Richard Wagner, best known for his long epic operas.

"Wer reitet so...": Lyrics from a famous "late night forest romp" song: *Der Erlkönig* by Schubert. Trans: "Who rides so late through the night and wind? It is the father with his child."

Acknowledgments

Thanks to my beta readers: Lt. Col. Mark Reidinger, Terry Borton, Willian Neussle, Bonnie Diemer, Steve Pivovar, Deborah Lynn, Katheryne Jennings, and my Zoom writers group.

Thanks to firefighters Justin Schorr, Lieutenant Curtis Kauffman, Falcon Fire Department, and Chief Bobby Halton.

Thank you to my 18th-century gurus: Linda Kerr, Chris Haas & Lindsey Wood.

Thank you, Kenton and Rebecca Whitman, for help with rappelling.

Thank you to my wonderful editor and advisor in self-publishing, Dave Pasquantonio.

Finally, thank you to my daughter, Annamarie, for thinking of the one thing a man would do that a woman would never take credit for... and also for getting Elly off the roof.

Made in the USA
Las Vegas, NV
09 April 2024

88422596R00215